PRAISE FOR

What Happened to Henry

"A striking debut . . . The novel is suffused with the characters' love for each other . . . A fascinating blend of family drama and metaphysical inquiry."

—*Kirkus Reviews* (starred review)

"An overpowering and life-affirming literary experience. At once joyful and heartbreaking—and ultimately unforgettable."

—Steve Kluger, author of *Last Days of Summer*

"As with the fiction of Ian McEwan, *What Happened to Henry* portrays childhood as a complex, contradictory world that is both dark and whimsical. Among the novel's many charms is a quiet suspense, a tension that resonates beyond its poetic conclusion."

—Timothy Schaffert, author of *The Phantom Limbs of the Rollow Sisters*

What Happened to Henry

Sharon Pywell

BERKLEY BOOKS

NEW YORK

THE BERKLEY PUBLISHING GROUP
Published by the Penguin Group
Penguin Group (USA) Inc.
375 Hudson Street, New York, New York 10014, USA
Penguin Group (Canada), 90 Eglinton Avenue East, Suite 700, Toronto, Ontario M4P 2Y3, Canada (a division of Pearson Penguin Canada Inc.)
Penguin Books Ltd., 80 Strand, London WC2R 0RL, England
Penguin Group Ireland, 25 St. Stephen's Green, Dublin 2, Ireland (a division of Penguin Books Ltd.)
Penguin Group (Australia), 250 Camberwell Road, Camberwell, Victoria 3124, Australia (a division of Pearson Australia Group Pty. Ltd.)
Penguin Books India Pvt. Ltd., 11 Community Centre, Panchsheel Park, New Delhi—110 017, India
Penguin Group (NZ), Cnr. Airborne and Rosedale Roads, Albany, Auckland 1310, New Zealand (a division of Pearson New Zealand Ltd.)
Penguin Books (South Africa) (Pty.) Ltd., 24 Sturdee Avenue, Rosebank, Johannesburg 2196, South Africa

Penguin Books Ltd., Registered Offices: 80 Strand, London WC2R 0RL, England

Cover art by Mug Shots/CORBIS.
Cover design by Elizabeth Connor.

PRINTING HISTORY
G. P. Putnam's Sons hardcover edition / July 2004
Berkley trade paperback edition / July 2005

Berkley trade paperback ISBN: 0-425-20261-5

The Library of Congress has cataloged the G. P. Putnam's Sons hardcover edition as follows:

Pywell, Sharon L.
What happened to Henry / Sharon Pywell.
p. cm.
ISBN 0-399-15168-0
1. Boys—Fiction. 2. Bereavement—Fiction. 3. Male friendship—Fiction. 4. Atomic bomb victims—Fiction. 5. Hiroshima-shi (Japan)—History—Bombardment, 1945—Fiction. I. Title
PS3616 Y94W47 2004 2003062239
813'.54—dc22

PRINTED IN THE UNITED STATES OF AMERICA

10 9 8 7 6 5 4 3 2 1

To Mark

PART 1

In My Father's House There Are Many Rooms

One

Lauren Cooper sat quietly in her assigned row watching a spider at work along the molding overhead, her legs swinging apart, together, apart, together. It was a late fall afternoon in Eleusis, New York, 1960. A dozen other potential first communicants sighed behind her, some preparing spitwads, others anxiously attentive.

Sister Leonarda's luminous eyes swam above little clusters of symmetrical moles. She limped, allegedly a victim of childhood polio. Everyone said she'd been disappointed in love.

"Now," she said melodically, "we will review the mystery of transubstantiation. Lauren Cooper?"

Lauren was a First Communion failure, repeating the curriculum for the third time at the advanced age of nine. Father Murphy had made it clear that no matter what she did this time, she was going to receive the sacrament along with the seven-year-olds. Lauren's first attempt had been foiled by multiple streptococcus infections. Twelve months later, bad judgment and temptation defeated her: a peanut had leapt into her mouth the morning she was supposed to take the sacrament. She had skipped down the stairs at dawn to find a glistening salted heap of them left over from a bridge party, and she promptly forgot the rules about fasting before receiving the host. Her brother Henry rounded a corner and saw the whole thing, making lying impractical.

Henry was mortified and protective in equal parts, ultimately deciding that he had to turn her in. Again she was banished from the lines of first communicants and had to watch them march down the aisle in cupcake-like dresses while she remained in a pew with her family, scuffing her Hush Puppies and moping.

So Lauren Cooper sat before Sister Leonarda now, struggling to focus on this question that she had been asked, probably, twenty times before.

"Miss Cooper. Transubstantiation."

"Well. It means that when the bread is blessed, it stops being bread and is changed magically into Jesus's flesh, but when we bite it we don't hurt Him."

"Not 'magically,' Lauren Cooper. The intervention of our Lord Jesus Christ is not *magic.*"

Lauren nodded, though this was precisely the kind of distinction that baffled her. It looked pretty darn magic to her, and Sister Leonarda's correction did nothing to shore up her thinning faith in adult guidance.

She had taken some of these problems to Henry, and he had reminded her that Jesus was capable, even eager, to forgive confusion about things that nuns said. There was no reason for her to worry. Yet she did. She stuck her hand up in the air now and said, "Sister, if God can forgive anything, why should we worry about being bad?"

Sister Leonarda sniffed. "Those who believe that they can evade judgment are generally struck down by trucks or disease before they can receive the sacrament of Extreme Unction or confess their sins to a priest."

"Trucks? But that's not fair!"

"There is no excuse for waiting until a truck comes at you. God appears to us every day in dozens of forms, offering chance after chance to those of us who wander the streets with our spiritual fingers stuck in our ears!" Here the Sister rapped a desk for emphasis. Just then Domenic Rumietti shot a spitwad into the neckline of the girl in front of him, who squealed. "You, Domenic!" Sister Leonarda cuffed the offending seven-year-old on his head. "Tormenting your classmates! Satan is just testing you little babies to see who's fertile ground. And you," she said, more in sorrow than in remonstrance, "are a very fertile little piece of ground."

Sister Leonarda blew her nose. She was just getting over a cold. "Of course," she sighed, "we all have some moist corner of our minds where sin can get its roots set down. Some of you"—her eyes swept over them—"come to me with the fuzzy idea that humanity keeps getting better all the time, and as history goes on we just keep rolling on together toward general improvement. Well, that is inaccurate. We all start from scratch. Less than scratch. We're all born into the same old war, each and every one of us, and History starts all over again with every child that's born. That's why we don't get anywhere here on earth."

This made a certain amount of sense to Lauren. Maybe she had some aptitude for religion after all.

"Sister." Lauren's hand crept upward again. The nun didn't seem to hear. "Sister," she repeated. This time Sister Leonarda turned toward Lauren, making a gesture like flicking a fuzz ball from a skirt.

"What?"

"Sister, how do you get to be a saint?"

"Why do you want to know, Lauren Cooper?"

"I just wondered, Sister."

"I know why you want to know: you want to know because you think you can be a saint. You will never be a saint, Lauren Cooper, because saints are selfless and don't waste their time worrying about whether they'll get turned into saints."

"What about martyrdom?"

"What about it?"

"I mean, if a person dies for religious beliefs. As a way to get to heaven."

"These people didn't check with their Religious Instruction teachers about potential sainthood before they martyred themselves."

"Yes, Sister. How about being a sister, Sister?"

"As a way to get to heaven? I presume that it usually works." Her fingers moved to her gold ring, tapping. "It's very simple, really. You just give yourself up. You surrender." The Sister leaned down beside her desk to reach a cardboard tube and from it she pulled out a picture, brown and cracked at the edges, which she unrolled very slowly. It showed a woman, tied to a stake, naked to the hips. For several of the children in the room this was a first exposure to a frank image of adult feminine breasts, and the attention level adjusted accordingly. Blood streamed from places on the woman's forehead and her left breast. Her face was turned toward the sky, leaving a white expanse of throat exposed. Her legs and lips fell open, gently parted. The lines of her thighs were so clear beneath the thin fabric of her robes that they looked naked, too. Her eyes were shining. Lauren's heart beat.

"Saint Margaret of Cortona," Sister Leonarda breathed, looking down at the picture in her hands. "A sacred martyr. This"—she held it higher—"is ecstasy. This is the reward of true faith."

"Sister?"

"Yes, Miss Cooper."

"What did she do that made her a martyr?"

"She retained her faith at a time when the faithful were oppressed."

"I know. But I mean, what did she do that made her a martyr?"

Sister Leonarda sighed. "You may borrow *Lives of the Saints* from me until our next class; any details you need will be found in its pages." Then the Sister leaned against the blackboard and drew one finger thoughtfully down her nose. "Remember your Communion gown rental money for next week." The alarm clock at the head of the room rang, signaling the end of class. Lauren took the book. The students scattered, leaving Sister Leonarda gazing upon the martyr with a kind of concentration that made Lauren anxious, though she did not know why.

Outside, she sat on the curb until her father pulled up in the family Chevrolet. They drove back to the little Cape Cod house where they all lived: Lauren, her brothers Henry and Winston, and their parents, Annie and Warren Cooper.

"Dad?"

"Yes."

"Do we really not get anywhere?"

"What are you talking about?"

"I mean, do we all have the same problems, and just repeat them over and over, parents and then children and then the children's children?"

Her father huffed. "Don't be ridiculous. Look at radio communication. Radar technology. Medical breakthroughs. We make progress every minute. This is the best time in all history that you live in. Think of running water! Blistering hot water anytime you just turn a tap! Presto! Central heating! The polio vaccine! Your grandmother didn't have this life, believe you me, and your children will have things we can't even imagine."

She watched her father's profile for a couple of miles, his happy profile. Warren Cooper designed missile launching and tracking systems. He was most fully alive when he talked about machines that threw and caught the different kinds of radio waves, and all his family knew that his work offered him a happiness he could not find bending over a homework paper or hurrying a child who was slow to pull on a coat.

Now Lauren sat beside him in silence as they drove along, thinking of the sacrifice on the cross and the hilly curve of the saint's thighs under her blood-spattered robe. These things seemed dark to her in ways that her parents never spoke of. Lauren doubted that her father ever felt the way she felt when Sister Leonarda showed them the ecstatic saint.

Once home, her father retreated to the basement, where he was supposed to be organizing pamphlets for the Knights of Columbus, but within a minute the *clickclickclick* sounds made it clear that he was playing with his Morse code receiver again. Lauren could hear the slam of the dryer door from another place in the basement: her mother, doing laundry.

She trudged upstairs to Henry's tiny bedroom. Her older brother sat among miniature box buildings they used in a game they called Apartment Complex. The cardboard apartments were occupied by imaginary residents—some of whom had tiny plastic representational forms, while others existed only in Lauren's mind. She was in charge of people; Henry was in charge of buildings and grounds. He loved to build. His most time-consuming projects were the meticulously constructed plastic fighter planes that now hung over their heads, suspended from the ceiling by fishing line in mock dogfights. Henry had shown her how to simulate the illusion of movement in a night confrontation by aiming flashlights at the planes in the dark and flicking them on and off. But Lauren hated the fake dogfights and left the room when Henry suggested them.

"What's Winston doing?" Lauren asked her older brother.

"He's in the garage playing with the cars. Trying to find the dipstick. He asked Dad where it was and Dad said he'd give him a quarter if he could find it by himself."

"Winston!" she heard their mom yell. "Winston, you come right here right now!"

Lauren glanced inquiringly at her older brother. "What now?" she asked.

Henry didn't look up from the door hinge he was attaching. "He took off all the doorknobs and electrical outlet covers in the house."

"Wow."

"I watched him do it. Mom was busy making something in the kitchen. He did all the rooms except the kitchen."

"Didn't you tell her? Didn't you try to stop him?"

"He had a sharp object in his hand," Henry replied. Both he and Lauren carried small scars from other failed interactions with Winston, who literally went deaf and dumb and maybe partly blind under the influence of rage. Their younger brother was sturdily built and surprisingly quick—small but dangerous.

They could hear their mother speaking sternly, calling their father up from the cellar to get involved, then Winston crying. Winston revered his father, and his disapproval made the youngest Cooper child unbearable for days. He would come stamping up the stairs soon, they knew, banished to his room. Sure enough, two minutes later Winston rumbled by, weeping. His door slammed, and within five minutes they could hear a regular rasping noise.

"Go see what he's doing now," Lauren urged Henry.

"I'm busy," Henry replied.

So Lauren made her way down the hall. She peeked through the keyhole and made out an elbow rolling back and forth, back and forth. The saw! How had he gotten his hands on the saw? She flung open the door. "I'm telling!" she said. Winston hesitated, then met her glare with one of his own and continued slicing a line down the center of his new bed's maple headboard.

"Good," he said grimly. "Tell."

"What do you think you're doing?"

"I don't know," he said, no longer glaring. He sounded sincerely confused, driven by some force he didn't understand but that had something to do with tools.

"I'm telling," Lauren repeated lamely. It was fairly clear to her now that she would not tell.

Winston twisted so she could only see his back and shoulders, not his face, and he kept sawing. The headboard would collapse noisily soon and there would be no need to tell. Lauren closed the door quietly behind her and went back to Henry's bedroom.

She wondered if some of the uneasy anxiety she felt was leakage from First Communion class and not Winston's current activities. "Henry," she said, "Sister Leonarda showed us a picture of a saint today."

"So?" Henry bent to attach a tiny door to a new building.

"Nothing. It made me feel kind of funny."

"Saints are nothing to worry about; you think too much. What did you dream last night?" Henry set his balsa wood and diagrams to one side. This was their routine—at some point in every day they asked each other this question.

"Circuses. Flying trapezes. I was on the trapeze." This was a lie. In reality she had dreamed that she had become lost and frightened, surrounded by unfamiliar trees and fences and cornfields, and that just when she couldn't bear being lost and all alone anymore she had seen

Henry walking across her dream cornfield to take her home. Such joyful relief! Henry had a phenomenal sense of direction, and whenever she was in his care she felt secure.

Once, in her real life, not her dream life, she had misplaced herself in a Smithsonian Institution building and after thirty minutes of fruitless searching, their parents had set Henry on her trail. Henry had come to her as directly as if she wore a homing device: he found her standing in front of the glassed exhibit of Civil War army rations and led her back to their parents. Henry had behaved as if there were no skill in doing this, but she regarded it as a kind of miracle. The Civil War ration of graying sugar cubes in particular stayed in Lauren's mind. They had been real, like Henry finding her; not a dream.

In her dream of the night before, a farmer sitting on a tractor saw them and flew into a rage. *You!* he screamed. *Thief! You get out of my corn!* In this dream, which Lauren had had many times, this man swelled up with an unreasoning rage, produced a gun and pointed it directly at Henry. In the dream Henry faced the furious man serenely, and then was shot. She had held her brother's dream body in her arms and thought, He's dying, and then, I don't know the way. Her chest had felt as if it were being pulled to pieces, a sensation she imagined was what people meant when they used the expression "broken heart."

The first two times she had dreamed this Lauren had woken with her blood banging up in her throat, as desperately frightened as she had ever been in her life. She had lain in her bed and tried to return to sleep but the image of Henry's body in her own arms, his blood, had been so powerful that she had had to go into his room and touch his moving chest in order to regain enough calm to sleep. He hadn't woken. Three times now she had lied about having this dream.

"What did you dream?" she demanded.

"I dreamed that I saw the explosion of the atomic bomb." Henry held the tiny plastic electric plate he'd made between his thumb and forefinger and filed some fuzz off its left side. "I dreamed that I was three thousand meters away from the epicenter and that I felt a big hot wave of air so strong it knocked me down. There were sirens and then the all-clear and I looked at the clock. I saw what I thought was a tornado spout rise up and then the top popped open, all boiling smoke coming out. Then fires started spreading out from the bottom and running in all directions."

"That isn't a dream," Lauren said irritably. "You read that in that book you check out of the library all the time—that *Disaster, Disaster, Disaster* one. Right?"

Henry didn't acknowledge her. He said, "I went running toward the fire. I had to find somebody. As I got closer I passed people on fire."

"Henry, cut it out," she demanded. Her voice had gotten frightened—skinny and bright.

"Winston!?" they heard. Their father's voice. "Winston, where's my hacksaw?" Then thumping steps on the stairs, the opened door, the *whooochk* of an open palm on a corduroyed rear end. "And you will stay here until I tell you you can move," their father announced. Then the steps descended again. They padded together down the hallway to Winston's room and stood shoulder to shoulder in its doorway, looking at him.

"Why did you do that?" Lauren demanded of her little brother.

Winston stood in the center of the room, tears running down his somewhat crumpled but still dignified expression, arms folded over his little chest. He didn't answer her.

"You're a weirdo, Winston," she went on.

"Shush," Henry said to her. He stepped into the room and sat on Winston's bed. When Winston sat down beside him Henry put his arm around his little brother's shoulders. Winston's arms remained stiffly crossed but he tipped a bit in Henry's direction.

Why are you so nice to him?" Lauren asked Henry when they had gone back to his room and resumed work on the complex.

"What do you think about putting more roads and kinds of trucks and cars in the design? Winston might want to play if we had cars."

"Nope."

"I'll bet Winston would be good at playing apartment if we worked on the roads. Put in a few tiered garages."

"I hate cars."

"Cars are interesting. They cause so much concrete, though."

"I want a swimming pool," she said, sitting beside his growing pile of neat boxes. "I want to make them swim." Then, seeing his new balsa wood door frames, she said, "Wow." Henry designed interiors to code. The wall sockets were never more than the proportional equivalent of twelve feet apart. He'd asked his father about it, and Warren called a local electrician to confirm the measurements.

Lauren had a different attachment to the apartment complex game. The whole while she chatted on about swimming pools and residents, she was thinking, I am God. I am God. In this little world, she could be. She propped up a tiny plastic person in the middle of a road, and when Henry turned his back to pick up something, she ran a little truck over the person. *Splat,* she thought, and an answering little thrill ran up and down her body. Then she slowly tipped the little person upright. Live, she said to it in her head, and it returned to life. She felt a little vibrating glow in her abdomen. Happiness.

"Nothing grows in swimming pools," Henry said, the better part of his attention still directed at a tiny window he was installing.

"What about a pond? I could make some modeling-clay trees. A rock garden."

"Okay. I'll float boats. I'll make the people walk on water. They'll do miracles."

"I don't think they should do miracles," Henry said.

"You know, you don't have to be nice to Winston. He isn't nice."

"What does that have to do with it?" Henry's tone was not argumentative. He was actually asking.

Lauren felt a bright little rush of gratitude toward Henry, and the old certainty that Henry's presence in this room with her, and in the world, made her safer. It occurred to her that her major complaint against Winston was that his corrosive and unpredictable temperament had just the opposite effect on her: it made her fearful and then evil. She did the worst things, said the meanest things, under Winston's influence. With Henry she was good.

He said, "You know, the model apartment complex needs more services attached to it. I should build a church. Maybe a temple for the Buddhist neighbors. A park." He tapped thoughtfully. "Can I borrow your crucifix for the steeple?"

"I guess. But you know, Father Murphy blessed it. Does that make a difference? What Buddhist neighbors?"

Henry shrugged gently, a gesture that simultaneously acknowledged her questions and indicated that he wasn't going to answer them. He returned to the four-inch-high door he was hanging on a small corrugated cardboard building.

"Henry?"

"What?"

"Do you think Sister Leonarda's right about what happens when you die?"

"That's a long way off. Hold this still for me while I attach shutters."

"But Sally died and she was little. You don't have to be old to die."

"Dinner!" their mother called from below them.

"Sally's in heaven," Henry told her. "I baptized her, Lauren. Remember?"

"You said, 'I baptize you in the name of the Father and the Son and the Holy Spirit' and you sprinkled her head," Lauren added.

"Right. That's all you have to do. The catechism says so." Henry stood abruptly and began packing loose apartment game parts. Then they made their way down the stairs to dinner.

"A hacksaw is for metal," their father said over the children's heads, his tone disapproving. "Not wood." Winston had been banned from the table; presumably he had already heard the lecture on appropriate hacksaw uses.

Their mother broke in, "The point is the destruction, Warren!" She had just bought that bed last month and she had had to scrimp on groceries for four months to do it.

"That's true. The waste is terrible. Of course."

It seemed to Lauren that her mother was tired. She tried to appear interested in the meal, pushing the gelatinous slush of summer squash around on her plate. Cooking, clearly, offered their mother no happiness.

"Eat your hamburger, Lauren," her mother said absently, petting the peony she had set at the center of the table. She was as good with plants as she was bad with food. Lauren pushed the hamburger to one side, knowing her mother was distracted and would forget about it. She was, and did.

That night Lauren sat as quietly as she could on the stairs, holding her knees as she listened to her mother's half of a telephone conversation with Aunt Honey.

"What would possess a child to saw a bed apart? I can't help but think that these things didn't happen before we lost the baby and now they're just the way we are. I hate it. Warren says put it behind us. He never talks about her. The kids don't talk about it but it has to be in their heads. It's in my head." She paused. "I love him but it's a mystery sometimes to me what's in that man's mind. This bed thing? He seems to think that what went wrong here is that Winston picked the wrong tool for the job." And though Lauren could not hear the response, it must have had something to do with gender, because her mother replied, "No, no. It's not just the men thing." Honey said something back, and her mother said, "Well. Maybe men."

Lauren retreated up the stairs, hugging the wall closely to prevent creaking, just like Henry's Boy Scout manual advised. She lay down in her bed and propped open *Lives of the Saints.* A smaller reproduction of the same painting Sister Leonarda had shown them faced a biography on the opposite page. There were the same beautifully molded thighs, blood streaming down and crisscrossing, a web of blood. There was the same face, thrown heavenward in an expression that was not anything, even to Lauren's youthful eye, that could be called pious. It was a look of a woman in the throes of something intensely mortal—not sacred. Or perhaps, Lauren considered, perhaps those two worlds were not contradictory. This thought disoriented her, so she abandoned it.

Two

Two years before, when Henry Cooper had been ten, Lauren seven and Winston five, their mother became pregnant with a fourth child. She knew right away it was a girl because she was so sick, as sick as she'd been with Lauren.

In her fifth month the neighbors' eyes began lingering at her waistline and she knew she could put the announcement off no longer. Each child accepted the news gravely, and then retreated to Henry's room to discuss the situation. There was general agreement that a new child would present more difficulties than advantages, the chiefest among them, as far as Lauren was concerned, the fact that she might have to share her room with a sister. Winston shaped scenarios in which he was utterly neglected while a baby cannibalized all the parental care and resources. Only Henry seemed reasonably happy.

"Anyway," he said to them, "it's not up to us to decide if we get a sister or not, is it? It's going to happen no matter what we think."

"It's going to be bad, isn't it?" Winston muttered to Lauren, for once seeking her out for solace.

Lauren didn't answer, unwilling to let agreement align her with Winston.

Their mother hemorrhaged on the middle day of the seventh month. Henry and Lauren came home that afternoon and found her, unconscious, sprawled over the bathroom threshold. Every part of her from the hips down seemed covered in blood. The sight paralyzed Lauren and galvanized Henry, who picked up the telephone and had an ambulance on the way within thirty seconds. The ambulance crew brushed the two children aside when they tried to climb in after their mother's body, saying, "Go to a neighbor's house, kids. You can't come."

Henry and Lauren sat in their front yard, stunned. A full half hour passed before it occurred to them to call their father. When they finally did, his secretary told them that the hospital had called and he had run out the door in a panic, not hearing her when she asked whom she should call to take care of his children.

"Who's with you?" their father's secretary asked. No one, Henry told her. It was Thursday—Winston's Hands-On Science Club day. He would be home in a matter of minutes. "You go to a neighbor's," she ordered, "and you tell them what happened."

Henry agreed, but when he hung up the telephone he announced that they weren't moving from the house. Winston would be home on the late bus any minute, he insisted, and could not come home to a parentless house full of bloody footprints. The two of them set to cleaning the gelatinous red fluids from the floors, following the darkening prints out the door and down the walk to where Annie had been lifted up into the ambulance.

When Winston came home the floors were unremarkable and a plate of cookies sat by a glass of milk on the kitchen table. "What's wrong?" he asked suspiciously. "Where's Mom?"

Lauren held her tongue. Henry said, "She fainted and she had to go to the hospital for a checkup to make sure she's okay. Dad's there."

Luckily their father called right at that moment. Henry made a quick strategic decision and handed the telephone to his little brother. That voice, so completely the voice of authority for Winston, set the little boy directly into their hands. "You do what Henry says," their father could be heard telling him, even from three feet away. "You be good."

"When is he coming home? When is Mom coming home?" Lauren demanded when he hung up. But Winston had forgotten to ask this question and Henry would not allow them to call the hospital.

The baby survived. The doctors calmed a distraught Annie Cooper by giving her a stethoscope and teaching her how to find the rapid little heartbeat just a bit below her own. She lay in her hospital bed with the instrument pressed to her abdomen day after day, listening. Bed rest, they were told, and quiet—these things would see her safely through to a delivery date that ensured the baby's survival.

Annie remained hospitalized for four long weeks, during which Warren proved to be fairly ineffective as the stabilizing adult presence at home. Lauren and Henry learned to rifle through the freezer and put things they found there in boiling water or in the oven. They set Winston on a chair and taught him to wash and stack. Their father seemed helpless, rudderless, wandering into the house at the end of the day to eat whatever the children put before him and then rising to leave for the hospital, apologizing to his children profusely as he set out, alone. He knew they wanted to come, but Annie's bloodless and depressed appearance frightened him, and his instinct was to protect them from it. He had confidence in them, he said every night, and knew they could keep order at home.

Henry and Lauren were indeed keeping order at home, in part because they had discovered that mopping and vacuuming were a defense of sorts against terror. Then one night Henry finally spoke up. Winston had left the room for a moment, and the second he was out of earshot Henry said, "Dad, we have to go to the hospital with you because Winston's afraid that Mom has died. Okay?" He looked steadily, hopefully, into his father's face.

That night they all went to visiting hours. When Henry saw their mother lying in the hospital room he started to sob, something his father had never seen. "Henry! Henry, please stop! Don't upset your mother! Henry, it's all right! Please stop!"

Annie Cooper's eyes flew open. The sides of her mouth wobbled upward and she struggled into a more erect position. "Hi, honeys," she said, reaching out a hand. "You come on over here. I'm fine." Her eyes were darkened into a raccoony mask, the rest of her face the color of school paste and her hands shaking visibly. "I'm fine," she assured them. If there had been any doubt in Lauren's mind before that moment that adults were not trustworthy, there was none thereafter.

Henry stepped right up to the apparition and took her hand, still crying. Lauren and Winston skimmed around the bed just out of reach. Henry divined the need for cheerful conversation and pulled himself together enough to rattle along about what Linda Jefferson's rabbit had done after it chewed its way out of its cage. His mother smiled gratefully at him, and gradually Lauren and Winston felt secure enough to come within her orbit. She reached out and stroked their hair, finally luring Lauren onto the bed by her side. But later that night Winston crept into his brother's bedroom. "Henry," he said, tugging at the bedclothes. "Henry, is the baby eating Mommy?"

• • •

The next evening Annie asked Warren to get a neighbor to watch Winston so he could bring Henry and Lauren to visiting hours. He protested, but complied. Ten minutes into the visit she tipped a container of hospital-issue applesauce onto her chest. She sighed.

"That's it," she said. "I've reached my limit. I've been spilling things on myself since I got here and I haven't had a decent shower. The nurses say they're too busy to help me get in the shower or that I'm not ready. Henry?"

Henry snapped to attention.

"Henry, you shut the door so the staff don't see what we're doing. Warren, this will only take five minutes if you help me. I'm going to get into that shower. Get the clean gown that's on the heat register. It's pink. In the plastic tub. Got it?" She was already throwing her sheets to one side. "Now. Lauren and Henry. You are the official guards, and you will patrol the entrance to warn us of any incoming nurses. Got it?"

"Yes, Mom," they said together.

"Ready, Warren?"

Warren did not look ready to his children. Annie's announcement had startled him, left him looking askew as well as anxious. "All right," he said.

He helped her hobble out of the bed and rolled the IV holder along after her as they made the long journey across the floor to the bathroom. As soon as their parents shut the door behind them, Lauren left her post and sidled back to shift from foot to foot in front of the closed door. Henry continued marching back and forth just outside in the hallway. They heard the shower start, and then a crash, and both children scuttled up against the closed bathroom door. "Dad? Mom?" they called.

Silence. Then the sound of their parents laughing. Something terrible was beaten back in an instant by this sound. "We're fine," their father called cheerily through the door. "We just slipped."

When their parents stepped out of the bathroom the mood had changed sufficiently to make the sight of Henry and Lauren bouncing on the bed look simply amusing, though fifteen minutes before it would have been a punishable offense. The children bounced off and helped their father settle Annie into her bed. He was dripping, even streaming little rivulets in places he hadn't reached with towels. Annie was in a clean and dry hospital gown.

"I was so scared," he said out loud, patting his wife's hand and watching Lauren and Henry try to figure out how to open the window blinds. He continued to dab absently at himself.

"I know," their mother said back. "Me, too."

This admission, and their parents' clear relief and affection, lifted Henry's and Lauren's spirits remarkably. "See?" their father said to them as they left a little later. "I told you that your coming to the hospital would do your mother a world of good."

Annie Cooper talked herself out of the hospital the next day by promising to remain in bed when she got home. Within forty-eight hours it was clear to her that it wasn't going to work—everyone, seeing her here, found ways to demand her physical attention. Hammering or weeping from distant parts of the house would draw her hobbling down a flight of stairs. Smells of burning things, actual clouds of smoke, wafted into her bedroom. The order that Henry and Lauren had maintained when they were alone dissolved when their mother was there as adult backup.

She had been told that if she could stay off her feet and keep the baby from coming for three more weeks, it would certainly survive. But if it was too premature . . . She called her beloved sister Honey and asked for help.

The moment their Aunt Honey entered the house, everything calmed down. Their cheery, disorderly aunt just made coffee and told jokes and left the household management to Lauren and Henry, but her presence kept their mother anchored and still, indifferent to the many sounds and smells that had plagued her before Aunt Honey's arrival. Honey laughed, and she made her sister laugh. Their aunt was careless, quick, affectionate. Normalcy streamed out behind her wherever she went. Burned bacon, misplaced sneakers or unfolded laundry were now powerless to disturb anyone in the house.

Lauren took up an after-school eavesdropping perch midway up the flight of stairs, just out of sight but well within earshot of their conversations.

"I've missed you so much," she heard her mother say to her sister one afternoon. Coffee and baking brownies perfumed the kitchen, sunlight flowed through the windows. Cereal boxes littered the kitchen counters and crunchy things lay underfoot. No one cared.

She heard her aunt say, "All my sick time and personal time is gone so I got to skeedaddle back. But I'll take unpaid time if you want when she comes."

"You're a saint, Honey. You saved us all from destruction."

"Just another day's work, my dear."

Then, as quickly as she had come it seemed, Aunt Honey left them. But the house was calmer—accustomed now to a mother who lay on the sofa all day and to the routines of cooking and sweeping without her. Honey had reshaped the household somehow in ways that left it at once more chaotic and more restful.

• • •

But the baby didn't quite make it to month eight. Henry found himself shaken awake and told that his father had to take his mother to the hospital—it was time.

"You'll have to get Winston and Lauren off to school alone. You'll do fine. I'll call home as soon as I can," his father whispered. "Don't wake anybody until it's time to get up."

An hour later Annie was being prepared for a cesarean section while her three children sat at home unblinkingly before bowls of Frosted Flakes and her husband waited in a green hallway.

Henry did his duty, making one last attempt to reassure his siblings. "Dad said it would be fine. All babies are born in hospitals. It doesn't mean Mom's sick," he told them.

"I don't want a sister," Winston said quietly. "This is a bad baby."

"Babies can't be bad or good," Henry sighed. "They're just babies."

Ten anxious days later their mother came home. Their new sister, named Sally the moment the neonatal staff offered her better than average chances of living, had to stay back at the hospital. It's only because of her teeny lungs, the children were told—Sally would come home soon. Lauren imagined little butterfly-ish lungs, beating and beating, too small to do their duty.

"Does it hurt?" she asked her father when their mother couldn't hear.

"To have a baby?" Warren looked down at her in surprise. "Well, yes, I'm told it does. But all women do it."

"No, I mean to be the baby. To have lungs that aren't working yet."

Her father looked at her. "I hadn't thought of it," he said blankly.

"I'm sure it doesn't, Dad," she said quickly. Her father turned away to go down to his basement workshop. She went straight to her older brother. "Henry," she asked, "do you think Sally's scared?"

Henry nodded. "She might be. But it won't last forever. We'll all be fine."

Sally arrived home swaddled in blankets whose volume exceeded that of her own body. She was lost in folds of white cotton. A tuft of hair sprang past the outer layers and the children were allowed to push them aside and inspect the occupant.

"Uch," Winston said.

"Oh!" Lauren exclaimed.

Henry said nothing.

"When is she going to look like a person?" Winston demanded. "She's all red with white scummy stuff on her skin."

Lauren thought she saw the top of the baby's head throb. She ventured a hand out, tentatively brushed the top of the baby's head. Something liquid and warm pushed against the skin at the baby's crown. She whipped the hand away as if a blowtorch flame had sprung from the infant skull.

"That's her fontanel," their mother said. "Her skull hasn't closed over the opening yet. You must be very careful not to let it be hit."

"Her head isn't finished?" Winston gasped.

"Nobody's finished when they're born, Winston. It's normal. You came the same way." Their mother's voice was reassuringly amused and the children breathed sighs of relief. "Lauren and Henry just don't remember you this little." Sally began to wail and push out in little spasmodic kicks. "Warren, go warm some formula. She's probably starved."

"What?"

"Go warm some formula. Show Henry and Lauren how to sterilize bottles so they can help when you're back at work."

"Now listen," their father said when he had them in the kitchen. "The doctor said your mother still isn't tip-top. So you two have to step up to the plate here and make sure Winston is taken care of. You'll have to keep helping around the house so your mom can stay quiet." They nodded soberly.

"Come hold your sister, Lauren." Their mother smiled when they returned to the living room.

They seated Lauren and placed the blankety mound on her knees. She propped up Sally's face and peered into it. The infant met her gaze head-on, utterly focused, penetrating, curious. "She's looking at me!" Lauren insisted.

"No, no," her father corrected. "Babies don't look at anything for weeks and weeks."

"Yes they do, Warren," Annie broke in. "Just for a little window in the beginning days they do. Then they get unfocused again. Like they go inside themselves. But every one of my babies met my eyes directly when they were first born."

"Did I?" Winston asked.

"You especially," she said.

That was a lie she told him just to make him feel good," Lauren muttered to Henry later that afternoon.

"Maybe," he said. "Maybe not."

In the following weeks they learned to mouth and clip diaper pins, to urge a bubble of air up from Sally's baby belly, to rock and walk until the gurgling breath at their ears took on an even rhythm. Their mother did her best but it was clear to Henry and Lauren that she was exhausted. They learned the baby's schedule, her regimented needs, and took her from their mother to walk and burp and change and hold as often as they could. On good days there was no better baby than

Sally. On bad days no amount of walking could calm her for longer than it took to try to lay her back into her crib, and then the howling would resume at the first step away from her.

"Sally cries so much," Lauren whispered on one such day, near tears herself. Her dreams were full of pins and bottles, and her back ached from walking Sally endlessly back and forth from one corner of the upstairs hallway to the other. "And Mom sleeps so much. She's like the baby."

"But Winston's behaving himself," Henry reminded her. "And I'm helping you with all your homework."

This was true.

And then one day as she changed Sally's diaper the infant looked up at her with a wrinkled old lady's face that suddenly, inexplicably, broke open into a smile that lit up her entire body. To Lauren, it felt more directed at just her than any smile she had ever seen in her life. It sent a tingling wave through her body—she actually jumped back from the table. Then she collected herself, kissed the baby softly on her fontanel and gathered her up. Sally's toes reached just to Lauren's belly button, and they tapped there for a few minutes until Lauren settled into a rocking chair with the baby draped over her chest. They remained there, rocking, all alone through what was left of the afternoon light.

She didn't tell anyone about the smile or how it had felt, but kept it for herself alone.

Three

Three o'clock in the morning and the seeping blood woke Annie Cooper from a dream of blood to its reality. She reached down and it met her searching hand, which left streaking prints on the doorjamb and doorknob as she made her way to the bathroom. It left a dripping trail between her legs all the long way back to the bed. Sweat covered her face and she realized she was desperately hot, panting—from fear or a fever she could not tell.

Once again Henry was woken in darkness and told that his parents had to leave them. "Call Betty Haffitz next door and tell her what happened," his father instructed in a whisper. "Stay here and don't wake anybody until it's time to get up. Then get the baby's bottle out of the refrigerator and run it under hot water for her. Get yourselves organized for school, and call Betty Haffitz next door to watch Sally until I get back. Okay. Can you repeat that?"

He could. Then he lay rigidly in the dark and waited until it was time to do all the things he had been told to do. He heard the car engine rumble to life, heard his parents back out of the driveway and leave, heard the night insect noises give way to birdsong, and then finally, finally, enough gray in the sky to justify getting up.

But before he could reach the kitchen and Sally's waiting bottle, he heard Lauren scream. He pounded into the girls' room and found his sister clutching Sally by the middle, holding the baby directly in front of her like a pot or a bag. A dripping bottle sat neglected on the crib-side floorboards.

"Something's wrong with Sally, Henry! What's wrong with Sally? I woke up early and I thought I'd feed her her bottle and I went and got it but she won't drink! She doesn't move, and she doesn't feel right!"

Winston stumbled into the room and took in the scene. Henry peeled Sally out of Lauren's firm grasp and lay her down on the floor just as he'd learned in Boy Scouts. He pushed on the tiny girl's chest. He breathed into her mouth. He told Lauren to call the hospital, and to call their next-door neighbor, but she was too undone to manage either task. Henry had thumped and breathed for several minutes, he didn't know how many. His brother and sister stood petrified by his side. When he gathered that no one, no adult person, knew of their situation, he placed Sally's body in Lauren's arms and sat her, with the corpse, on the rocker. "Hold her and don't move," he ordered. He ran to the telephone and called the emergency number, told the adult who answered what he thought was happening and where he was and then dashed back into the girls' bedroom. His siblings stood and sat, frozen, uncertain. What should they do now? What could they do? An immense icy quiet lay around them—a terrible quiet. His younger siblings turned to him as they always did, asking what would happen now.

"An ambulance is coming," he told them.

"She's dead," Lauren whispered. "Isn't she? And she hasn't been baptized."

"You have to do it," Winston cried. "You have to do it, Henry, or she'll be stuck in the limbo place! We have to baptize her!"

"But last week in catechism the Sister said you had to do it when they were alive," Lauren said. "What if it doesn't work? What will happen?"

"She won't be stuck. We can do the baptism. Anybody can." Henry spoke with so much authority that Winston turned on his heel and came back with a glass of water, which he handed to his brother. He took it, dipped his fingers in, approached the rocking chair, and braced himself. He spattered drops on Sally's now silent fontanel. He said, "I baptize you in the name of the Father and the Son and the Holy Spirit." They all three said, "Amen." Then Henry and Winston sat down on the floorboards by Lauren's feet and waited for the grown-ups to find them.

The doctors called it a mystery. It happened sometimes, they said. It just happens.

"If God took Sally he must have needed her," their father said soberly. "She's in God's hands now."

"It is not your fault," Annie Cooper told her children, better able to divine their fears than her husband. "It is nobody's fault."

Henry and Winston absorbed what their parents said soberly. Lauren didn't. She said, "Henry, what could God need from Sally?" Sally was just about the size of a roaster chicken. What could she do for God?" Lauren remembered one afternoon when she had gotten impatient with Sally and put her in her crib roughly, the baby still crying. She remembered the smile and the way Sally's little tapping feet just reached her own stomach when she lifted the little girl up. The two memories came together and emptied all the air out of her lungs.

Henry said, "It's not so bad to die. It's just going somewhere else."

Henry laid one hand gently on her arm. He didn't make the dark ideas vanish but he dulled their power over her. She eventually tipped over onto a pillow at the bottom of his bed, where the next morning she woke covered with his second blanket.

A new and thicker kind of darkness fell down on their household. Lauren could see her mother struggle almost every moment with a desire to sleep. She had come home from the hospital like this, and they had waited for it to go away but it hadn't, even after the doctors said she was healed. Lauren hid and watched her, though she needn't have bothered hiding; their mother's state of mind kept her children invisible to her. Lauren could plainly see that something had her mother in its teeth and that Annie was helpless now.

Had Lauren been able to hear her mother's thoughts, they would not have comforted her. She would have heard Annie Cooper think, as she passed a building with a plaque bolted to its side, reading "1901": The man who laid that cornerstone is dead. If her mother then lifted her eyes and saw a bridge, she would think, And all the men who built that, too. The engineers. The men who worked underwater. How horrible, to work underwater—to maybe die contained in dark spaces underwater. Annie would imagine these people getting up in the morning so proud and happy to be working on these things that didn't care a bit about them, that stood long after they were gone and felt nothing but the weather. Were these men frightened when they died?

Lauren could feel the cool sharp change in the way her mother looked at her and her brothers. She didn't talk to her brothers about it but they felt it too, she was sure. It was just another mystery. Now she refused to join Henry when he looked at *Disaster, Disaster, Disaster.* The pictures had taken on a different, closer meaning.

She watched her mother for clues as to what made her happy, and what made her sad, but her mother hid from her—she was the kind of parent who believed in protecting children from adult troubles. Some kinds of telephone conversations now took place after bedtime, when eavesdropping children could not hear them from the stairs. Then there were the silences, long silences, which were perhaps worse than what could be made out by eavesdropping. Lauren tried to think of the sadnesses she felt in her house as having nothing to do with her—she was only a child, after all. But it didn't work. She knew that no one was safe here.

They sat at the kitchen table listening to the same music that had drifted over an entirely different household a few months before. Her mother always had the radio on now: "Moon River," "Those Lazy Hazy Crazy Days of Summer," "Love Makes the World Go Round," "Call Me Irresponsible." Lauren put away her *My Fair Lady* and *Christian Songs for the Young* records and practiced these other songs. She watched her mother's feet shuffle and tap as she squeezed orange juice in the morning, the two-tone blue radio that their father had built playing at her elbow. Evenings, after dinner dishes, Lauren thumped around in her room, working out steps to go with the lyrics. In the afternoons she began assembling parts of a costume. In her own mind, she planned a surprise performance that would be so brilliant and so tactfully timed that it would leave her mother permanently charmed, happy again.

Much as she wanted to drag the whole show downstairs, however, she was too much of a coward to manage it alone. Winston helped her in the end. He turned to his mother one morning as they were all eating breakfast and "Moon River" floated out of the blue radio. He said, "Lauren sings that song in her bedroom all the time. Right, Lauren? Show them. Go get the tutu and show them the song."

Lauren lowered her face closer to the cereal bowl.

"Come on. I've seen you." He turned to Henry and his mother. "It's weird. Wait'll you see."

"It is not weird."

"Whatever. Come on and do it. What are you, scared?"

Lauren pushed away from the table, went upstairs and yanked on the pink tutu and the plastic sequined shoes. She jammed a torn straw hat on her head, made her way back into the kitchen and did her number to "Moon River." Her mother watched politely, but Henry and Winston banged the kitchen table and howled, inspiring her to even more, entirely improvised steps. They pleaded for more, but their mother said they were to thank her for the entertainment and clear the table now please. There were things to do.

So in the end Lauren's intended audience smiled thinly and thanked her formally, and the effort she had spent was lost. But Lauren noticed that she herself felt immensely better. So, it seemed, did Winston. The dance had missed its target, but still, it had a curative effect.

"Where did you get that idea?" Winston asked her later.

"I don't know," she said. "Maybe from Henry."

"Well," Winston said. "I liked the part where you tipped the chair over and fell on your butt."

"I saw that in a movie with Fred Astaire. He didn't fall, though," she added.

Four

Two years after Sally's death, two years after her first failed attempt at becoming a first communicant, and Lauren Cooper sat in the third chair in row three of Sister Leonarda's class—its only nine-year-old member.

The Sister had pulled down a chart that she then turned her back upon and ignored. The horizontal values were labeled PENANCE; the vertical, PURGATORIAL BENEFITS. This particular chart showed how much time each kind of prayer or mass offering was worth, in terms of time knocked off a stay in purgatory. Mass cards carried the most weight, valued at a full decade.

Domenic had his hand up. "So you can, you know, get out of even mortal sins by, you know, buying mass cards and saying rosaries?"

"There has never been a mass card printed that could address a mortal offense," she sniffed.

"Like what?" Domenic persisted. "I mean, what mortal sins?"

The Sister's eyebrows poked up into two little V's. "You have some particular offense in mind, Mr. Rumietti." It was not a question. "Mr. Rumietti, you are too young to know how to commit a mortal sin." A general embarrassment spread through the classroom as the future communicants imagined what was on Mr. Rumietti's mind, scanning their charts busily to place their own theoretical offenses and see just how much trouble he was in, spiritually speaking.

"My dears," the nun said then. "You are safe. Mortal sin requires some experience—generally even skill. Seven-year-olds are not yet reflective enough to commit such a thing." She turned to Lauren. "Also nine-year-olds," she added.

Lauren had scenes from *Disaster, Disaster, Disaster* on her mind. Lately she had found herself opening the book when she was alone. The Hiroshima chapter in particular had power over her. And among the Hiroshima photographs, the one of the ravaged woman drew her most irresistibly. The woman's arms were lifted as if in prayer, and behind her a man ran through the ashes and embers, his hands stretched toward her. Her clothes had been burned from her body and the skin of her arms was charred and hanging slack from the bone. In the place on her chest where there had been a second breast there was only a gaping mouthlike wound. There were other people in the picture but she did not remember them after she closed the book.

Sitting here in Sister Leonarda's presence, she wanted to say that the photographs from *Disaster, Disaster, Disaster* looked like Calvary. Surely sins, mortal sins, had led to the things she saw in these photographs. Surely suffering was not Jesus's alone.

Also, she had begun to read the newspaper. Only the week before she had asked her father the meanings of "rape" and "nude." She already knew the significance of "abandoned" and "garbage Dumpster." Warren had told her gruffly to go to the dictionary. She had not. She had gone to Henry, and he had solemnly explained these words.

"The crucifixion," the Sister was saying, "is the defeat of death. It makes mortal suffering meaningful and insignificant at once."

Lauren thought of the weight of Sally's body the morning she had not woken up. She tried to imagine her own father giving her up to be crucified for somebody else's good. It seemed to her that it would be a bad thing, a very bad thing, to pass her or Henry or Winston off to a mob that would effect their humiliating, violent deaths. It didn't matter for what or for whom.

What would happen to her, Lauren wondered anxiously, if she found herself thinking of God as a figure from *Disaster, Disaster, Disaster*? That had to be wrong.

"Name the sins against hope," Sister Leonarda demanded. She waved three fingers at the first raised arm.

"The sins against hope are presumption and despair," a student in the second row called out.

"Such temptations." Her hand flew suddenly to one of the larger moles on her face. "Open to page seventy-three," she called out, once again brisk and certain. They did. On the top of page seventy-three was an illustration showing the soul, in the symbolic form of a diesel locomotive, leaving Station Earth, in the form of a church with "Baptism" written on its side, and making its way past all the holy sacraments, which appeared as grocery stores, suburban homes and other interesting buildings with the sacraments' names scrawled on their sides. At the end of the tracks the train shot into a dark box labeled "Extreme Unction" and popped out the other side directly into a cloud.

Father Murphy knocked on the classroom door, and the Sister excused herself to speak to him in the hallway. When she returned she looked very tired.

"Children," she said. "I stand reminded that when the Father visited us last and asked questions about insurgencies, your answers led him to believe that we had work yet to do. Still, I want you to know that none of you, I repeat none of you, will get two weeks knocked off your time in purgatory for saying two Hail Marys. Pay no attention to me now, but it is my duty to stand here and point at the numbers."

"Sister," a dissenting voice piped up. "I had Sister Paula last year and she said she was relieved and grateful for insurgencies. She said they were one of God's greatest gifts."

"Sister Paula," Sister Leonarda replied, "is a lovely young woman with warm reserves of faith, but an unfortunately literal idea of dogma. Insurgencies mean nothing. What you do while you're here means everything."

Sister Leonarda says insurgencies are bunk," Lauren announced at dinner that night.

"Certainly she didn't," her father scoffed. "Insurgencies are a serious subject."

"But she did!"

"Lauren, I'm sure Sister Leonarda never said anything at all like that," her mother said quickly.

"They never believe me," Lauren complained later that evening to Henry. "But she told us insurgencies were a lot of hooey and that Sister Paula is stupid."

"I know. I had Sister Paula when I was in first grade and Sister Leonarda last year."

"Well, why didn't you say so at dinner, then?"

"It would have made Mom and Dad very unhappy to think you were telling the truth, maybe so unhappy that they might call Father Murphy, and then Father Murphy would make Sister Leonarda unhappy. Not to mention all the masses Mom and Dad have bought for Sally's soul."

"Sister's already unhappy."

"No, no. She's very happy most of the time. She's just unhappy when Father Murphy makes her do things she doesn't want to do."

"Do you think Sister Paula is stupid?"

Henry nodded. "Yes."

"Sister Leonarda isn't normal. I think she has a lot of problems. And she's a nun. Nuns are Jesus's brides. So what does that mean about God?"

"Probably God has a lot of problems." Her brother looked at her anxious face and sighed. "You're nervous about things because Mom's been sick. Because of what happened with Sally. Lauren, Mom is better now, and everything will be normal again."

She retreated to her bed and anxiously opened her catechism to the section on the sacrament of penance. She studied the illustration of a little boy and girl, wearing a suit and pinafore, respectively, kneeling under an open-winged dove signifying the Holy Ghost. Over their heads a little balloon contained the words *1-Examine, 2-Sorrow, 3-Sin No More.* At the bottom of the page in another bubble two soldiers in World War II Allied uniforms marched with guns over their shoulders and the words *Onward Christian Soldiers* below their feet. She shut the book to think about that.

Five

Two years went by. Slowly, almost so gradually that she hadn't seen it happening, rage had sunk its teeth into Lauren's eleven-year-old heart and she couldn't get free. Right now, as so often lately, her rage was directed at Winston.

"It's not you. It's him."

Henry was speaking to her, patiently working his way through the feelings that kept her from hearing what he said, kept her from caring about his fascinating planes. Lauren moved in the lower steppes of junior high school now, and from the elevated position of seventh grade, Henry's planes looked like a childish preoccupation that her older brother should have abandoned long ago. But she never said that to Henry because it was one of the things they didn't talk about, like Sally. Though Sally had died four years before and the half of the room that had held her crib was empty, nothing of Lauren's had bled into the space. It was as if the baby's things were still there but invisible.

Henry held out a model of a glass-nosed Heinkel He 177 Greif that looked like a great bug. "What's that?" she asked, not particularly caring, only asking the question to repay her brother's kindness.

"Six-crew bomber. German. Maximum speed three hundred three miles per hour with a climb rate of six hundred twenty-three feet per minute."

"It looks like a bug. A praying mantis." She picked up another one, rolled it over and examined its belly. If she were honest with herself Lauren would see that the planes did indeed have a compelling quality for her—toys yet not toys at all. Directly beneath the impatience she felt with Henry's interest in them she felt something else—a rippling sweet anxiety. This other, hidden feeling made the planes harder to ignore. She peered closely at the fuselage in her hands. She said, "This one looks like needle-nosed pliers with wings."

Henry looked up. "Isn't it something? It's the Messerschmitt Me 262, the later model of that plane. Maximum speed five hundred forty-one miles per hour. Single-seat flyer. There's a two-seat model—the Sturmvogel—but I haven't been able to find it. They had radar equipment that kept them in the air day or night."

"This one looks friendly." Lauren pointed up at a model that was banking at fifty degrees right above her head. She knew it was Japanese because it had that red dot on its side. "It's got a nose like a cocker spaniel." The plane struck her as cozily boxy, thick in its middle and blunt on its snout. It looked, unlike many of the planes hanging from the ceiling, like a toy.

"That's a Mitsubishi A6M 'Zeke'—the Zero. It was the first carrier-borne fighter that could shoot down any land-based fighter it found. It could climb about twenty thousand feet in seven minutes. Flew up to three hundred fifty miles per hour. If the Americans hadn't gotten their Hellcats into the war right after them, there wouldn't have been a thing in the world to stop them.

"This is a Boeing B-29 Superfortress," Henry continued, holding up a piece of the plane he was completing. "In two days in 1945 a B-29 firebombing raid on Tokyo leveled most of the city." He revolved the plane slowly in his hands. "They say the canals and rivers boiled."

The Boeing bomber was black. Its wingspan was three times that of the Zero or the other fighters in the air above their heads. Its nose was blunt, made of squares of clear plastic that rolled up over the pilot's head and into a smooth line with the thick cylindrical roof of the plane's body. It dwarfed the models around it, and it did not look at all like a toy.

She thought she heard adult footsteps on the stairs and she started. Henry should hide that thing! was her first thought. It was an adult thing, a bad thing, even a mildly pornographic thing, and the adults would disapprove and take it away. But before these thoughts had even gotten finished in her mind she realized that this was not true. The adults knew all about Henry's fighters and bombers and in fact their father took some friendly interest in them. He told stories about seeing them in action.

Her father, she knew, regarded these planes as a kind of high point of civilization—enormously complex and exact creations that reflected the highest intelligence in his species. He clapped Henry on the back in a manly fashion when he looked at the planes. Their father did not sense, as Lauren sensed, that his interest in the planes was not a bond with Henry. They did not see the same things when they looked at the models.

She would change the subject back to her original complaint. She said, "He ran that tape recorder into my room and hung a microphone above my closet! He played it at school!"

Winston's recording had included several numbers from *My Fair Lady,* all sung by Lauren in what she had assumed was the privacy of her own bedroom. He had played it for the family only last night, blocking his enraged sister's attempts to hit the off button until their mother intervened, telling him to turn it off because it was not kind to mock his sister. As far as Lauren was concerned, Winston Cooper was only getting worse, and nobody was doing a thing about it.

"Mom and Dad let Winston get away with murder," she grumbled, absorbing but pretending to ignore the exact date of the firebombing.

"They don't have to punish him," Henry told her. "He feels bad enough without their punishing him and they know it. This particular B-14"—he held up another model, abandoning the B-29 for now—"was known for complications in the landing gear. I've actually modified it to reproduce some of the faulty hinge joints that caused the most problems. See? They stick. Isn't that great?"

Lauren put down the record she'd been holding. Henry had known from the way she'd held it and from the funny bend in her neck that *The Sound of Music* was in danger. "Last summer, for example," she said.

"Last summer what?" Henry laid an incredibly small decal to soak in the also very small bowl of water that he kept in his room for this purpose. He so loved this kind of detailed exactitude. The perfect little strip of trim floated for a moment before drifting downward.

"Last summer when Winston ate all the aspirin and had to go to the hospital, Mom said it was an accident. She said he thought it was candy."

"He likes the orange-flavored ones." Henry nodded.

"He didn't think it was candy."

"I think he did."

"He didn't think it was candy. Maybe the first time he did it he thought it was candy. Not the second. And when I said that, Mom and Dad said I didn't know what I was talking about. I did."

"Maybe you did." Henry swished the water gently.

"I'm not crazy."

"Nobody said you were crazy."

"Yes, they did. They keep saying that Winston is normal and I'm not. But I know there's something wrong with Winston, Henry." She was also thinking, There's something wrong with me. I can't control my mind. People tell me that what I see isn't there. Things come into my head that are definitely not right. God is not a character in *Disaster, Disaster, Disaster,* for example. Yet that is how He is in my mind sometimes. Winston ate the aspirins on purpose. I am not crazy; Winston is crazy. Everybody else is afraid to see that Winston ate them on purpose.

"No. He's all right. He was just mad, Lauren, angry, like you are right now."

"But I don't go around eating bowls of aspirin, do I? I never sawed things in half or took apart locks, or built little death traps for insects, did I?" Winston had developed anxious feelings about spiders and ants recently, and had begun building traps out of sugar-baited boxes for them. He passed entire afternoons waiting for insects to enter. Then he crushed them. So far he'd had no luck with spiders, which preferred live food and were too busy working on their own traps to notice Winston's. But he was getting very good at finding high-traffic areas and arranging lures attractively.

"You're different than Winston." Henry had spent a good deal of the morning putting a television back together that Winston had dismantled. Henry had argued that it would only upset their mother to see it in pieces and it would be amusing, anyway, to get a close look at a television's insides. He enlisted Lauren's help and the two had worked side by side until it was done. And as usual, Henry was right. It had been fun, just the two of them solving little puzzles, making the world right again behind the grown-ups' backs. She knew Warren's workshop as well as Henry—probably better—and it was Lauren who found the tools they'd needed.

"You're not kidding." Lauren kicked the plastic molding that ran around Henry's walls. She kicked it so hard that the plasterboard behind the molding cracked and the water in his stencil-soaking bowl jumped. "Maybe God is trying to tell me something through Winston," Lauren said. "Maybe I'm not listening right."

"You're a good listener, Lauren. Here. Hold this." Henry held out the bowl and she cradled it while he removed the stencil with a pair of tweezers and gently separated the back from the design itself. Henry didn't even breathe when he applied decals, and Lauren knew that she, too, was expected to maintain an unnatural stillness. She counted to ninety-eight, barely filling her lungs, almost hissing as she let the air out so carefully, until the red spot was in place.

Free to speak again she resumed her complaints. "Nobody hears me."

"Who doesn't hear you?"

"I just told you, Henry! I just said that Mom and Dad tell me I remember things that didn't happen. I just said that!"

"You really should look at this landing gear design."

"You aren't listening to me!"

Lauren stamped around the room for a few seconds before her feelings simply blew her out into the hallway. What was wrong with Henry, anyway? Why wasn't he paying attention?

She went to her room and prayed not to lose Henry, who seemed to be slipping out of her grasp. She then searched the room for hidden wires and microphones, and invented four different unworkable and detailed plans to make Winston miserable. The plans only made her miserable herself. She struggled against these feelings about Winston, but she only felt eviller.

Footsteps outside her door.

"Go away, Winston!"

No answer.

"I said go away! Go away or I'll make you sorry! Leave me alone!"

Footsteps padded away and Lauren sank to the floor in relief. The desire to hurt someone faded as the intruder—certainly Winston—retreated. She spent the remainder of the long afternoon simply sitting on her bed waiting for whatever was driving this mood to let go of her.

Annie Cooper had seen sadness come and go, sometimes cripplingly sharp, sometimes just enervating. She never got the knack of predicting how bad it would be or how long it would stay, which made her feel helpless against it. One morning she woke up feeling a bad patch coming on and decided she couldn't face it alone. She announced that she was going to visit her sister Honey.

Except for the terrible times around Sally's birth, the family had never been without her for more than a few hours. After she made the announcement Warren took her aside to say that she could not possibly go, that she was needed here at home.

For once Annie didn't accommodate his fear. She would yield to this pressing need and so would everyone around her. "Warren," she said to him at the dinner table the night before she left, "I'm going to get on an airplane and order a martini on the flight. When I get there I'm going to make Honey tell me jokes, and I'm going to go shopping, and we'll eat whatever we want and we'll smoke cigarettes. We'll drink beer on the back porch and throw the cans into the parking lot behind her house." Her family was as dumbfounded by the speech as by the fact that she was going to do it.

Back at home things began unraveling the moment she got out of the driveway. Lauren watched her father pace around the kitchen table for an hour one night before his anxiety drove her into hiding in her usual retreat in the stairwell. From there she heard him pick up the telephone and dial. She made out "Are you having a good time with your sister?" and then "You know, you can change your ticket for an earlier flight back."

She said she didn't know how to change plane tickets.

In the end it was Winston who forced the issue. The first few days Winston did what Henry told him to do; he tried to be good. Then he got mad and stood in the street defying oncoming traffic, just to scare Henry and Lauren, who were responsible for him while their father was at work. He stopped doing what he was told and started talking about what bee stings could do to you, and spider bites. A few days later he put a clock, a cellophane package of Oreos and a pair of underwear in a paper bag and ran away from home. He left a note explaining that he would never be found again. Henry called the police, who plucked him from the roadside a thousand yards from their door, sitting in a stranger's front yard crying and eating Oreo cookies. The police took Winston to his father's office to discuss it.

Warren Cooper called his wife. "Annie, you are needed here!" he pleaded.

That night as she and Honey rocked and drank beer on the porch, Annie said, "I'm not just running away from home, am I? Maybe Winston just gets it naturally from me. Maybe I'm just selfish, letting myself feel like this. After all, I'm not the only one who lost that baby."

It was the only mention of this loss, this reason for her fleeing her family, that she had made in the entire visit.

"Men," Honey replied, which was comforting to her, in a strange way.

The next day Warren called to say that they couldn't even carry Winston out of the house, he was so afraid of the bugs. He'd spread-eagled himself at the door. The child was unscrewing and puncturing and sawing everything he could get his hands on. It was hard to fall asleep sometimes, waiting for the squeaky sawteeth sounds or the rasp of a screwdriver on a bolt.

She came home.

The children circled their mother warily in the weeks that followed, looking for a change, fearing the times she slipped into glazed and absent states. Lauren found little jobs to do around her, as if keeping her mother within eyeshot provided a kind of protection. Henry soldiered on, rummaging in the freezer every morning and defrosting things for dinners. Then their mother found Winston struggling to tie a pillowcase onto a stick. The pillowcase, upended, revealed a loaf of bread, a handful of miniature cars and a carton of orange juice: another escape attempt. His mother spanked him.

She spanked him harder than she meant, lost in a dizzying and satisfying rage. Tears sprang out of Winston's eyes and fell on her knees, the first he had ever shed in front of her, and this shocked her back to her right mind. She came to consciousness as if from a distant place where a woman overcome with anger was hitting a small child as hard, as absolutely hard, as she could. She began to cry herself. "Oh Winston," she sobbed, "I'm so sorry." Her head sank down onto the child's as she wept. This frightened Winston, who broke free and ran to get Henry and Lauren. The children gathered around their mother in a little gaggle of petting hands, stroking her face, crying themselves when it became clear that she couldn't stop.

Then finally she did stop. She suggested that they eat hot dogs. They agreed enthusiastically, as they would have had she suggested they eat mud balls. Halfway through her hot dog, her eyes popped completely open. Annie lifted the wiener to eye level for inspection as if it were an entirely foreign substance. "I can taste it," she whispered. "My God, I can taste it."

She was coming back for sure.

It was happening just in time, because there were things to be dealt with. Winston was beginning to experiment with rewiring things in the night when they slept. Lauren had woken her father only the night before to report that she had found him fiddling with a smoking electrical socket.

"How do I make him quit it!" Lauren had begged Henry.

"You don't have to make him quit," Henry had assured her. "It's not your job."

"Someone has to!" she argued.

"No," Henry said, patting her head absently. "No, no. Winston will be fine. He'll stop on his own."

And Henry would move his models into Winston's room for a few days and work there. Some nights he slept on the floor beside Winston's bed. Lauren hated this because the steady low murmuring between her brothers was a barrier that stood between her and Henry. But it made Winston better, so she tolerated it.

At school there was no Henry to stand by Winston's side because Henry had moved on to the high school, where he was probably the ninth grade's youngest student. Lauren, though she was in the seventh grade, was in the same building as the fifth-graders. Keeping an eye out for Winston thus became her patrol, her watch, her grim solitary responsibility.

One afternoon a telephone call summoned Annie to her children's school: Lauren, she was told, was not in control of herself. When she arrived a blotchy-faced Lauren was sitting cross-armed in a chair outside the principal's office door. "Please come in, Mrs. Cooper," the principal said coolly. Lauren was not invited in, though the door was left ajar so she could hear herself being discussed. She had punched Timothy Hanover so hard that she might have broken his nose, the principal reported. She had then punched Timothy Hanover's brother Tommy in the ear when he came to Timmy's aid. Told to report to the principal's office, she had refused. In fact, when pursued she had locked herself in the bathroom on the first floor and refused to come out.

"Well," Lauren heard her mother say at last. "So how did you get her out?"

"Is that all you have to say, Mrs. Cooper?" the principal asked her.

"I don't know. I haven't spoken to Lauren."

"The janitor had to remove the bolts and lift the door out of the jamb," the principal told her.

"This isn't like Lauren," Annie told him.

"Whatever she is like, Mrs. Cooper, she did these things today and she will go home with you now. I am expelling her from the building for the remainder of the week."

"Humph," Annie said. "Humph."

"Mrs. Cooper, I know that your family has had difficult times . . ."

"Our difficult times need not concern you," she said dryly.

Once she had Lauren alone in the car she began a firm lecture on appropriate behavior. Lauren responded with rage: she had only done what had to be done! Timothy Hanover had been trying to force Winston to eat dirt on the playground, which Winston imagined to be full of bugs, as if the dirt itself weren't bad enough! Timmy, Lauren pointed out, was just as tall as she was and ten pounds heavier, nothing but a bully. And she hadn't bitten him! He had tried to jam his elbow into her mouth and her teeth had cut through his skin! Didn't the principal want to see her own bruises? Didn't anybody want to hear her side?

Lauren certainly hadn't heard the principal outlining her side of the story in his interview with her mother. In fact, he had concluded by saying that Lauren had an immature and violent temper and that perhaps outside assistance was called for. Perhaps, he had said ominously, perhaps Lauren Cooper was a narcissist.

It was clear to Lauren that though her mother was enraged, she was not enraged with her daughter. She slammed every door she moved through that afternoon, and when her husband got home she repeated everything the principal had said. Lauren took up her post on the fourth step and settled in to listen. Her father actually looked up the word "narcissist" in a medical dictionary and started explaining how the man might have arrived at this word.

"No," Annie said. "You are on our side, Warren; that man is not. We are not the school's Defective Family. We are not what he thinks we are."

"Be reasonable," Warren said to her.

"Be on my side," she said back. "Be on our side."

"Well, Lauren has to learn to behave herself, even if the principal's judgment isn't good. He's the principal. She has to learn to acknowledge authority—she'll have a hard life if she doesn't."

"Oh, Warren!" she said in disgust. "She was protecting Winston!"

"Well, she didn't manage to communicate that to the people in charge, did she? You have to learn to work with the guy in charge. That's the way the world works, Annie."

Her mother told Lauren that she would have to go in and apologize to everybody involved. Lauren's eyes narrowed into wolfy green slits. "Lauren," Annie said, "you have to help me. Don't attract any more attention, all right? You have to help me with this. Do you understand?"

The canine sag to Lauren's head and the sharp predatory look in her eyes went away just like that. She nodded. You and me, Mom, the nod said.

"Baby," she said to Lauren, "would you do that 'Moon River' thing you did a while ago for us after dinner?"

Lauren brightened significantly. "Sure, Mom."

"You're a good girl, Lauren. It was a kind thing for you to do that dance for me when you knew I needed cheering up. It was a good dance."

Lauren found the record, the tutu.

"Thank you, honey," Lauren's mother said when it was done. "That was lovely."

Six

THE CHRISTMAS OF 1962, Henry was fourteen years old, Lauren twelve and Winston ten. Christmas was Henry's happiest time. If Winston or Lauren sliced themselves open on a rock or branch, if they suffered humiliations at school, Henry had the same advice for them: Think of Christmas.

Two weeks before Christmas Eve Lauren slid off the McGrath's icy barn roof trying to help Winston, who had wedged himself on a shingle halfway down and didn't need her to save him at all, it turned out. The McGraths lived at the very edge of their residential neighborhood, corn and pasture land stretching away for seven miles behind their barn. The McGrath children were close in ages to the Coopers so the families had known each other for years; the mothers had long observed the tradition of exchanging holiday cookies or cakes. Thus, the visit.

On this particular day, Lauren and Winston had squeezed out a hole in the McGrath barn's loft wall to look over acres of new snow while Annie sat drinking coffee with Mrs. McGrath, her children far outside the range of adult sight. Once on the roof, Winston lapsed into the usual dares, threats, shoves. Lauren saw it was all going in the wrong direction but she couldn't get Winston to scramble back up into the barn. He said he'd jump off, that she couldn't stop him. She said she could. He stretched his feet out in front of him and pushed off and she had no choice at all but to go after him. Winston had managed to wedge his heel in a split roof tile; she sailed over the edge and broke her lower leg in two places. Winston had been spanked. Think of Christmas, Henry had told them both when the spanking and cast-setting were done.

Their mother taught all three of them to cut snowflakes and reindeer and snowmen from white paper. When Winston destroyed or broke too many things in the process he was swept to the busy circle's outside edges, forbidden scissors and glue until he was forgiven. Usually this took about an hour. They plastered so much aluminum glitter and foil to their paper creations that the gluey wreaths and doughy Santas made a soft little clanking against the windowpanes and walls when the forced hot air heat kicked on. Lauren thought of this as a distinctly Christmas sound: *pshwewww, pshwewww, pfunk-pfunkpfunk.*

Henry and Lauren strung miles of popcorn, leaving about half of the snowy kernels splashed with blood from their pricked fingers. They stood on kitchen chairs through entire mornings with their tongues jammed between their teeth, forgotten while their owners struggled to cream butter and sugar. Lauren clumped back and forth on her cast from the backyard where she cut pine greens. She wedged them wherever they could be smelled without being stepped on regularly.

In her own childhood, their mother told them, parents were

expected to manage the tree's arrival between Christmas Eve and morning. But here in her own household, tree selection was a committee process that took place about five days before the Day itself. Winston typically had the final word because he was most insistent, most inflexible and most likely to spoil the event with a tantrum if everyone else didn't give in. They gave in at Christmas. This didn't make Winston any more satisfied. He changed his mind over and over in the aisles of furry little saplings. He changed it as they waited in line to pay for his absolutely final choice. He was tormented, understanding that everyone was going to go along with him and the final responsibility was entirely his. But there was always an end to it and they wedged Winston's selection into the trunk or tied it on the car roof, holding onto branches as they drove. They wrestled it upright and struggled to agree on how to make it erect, an almost perfectly ninety-degree angle to the earth. Then they hung things on it.

When their father got home from work, he'd find his wife and children sitting in a quiet circle, watching the tree in a trance-like state. No one would have made dinner. He hated disorder and disrupted routine, but he bore the disruptions patiently, stepping around piles of glitter and paper.

Henry served as luminary advisor, heading up the efforts to untangle last year's quickly stripped tree lights. He ran the entire length of them down the hallway and into the kitchen, spotting shorts and burned-out bulbs. Henry had nothing but disdain for blinking lights, silver trees, or any departures from traditional schemes. He was persnickety about getting spaces right between lights on the outdoor shrubs and he bossed Winston and Lauren around while he did it, standing in the relative calm of the front yard and barking orders as they ripped their winter jackets climbing around in the briars with strings of lights. This year he occasionally stepped directly in to relieve Lauren, who had a cast as an excuse. They had sealed it up in Wonder bread bags before setting out into the front yard together.

Then, presents. Henry loved shopping for presents and helping Lauren and Winston shop. He had a special Christmas piggy bank, and everyone knew he monitored its contents all year. He thought and planned, unlike his brother and sister, who did all their shopping for the year in one fell swoop in a concentrated half hour at Gerry's Five and Dime. Not Henry. Henry made things for people, and inside or alongside what he made he offered up some other gift that not only fit the homemade item but suited the recipient. In the years that Lauren loved stuffed animals, he made burrows or cottages for them out of plaster or cardboard. He would set the stuffed animal he had chosen for her gently inside its personalized home and then wrap the whole package. Winston never tired of vehicles, and Henry designed and constructed garages and pit stops, bridges and tollbooths for them. As Winston's feelings about bugs got more complicated, Henry designed little houses for bugs, which Winston could not bear to use. Then Henry tried bug jails, which Winston thought were very wonderful indeed.

When Henry was thirteen years old he had presented his mother with a diamond chip in a necklace pendant. He had mowed thirty-seven lawns for it. For Henry, the maneuver was a triumph. He had out-Santa'd Santa. A Superman cape was among their gifts that year, and Henry wore it for weeks without a trace of irony.

During the week before Christmas, when the tree was up and wired, Henry regularly woke in the coldest part of the night and tiptoed down the stairs to sit in front of the heat register in the dark with the tree lights lit. If neighbors were awake, they would see the tree ping into life at around three A.M. and then vanish into darkness an hour later when he returned to bed. One night Lauren woke and saw the light from the first floor seeping up into the upstairs hallway. She poked her head over the banister and squinted. She slid along the stairway wall to avoid making any creaks, and slowly moved her head (at the bottom of the wall, so as to appear in a place that is not expected) past the doorjamb to see what was in the living room. She saw Henry, transfixed. She watched him for a few minutes before the cold drove her back upstairs to bed.

Children were not allowed, if awake, to make that fact known before six A.M. on Christmas morning. They were to remain upstairs pretending to sleep. On this particular morning Henry woke them all at four-thirty, unable to restrain himself. They paced up and down the hallway overlooking the narrow stairs, and finally retreated to the foot of Winston's bed. The bed board was still sliced halfway down its center but holding. A heat register warmed the air at the foot of Winston's bed, and here they spread a quilt on the icy floor and draped another blanket over their shoulders, shaping a tent that kept the hot air from blowing into the darkness around them. The night that shone into Winston's window was full of stars and their shadows. A full moon nodded down toward the top of the Haffitzes' garage roof. Its light cut a line like a pencil drawing down the incision in the bed board and lit up the outlines of a corner chair, a pile of discarded clothing by the bed, a bookcase and the little hamster cage, now empty, jammed against the far wall.

"I miss that hamster," Winston said suddenly.

"He misses you, too," Henry reassured him.

"How do you know that?"

"I just do. Hamsters are good souls. They're generally rememberers."

"How do you know that?"

"I've known hamsters," Henry replied.

"How much longer?" Lauren asked her older brother.

"One more hour," Henry replied. He was the only one among them with a watch and he kept it in his pajama shirt pocket, checking regularly to see how long before they could wake Warren and Annie.

"Animals are here to serve us. They're our food," Winston persisted.

Henry plugged in the Bozo record player and started the turntable spinning. Winston had started using the turntable as a track for his toy cars about a year ago, and it no longer moved at standard speeds. This gave all their records a loopy sound, either chipmunky or lugubrious. Henry set two or three cars on the turntable and slowed it. Winston rose to the bait and flipped the dial to 78, sending the lightest car on the platter skidding under the bed. He crawled off to get it, returning with a small front-end loader, a dump truck and a convertible roadster with doors that really opened. They divided these vehicles among themselves and set them in various patterns on the turntable, sometimes helping them along with little careening crash noises or aggressive tailgating. It took about twelve minutes for a sideswipe (Lauren did it—it was her fault, but he had been crowding her and crowding her) to drive Winston to his feet and then onto the turntable, crushing all the assembled little vehicles and spinning around himself. The weight of an entire child's body slowed the little turntable to a wobbling, grinding motion.

"Something's burning," Winston observed. Then he said, "Yikes!" and hopped off the turntable, which was very hot. Smoke poured from Bozo's mouth.

"Get back," Henry said calmly, pushing his brother and sister away from the machine. Then the thing happened that marked, in Lauren's mind anyway, the moment when Henry changed beyond any hope of turning back.

Her older brother reached forward, yanked the frayed cord out of the socket and in the process received an electrical shock that jolted him backward three feet. He would have gone farther but he collided with the bed board.

"Henry! Henry, get up! Henry?" Lauren tried to struggle to her feet, the cast tripping her and sending her careening back down and onto her prone brother.

Winston started screaming. Within twelve minutes their disheveled parents had dug the car out of the new snow while Lauren—her cast taped into plastic bags again—sat by Henry's side in the living room. Then they wrapped the unprotesting Henry in blankets, packed him in the backseat and skidded down to the end of the street onto plowed road, then on to the hospital emergency room. Henry's heart was listened to and pronounced still running pretty evenly. His blood pressure was checked, his temperature taken and his cheerful affect complimented. "Merry Christmas," he said to the sleepy resident attending him. "Merry Christmas," he greeted the nurse who wrapped the blood pressure collar around his arm. "What are you getting for Christmas?" he asked a young cardiologist. "I'm giving my little brother a spider jail. I've put in windows at adjoining walls to allow strategic drafts. Spiders like to build in drafts."

"Tell us your name," they answered. "Count backwards from ten. Are you thirsty? Are you nauseous?" They pried open his eyes and compared his pupils. They told him what they hoped to get for Christmas. The nurse flashed an engagement diamond and told him it was her best present.

"Beautiful," he said.

"This kid isn't disoriented," she told the resident.

"He's always like that," Lauren said.

"Well, that's good. We want him to be like he always is," the resident replied. Then the people in the emergency room told them to take Henry home and watch him. If he is in pain in forty-eight hours, they said, if he has a fever, if red streaks extend from the brown burned fingers, if the fingers swell, if there is a discharge, call.

They took Henry home and set him in the middle of the living room floor on a bank of cushions, and there he sat like a pasha, eating coffee cake and receiving presents. "Don't you love Christmas?" He beamed in the red and green and orange tree lights. "Isn't it just great?"

That afternoon the smell of roasting turkey and boiling potatoes rolled up the stairs and into every bedroom. Winston's toys lay around him in his bedroom in neat stacks—he always hamstered them away upstairs as soon as the morning was done. This year the gifts sat ignored while Winston lay on the floor among the Bozo record player's parts. He held each wire up to the light, rewound, reassembled. At the more confusing points he carried things to his father, who was spending the afternoon in his workroom listening to Christmas music and receiving ham radio messages from around the world. Sometimes his father traveled up the stairs with Winston to show him how to check a part or reconnect an electrical pathway. He found a new electric cord and taught Winston how to connect it. He patted Winston on the back, sometimes on the head. Good boy. Good boy. Keep working, he'd murmur as he walked back down to his workroom.

Annie Cooper had gone next door to borrow confectioners' sugar and stayed for a glass of wine. Henry and Lauren sat in his room under the model planes. She struggled with an irrational sense that Henry's accident had something to do with her—that she had left him vulnerable and open in a way that the electrical shock had found and moved through.

But he looked fine now and she herself was full of grateful relief. "Boy, I was scared when you got shocked," she sighed. "Wasn't Mom's coffee cake good?"

"Food is a wonderful thing," Henry replied. "Sometimes all it takes in the world to make a person happy is food."

"Yeah."

Lauren had gone to Henry's bedroom and found him bent, again, over *Disaster, Disaster, Disaster.* The terrible atomic bomb pages were open, with people in burned pieces spilling over the book's gutter. There was the one-breasted woman again, holding Lauren's eyes on her and not letting them go, and the man behind her, running toward them.

"Don't look at that," Lauren said impulsively. She turned her head away; she had to use some force to make it turn but she accomplished it.

"You know they called the years before the war the *kurotani.* It means the Valley of Darkness. There was nothing to eat but railroad grass fried up with soybean sludge."

"Where?"

"In Japan." He turned the page: still more photographs of Hiroshima. An armless boy stood over the corpse of a baby, his eyes hard and mottled like marbles. Henry flipped the page back again: the breastless woman; the running man.

"There." Henry pointed. His index finger drifted to the running man.

"What?"

"This man." Henry touched the page lightly. "He is running back into the center of the blast. He was further away from it; safer. He's trying to reach this woman. He's going to be a survivor—a *hibakusha.* I don't know what his name is." Henry's brow furrowed in concentration. "I can't . . . I don't know his name."

"You're making up stories about people in a picture? Or is there, like, writing about them? Where did you read that?"

"I didn't read it."

"So you made it up." Lauren flipped the page and scanned the text.

"No. It feels different from that. Lauren." Here he bent conspiratorially toward her. "I'll tell you what it feels like. It feels like I'm in this man's head." His fingers moved over the page again as if they were working over a Braille surface, coming to rest at last on the head of the figure who ran toward the one-breasted woman.

"Maybe the idea flew into your head on radio waves." She laughed uneasily. "Except the only stuff coming in right now is like *Big Bands at Four.*" She tried laughing again to see how it felt.

"Sound waves are very real," Henry said, as if this explained something.

Lauren ran through all the things the doctor had told them to watch for in the hours after the emergency room visit. There was no puffy red swelling, no red line radiating from the burn site. She put her hand to Henry's forehead, which was cool and smooth. He smiled at her.

"You know, Lauren, that dream I tell you about, the dream of the atomic bomb? It isn't my dream."

Lauren felt an icy thing, like a rush of liquid, roll from her feet to her head.

"Yeah. You said the hot air knocked you down. But it didn't happen, Henry."

"It did. It happened to these people, and I remember it from inside that man's head. He was there and I can remember his memory of it—sheets of fire and ash and people walking away from the blast. Lines of them like lost ants." Henry grew more animated as he spoke; less like himself. He said, "After that, this man lived for another year, but all the rest of his life he lived with a dark feeling, and people looked at him with white eyes."

"White eyes?"

He looked at her but his eyes had a nacreous, shallow quality. Not like his eyes at all. "Suspicious eyes. Distant eyes," he explained.

"But it didn't happen to you," she said. He didn't answer her. "Henry?"

"It's all right," Henry said to her. He was suddenly himself again. "I'm all right. I know what you're thinking. You're thinking about the electrical shock. But I'm fine." He patted her hand. Henry leaned forward and lowered his tone confidentially. "It's all right. I'm all right."

"We should tell Mom," Lauren decided aloud. "That you don't feel good."

"Why would you do that?"

Why indeed. What could their mother do to make Henry never have said the things he had just said? "No need!" Henry beamed. "I feel wonderful!" Henry laughed a great big Santa hohoho laugh. Christmas turned to ash right at that moment for Lauren.

"Oh, Henry," she said.

"Don't feel bad." Henry looked down at the picture again. "I felt so bad, looking at these pictures. I felt so bad that there was a time, just for a little while, when I wondered if it might not be better not to be here at all so I wouldn't feel anything. But you know, *Mono no aware*—it's just the suchness of things. I shouldn't necessarily see these things as bad. They're just things. Just there. And what we see here, what we're attached to . . ." Henry's arm swung to encompass the plastic airplanes, the chipped wall paint, the glare on the snowbanks outside and the dented pine boards beneath their feet, "Maybe it isn't there. You know?"

"No."

"I mean, it's . . . an illusion."

"What's an illusion, Henry?"

"It's something that looks like it's there but really isn't."

"What are you talking about?"

"Basically what I mean is that there's no reason to worry. I can't change what destiny has arranged. You can't change it, either."

The door slammed. Boots banged on the mat, and then the oven door creaked and banged shut again. "Mom's home," Lauren said.

"Yes."

"Come set the table!" their mother called up the stairs.

"That's us," Henry said. "Let's go." He smiled. "Turkey and stuffing destiny."

Lauren put her fingers to her lips. Silence, the fingers said. No talk of destiny. Henry nodded and placed his own fingers to his lips. Got it, his fingers said. Just between you and me. He smiled. They went down to Christmas dinner.

Seven

In the first week of the new year there was a wonderful blizzard. Lauren's cast had just been sawed off, and though it ached considerably, she was able to put a boot on the foot and join Henry and Winston when they went outside to make a snow house. She took care not to complain about the pain in her lower leg because Henry would make her go inside if she did.

Henry had grand plans, and the house grew a two-foot-thick exterior and rooms divided by snow walls and furnished with snow chairs and snow tables. Lauren molded a little sink and a counter for a snow kitchen. Winston made a snow sofa. When dusk came at around four o'clock that afternoon they marched into the house exhausted and perfectly pleased with themselves.

That month a full moon reached its fullest moment on January fourteenth, and when Lauren woke in the middle of the night her room was full of deep shadow. She sat bolt upright, certain that something in this glistening white and black night was wrong. She stumped down the hall to ask Henry what it was. Henry was not there. Drawn as if by cables, she stepped to the little window overlooking the backyard. From this window she saw the igloo's windows and door lit and flickering. Buttery illumination gave the little building something like a human face as it poured out onto the packed snow around it. A few minutes later she stood in its doorway.

The scent of pine was everywhere, and branches jammed into the rim of every archway in the little ice house. Candles stood lit and warm on every flat surface, flickering behind rows of upright icicles. Henry lay comfortably in the center of this splendor, his Boy Scout–issue sleeping bag wrapped snugly around him.

"Henry," was all she could think to say.

"Oh, I'm so glad you've come! I have cookies! Hot chocolate!" He waved Winston's old Roy Rogers thermos at her. Even in the light refracted through the icicles she could see the chips on Trigger's tail.

"Henry," she repeated.

"And where's your blankets? Or are you just visiting?"

"Henry, it's cold. Come in."

"No, no. Tonight I have to stay all night, and give everyone who comes something to eat and drink."

"Henry, no one will come! It's the middle of the night. And the only thing you have to do is make sure Mom and Dad don't wake up and find out you're not in bed!"

"They won't mind."

"Of course they'll mind."

"But it's *Kamakura matsuri!*"

"Henry, please. Please!" She started to cry, which upset him. He struggled to his feet and hopped over to her, still zipped up to his chest.

"It's just fun, Lauren. I'm having fun."

"What's a kamakazi matsis?"

"It's a holiday! You build snow houses and stay in them all night, like we're doing."

"Who does this stuff?"

"We do."

"We never did this stuff. You'll get in trouble."

"How could I get in trouble?" He seemed sincerely confused.

"You'll get sick. Aren't you scared out here alone?"

"Oh, no! Isn't it beautiful in the snow house? Isn't it just perfect?"

She looked around again. Yes. It was beautiful. "You'll come in before they wake up?" she whispered.

"Oh, tomorrow's Saturday. I'll get in before they wake up."

"You promise?"

"Oh, yes." He grinned. "Why don't you stay? Please stay! We can put these blankets under you and you'll be dry and warm!"

"No, no!" she cried. But an hour later, after standing helplessly at a window and watching the buttery candlelight in the ice house windows, Lauren pulled all the bedclothes from her room, climbed back into her boots and stalked into the backyard.

"I'm so glad!" Henry greeted her. "Isn't this fun!" He gestured to the little snow bed he had fashioned against a wall. "Just for you."

She shivered at his side until the moon settled down beneath the highest trees and the last of the candles Henry had lit sputtered into the snow shelves and the snow tables. As the last three candles burned into oblivion it occurred to her that it was indeed fun, and so very lovely. She had never been like this, awake and watching in a glistening black-and-white universe anchored by a heavy moon. There are no grown-ups here, she thought. Henry and I are alone. She waited for the moon to sink, and it did. She slept until the first bit of morning made the world full of shapes again, gray and blue-beige snow walls and shrubs. Houses.

She woke Henry and pulled him into the house, where he resumed his old responsible roles. He took away their sleeping bags and stuffed them, along with their wet blankets, into the dryer in the basement. Then they crawled into opposite ends of his bed, her toes to his head, his head to her toes, because there was no dry bedding left in her own room.

"Wasn't that fun?" he murmured sleepily, drifting off as the sun bellied up above the roof line of the house behind them, sending clean pink light across the wall and onto the hanging planes. "I love *Kamakura matsuri.*" Then Henry fell asleep, but she did not.

You're looking disturbed, Lauren Cooper. And you're limping."

"I know, Sister. The doctor says I'll limp for a while. But the cast's off. Sister?"

"Yes?"

"Sister, what would you think if I started speaking in Japanese?"

"I would think you were learning Japanese, Miss Cooper."

"But I mean, if I started speaking it but I hadn't taken any classes or anything or studied it on my own. Nothing. Just *wham,* Japanese."

"Why do you ask, Lauren Cooper?"

I am asking, Lauren thought but did not say, because I don't have anyone else to ask. Henry was her usual confidant, and she couldn't go to him. Winston was out of the question. Telling parents? No. This left her at a loss, and finally she had decided to ask Sister Leonarda. Now she wasn't so sure this was the right thing to do. "I don't know," she answered. The nun regarded her for a full minute.

"You say that quite a bit, don't you?" the nun asked. But she was paying attention, that was clear, so Lauren pressed on.

"The Catholic Church has people called exorcists, right?"

"Yes."

"And sometimes they can push certain . . . forces . . . out of people. Right?"

"Miss Cooper, are you saying that you think the Devil goes around jumping into people's bodies so he can babble in Japanese?"

"Oh, no, Sister!" But of course that was what she was saying.

"I think I can reassure you. This is unlikely." The nun studied her student. "You are still anxious about something."

"No."

Sister Leonarda sighed. "Young woman. You waste my time, and time is all we have here. Tell me what's on your mind. Or don't. But do not sit there prevaricating."

"Well, if someone started talking about the Great Void as the place where you go after you die, is that a sin?"

"Not if you are Buddhist."

"I mean if you aren't Buddhist."

"Lauren Cooper, there are many names for the same things. Perhaps the Great Void is only another way of saying what we, as members of the Catholic and Apostolic Church, call Heaven."

"Or Limbo."

"Perhaps."

"And . . . the influence of people you can't see? Like spirits?"

"Who are the communion of saints if not people you can't see? What is the Holy Ghost if not a spiritual force whose influence lies beyond our comprehension?"

"I don't know."

"Neither do I, Lauren Cooper. And it doesn't keep me awake at night." And with that, the Sister turned and limped away.

Henry's conversational topics continued to alarm her.

"You know, he's afraid that he's wandering around still because he's a *gaki,*" he said out of the blue one afternoon. "And he's confused."

"What's a *gaki*?" she asked. She didn't want to know but she had to ask. She knew what person he meant—he meant that man running toward the woman with one breast and a mouthlike red place where the other breast had been. She wished, standing here at the sink peeling potatoes for dinner, that she did not know which person he meant.

"It's someone who got stuck on earth after they died and didn't pass on to another life because they were attached to something or someone here. He was alone after the *pica-don,* and nobody offered him *chinkon.* I think that happened to a lot of *hibakusha.*"

"Is that a kind of food?"

"It's a kind of honoring. Every day you burn candles and set out little bowls of the dead person's favorite food. They visit during the holidays, especially the Festival of the Dead, and you make them party food and get them flowers. It calms the dead people down and then they're less likely to bother the living. Maybe this particular person has no grave, so no one knows where to go at the beginning of the Festival of the Dead. Maybe . . ."

"Henry, is he bothering you?"

"Oh, no. It's just that I seem to have slipped into his head. He isn't doing anything to me."

"Does he talk to you?"

"Nope. I don't think he knows I'm here."

"Henry, what the heck is the matter with you? This isn't a game, is it?"

"I don't even know his name." Henry's whole face crunkled around that problem, concentrating. Then his face smoothed and brightened. "Maybe if we honored him here it would help him. And in July we could celebrate the *Bon-matsuri* and put little lanterns and food on a boat for him, light the candle and push it off into a stream. His spirit would follow it, maybe, and be settled down."

"Did you take out books about this from the library or something?"

Henry shook his head from side to side: no.

"You're lying."

"No."

"Then what's all this Festival of the Dead stuff? Sister Leonarda didn't put it in your head. I think it may even be a sin. Lanterns and dead people visiting?"

"His name is right at the edge of my mind but I can't get it. You know, people don't use their own names when they're thinking. Hardly ever."

"Forget about the name." Lauren could see that her brother might actually have wanted to forget about the name at some point, but it was beyond that now.

No one else seemed to notice anything odd about Henry except for Winston.

"Henry's getting a little weird," Winston observed. It was clear that Winston didn't like this. "He doesn't hear me a lot when I talk to him. Did you notice he's stopped building airplanes?"

"You shut up." Lauren knew this wasn't a good response but it flew out of her mouth anyway.

"No, you shut up," Winston replied. Then he hit her directly on the bridge of her nose. The sudden bright pain released her instantly from the feelings that had plunged her into hapless wandering about the house. She was mad, and the anger was such a relief that she didn't get in its way when it progressed into thoughtless rage. She returned the blow. He stood his ground and raised his fists.

They then engaged in the first serious physical confrontation of both their lives. None of the swats or taunts or scuffles that preceded it had, at their core, a sincere desire to hurt. But this one did. Lauren was taller and older, but Winston was heavy and concentrated, more than able to compensate for his sister's height. She wanted Winston to cry; he would not. She swung wildly at his face and bloodied his nose. He caught the back of her legs with a kick and fell to his knees on her chest when she went down. They fought in an eerie glaring silence, both intent on inflicting significant damage. "Cry," Lauren hissed at her brother, but he wouldn't. She knew he wanted to. She had seen Winston weep over imagined insults, skinned knees and the tiniest of scratches, but this was a different matter. He met her eyes and would not cry. He swung again. They were both bloodied and bruised by the time a leg colliding with the wall abutting Henry's room brought him hurrying in.

Henry pulled them apart and stood between them, absorbing the blows that had begun before they were able to understand that Henry would receive the impact. Their older brother braced himself and gasped. When Winston realized that he had hurt Henry by accident he did, at last, begin to cry. "I'm all right," Henry said, draping an arm over his brother's shoulder. "Don't worry at all. I'm fine." He turned to Lauren. "You're the older sister and you have to act like it," he said sternly. She started yelling then, enraged that Henry was taking Winston's side, again! For a minute they stood together in a little circle, Henry with his arms around both of them as they wept and pleaded their cases.

"Henry, he just hit me! He wanted to hurt me! Why are you taking his side?"

"It's not sides."

"It's not fair!" Lauren protested.

"It's not about fair."

"He hates me!" she raged. "I hate him!"

"No, no," Henry crooned. "It just feels like that because your feelings kind of overloaded and blew out a fuse. You're confused. Your nature tends to these big mistake attacks on things you don't really want to hurt. Remember, you are little brother and big sister."

Lauren could hear a foreign influence in that syntax. She pushed the palm of her hands over her ears. "AieAieAie," she wailed.

"You two!" Henry said sternly. "Stop it before Mom hears." He led them into the bathroom and washed their bloody noses. He inspected their bruises and then sent them to different corners of the house to stay put. That afternoon Lauren looked out the kitchen window and saw Henry sitting on the swing, crying.

Even before the sight of Henry crying could dislodge the satisfaction she had felt in giving way to destructive rage, something else intruded sharply: a smell. She whipped her head around to see what was on the stove, expecting to see some smoking oil, a piece of fish. There was nothing. She sniffed again, and surely, surely, it was there as clear as her brother in the backyard—an almost motor-oil kind of smell, and some oily fish. Greasy ash. She looked in the air for smoke: there was none. She ran a finger over clean plain surfaces for evidence of grease left there by some earlier smoking oil. None.

"Henry!" she called, and Henry's head lifted. "Come here!" Henry dragged himself into the kitchen, clearly struggling to look less disheartened as he got closer. He was actually smiling when he stepped across the threshold. "Smell," she commanded him. "Tell me what you smell."

Henry sniffed obligingly. "Dishwasher soap," he said.

"No. Smell again."

He smelled again. "Well. Maybe it's the old sneakers in the hallway here."

"Don't you smell the fish? The oil? Heavy oil, like the smell of a car engine?"

Henry shook his head slowly. "Nope."

Then the smell vanished as suddenly as it had arrived—as though it had tangible parameters and it had simply passed by, leaving no trace of itself. No clinging oil. No fabrics tainted with its little molecules of fishiness. "Well," Lauren said doubtfully. "It doesn't matter."

"Don't worry," Henry told her, patting her shoulder. "It happens."

"What do you mean?"

"Just that it happens."

"Does it happen to you?"

"It doesn't matter, Lauren. I'm going upstairs now." He drooped a bit again as he climbed the stairs. She watched him, wondering.

Sister, what about anger?" she asked Sister Leonarda at the next class.

"What about it?"

"Is it a sin?"

"Depends. Anger when? At whom?"

"Say, anger at a somebody you're supposed to love, like a brother. When he does something that hurts you."

"So who else could make you feel anger but someone you love?" The Sister scrutinized her, peering down from her wimple. "You, Lauren Cooper, are very upset right now. Don't do anything hurtful to anyone you love simply because you are upset. Wait for calm."

"And what if I still want to hurt them when I'm calm?"

"That's another subject. Not this subject."

A bit of light glanced off the gold band around the Sister's ring finger. "Sister?" she ventured. "Do you get angry at God? I mean, so mad you want to do something very very terrible?"

"Well, of course," she sniffed. "But He releases me from that state eventually."

Lauren pressed on. "Don't you get, like, anxious with all the stuff you say is a mystery? Do you get mad that He made it so confusing?"

"Of course." The Sister sighed. Lauren had come in early to ask these questions, and the children would be filing in soon. There were things to write on the board and a quiz to mimeograph. She put a wrap-up tone in her voice. "Strong feelings aren't always something we want. But we have them, don't we? Some of us, anyway."

Lauren nodded. Yes, indeed. A photographically clear memory of the saint with the beautiful hilly thighs and upturned bloody face came to her. Sister Leonarda saw something in her face and asked, "Lauren Cooper, does your faith make you frightened?"

Lauren nodded miserably.

The Sister considered her for a moment. "Be patient," she said at last. "Things will change."

No they won't, Lauren thought. No, they won't.

Once home and alone again Lauren considered her situation, and her brothers'. She thought of Winston's refusal to cry; his grim dignity. She thought of his determination and the sight of Henry in the windy backyard with tears running down his face.

She went to Henry's room and sat on the floor by his bed and watched him doing his homework. He proceeded as if he were entirely alone. Only a week ago Lauren would have protested, interrupted, gotten his attention. But today she simply sat in the room with him and watched him work. She wished, watching his peaceful expression and effortless concentration, that she herself had visions of little candle-lit boats floating to the sea, of icy houses full of balsam and hot chocolate, of people whose names escaped her. She would simply be accompanied by them—not so alone.

All her life she had admired Henry and hoped to grow up to be like him. She knew already that this wasn't possible. Perhaps, worse yet, it was not desirable. Henry looked up from his work and saw her shifting uneasily. "Come out and ride bikes," he said. "We can see who can run over the most leaves with their tires." This was one of Lauren's favorite games, in which quick turns, pitches into neighbors' front yards, and occasional collisions with parked cars were inevitable parts of trying to "tag" a leaf as it skittered across the road. Henry was not as good at it as she was, because he simply wouldn't take as many chances. He would choose leaves carefully and pursue them until they blew into a yard or became fully airborne and then he would give up and choose another. Lauren pursued no matter what—anywhere.

By the time their mother called out for them to come in to dinner, Lauren had inhaled hundreds of pounds of crisp air. Her face was red, one shin a bloody lacework from the knee to the ankle. Her pants were torn, and her throat hurt from screaming and laughing. Henry was still neatly put together. Her worries about Sister Leonarda's lessons, about Winston's moods, about Henry's mind, all were gone. She was happy: dirty and tired and satisfied with herself. When their mother saw them walking into the kitchen she smiled, which lifted Lauren's heart further.

They sat down at the green linoleum table in their aluminum chairs. For perhaps the four thousandth time they recited the Catholic grace in the dactylic meter that their father preferred. Winston's feet tapped against the aluminum table legs on the stressed beats, and no one berated him despite the jumping saltshakers and rattling plates. Then, spaghetti and meatballs, cookies in the backyard, baths and beds. Another day.

Eight

On Family Day, Warren Cooper's corporation opened up its laboratories to employees' families and gave prizes, tours, gifts and talks. The family attended faithfully every year.

Lauren had always really thought of her father as living here in the glamorous country of Work, where people went to meetings in airplanes and had limitless access to vending machines. He wasn't really fully alive at home.

On Family Days the children and wives were guided through the site in a path bordered by ropes, like the ones shaping the lines that led to bank tellers. Wives received coffee cups with the name of the company on it; children received balloons and cookies. The tour led them through offices, laboratories and finally, the dramatic finale, into the cathedral-sized amphitheater whose upper beams mirrored the open gridded radar dish beneath them.

Henry was almost fifteen years old—a child no longer. His father took him by his side and introduced him to the men in his work team. Seeing that his older brother was going to be included in the inner-sanctum tour this year was more than Winston could bear. He would not be left behind, and rather than have his colleagues see his younger son throwing a tantrum, Warren acquiesced. They moved away from the women and children toward their actual work places, Henry and Winston attached to the little flock of sons who tagged along after their engineer fathers.

Henry had very good manners. From across the plant floor, Lauren watched him shake hands with all the adults and saw that Winston had the good sense to imitate his brother exactly. Henry, in this convivial confident group, had looked small. Winston, on the other hand, was so pleased with the situation that he seemed to physically expand.

Lauren's gender relegated her to the children's game of guessing the radar dish's height. A young civil engineer in a clown suit handed her a tiny square of paper and a mechanical pencil. "The prize is a box of drafting pencils and a ream of graph paper," he told them soberly. "Stay here, little girl!" This to Lauren, who had leaked to the edge of the group and begun to move off after the boys. It was Henry she needed to see about. Winston was fine.

She won the box of pencils, which were handed to her at the conclusion of what felt like a brief business meeting on the subject of how to best calculate the height by estimating a single grid unit's dimensions and multiplying. None of the children listened.

Lauren had rejoined her mother and begun scanning the crowd for a glimpse of her brothers long before they returned. The men were all poking the air with happy animation, their mechanical pencils and slide rules knocking on their clipboards as they approached. She heard the words *Tiros I, satellite, moon's surface.* One of the engineers wore a black band on his arm in memory of Lee De Forest, inventor of the vacuum tube, who had died six months before.

Henry's face made Lauren's throat close up. It was plate-like, devoid of intelligence. He stood in the center of the happily gesticulating men, a little absent vacuum.

"Mom, what's wrong with Henry?" she had asked, right in front of him.

"Nothing," her mother answered. But Annie clearly thought something was wrong because when Warren rejoined them for a moment and Henry had ducked into a bathroom, she repeated Lauren's question. What had he shown Henry? Why was Henry so quiet? Why did he look like that?

"Like what?" Warren asked. He was here in his native country.

Winston's face was flushed with happiness. "Look!" he cried, dancing in place, holding up a little something that looked like part of an iron gate. "It's part of a real launching platform! I'm taking it to school! I can keep it!" Warren smiled vaguely down at his younger son as his wife asked him, again, what was wrong with Henry. He looked at his wife and daughter over a great gulf. Like what? he repeated; quizzical, cheerful, uncomprehending.

That night at dinner Winston glowed. He wanted to describe every instrument he'd seen, and every tube and dial he'd been allowed to touch. He babbled happily about being admitted to rooms with radioactive waste danger signs posted on their doors, rooms that were as large as high school auditoriums, full to the ceiling and out to the walls with the company's actual computer. And yes, there had been real bugs flying into the mazes of tubes and there had been special shoes for walking through a room that had been contaminated by something so dangerous that the men wouldn't explain it to him, which he thought was wonderful. He had wanted to keep the boots but the grown-ups wouldn't let him. The only reason he didn't cry was his terror of being banished again to the anterooms of children and mothers. It was clear that Winston felt like he'd finally made it to the beating breathing middle of things, and he would never be happy until he'd grown up and surrounded himself with the world he'd seen today.

That night Lauren crept yet again into Henry's room to make sure his chest was moving. He was alive—not like he had been in her dream. She pushed open his door and whispered, "Henry, what happened on the tour?"

"I know his name," Henry said back to her in a normal speaking tone. And then he would say no more.

Soon after this things began to disappear from their father's workshop. The planes that had hung on invisible wires over Henry's bed also began to vanish. It took their father about a month, given the state of his workshop, to notice. He'd been looking for a particular kind of wave-frequency meter. When it couldn't be found he trudged up the steps to Winston's room and demanded to know what had become of it.

"You've taken it apart, haven't you, and you didn't know how to put it together again. Just admit it and give it back and I'll show you how to reassemble it."

This was so likely that Winston had to consider for a moment, but the fact was he had no idea where the meter had gone. "Well," his father sighed, "you will be punished while you think about it. You are confined to your room. You will not have your dinner. You will remember this the next time that you go to confession."

For two hours the family was subjected to the sound of Winston being confined to his room. They sat in the living room, directly beneath the bedroom, and listened to things breaking. No one said a word. The punishment didn't produce a confession.

Henry looked positively haggard when he went to bed. The next morning Lauren sat bolt upright feeling the familiar ringing in her chest that she had whenever she dreamed the Henry-getting-shot-by-the-farmer dream, and she padded quickly to his room. He was not there. She searched, and found him in the backyard gently setting one of his beloved plastic model airplanes into a hole in their dirt pile. He had packed it in a shoe box, wrapped it in tissue, and his eyes were full of tears as he committed it to the earth.

"Henry. Tell me what you're doing."

"The planes are very disturbing," he said. "Very distracting."

"But you love them," she protested. "You made them!"

"But they need to rest now," Henry said. "They have to go away from me."

"Plastic toys don't rest, Henry."

"These planes are so . . . very powerful—exciting and terrible at once, you know?" He looked up at her, his eyes catching every bit of morning light because of the tears they held. "Whole cities turned into firestorms. Rivers boiling and burning."

"Henry, they're toys."

"I know. Yes, I know. So strange."

She wanted to leave him but she could not. She stood while he dug and then she bent and helped him arrange the box in its finished hole, and remained until the dirt was replaced.

"They look honorable. Noble. But they are not." Then he worked silently, only morning insect sounds breaking the silence.

"Do you hear the bell-ringer?" he asked.

"The what?"

"The *kuro-hibari,* and I hear also the *kanetataki.* There is a beautiful poem on the *matsumushi* by Tusrayuki. Someone I loved but cannot remember used to say it: *With dusk begins to cry the male of the waiting insect; I, too, await my beloved, and, hearing, my longing grows.*" Henry began to cry.

"Henry, what is it?"

"I don't know. I lost something. No. No, it isn't something. It's someone. I've lost someone."

He picked at the dirt with his shovel and it shifted the soft mound by his plane's grave. A shiny thing lay there in the dirt. Lauren bent and swept the dirt aside. It was their father's wave meter.

"Henry, what's this?" she whispered.

"It's a bad thing. It had to be removed."

"Henry, why did you let them blame Winston? What else is here?"

Henry hung his head. "I didn't want to dishonor Winston, who did nothing. But I couldn't sleep with these things under my roof. I will find some way to make amends." Then Henry looked to either side, as if making sure no one could see. He grinned, put his finger to his lips as a sign to make her quiet and hissed, "There are many more of the radar-electricity-wire things here in the earth! I have been spiriting them away!"

"You mean you've got more of Dad's workshop back here?"

Henry nodded. His expression was satisfied and secretive. Utterly unlike himself.

"Henry! Lauren! What are you doing back here?" It was the voice of their mother, and it was not inside the house. That meant she had been watching them from the window long enough to decide to get a robe on and come outside. Her voice was not sleepy and her eyes were very open. "Henry, why are you burying your models?" Their mother clutched her robe around her and held it at her throat like women in movies did. Her hair was so soft in the morning, the gentlest frame to her worried face. Lauren stepped between them though she knew it did no good. "It's a game, Mom," Lauren said. "Henry's pretending to be the Zero pilot and I'm pretending to be the bomber pilot."

"You don't play war planes," she said to her daughter. "You don't even play Apartment Complex anymore. And why would someone playing with airplanes bury them? Henry. What is this?" Their mother bent over and dug at a piece of glass—a radio's face. She yanked it out of the ground. "Henry?" she said firmly. "Tell me about this."

"They make the city into rivers of fire," he whispered, hanging his head.

"They what?"

But Henry said no more.

"Come inside. Now." Their mother took their hands and dragged them into the house. She sat them down side by side on the sofa. From that moment Henry answered no more questions. He sat very still and refused speech, even though she continued to pepper him with questions.

"Henry," she finally said. "I think you are not feeling well and I'm going to call Dr. Simmons." Henry nodded.

The doctor came immediately because Annie Cooper had never called him at this hour in the morning in all the years he'd known her, not for gashes or earaches or whooping cough. He arrived to find the entire family sitting in the living room waiting in their pajamas.

"Henry," he began cheerily. "Tell me how you feel."

Henry would not speak. Dr. Simmons, a busy man with half a dozen children of his own and a large practice waiting for him over there on Brewer Street, gave this patient another ten minutes and then sat down in the kitchen to have a conference with the parents. Warren shooed Lauren and Winston up to their rooms, but Lauren crept back as soon as the adults were in the kitchen and out of immediate earshot.

Alone with her brother again in the living room, Lauren hissed, "Henry?"

He nodded but did not speak.

"Henry," she whispered. "What's his name?"

Henry whispered back. "His name is Suriyu Asagao."

"Tell me what he's thinking." They were still whispering. "Are his thoughts in your head? Is that what's happening?"

Henry nodded soberly. "The *pica-don* came and made the world fire—like the Hell that *Genshin* wrote of. He saw ghost people holding burned arms and hands out from their bodies drifting by in lines, going away. They did not know where. Only away. He said, 'Where are you going?' and they pointed to the mountains and said, 'Over there.' He said, 'Where did you come from?' and they pointed back toward the pillar of flames and said, 'Back there.' He saw hands burning like candles. People with no faces, walking, walking."

Her brother swiveled around and looked her in the eye. He said, "I know that being afraid is not wise. Long life or short life, one poisons the gift of life by worrying about its size." He stopped for a moment, seemed to gather himself, then said, "You mustn't worry."

The grown-ups returned, and Henry turned a sober face toward them. He winked at Lauren.

"Henry, the doctor would like you to meet another doctor. He thinks we need some tests."

"I'm fine, Mom. I feel fine." He smiled beatifically.

Then Henry closed his eyes and fell into a sleep from which no one could awake him for three days.

The Henry-being-shot-by-the-farmer dream woke her and, as she always did at these times, she rolled directly from her bed and trotted into Henry's room. On this night, though, when she arrived at

Henry's doorway she knew his bed would be empty; he'd been sent off for "observation." Still, she felt Henry's empty room like a vacuum, pulling, so she had risen and crept along the cool hallway to peer through the gloom at his bed.

She froze in the doorway. The bed was lumpy. Those were feet at the head of his bed and as she quieted her startled breathing she could see the rise and fall of another chest admitting air, expelling air. He had escaped and returned! She stepped forward and touched the warm head. Its hair sprang up in a curly mass.

"Hello," Winston whispered. He slid to one side. Had it been daylight, with their parents moving purposefully through the rooms beneath them and Henry in his rightful place, she would have scorned an invitation from Winston. But it was night, and things were different now. She sat down where he had made room for her, swung her feet under, tugged the blanket up to her chin.

"What do we do?" Winston whispered again. It was suddenly clear to Lauren that Winston loved and needed Henry more than any of them; that Henry might really be Winston's more than hers or their parents'. Lauren summoned the things she knew Henry could do, would do right now. She borrowed them from Henry just for a few minutes while she took Winston's hand.

"Henry will be back," she said, just like Henry would have said, not because it was the right or true thing to say but because it was what Winston had to hear in order to sleep that night.

"He didn't have to go anywhere," Winston replied.

"Maybe he did. We can't understand everything." Now she was borrowing from Sister Leonarda. Such a ragbag, she thought. Had she nothing of her own?

"I don't want to understand everything. I want him back."

"We don't get to pick and choose what we get." There. That was her very own.

"I'm going to get to choose. When I grow up I'm going to get to choose."

"Choose what? You can't change that they sent Henry away, Winston. And you can't change Henry, or anything that's happened already. It's happened."

"I'll be rich and nobody will be the boss of me. I'll have a separate house on my property for Henry so he can live there and nobody will bother him, no matter how he wants to act."

They lay silently for a full five minutes and then Winston said, "Could you do that 'Moon River' thing again? Do you know where the tutu is?"

She found the tutu. She jammed on a hat and the tutu and a few things that suggested the old costume and she performed it for Winston as quietly as possible. Miraculously, they woke no one. Winston sighed at the number's conclusion.

"Thank you. You know what, Lauren?"

"What?"

"I'm going to have at least six children. And a beautiful, kind wife."

"He'll come back, Winston," she said. She patted her little brother's hand, and they lay there through the night with their eyes fixed on the airplane-less ceiling.

Henry did come back. For a week he was pale and soft in all his movements. Lauren did not ask him what had happened to him when he was away. No one talked about his going to school that first week he was home, and even after the first week Henry sat on and on in his room, staring away into nothing. At night Lauren sometimes made her way to his room and they talked about nothing that mattered. Other nights she pressed her ear against the common wall between their rooms and she could hear him murmuring.

Lauren went to his teachers and got work, which she took home and carefully explained to him with exactly the inflections and concerned expressions of his teachers. They had been told he had pneumonia. Henry offered up brilliant appreciative smiles and left the books and graph paper and pencils untouched. Lauren removed them and brought more, every day laying fresh needle-sharp pencils down like a child pressing food upon an animal who had died; an animal the child hoped, though it was clear it would never happen, might be stirred back to life by the smell of what it had once loved.

Gradually Henry did stir. He picked up a book one day, and then a pencil. He began to talk, but not about where he had gone when he was sent away. "Henry," Lauren said to him one afternoon when she crept in with homework. "Henry!?"

He looked up vacantly.

"Henry, are you all right now?"

"Sure I am."

"I mean, more all right than you were when you talked about *matsuris* and bombs."

"I'm fine."

This was not exactly an answer to her question. She said, "Henry, everything's bad now."

"What's bad now?"

"Well, for instance, now I have to walk to school with Winston. Last week he pushed me into the street, and when I told Mom, he said it was just a joke and he didn't mean anything. But I felt the push so I know what it was."

"Were any cars coming?"

"No," she admitted reluctantly. She realized that it would have pleased her to be able to describe Winston as dangerously mean instead of simply annoying. A part of her wanted Winston to be evil. For a second she allowed herself to examine this idea of herself as somebody who liked Winston just the way he was, but then shook herself as if this action could literally spin off the questions it raised.

Henry said, "You know, on the island across the bay from *Kagoshima,* there was a volcano—Mount Sakurajima. This volcano was on fire the whole time, every day. When Asagao walked to school in the morning his mother put a hard hat on his head so the chunks of rock flying through the air wouldn't hit him. His father told him that the volcano was restless because all of Japan lay on a dragon's back. When the dragon moved he shook Japan." He grinned.

Lauren pushed Winston out of her mind. She saw the dragon lying directly under the water under miles of islands, restlessly flicking its tail, causing earthquakes: a satisfying image. "Baloney," she said.

"Oh, he did. He wore that hat walking to school along a path that smelled of cedar, camphor and pine. And his teachers told him that Japan was the throne coeval with heaven and earth, and the emperor was God."

"Henry, you know that rule about not putting false gods before the true god?"

"Sure."

"Are you breaking that rule?"

"No."

"Some rule, though. You must be breaking some rule."

"Rules aren't everything, Lauren."

At least he had begun to talk again. More important, he seemed to be able to distinguish the kinds of ways in which he spoke—the Japanese way as opposed to the normal one. Asagao's mind as opposed to his own mind. She was not entirely at ease, though. While her conversations with her brother all seemed to draw Henry closer to the conscious world where children took yellow buses, they drew Lauren deeper into the parts of Henry's mind where volcanic ash ponked on children's hard hats as they skipped past cypress and pine.

"I want that Japanese guy to just vanish," she said to her brother. "Like right now."

Her brother shook his head. "So impatient," he sighed. "And stubborn. So much wood in your nature."

Winston and Lauren, unlikeliest of allies, now watched over Henry together, united in this doomed effort to protect their older brother from something they could not touch or name. Sometimes Lauren thought of the enemy as a thing called Asagao, but when she was with Winston, talking about Henry, the enemy was referred to as The Grown-ups—those ones who had sent Henry away once and might do it again.

"You know," Winston said to her during this anxious watching time, "I pray to God to make Henry normal and I don't know why He's not doing anything. Does God not hear me, or is God saying He won't help?"

"I don't know," Lauren said.

"In my catechism it says that hell is the place where bad people live and where nobody gets to see God," Winston said.

"So?"

"So," Winston said. "So what's the difference between here and there?"

"Not everybody here is bad. It snows here," Lauren said.

"What's so good about snow?"

"It's beautiful here. There are trees. Bicycles. Macaroni." She was thinking about the way she felt going down a hill when it first got warm enough to ride a bike, her hair in a whipping ball moving between her face and shoulders and warm dirt smell in her nose. "There couldn't be those things in hell."

Winston said, "Sister Leonarda says we're here to adore and serve

God. But if I met a kid who was only interested in people adoring and serving him, I wouldn't cross the street to play with him if he was the only kid in the universe. He could break my nose before I'd give him my lunch money, which is what that kind of kid usually does. That's God? So, I mean, what does that mean?"

Lauren nodded. It was her idea of God exactly, the God from *Disaster, Disaster, Disaster*—silent, demanding, punitive, irrational, enormous. Crazy. Sister Leonarda would say that she was too young to really understand her faith.

She hoped so.

Nine

During these months their father retreated to his workshop, a peaceful backwater whose shelves and flat spaces were littered with machine parts and technical manuals. Lauren followed him, partly to have better information about the enemy's plans, partly because she loved her father in this place and she loved the workshop itself.

Oak shelves rose up behind the main bench, and on these shelves flickered the visible manifestations of radio waves. Round instrument panels, most etched with degree lines or wave frequency numbers, glowed from neat rows of glass faces. Wave patterns pulsed along them like dozens of electrocardiograms. As he worked on one thing or another at this bench or the one facing it on the opposite wall, her father always had at least one other transmitter and receiver within reach. These instruments would sit by his side and he allowed Lauren to tinker with the knobs in an ongoing search for messages from as far away as possible. He allowed Lauren to fiddle with dials and hunt for voices. Once she had gotten a babbling stream that could only have been Russian. Every Saturday they made a point of trying to capture a signal from Nome, Alaska, that carried *Big Band Afternoons at Four.* It broadcast at noon.

Other times her father made her sit with a pencil and a Morse code workbook, an unwired transmitter by her right hand for practice. He reasoned that his most powerful receivers and transmitters could get messages from much farther away in code so she should master it. And what a savings in telephone bills! They would communicate with one another by Morse code when she went away to college. She would sit for the test and get her license. Learning Morse code, clearly, was an Important Activity, unlike tree climbing or Apartment Complex. She studied the manual and sat by the radios for hours but she still preferred the scratchy Colgate toothpaste advertisements to the military darkness of the coded beeps and dashes.

Still, her father loved the code and she loved his approval, so she kept up the losing battle with the tapping instrument. She understood that her failure to master what he considered an elementary skill was a disappointment to him. But she also understood that had she been Henry or Winston, the disappointment would have been more profound because they were boys and she, after all, was a girl. She and her father both regarded the wall of radio wave dials and receivers as lovely, but they loved them for different reasons. He adored their physical selves: the little wires, the tubes, the etched glass, the currents they attracted and tracked. Warren believed that if he could track something he controlled it; it became, in some way, his possession. It enlarged him.

Lauren didn't think that. She had tried to control the currents—had spent hours trying to make the waves spike or drop or roll with her mind or her hand on the dials, and she couldn't. When she stopped trying she found it was more satisfying to simply follow what came and forget about herself. It made her disappear. Then she found that the waves carried her along, and she felt the spikes and drops in her belly as she tracked them with her eyes. She tried to find patterns among them, and sometimes did. She imagined them coming toward the workshop from all over the Western Hemisphere, invisible and indifferent to her and to her father, unaware of the little glass and metal screens that would manifest them here in the basement of this blue-shingled house in Eleusis, New York, while *Big Band Afternoons at Four* played in the background. Sometimes she imagined that there really was no Big Band. But there were the waves, right there on the dial so there had to be a Big Band.

Her brothers didn't come here as much as she. Their father was more critically demanding of them, and their presence in a workshop was treated as serious business. In his workshop, they were compelled to build things and explain things. Winston preferred things that could be modified with a screwdriver, and the invisible waves frustrated him. He took a few too many things apart and made himself unwelcome; he failed a few workbook exercises in Morse code. Finally he started finding other places to take things apart. Lauren failed the workbook exercises, too, but it didn't keep her away. Unlike her brothers, she was free to sink into a hypnotic trance in front of the meters and tubes. She was free to fail technical tests with impunity. And when Lauren came down here to her father's workroom, her mother didn't worry her about folding clothes and vacuuming. So she lingered before the beautiful wave patterns, pretending to practice her Morse code.

Her father talked to her here. He talked about stocks, and fighter plane radar design, satellites plummeting through space directly above their heads sending information about cloud patterns and the surfaces of other planets and the Enemy that was the Soviet Empire.

He didn't talk about Henry, which caused her both anxiety and relief. She listened with an attentive expression, understanding nothing but enjoying the flow of sound. Upstairs, in the rooms where the entire family lived, her father was generally silent; here in his workshop he was a running stream of talk.

Her mother seemed to have no comparable safe place, no real retreat from confusion. In fact, she drove right into the teeth of trouble. She'd put on her hat and her high heels and head out to see doctors or experts, leaving Lauren and Winston with Henry and clear instructions about what they could and could not eat. Sometimes she took Henry himself. Lauren and Winston were too frightened to ask Henry what happened to him when he went away with her. The children knew more about Henry's Japanese tendencies than their mother did; she knew only that Henry sometimes spoke in a strange voice, sometimes wouldn't speak at all, and once had slept on for three unbroken days.

The children did nothing to enlighten her. This unspoken pact drew them closer together as it pushed them further away from the adult world. Had they seen this, they would have chosen it anyway.

By daylight the children behaved as if they didn't suspect their family had a care in the world. But at night Lauren and Winston crept into Henry's room as soon as the house was quiet. Henry let them stay, the three of them in an uncomfortable heap until sunrise when they parted again. When all three of them were together Henry amused them with imitations of teachers they all knew and various psychological experts that only he knew.

On nights when Winston did not come Henry spoke to Lauren about the wandering lines of people leaving the epicenter of the blast. He talked of trying to fold a thousand cranes because if you offer a thousand cranes, children will survive even the leukemia left in the explosion's aftermath. She let him talk.

Perhaps if we had offered a thousand cranes, she would think, lying in the darkness. But they hadn't had time. There was never time to fold a thousand cranes. That was why they told you that it would work. It was impossible, so they knew ahead of time you would fail. You could rush to the crib but there your fate would be.

One night Henry taught them a game with rocks and hollowed spaces in a board.

"Did Asagao teach you this?" Winston had asked.

"No. But it was in his head."

They nodded and played on.

Lauren and Winston began to accept Asagao as a member of their sibling group without even thinking about it. It happened slowly. They played games by flashlight that Henry had learned in Asagao's head until arguments about rules got loud enough to threaten their parents' sleep. They found themselves considering Asagao's point of view on things. They imagined him.

In the parts of Lauren's and Winston's minds that controlled things like what they said at the dinner table, their parents were crazy and there was nothing at all the matter with Henry. But other times the parts of her that feared for Henry gained ascendance.

Lauren looked up from her little Morse code lever one afternoon to ask her father, "Do you think there is something wrong with Henry?"

Warren continued working intently on the pile of wires before him. He hmmmmmed and cleared his throat and waited for Lauren to forget that she'd asked a question. She repeated it.

"Well," he said, "it's hard for a girl to understand."

"Why?"

"Girls don't feel the kinds of feelings that young men feel."

"Like what?" Lauren was imagining hunger, impatience, but at the same time, under these initial imaginings, the word "sex" had formed in her mind. The painting of Saint Margaret of Cortoner floated into view as well.

He said, "Well, boys have these feelings, confused feelings that are very strong, right about the age that your brother Henry is right now. And they can make boys behave in ways that are not like the ways they normally behave. And these strong feelings are caused by things called hormones and they go away as the boy gets older. As it will with your brother. But in the meantime hormones can cause some difficulties."

"What does Mom think?"

"Your mother agrees with me."

Even Lauren, at thirteen years old, knew that this was a lie. She had seen her mother's face when she came and went from the meetings with the Experts. Lauren's heart thumped upward and into the base of her throat. She had her answer: she was in danger. Her father had no idea what he was talking about.

"What's dot-dit-dit-dot-dot-dot?" he asked.

As far as Lauren knew, it was nothing. It was her father's way of saying that he would say no more. She turned her attention to the flickering tracks of radio waves.

Ten

Winter came down like a hammer that year. Sister Leonarda was once again their teacher, in charge of the Tuesday afternoon religious instruction that was mandatory for all public school students who were members of the church.

She was cheered by snow, especially in its more dramatic forms. Glaring blowing white-out conditions left her literally skipping down the aisles between dripping coats and Tuesday afternoon religious school students. But the paralyzing cold had a very different effect on Lauren Cooper's mood. The freezing expanses of shining ice around their home seemed to her like the very manifestation of her family's state of mind. In the end, finally, two things shattered the season's grip on her: Henry's reentry into the life of the family and the Sister's Easter play.

The Sister personally preferred winter to spring, but what can you do. Spring's muddy succulence simply wasn't as True as winter's icy brilliance. The flesh as opposed to the spirit—this was how spring as opposed to winter looked to Sister Leonarda. And the Sister clearly felt more at ease with the spirit than with the pliable, muddy chattering flesh.

On the first day of Lent she accompanied her students to confession, it being a mortal sin not to make a worthy confession during the Easter season. She marched them into the church, calling their attention to the rising light in the stained-glass windows to either side of the pews. "See the black maroons give way to deep blood reds," she said, "which in turn rise up and give way to pinks and ethereal golds? See the brown robes yield as they ascend, become bristling clear light at the crest of the upper windows? It is time," she announced solemnly, "to start work on our Easter play."

Most of the nuns were more attracted to the Christmas plays with their furry lambs and babies in mangers and carols, and so the Easter play always fell to Sister Leonarda. The reenactment of the march up Calvary—the jeering Roman soldiers, the crown of thorns, the stumbling falls under the weight of the raw timber, the nails, the vinegar offered up on the end of a weapon when Jesus pleaded for water—all this was left to Sister Leonarda to interpret with her small charges. "When the Christ Child lay in His manger the first gifts brought to Him by the Magi were incense, myrrh and gold. Myrrh, of course, the oil used to anoint the dead before burial. This is the moment Jesus Christ was made for—His death. It is His purpose, His fulfillment."

Oddly enough, this kind of talk cheered Lauren. She was particularly reassured by the idea that the baby chose death, had known all along that this was its fate and had accepted it with his whole heart.

"There are some people in the modern religious world," Sister Leonarda admitted, and everyone understood her to mean Father Murphy, "who believe that plays like this are frivolous or even pagan. They forget the importance of dance and drama in the earliest churches. You see, children, in the confused pagan mind," Sister Leonarda said, "dance and drama were religious offerings to a god. But the wrong god. Then, when the only true Catholic Apostolic Church was revealed, humans offered them to the right god."

"Who was the wrong god?" Domenic asked.

"The most popular wrong god was Dionysus—the god of physical suffering and physical joy—the only Greek pagan god who died and came back to life. His worshipers honored him through dance, through theater and through other less acceptable practices. Like our Lord, he had a god as a father and a mortal woman as a mother."

"So what was he?" Domenic pressed.

"What?"

"I mean, was he a god?"

"Of course not. None of the pagan gods was a god. They were simply stories. But the pagans believed he was a god, and they told stories of his performing magic tricks to prove that he was a god, like turning himself into a dolphin and then back into his human form again to convince a boatful of fishermen that he was divine. True saints and holy people do not resort to magic."

Lauren decided not to ask about loaves and fishes, blind men given sight, or the business about turning water to wine at the wedding. The children were fully attentive. They knew that the classroom next door was filling in worksheets on indulgences and commandments, and there was no discussion of pagan gods, dancing, drunken sexual excess or playacting. Sister Leonarda's charms were being revealed at last.

"So was Dionysus, like, related to our God?" Lauren asked.

Sister Leonarda began what was certainly going to be a curt dismissal of this question, but she stopped with her hand still in the air where she had raised it to bat the question away. "Perhaps," she said slowly, "perhaps some of the pagan gods were the dim reflections of the glory to come."

"Wow," Domenic said. "Reflections going backward in time. Like space travel."

"Indeed," the Sister replied, no irony in her tone. "We have children of different ages and abilities here and we should take advantage of this wealth. I want people who want to be dancers to the right. Actors to the left. Actors, you will be reenacting the stations of the cross. Dancers, you will be creating an original dance made to honor the glory of Jesus Christ, the Lamb of God."

"Baa-aaa-aaa." Domenic fell onto all fours.

"Domenic, you will be banished from the play for disrespect."

"I wasn't meaning to be disrespectful!" Domenic cried, his pained sincerity changing the Sister's stern expression to a milder one.

"Lauren Cooper, you have a limp." This was true—a reminder of the day she flew off the barn roof. "Leave the dancers and join the actors."

"But, Sister, I can do whatever they do."

The Sister hesitated but yielded. "All right. Unless you prove unable." She addressed the cluster of students who wanted to dance. "Dances are symbolic," she said. "Abstract. Do you know what 'abstract' is?" The communicants looked at her in amazement. Of course they didn't. She sighed. "In this case it means that you show how something makes you feel—not what it looks like on the outside, but what it makes you feel on the inside."

The communicants continued to stare, though the Sister seemed confident that the confusion was lifting. She said, "Here is an example. A starting point. The idea of Jesus fills us with joy. Can you all dance a dance about joy? A joyful dance?" Now they nodded. They could probably manage that. "Fine," she said. "Do so."

They did. "Not bad," she offered, and they beamed. "We can get to the more complicated ideas in time. Besides, a bit of literalness can be a good thing."

The rehearsals began openly. Father Murphy passed by the doorways of their classrooms, looking pained. When the rehearsals continued despite his clearly communicated pain, he began to pass by looking more like what would be called furious. Arguments in the hallways between Father Murphy and Sister Leonarda followed. The rehearsals continued more discreetly, indicating to all involved that the Sister had lost her argument and the little drama was never going to be publicly presented. This deterred them not at all. They knew what waited for them the second the dancing stopped—workbook sheets on Feast Days and quizzes on venial versus mortal sin. So they guarded the Sister's work and answered questions from home with evasive little grunts.

In front of her charges the Sister behaved as if no conflicts existed, and the entire diocese looked forward to seeing the fruits of their labor. But she was lying, and what's more, she knew that they knew she was lying. This gave them a terrible freedom from her authority. The drama began to take unorthodox turns, and the dance looked unsnapped in places. The Roman soldiers grew more brutal. Mary Magdalene began wearing interesting underwear, which she showed to the Roman soldiers, and the disciples became more tragically grieved. But even as the drama began to feel out of control, a centrifugal force developed, holding them all together at the same time that it left them feeling a bit crushed and breathless by the story's powerful movement.

"Stop!" the Sister commanded midway through Jesus's entrance one day. They stood motionless as if she had flicked a switch and left them inanimate. But they could turn their faces to her, and they did, magically attentive. "Jesus comes to His death like a lover," she said, and the group seemed, by this time, to actually understand her. "He achieves His destiny in this act. We gain forgiveness and thus life through His sacrifice."

A crown of thorns was fashioned from coat hangers; the pike a Roman soldier drove between the ribs and into the lungs had begun its life as a broomstick. Rags and blood, the stuff of dozens of other narratives, were available in the form of ripped sheets and ketchup. When the ketchup was pooh-poohed at a secret dress rehearsal in Domenic's basement, Eddie volunteered to take the city bus to the joke shop his older brother frequented. There he found a more reliable blood substitute, manufactured and distributed from Paterson, New Jersey. The dancers attended this dress rehearsal, and structured their big finale around the risen Lord—the narrative extended to Easter itself to provide the satisfaction of the Resurrection. They did this on their own now—it was not the Sister's story. Her description of how the play should run ended at the moment of His death. But alone, in each other's basements, they had gone on.

By the time they showed the final production to Sister Leonarda, the single Roman soldier's pike had multiplied, like loaves and fishes, into a small armory. Jesus bore his cross through a frenzied crowd of tormentors. The Sister watched, transfixed, as the entire scene took on a kind of austere dignity. A moppy-headed Jesus was lifted over the heads of a swarm of little actors moving like so many ant scavengers. He vanished, cueing Eloise Gorman, playing Magdalene, to rush smack into another assembled knot to announce he had risen from the dead.

This cued the dancers. When they first began they had hit on the idea of flinging hosts all around their heads as they made their entrance. This idea had happily been rejected along the way and now they came empty-handed. At the same time the host idea had been killed, the costumes became more subdued—white shirts, white skirts, white pants. Initially those who had taken dancing classes had worn leotards. Mary Haffitz had insisted on a spangled stars and stripes outfit designed for a July Fourth patriotic event. Those with fewer concrete notions had stumbled on the idea of wrapping sheets around themselves. An emergency meeting had been called, and as if some visitation from the Holy Ghost settled on them all at once, a moment came mid-argument when they threw aside the more jarring choices.

What remained looked like prayer. They performed it for Sister Leonarda and waited solemnly to hear her verdict. Lauren was sure she saw tears forming in the old woman's eyes.

"Sister Leonarda!" This from Father Murphy, whose black robes suddenly, horribly, filled the doorway.

Whatever might have become a tear was dry before she stood and turned to face Father Murphy. Everything in her posture radiated disapproval. The Sister swept regally to the door, brisk and quiet and hard. Her eyes were very small. Father Murphy's voice rose, and he closed the door to keep the students from overhearing. But through the narrow glass window they could see his face darkening unevenly and hear the repeated words "submit" and "irreverent." There were many other words that began with "un" and "in" sounds, as in "inappropriate" and "unacceptable." When Sister Leonarda returned to the classroom she did not look chastised. She looked like a woman pushed into an arena with a large unpleasant animal that she had every intention of killing before she left.

She instructed the group to reenact the resurrection dance, and she clapped when it concluded. She told them to sit quietly, and wait. When she returned from the room with the copying machine she had a sheet of paper for each of them to take home to parents. It said, "The children have created an original play that will be performed directly after the First Communion Mass. Please R.S.V.P. to Father Murphy. Relatives and friends welcome." It was dated the previous day.

Father Murphy was deluged with calls from parents happy to see their children in a play. He told the first three callers that there had been a mistake. These initial callers were told, by their children, that there was no mistake. The play existed and they had worked very hard on it. Other parents were called, incited, and they in turn called Father Murphy.

In the end the play was performed complete with pikes, all the way to the end of the long three days and the resurrection of the flesh. The Sister triumphed on that day, departing the scene with roses and chocolate while the thespians skipped off happily to Easter breakfasts.

But Father Murphy was not done. He brought charges of insubordination to the Bishop, who took quiet steps. The Sister vanished for six months. She did not seem chastened when she returned. It was Father Murphy who seemed diminished, smaller somehow after her departure. The Sister had won, really. That was how the children saw it.

The victory was linked inextricably in Lauren's mind with Henry coming back to life after his absence. He talked to them again, and laughed at dinner, and did his homework. But behind the grown-ups' backs Henry hummed things Winston and Lauren had never heard and began hunting insects with Japanese names for whom he had fashioned little cages. When the cages began to pop up in his room Winston and Lauren shoved them under his bed and hissed, "Don't upset Mom!" Henry would shrug and say what will be will be, and there isn't much to be done. *Shikata ga nai,* after all. What did they think would be for dinner?

Henry's enthusiasm for dinner, for ice-cream cones and walks in grassy summer paths increased tenfold in these months. He regarded every good food as delicacy, and rejoiced over things like the shape of a stone or the sound of running water in ways that he hadn't ever done before. "This Italian ice," he whispered once to them, "is so like the shaved plum ices. But coffee ice cream! A miracle!" The sight of Henry weaving a bamboo door for a miniature cage cost Lauren all her patience one afternoon.

"What do you think you're doing?" she snorted. "What are you making these things for?"

He smiled up at her and held out another, smaller cage. There was an insect in it. "This one doesn't breed well in captivity so it is very treasured. Very brief life," he said, holding up a blue and green creature with what looked like mantis legs. Winston had walked into Henry's small room directly on her heels, and now he tapped his sister on the shoulder.

Lauren began to say something else, and Winston interrupted her abruptly. He said, "Just shut up." She replied in the same vein, and the exchange drew all the pained frustration that had initially been directed at Henry. The two were on the verge of blows before Henry simply stepped between them. "Stop it," he said sternly. "You must treat one another as brother and sister."

"That's just what we're doing," Lauren shot back.

"Oh, Lauren," Henry sighed. He slumped down by their sides, still between them. "It isn't Mom and Dad who needs me to stay away from Asagao. It's you. Both of you." They didn't say anything back. Henry was concentrating, looking exhausted but struggling to rise to a difficult problem. Finally he spoke. "What if I manage not to sound . . . different than I used to sound? What if I just hid Asagao's thoughts even from you and Winston?"

"What would that be like?" Lauren demanded. "I mean, would you feel all right?"

"I don't know. I won't know until I try."

"You mean you would never talk about what it was like to be a *hibakusha?*" Lauren asked. "The insects would go away, and the altar and the talk about the Meiji Empire and the bomb and all that?"

"All that," Henry said.

"But it would all still be here?" Winston asked.

Henry nodded. "But only . . . quiet."

"Would you be the same again?" Winston asked.

"The same as what?"

"The way you were before you remembered this guy's name."

"Asagao," Henry murmured. He thought for a while and then said, "I don't remember before Asagao."

"Christmas, Henry! There were Christmases without Asagao," Lauren protested. Certainly this would jog his memory.

Henry smiled brightly. "Oh yes. You're right. There was the year we got the chalkboards. I don't remember any of his thoughts when we opened the chalkboards."

"I got the yellow truck with the doors that opened and the front-end loader with the shovel that really worked that year," Winston urged. "It was just us."

"Just us." Henry smiled. "I remember."

But his smile looked odd—not the way it had looked before Asagao. Weeks went by and Henry went to school and ate baloney sandwiches in the cafeteria and helped her with her homework and it seemed to be working. But she was on edge—waiting for it to stop working. She felt sure that Henry had offered them something that he didn't have the strength to give.

One Tuesday afternoon at the end of class she did not hear Sister

Leonarda dismiss them. Students filed out, leaving her alone at the third desk in the first row, staring blindly out the window.

"Lauren Cooper," the Sister said. "Lauren Cooper, class is dismissed."

But Lauren did not hear her. She did not look away from the window until the nun had walked up to her and sat down in the seat directly by her side. "Lauren Cooper, is your father picking you up today? Or is your brother going to be waiting to walk home with you?"

At the word "brother" Lauren turned to her. "Both my brothers are home today with colds," she said.

"What are you looking at?" the Sister asked. "What is so fascinating out that window?"

"Nothing. I don't know." The nun did not move and the next words tumbled out in a little heap. "Sister, if Jesus comes to you in many forms and sometimes it's hard to tell if it's really him, how can you know? How can you be sure it isn't the devil or something else, pretending?"

"You must look to the effect. Does this person who might be Jesus make you happy, better—or does this person make you evil? Miserable?"

"Maybe Jesus can make you miserable."

"It is not Jesus who makes us miserable. It is our resistance to Jesus that makes us miserable, and it is easy to confuse the two things. What is the trouble, child? You've been trying to tell me something."

"Sister, there's a Japanese man in my brother's mind. He didn't have pneumonia like my parents said that whole month he missed CCD, Sister. He went to a sanatorium or something to see doctors. They were trying to get the Japanese man out of his head, only they don't even know the Japanese man is there. All my mother and father know is that Henry wasn't himself. He got strange, and then once he fell asleep for three days and they thought something was wrong with his brain so they took him to all these brain doctors."

"And how do you know about this Japanese man, then, Lauren Cooper?"

"Well, Henry lets us know about him. Me and Winston. But not our parents."

The Sister considered this. "Your parents have taken Henry to doctors? Did your parents explain what the doctors said?"

"They didn't tell us, Sister. We don't know."

"And you don't tell them," the Sister added. "So they don't know."

"I guess so. But they took him to doctors. They've gotten him all the help that they know how to get him. I don't know if he needs any help, really. Because he's happy. It's me who isn't happy."

"Do you think you should talk to one of these doctors, Lauren Cooper?"

Lauren whipped her head back and forth vehemently. Absolutely not.

"Tell me about your brother's Japanese man."

"His name is Suriyu Asagao. I don't know how he got into Henry's head. Actually, Henry says that the man isn't in his head; Henry says that he's in the Japanese man's head. And that the Japanese man doesn't know he's there. It's not like he hears voices—it's more like he's watching a film of the Japanese man's life. That he can hear his thoughts. And, Sister, he's real. I've seen him."

"Excuse me?"

"He was in Hiroshima when the atom bomb was dropped. He's one of the people they called *hibakusha,* people who survived the atomic bomb. Henry has a book with his picture in it. I've seen him."

"So your brother has invented a story to go with this picture?"

"No. It's not like that. It's not made up."

Sister Leonarda sighed. "How does this Japanese man influence your brother? Does he want your brother to do things?"

"He doesn't talk to my brother. I said that."

"Very well. Does his influence make your brother feel or behave badly?"

"I think he makes Henry feel happy. Henry doesn't make airplanes anymore. He makes insect cages. Asagao's family were insect merchants."

"I didn't know there was such a thing."

"I guess there is. Or was. Henry just woke up one morning knowing which insects live in captivity and which don't; which ones get attracted by light and which ones don't; what kinds of noises they make. He knows a lot now that he didn't before. And he didn't take books out of the library or stuff, Sister, which is why I'm saying that this isn't just something he makes up for fun. It's something that's inside him. The thing is, Sister, Winston and I got Henry to agree to pretend that he doesn't know this stuff. We told him to pretend that this Asagao was never alive, and that he doesn't hear any Japanese thoughts."

"Did your brother agree to this?"

Lauren nodded unhappily.

"Why does it make you sad that he agreed to this?" Sister Leonarda asked.

"Because I don't think Henry can keep the promise. And it feels like we've made a mistake. It only feels like a bigger pile of secrets. And I'm afraid that it will hurt Henry to do this."

"Why would it hurt Henry, Lauren?"

"I'm not sure. But I think it hurts to keep secrets. And it hurts to hide what makes you happy. Doesn't it?"

"Yes. I believe it does." Sister Leonarda waited but Lauren had stopped. "Miss Cooper, are you asking me for advice?"

Lauren nodded dumbly.

"You do not know what is going on. Neither do I. But I know that Jesus comes to us in many forms. He does not take only one form, and he does not live only one kind of life. He is infinite. Now, you say that this Japanese gentleman makes your brother feel better?"

Lauren nodded miserably. "And when he's feeling this other person's feelings he's happy. He feels differently about things like ice cream."

"I don't understand."

"Well, Henry treats food like some miraculous thing now—not like something that's just there. He's like that about more things now, with Asagao in his head, than he was before."

"Do you think the Japanese gentleman has your brother's best interests at heart?"

Lauren nodded again. "I know that Henry likes having his thoughts."

"But these thoughts of your brother frighten you?"

Lauren nodded.

"Your brother is not the first person to have an Asagao," the Sister said. "They have always come to us. Some of them are sent by God. Some are not. Some, I believe, are some fragment of God we have in our minds. They mix in our affairs for reasons we do not understand."

"Who else has had an Asagao?"

"Oh, many people. Do you remember what I told your class about the Immaculate Virgin's appearances at Fatima?"

"But that was the Virgin Mary," Lauren protested.

"The three children did not see just the Virgin Mary," the Sister sighed. "There were other visions. Visions that came to the little brother and sister who were taken from this life the year after the visitations, when they were only nine and ten years of age."

"What other visions?"

"You say your brother's imaginary friend died because he was in Hiroshima. Does your brother think about war a lot, Lauren Cooper?"

"I don't know, Sister. But he describes things. People with their hands burning like torches at the ends of their arms. People with bubbling skin. Rivers full of bodies and ash."

"I see," said the Sister. "And you?"

"Oh, I don't have an Asagao."

"I mean, Lauren Cooper, do you think about war a great deal? About the scenes your brother describes?"

"I don't know."

The nun waited for more, and when it was not forthcoming she took a different tack. "Does your brother honor the Immaculate Conception?"

"I think so."

"Has he made the five reparations that the Virgin asked us to make on the first Saturdays of five successive months?"

"Yes. We all did last year with my mother."

The Sister considered this for a moment. "And when he was celebrating the mass, during those five Saturdays, did he seem distressed?"

"I don't think so."

"How did he seem?"

"I don't know."

"In other words, his appearance was peaceful?"

"Yes."

"Then, Lauren Cooper, I believe your brother is under the protection of the Virgin. Your parents, you say, have taken him to the so-called experts, so the rational adults have had their day here. Now we are in the Virgin's hands, which is not such a bad thing at all. She promises this to all who make the proscribed Reparation of the Five Successive First Saturdays. And to these people also she promises her presence at the moment of death, and support in the subsequent journey."

"So you think Asagao is the Immaculate Virgin?"

"I did not say that. But I believe your brother is in Mary's hands and no harm will come to him. I can also tell you this, Lauren Cooper. I prepared your brother for his First Communion, as I prepared you, and it was clear to me that he had a sense of the Child Jesus that was simple, and radiant. I have no fears on your brother's behalf."

"Asagao doesn't seem to think a lot about God."

"Sometimes they do not. Who does Asagao think about?"

"Shaved plum ices. Rice balls. Insect songs. Honorable boiled food. Honorable uncooked food—*O-sho-gin-gu. Dango* dumplings. *Gozen* noodles. Charlie Chaplin. Henry can describe Chaplin's movies. He really loves the scene where Charlie Chaplin tries to boil and eat his shoe because he's so hungry."

"That is merely your brother speaking, Lauren Cooper."

"Sister, Henry has never seen *The Gold Rush*. How would he know what *O-sho-gin-gu* means, much less tastes like?"

The Sister regarded her silently for a moment. She said, "Prayer can help. Prayer is more powerful than we know."

"Henry prays a lot, but lately it's to the spirits of departed ancestors."

"What I mean, Lauren Cooper, is that I advise you to pray for Henry," the Sister said. "And yourself. And I myself will pray for you both. Observe the rosary daily, and pray particularly to the Virgin Mother of God."

"Will that do it?"

"Do what?" the Sister asked.

"Make him . . . safe." Lauren didn't dare ask about herself, or what her own prospects might be.

"I don't know."

Lauren stopped talking altogether, dumbfounded.

"You don't know?"

"Right." The Sister nodded.

"You mean, maybe God won't hear me?"

"I didn't say that. I am saying that we might not understand God's answer. If Asagao is God's, we need not concern ourselves. It is between God and your brother. Your brother honors the Immaculate Conception. And we know that Mary has her son's ear, and the love of God the Father. If Asagao is not God's, it is still, in the end, between your brother and God. We can only pray to God for Henry's sake."

"Yes, Sister," said Lauren, but she felt a full-blown rage coming on. How could Sister Leonarda think she would be satisfied with this ragged little offering when she so clearly needed something certain—something firm and sure? "But, Sister," she said, "there has to be something besides that."

"I think you might do one other thing," the Sister conceded.

"What?"

"You might allow your brother, when he is alone with you, to share this Asagao's thoughts. I know this is a burden to you, but it may be a gift to your brother."

"And if I don't tell other people, like my parents, is that lying, Sister?"

"I'm not sure," Sister Leonarda answered. "I'll have to think about it."

"What about Winston?"

"Your brother? What about him?"

"Should Winston do the same thing?"

"I believe so," the Sister said. "If he can."

"Sister, what else did the Virgin say to the children?"

"There were three children, and she revealed three mysteries."

"What were they?"

"The first was a vision of hell. The second was the prediction that there would soon be a second and more terrible war, a punishment for our offenses against God. The visitations took place in 1917, so the Virgin was referring to the Second World War, which came to pass, as you know."

"And the third?"

The nun hesitated. "The Holy Father has said that he feels this last vision is not for public knowledge."

"It doesn't sound like having other people in your head is a good thing," Lauren said.

"It depends, I am sure, upon the head. Now if you don't go home your mother will think you are lost."

Lauren stood up and gathered her catechism, pulled on a sweater. "Sister, do you believe in the mysteries?"

"Our faith only leaves you frightened, doesn't it, Lauren Cooper?"

Lauren nodded.

"And that is why you seem to be angry all the time," the Sister sighed. "Lauren Cooper, I have something to give you."

"What, Sister?"

"I give you permission, if you need it, to leave the Church. I think that what is Divine is so enormous that almost all the roads lead to it and I am sure that you will find a road of your own."

"But Father Murphy says there is only one way."

"Indeed. Father Murphy says many things."

"Have you ever met a real Japanese person, Sister?"

"Once."

"Was he a Catholic?"

"No. I don't know what he was. I asked him how he honored his own faith, and he said something that at the time I thought was very un-Catholic."

"What did he say?"

"He said he danced."

"Oh."

"Go home, Lauren Cooper. Your brother, I think, is a good boy, and though the devil is drawn to the good boys he usually does not succeed with them. Henry has you, and your little brother, and the Virgin, and your parents. The dead will protect him. Perhaps this Asagao is here for that purpose."

"Which dead, Sister?"

"Members of the Holy Catholic Apostolic Church, which is made up, you know, of the spirits of its members both living and dead. So you must not worry if your brother honors the spirits of the recently departed." The Sister's tone left off its stentorious classroom ring. "Lauren." She took Lauren's hand. "Perhaps Asagao has come to offer you a challenge. Not Henry but you. Loving Henry does not necessarily mean keeping Henry safe. None of us is safe. But some of us are loved. That is better than safe."

"Sister, did you really mean it when you said you thought I'd be fine?"

"Absolutely, Lauren Cooper."

Lauren went home and considered all this. As to the idea that prayer would accomplish something, she was of two minds. Prayer offered relief. But in her experience it effected absolutely no other change, and she wanted change. She wanted Henry back entire and whole with no Asagao attached.

She apologized in her mind to God for her bad manners. Then, out of habit and limited alternatives, she took her state of mind to Henry, carefully leaving behind specifics about her conversation with Sister Leonarda and about Winston's anxieties.

"Henry, are there Catholic Japanese people?" she began.

"Well, yeah. There were Jesuit priests there."

Lauren looked around at the room. She noticed for the first time that the room had several dying plants in it, and the smell of dirty clothes. Staleness. Crusty things. Surely Henry could see that he was killing the plants.

Henry smiled and said, "Look. I have the most beautiful design for this year's ice house! Lauren?" He took her hand in his own.

The sound of her own name spoken in Henry's much trusted voice felt like a little blow inside her chest. His warm, engaged attention, his deep native goodness, and the fact that he was moving steadily away from her into a foreign state of mind—this unbearable combination of forces was taking on a tangible shape somewhere at the base of her throat.

Eleven

Things worked and then again they didn't. Henry did his best, but his siblings could see the difficulty he had keeping his Japanese tendencies out of any public discourse, especially given that once again he had complete freedom to speak freely of Asagao with Lauren and Winston. Henry inhabited two worlds—the real one and the Japanese one—and it was clear that the internal pressures he suffered had punched little leakage points between the two. His speaking voice, his opinions, his food preferences, even some of his memories, continued to sometimes meld with Asagao's. He matured into one of those people with non-native syntax—someone who could send unfamiliar signals in such intangible ways that new acquaintances found themselves wondering where he had lived in the past or where his parents were from.

In the last years that Henry lived in her house, Annie became committed to keeping him away from professionals who used words like "schizophrenic" in order to make a living. Warren had more faith in authoritative figures with technical degrees. He also tended more to view his children as logically comprehensible collections of parts that occasionally broke down but could be fixed.

Henry resisted fixing; he clung to his little *Meiji* period ways. *Matsuri,* in particular, had an irresistible pull on him, particularly the winter *Kamakura matsuri* and the summer *o-bon,* the Festival of the Dead. The years went by, and Lauren and Winston learned to listen for the door softly closing behind him on the night of January 14. It would be Henry going out, armed with cakes and thermoses of tea and chocolate. The first year Lauren alone had joined him. The second year she bumped into Winston in the lightless hallway as they both tried to sneak out unnoticed. The third, the last year before Henry left for college, Winston and Lauren told him to just wake them up so they could go together to light the candles he had set into his ice house's shelves. There they sat in a row, all three, until the hot chocolate was drunk, the cookies eaten and the candle flames had guttered into the puddles their heat had melted around them. It was fun. They agreed this practice was harmless as long as their parents remained at a distance. "They don't check beds," Lauren assured her brothers. But she was wrong. Their mother checked beds.

Every July *Bon-matsuri* Henry built lantern boats and loaded them with tiny bowls of food offerings for his spirit visitors. Modern people, Henry told them, built small platforms that held only the rice paper lantern. But he built traditional miniature boats, every year making a special place on the foredeck of the largest boat for small satin-bordered blankets or pacifiers. These baby possessions floated off in their boats without a single mention of Sally. Winston and Lauren began to build their own boats and push them off laden with things that the very young dead might want. They had not noticed that they were happy building the boats and lighting the candles;

their happiness was hidden from them behind their complaints about Henry's behavior.

On the last night of *o-bon,* that long week of visiting spirits, Lauren and Winston would help Henry carry the whole flotilla to the creek that ran behind their house, bordering the cornfields and marshes that resisted development. There they perched the bowls and toys on the tippy little boats, lit the lantern candles and let them slip away in the thickening darkness, off no doubt to some septic system on the other side of town. Every year Winston and Lauren told each other that they hoped Asagao and his thoughts would leave with the other spirits. Every year Asagao stayed. "So beautiful," Henry would say, watching the little boats' lights stream away.

Lauren and Winston coached Henry on public behavior that would keep him in the mainstream of anonymous student life when he went off to college. "Don't tell anybody about volcanic stones punking on your head when you walked to school," Winston would remind him. "Don't talk about insect sounds."

"It is not 'insect sound,'" Henry corrected. "It is song."

Lauren didn't like the syntax of his response. "We're talking to you, Henry." Henry's face swiveled toward her—his face, but not. It wrinkled in concern. "No holiday talk." Lauren jabbed the air with a pointer finger.

Winston tapped his older brother's arm. "Just the usuals, like Christmas. Maybe Easter if you have to, but only the bunnies and egg stuff. No death and resurrection."

"Maybe the major feast days," Lauren added. "To Catholics, I mean."

"Don't you worry," Henry reassured them. He actually patted Winston's knee. "I'm completely invisible. I draw no attention to myself whatsoever."

What could they do but take him at his word? Still, a week after this conversation Lauren found Winston sitting alone in the garage, clutching a car jack. "It makes me so nervous," he whispered. "I just want to take something apart."

She knew exactly what he meant, though she didn't seek comfort in the same places. Winston also attended mass almost daily. He swore by its beneficial effects. Lauren had taken the opposite tack. Where did ideas like saints and holy ghosts lead if not to ideas like Asagao? She never entered a church.

"Don't worry," she said now. She reached out a hand to touch him but changed her mind. The jack in his hand bounced up and down, up and down. She tucked her hand back into a pocket. "It'll be all right."

Twelve

There are many things that are no longer mine, but I still possess the memory of having been born in the Center of the Earth. There was never a moment when my parents did not look at me with eyes that placed me firmly there. My honorable parents—I never thought of their love because it was the air, the sky and myself below it—not the kind of thing you name in your waking mind until it is gone and you must name it to recall it. When they died, because I was so young, I lost the memory of being in that perfect state. It did not return until I gave myself to Ishiru, whom I loved entirely. Once again I lived in the Center of the Earth. The volcanoes above us and the sea before us caused me no concern.

My father said that Japanese had to live with volcanoes and earthquakes because our country was stretched along the back of a dragon who lived beneath us, and when the dragon became restless we were shaken. I grew up beneath a volcano's fiery breath, and walked to school with a helmet on my head on the days that its rocks flew through the air.

We lived beneath the volcano because my mother was afraid of the tsunami that comes from the sea. When she was a little girl she went to hunt berries one morning on the cliffs behind her village. She had climbed only a short chi from her mother's house when she turned and saw her entire village swept into the sea by a single wave that carried away every dog and wall and tatami mat. Every person.

My father's family took her in, and she married my father and learned his family's trade. Though I know she loved my father I also know that she could not have married him had he been a fisherman who made his home upon the beach with the waves hissing on the sand just outside her windows.

My honorable father was not someone who worried. He would say, "Do not waste your heart wishing for safety. Life is lived between the volcano and the sea, and one dishonors life by worrying about its size."

In the end, both my honorable parents' lives were quite small. They died of a sickness when I was eleven, and my uncle adopted me into his house as a younger brother to his own son. This son longed only to make mechanical things. If he found a stream he built little wheels that twisted in the running water, and attached the wheels to other moving things. Everything, to this boy, was material for some other thing. Nothing was itself. When he was still very little he sent away in the mail to western addresses to get books about inventions, and was mad with disappointment that in his simple family of insect purveyors there was not means or understanding to help him follow the instructions which were in English.

This boy, I think, had made a mistake in the drifting void between lives where spirits choose their next families. This happens. He had chosen these people to whom he was a mystery, and he walked the earth in a rage because of this terrible mistake. He and my uncle loved one another but fought all the time, the son hating the insect trade and begging to be freed of it. "You cannot free yourself of your own life," my uncle would tell him, "or the obligations of son to father." But the son managed, I think, to do what my uncle said was impossible: he ran away. My uncle spent the remainder of his life waiting for his son to return. He spoiled his own heart with waiting.

I could not replace my uncle's son, but my lively feelings for his work offered him some comfort, for which I was grateful because I loved this gentle uncle. I learned the business at his side and he told me I had a fine stomach for it. When we went out to hunt night singers with lanterns, we would wade through meadows into groves full of the jingling and ringing of the bridle-bit insects and the gotcha-gotchas. The broken grasses opened a wake of their scent behind us. Night insects sing more beautifully than day insects and attract the highest prices, so there were many flawless nights like this.

We drew them toward us with our lanterns, knowing that they could no more refuse the heat and light than stop their singing. They mistake the flame for love and they come; they are caught. Insects are full of the forces of fire and water, yet they fit into my pretty cages. They were the first to reinhabit Hiroshima with any real life and spirit after the pica-don. *Their sawing filled the night air before the end of that August, while the humans left behind wandered in a* hippon *haze from gutter fire to gutter fire, eating things fried in motor oil and robbing from the dead. The insects are the ones with the true* yamato dasai *spirit—so brave, so heedless of the limits of their lives.*

We always had a booth at the Bon-matsuri *so that those seeking offerings for their own visiting spirits could place their ancestor's favorite insect singer on the lamplit boats. Many shopkeepers, like us, did their best business during the July Festival of the Dead. Oh, the lanterns floating in the darkness! Like calming oil on rough feelings.*

Ishiru's family did not rely on the festivals for their living—they were stone sellers, builders of the most beautiful gardens on our island. Very famous for their stones. I watched her from a distance for two summers, and finally I knocked down two little boys to force myself beside her in the line of bon-odori *dancers so that I could take her hand. The memory of that first pressure of palm upon palm is mixed, in my mind, with the taste of plum ices and the night parting to let the floating lanterns in the stream pass on to the sea. When I touched her the place where our hands met rang.*

I go on and on remembering though I know it is not wise. It is the reason, I am sure, that I wander between lives like a gaki, *trapped by my attachments to my last life and unable to go on to my next. And so I am lost. I do not know where I am. I try to stop thinking about Ishiru. I fail, and remain lost.*

Ishiru's family had gained their feeling about the stones from the Buddhist priests, who made the most beautiful gardens. She showed me gardens that her family had built, some all sand and stone; some masses of plants anchored in black stones and little pools. Her family especially honored chodzu-bachi, *the water-basin fountains formed of granite that had been worn over centuries by dripping water. These* chodzu-bachi, *or the river stones, were her family's fame. They are valued also because their water attracts butterflies, cicadas, dragonflies and the little semi who sing kana-kana-kana.*

Ishiru had a reputation in her family for finding stones in the shape of tortoises, which she especially loved because the turtle is the servant of the Dragon Empire under the sea. And each garden her family made has the lucky Yuzuri-ha tree, whose old leaves never fall before the new ones come to take their place. Fathers especially honor this tree, as it assures them that their sons will be ready to take their place before they die. Her family shaped her feelings in the Shinto way, seeing the stones they found and placed as having spirits.

The other boys said she was too bold, not modest. She did not have a flower name, like other girls of her class—Plum Blossom or Golden Chrysanthemum. She was more like her family's beautiful stones than like the fragile flowers, which for most boys meant that she was undesirable.

The first year I noticed her she was calling out to friends in an immodest way. She sang out loud. Very loud. She stood before her family's stall and recited poems. The next year I pushed down the two little boys to reach her side in the dance line.

Later she offered more poems, now looking at me, right at me. The nature of the poems changed. She became all that I thought about. She became the feeling in my heart when I read the lines "O insect, insect!—think you that Karma can be exhausted by song?" She became an answer to the longing in the insect voices I listened to all my life, the voices that seemed to sing of impermanence and brief life, of the pain that colors all desire.

Pain does cling to desire. It is the combination that gives longing its sharp taste, its long memory that stretches back over all the lifetimes.

PART 2

Unidentified Bright Objects

Thirteen

Henry had promised to move through his public life with apparent complete normalcy and he kept his word. He graduated from high school and packed his bags for college in Boston. The departure created a kind of vacuum in the house—a vacuum with a sucking pull.

Over the next few years Lauren and her parents followed him to New England. Warren heard of an opening at a firm in Lynn, just a few miles from where Henry would be, and Annie surprised him by suggesting he apply for the job. She dug up all the perennials toward whom she had sentimental feelings, and they moved. When Lauren's turn came, she chose a college within a half-hour subway ride from Henry's dormitory. Only Winston balked. He determinedly avoided New England colleges, heading off to a school in the Midwest.

"Lauren," her mother told her the night before she left to begin her freshman year. "I know you like to stay close to Henry and that you worry about him. But Henry is all right. What I'm saying to you, honey, is that I want you to let go of this responsibility I know you've felt. Do you know what I mean?"

Lauren was surprised that her mother had paid so much attention to her and that she herself had been so transparent. But she was more surprised to realize, listening to her mother, that underneath this feeling that she had to take care of her older brother was a larger feeling: the feeling that Henry was just on vacation but that it was still his job to take care of her. Wasn't she just trying to make Henry normal again so he could keep up his old austere offices of love? "Sure, Mom," she said. "I know."

She examined her mother's face carefully and saw only perfect trust. She doesn't know me, Lauren thought. Her mother thought Lauren was generous and caring, when in fact she was only self-interested and afraid.

So off they all went, Henry majoring in civil engineering and talking about highway lighting patterns; Winston majoring in electrical engineering and happily immersing himself in the world of large and technically delicate machinery. But Lauren, to everyone's amazement, simply seemed to get lost. She enrolled in too many, too difficult courses. Every week the pile of uncompleted work rose, and Lauren, who had always been an organized and accomplished student, faced the real possibility of flunking out of school.

Into this jumbled state entered a young professor who saw her clear distress and offered to help. But he was only one of those men with an antenna-like sensitivity to weakness and a muddled sense that confusion and academic failure were sexually provocative feminine qualities. This was Lauren's first contact with the type, and she mistook it. She thought he was in love. She thought she was in love. She felt powerful and light. Her study habits returned overnight and she sailed through her examinations with solid grades after an entire semester of disastrous inattention.

The object of her love returned the feeling until he realized that Lauren believed they might continue on like this forever, and then he got uncomfortable. The spaniel-like devotion that at first had so charmed him came to have an opposite effect. He stopped returning Lauren's calls. He failed to explain his silence, his evasive manner, his appearances in various places with other women. Finally he vanished as suddenly as he had come into her life.

Lauren was too young to think of this as something that happened to teenaged people like herself—people practicing at the ideas of commitment and betrayal on the adult scale of full-blown sexual infidelity. She didn't see that she had simply had the benefit of practice in the world of romantic love, and that the world itself was still intact if a little less shiny. As far as she was concerned, the world was ruined.

She was startled one afternoon during this terrible time by the smell. It filled her nostrils for the second time in her life as she walked across campus early one morning: the acrid scent of fish frying in motor oil. An aftertaste in the mouth of something ashy.

She went to bed for two full weeks. The smell persisted, appearing every day before lunch and staying for perhaps the amount of time it took to shower, or make toast.

When she got out of bed it occurred to her that she had not gotten her period that month. An appointment at a clinic and a test confirmed her fears—she was pregnant. The protocol of the time demanded that whether the test result was positive or negative, the woman requesting the test had to appear at an appointment to get the results. It poured down rain as Lauren stood on the street waiting for a subway car to the clinic. She sat dripping in the waiting room, received her news, and stepped outside into incongruous and disorienting sunlight. The day had cleared into a cloudless perfection. She stood on the side of the road once again, waiting for a trolley car, this time clutching a small body of literature on adoption and abortion options and costs, counseling telephone numbers, a suicide hotline, pregnancy health issues and birth control options to consider at a later date. The world had changed.

She called Henry. His line was busy, then it was busy some more. Her mind had fixed on the idea of talking to Henry and it was difficult to think of anything else to do, but do something she must. Finally she decided to go to a party she'd been invited to that morning by someone in her dormitory. She put on a snug orange dress covered with red palm trees, a gift from the faithless lover. She set glass diamond earrings in her ears and feathers in her hair. She strapped on one of those pairs of sandals that are primarily strings and strips of leather all leading up to four-inch penknife-sharp heels—also a gift—and clicked purposefully toward her evening. Lauren was fully aware that she was in a kind of costume, carefully assembled by the young professor, that it had nothing to do with her own tastes or inclinations whatsoever. It didn't even fit the fashions of the time and place. Still, she fastened the shoe straps and jabbed the feathers in place and strode out the door. *Clickclick, clickclick.*

Not surprisingly, the evening did not turn out well. In the middle of a conversation with someone about a movie she had not seen, her hands got the better of her and banged straight through a glass window. Four windows, before they were done.

The ambulance responded quickly, and the EMTs wrapped her arms from the elbows down. The orange dress was ruined. Was she drunk, they kept asking, but they were so sure about the answer that they denied the evidence of their very patient's clarity and coordination. Lauren's protests grew more vehement as they ignored her responses. She struck at someone who had grabbed her a bit too firmly by the shoulder. They forced her into overnight observation.

She put the sedatives they gave her under her tongue and spit them into a corner of the room the moment she was alone: they bounced and clicked before coming to rest in a corner. She lay back on sheets so starched they crunched. The smell of bleach burned her nose. She counted minutes at first and then, in her despair, forgot to count or wait or hope and just gave herself up to how miserable she was, and this seemed to free her to lift up out of herself and over her own exhausted body, which she could see lying there in the bed with its brute pawlike hands and reddened face, its bony knees poking up in the sheet, its brown hair splayed like so many exclamation points on the pillow around her head. Poor silly silly girl, she thought, watching herself tenderly from a distance. Poor fool.

Her resident dorm advisor conferred with college administrators about the event, called her parents, and asked them to come take her away. The infractions, she explained, were beyond standard disciplinary procedures. Actually, the resident and her colleagues were frightened because Lauren had broken the windows with her bare hands and the visual effects had been shocking, though she had miraculously avoided major arteries.

Things had not been going well, the resident advisor explained when her parents arrived. Even though she earned remarkable grades on the last semester's final examinations, Lauren's attendance and grades before then had been entirely erratic and she did not seem to have attended classes at all in the last two weeks. Her dormitory room looked like the nest of an animal struggling with an incapacitating illness. And then there was the incident with the windows, the resident finished, her hands rising at her sides to provide a final flourish, a sign that all that could be said had been said.

Lauren's father was dumbfounded. In her telephone conversations with her parents Lauren had regularly reported facts that directly contradicted this picture; only the week before he'd been assured of good grades, friends, happiness. The Lauren that the resident advisor described was no one he had ever met. Her mother was not so dumbfounded, but she was frightened. The Lauren these people described was someone whose parents should be talking to a psychologist.

The doctor advised them to wait and let Lauren stay another day and night in the campus infirmary. They sat awkwardly by her bed talking about what they'd eaten for dinner on each evening of that week until visiting hours ended. They had managed, they told her before they left, to talk the administration into giving her one more chance.

As soon as they were gone Lauren struggled out of bed and down the hall to the one telephone on the patient floor. This time Henry answered. She slid down on the linoleum floor, her back against concrete blocks and the telephone receiver cradled awkwardly in both her bandaged hands. "Oh, Henry . . . ," she began, and then she sobbed.

It was as if the sobbing popped a cap off her sadness. Of course she had been entirely deluded and stupid—how could she not have seen there was something wrong with the man when he had presented her with those shoes? Then she told Henry the worst of it.

"What will you do?" he asked.

"I don't know. I'm trying to imagine adoption. I can't have this baby. I can't right now."

Henry said, "But, Lauren, the child picked you of all the people in the world. She did it for some reason."

"Oh, Henry, please! Fetuses don't pick somebody. And at this stage it's about one half of a centimeter long—not that different from the cells under my fingernails when I scratch my forearm."

"But of course you wouldn't get an abortion?"

The whole thing made her furious all of a sudden. "You don't know anything about this, Henry. You'll never be in this position." She had never spoken to Henry like this—so bitterly.

"I'm on your side," he said. Then, "I'd be so grateful if I could be pregnant."

"No you wouldn't. No you wouldn't."

"Maybe the baby's confused about timing. She's just picked a bad time. But that doesn't mean you should stop her, Lauren. Why are you snorting?"

"There's this smell. I've had it before, and nobody smells it but me. Always the same smell. It's like a hallucination in my nose."

"What's the smell?"

"I don't know. It's like some kind of car fuel or oil, and frying fish. Both smells together. It wasn't here at all a second ago. There isn't even a kitchen in this wing."

"I would help you with the baby, Lauren."

"Henry, for Christ's sake. I just turned eighteen. You have no idea. Do you lack imagination, or is it something worse that makes men talk like that?"

"Don't be like that, Lauren."

"I could be much worse. Much, much worse."

"It isn't true that I don't have an idea. You know I do," he protested.

"I know what you're talking about, Henry. But when we took care of Sally we were just little kids. And look at what happened." Henry said nothing. She said, "I have to hang up now." Her voice was dry. It sounded as if it had been caked with something and left in the sun.

That week she did not sleep a single night. She tried to imagine herself giving birth to a child whom she then gave away; she tried to imagine herself stepping past the demonstrators waving pictures of bloody six-month-old babies to enter a clinic; she tried to imagine herself caring for an infant. At some point in every one of these very different scenarios she would see Sally. Sometimes she saw the Sally who smiled at her before she had smiled at any other living thing. Sometimes she saw herself clutching the white lumpish form that was Sally on the last day of the baby's life.

She called her brother. "Henry, let me stay with you tonight, okay? I can't sleep. It's been a week and I can't sleep."

"Sure you can stay with me, Lauren. Of course you can."

At two o'clock that morning deepening waves of cramps woke Lauren. She struggled to the bathroom doubled over in pain. Henry found her there at six A.M., her sleeping body curved into a moon-like crescent on the linoleum. She had dragged a large towel over herself, blanket-fashion. In her hand she clutched a facecloth that still held traces of the blood she had struggled to clean up. The tub rim, the floor by her face, the door molding, all had bloody fingerprints that she had missed in the darkness of the night.

"Oh, Lauren!"

His sister raised her head, turned her perfectly white face toward him. "I didn't do anything to make it happen, Henry. It just happened," she whispered.

"I know," he answered, lying down on the linoleum by her side, stroking her face. "You'll be fine."

Lauren refused to let Henry tell their parents or Winston that she was kept overnight for observation in the university health clinic. As soon as it became clear to her that she was not going to bleed to death she regained some of her stiff insistence.

"So much wood in your nature," Henry muttered. But he let her have her way. "I'll be back tomorrow and you're not going back to the dormitory when you check out of here. You're staying at my apartment, at least for the next couple of days."

The next afternoon while Henry attended a class she crept out of his apartment and found herself poking her head into the campus Catholic church. She kept an eye out on the street for trucks, which she expected to swerve in her direction. She stood patiently in line, resigned to the impulse, and when her turn came she stepped into the dark confessional booth and knelt. The little screen clicked open between her face and the priest's. "Bless me, Father, for I have sinned. It has been three years since my last confession." But when the inevitable came, and the priest was waiting to hear her sins, she stopped. She couldn't name what she had done—not because she had lost her voice but because she wasn't exactly sure what it was. There would be no help for her here.

"Daughter?" the priest prompted.

She peered carefully through the screen and could just make out a razor burn on the man's face and what looked like a chocolate stain on his collar. He had a friendly face. The motor-oil fish smell seeped into the little box where she sat, squinting through the grate at the man on the other side.

The priest asked, "Do you want to make your confession?"

"No, Father. Thank you, though." She rose and left the confessional. The priest did not call out after her or open his booth door.

She hesitated for a moment at the doors of the building, looking up at the rising glass figures of the Stations of the Cross. A dark feeling swept up her—the feeling she'd had the day Sister Leonarda described the Virgin opening the earth to reveal Hell to the children of Fatima. She remembered the white expanse of the Sister's palms as she showed them how the Blessed Virgin had opened her hands, how light had flowed from their palms, downward, tearing open the earth and revealing what lay beneath. Poor little children, Lauren had thought, suffered to come unto the Virgin.

She was so sorry—so sorry to have sent the little child away.

And though she consciously told herself that she did not think of souls wandering about the universe any more than she thought of a literal blast-furnace hell, she wondered where the child had gone next. The thoughts kept going, no matter her efforts to quiet them.

"Henry," she said at dinner that night. "Would Asagao know where a spirit went in between lives?"

"Oh, I doubt it." Henry shook his head. "I have to tell you, he's a very confused individual. I don't think he's ever going to be any help in a concrete thing like that—a particular question, I mean."

"Henry, I feel so terrible. I want something so badly but I'm not sure what it is."

Henry nodded. "I know."

Lauren fiddled with her green beans and thought of things her lover had said to her that were not true. She was thinking about things that she had said to the lover that now didn't mean anything at all. The diesel-oil–fish smell flooded her senses. It was popping up all the time now, not just in the mornings. "I'm so tired. My arms hurt so much. My hands. I still have these cramps."

"It will get better," he said to his sister. "Go to bed. Think of something beautiful." He put his hand on her head. "You have a fever. I'm going to give you some aspirin and that painkiller they prescribed. Meanwhile think of something icy cold. And if you're still like this tomorrow we're going to go look for a doctor and some antibiotics."

She lay down. She thought of all the big snowstorms she had known that brought normal life to a halt, that stopped time and altered space. Then she picked one particular storm to remember, a five-day blizzard with a warm spell in its middle that melted the top layers of snow into a crust that froze like a boiled-sugar frosting when night came. On that night Henry had floated noiselessly into her room at around two A.M. and convinced her to go outside with him and explore. They jumped out the window—the only way out since the doors were banked with snow—and glided around a hypnotic expanse of frozen white. The storm had passed, and the moon was full, transforming all the backyards and fields and gardens into luminous mirrors. She felt quite keenly that she was seeing another world.

"What do you think?" Her brother had beamed, standing on top of a clothesline and spreading his arms wide.

"It's magic," she'd said. "It's just magic!" Then she'd sat down on the top of the McGarry's clothesline just long enough to freeze to it so that when she stood she ripped a hole right in the seat of her pants.

She fell asleep cooled and calmed by this memory. "Thank you, Henry," she breathed as he put a cool washcloth on her head.

When she woke up the next morning she was calm. There were no smells. The bleeding had slowed, her body cooled and the cramping diminished. Henry hovered anxiously but she told him she had to go pack her things before the dormitories closed for the semester. She had to face their parents. Though Henry had found a summer sublet and a job, she was still only at the end of her first year and her parents insisted she come home for the summer. Her mother had been frightened by the look of her in the infirmary, and she had insisted that Lauren come home with an unprecedented determination and rigidity. Lauren had not been able to resist it.

"I'll be sure to be there on Wednesday after your last exam when Mom and Dad come to pick you up," Henry offered. "They'll be more reserved if I'm there, too."

"No. Thanks. I am going home with them, remember, and we

won't have you to help us get along all summer. Might as well start now. It's okay, Henry. I'll be okay."

It was okay. Lauren struggled to look engaged and normal. She was thinking of how the perfect sheet of white had rolled away from her in the moonlight that night of the storm long ago. She was thinking of the faithless young man she'd believed she loved and the wandering loose spirit of the child she might have sent away. Her father didn't see that he had only the smallest part of her attention but her mother did.

"Lauren?" Annie said sharply. "Lauren, did you hear your father?"

"Yes, Mom." Lauren smiled persuasively. They peered into her face anxiously but saw nothing but tired confidence. They sat back, relieved. She would be all right.

Fourteen

During the fall of Lauren's senior year of college, Henry got a job with an engineering firm that specialized in lighting technology: highway lighting, football stadium floods, monument lights. But their future, they told him breathlessly, was lasers. They were combing engineering schools looking for talent, and Henry was some of the talent they unearthed.

Warren was proud: worthwhile work, proof of Henry's sound upbringing. Annie was relieved. Winston and Lauren were watchful and anxious. Would there be any discussions of bell-ringing mating seasons or *o-bon* dances that caused new colleagues to isolate or mock Henry? Would he fall asleep for three days and not go to work? Could they possibly control anything at all in Henry's new life? Did they need to?

Everyone but Warren held their breath and checked in frequently, but Henry seemed to have finally gotten to where he wanted to go all along. In his first year he was assigned to a group working on the illumination of five hundred miles of state thruway in Pennsylvania. He loved it. He loved the distance and geographical charts and the careful mapping of wattage and the delicate internal workings of bulbs.

"And who knows what's next?" he said to Lauren. "Everyone, everywhere, needs light of some kind."

By the end of that year Lauren managed to complete a haphazardly designed degree in the humanities. Her father stepped forward to advise her professionally, suggesting the military. "You could retire in twenty years," he said. "And you could get a real education there. Learn something you can trade on later in your life, not like the stuff you studied in college. You could go anywhere after those twenty years. Twenty years go by in a blink. And I can tell you with complete confidence that just about everything we have come to think of as important in modern life we owe to the military. Space flight, plastics, heat conductors, satellite technology! You could be part of that!"

"I don't know if I'd fit in, Dad."

"They would shape you so you'd fit. That's what the training is all about. It leaves you changed forever—you leave yourself behind and become part of a team. You become more than yourself—better. You can tell a military man within minutes of doing business with him, with or without the uniform. The background tells in a hundred ways."

Lauren resisted with silence and an owlish expression. After a period of head-shaking, her father suggested the insurance business. "The benefits are unbeatable, and a young person can't begin saving for retirement too soon," he told her. But when she countered with advertising, because it seemed less bleak to her, he agreed that advertising, too, was a product that would always be with us.

She got a job with an account executive in an advertising firm, tracking product sales for the agency's smallest clients.

"Well?" Henry asked her a few months after she'd started. "How is it?"

"All the people look like transvestites to me—the ones in the account side. And the people on the creative side all look costumed, too, but for something else. You know? I don't know what."

"You're miserable?"

"I don't know, Henry. It doesn't make any sense to me. I don't understand why all these people care so much about making people think they need stuff. I know that's just business . . ." She broke off. She grimaced.

"What? What is it?"

"That smell has come back. I went to a doctor about it and he told me he thought I had a sinus infection. He gave me this." She pulled a nasal inhalant canister from her purse. "But I don't think it's making a difference."

Henry had nothing to say to the canister. "Come with me on Wednesday. I'm having lunch with a guy who might know about a job opening. Something with no benefits. Something with no job security. Lots of hours."

"How do you know this guy?"

"He's a dance company manager. He called the division I work with because he needed lighting directors and he thought we could help him."

"Could you?"

"Of course not. He just got the number in the yellow pages or somewhere under 'lighting.' We don't do work like that."

"Then how did you get to know him?"

"We got talking on the telephone. I liked the sound of his voice, and the warehouse space they're using now for offices and performance space had lighting problems that I knew I could fix for him more inexpensively than the kinds of people he'd call in from a construction firm. I have lunch with him now and then. I did the work for him pro bono."

"He has a job?"

"He needs an assistant. But I also happen to know that he's not going to stay at this company for long. He's got his name in for general manager positions in larger companies in San Francisco and New York. He's looking for somebody to groom as a replacement."

So she joined Henry at his lunch with Dick, who greeted Henry with noisy enthusiasm and made it clear that he trusted Henry's judgment implicitly. Lauren, for her part, did not trust her brother's judgment implicitly but she knew that his impressions were usually sympathetic to her own.

The deciding factor, for her, was the studio. Entirely empty when they arrived, the vaulted dusty box took up all of the fifth floor of an old federal-style brownstone. Motes drifted up and down in the drafts from the twelve-foot-high windows. Lauren turned to her brother and grinned. "Sister Leonarda would love it here, wouldn't she?" she asked him.

"Oh, yes." The light rising up through the very tops of the arched windows was so brilliant that it blinded. "Dick," he said, "show her your office so she knows how glamorous your life here really is."

"Oh, God, yes!" Dick cried. "My closet! Pounding feet all day over my head, plaster coming down during the five-o'clock aerobics class that rents the space, no hot water half the time. But it's a pre–World War Two sprung-wood ballroom floor. No pillars. Open to any line of movement you make. There isn't anything better in the city for my money."

"And of course," Henry added, "you have remarkably little money."

"But look how far I can make it go. You, for example. A total freebie. And I learned so much about insects that I didn't know. It was an unbeatable package deal."

Lauren looked at Henry with what he called her white-eyes look.

"So how is Asagao?" she hissed at him when Dick answered the telephone a few minutes later.

"Not to worry. I am entirely in my right mind." Henry smiled.

Just then about a dozen dancers jostled into the space. As they scattered around the studio, stretching, Dick led them back down the stairs to his office.

"I'll offer you the job on the spot, but you can't accept," Dick said to her before they left. "Until you've seen them perform you can't know what you'd be helping to manage. But I feel entirely confident that you'll say yes; they're the best repertory company in the East. Saturday night we're doing a visiting choreographer's open rehearsal at eight right here. Come."

She wasn't sure at all if she would go. She found herself wondering what Sister Leonarda would make of Dick and the dancers and the studios and the job, and this line of thought was one of the things that drew her back that Saturday night.

The company was just what Dick had said—shockingly good. At one point a line of three men moving like a crowd of twenty all stopped at the height of a roll and paused for one preternaturally still instant before they swept the upbeat with what appeared to be a cascade of legs. A whispy cloud made up of only two women entered stage right. The men sliced into it and it parted.

At some points Lauren forgot that the dancers were people at all. She was startled to see sweat fly off a dancer's face as she spun because she had temporarily forgotten that the soloist was a person. She imagined that the dancers themselves probably forgot they were people too.

It made Lauren happy. Moreover, she had the unusual experience of knowing she was happy. She approached Dick in the crowd before she left. "I want the job," she said. "Tell me when to come back."

"Tomorrow."

"I have to quit another job first. Give me a week."

"How about two days? I have a monster mailer to get out and nobody to help me."

"Done," she said.

At the next weekend family dinner she told her family about the job switch.

"And what exactly is the pay?" her father asked.

She named an embarrassing figure.

"This is a nonprofit institution?" Warren pressed on after a terrible few moments of silence. "You're going to work for a nonprofit institution?"

"Well. Yes."

"Does this dance company offer any pension benefits?"

"No."

"What about health insurance?"

"No health insurance."

"You can't be serious," her father said.

"I'm a very healthy person."

"Well, besides this whole issue of being responsible to your own financial well-being, what does it contribute to society?"

She sighed. "Think of it this way, Dad. Think of a culture's artistic vitality as a kind of indicator of its psychological health." She smiled. "I'll be contributing to our society's well-being, defining it for history the way it will want to be seen."

Her father looked pained. "Dance doesn't protect anyone or feed anyone. You can't put your hands on a dance. It's not . . . real."

"Well, what about church?" Lauren countered.

"What are you talking about?" he huffed.

"Church isn't something you can put your hands on, Dad, but it's important to you. Right? It doesn't make anything or feed anyone. It's a spiritual resource. Very important to lots of people, but intangible. Not . . . real."

Everyone but Winston had stopped eating. He chewed on, apparently unmoved by the tension between his father and sister.

"Well," her father said grimly. "You can still tell the dance company you made a mistake."

Lauren set her fork down. "I'm sorry, Dad."

He pushed himself away from the table. "This is what I think. I have never been the kind of father who insisted on obedience first. You know that. I didn't force you back to mass when you stopped going because I knew that sooner or later you'd figure out your mistake on your own and go back to church. But it's my job to tell you when you're making a mistake." He rose and walked out of the room. They sat around the table in silence. Finally it was Winston who broke the long silence.

"Well, Lauren," her younger brother said between bites. "He was only trying to help. And he did pick up most of your tuition, you know."

The next morning Lauren gave her notice at the advertising firm and called Dick to name a starting date. When she hung up the telephone on that second call a new smell happened: pine and camphor. She sniffed, looking for a breeze that could have carried it in. The scent hung there for another minute.

"Dad didn't give you a hard time about job decisions," she complained to Henry later that week.

"I'm an engineer, Lauren. I'm working for a company that's publicly traded. What could he think was wrong about that? And it also matters to him and Mom that I still attend mass. You don't want to think that your nonobservance sets up a tension, but it does. They just have this idea that you're on an uncertain path. They worry."

"Do you attend mass because they want you to?"

"Nope."

"Why do you go?"

"I like it. The whole story makes sense to me, you know, the cross and the resurrection and all."

"It made me nervous. Every week, slurping down Jesus's blood and chewing on his flesh—God pitching his favorite son to the homicidal thugs."

"But there's a kind of emotional logic to it. And so much generosity in that sacrifice. Think of the purity of that gift—the enormity of it. The bread and wine. Repeating the same story over and over."

"Henry, how can you believe that somebody's death—especially that kind of death—was a good thing? How can you think that what happened there on that hill thousands of years ago will benefit you?"

"Now you sound like Asagao," Henry said.

"I couldn't possibly."

"But you do. He thinks the same thing—that it's a crazy *hibakusha* thought to imagine that one person's death will do another person any good."

"How does Asagao know about Jesus?"

"Black robes. Missionaries. He didn't think much of them."

"It's not a very happy idea, dying for somebody else's good," Lauren finished.

"Nobody said anything about happy," her brother replied.

Lauren steadily gained authority and expertise at running a dance company. With only she and Dick and a gaggle of consultants to manage the company's affairs, she could take on any kind of task she wanted. She wanted them all, tracking cash flows and negotiating loans and contracts, calming down underpaid and frequently injured dancers and figuring out the intricacies of their unemployment benefits. She dreamed about advertising bills and shipping arrangements for portable dance floors. She discovered a particular gift for generating faith—the company's creditors all loved her. She had an unerring sense of just how small a fraction of an outstanding bill she had to pay each of them to maintain goodwill. She knew their children's names, their own creditors, their own business woes. She listened. A year after she began, Dick moved on to a bigger company and she stepped confidently into his place.

The dancers adored her, and this made her happy, which in turn contributed to her seamless competence. She listened to everyone and betrayed no secrets. John, the artistic director, came to her office to bemoan the dancers' shortcomings; the dancers came to blast the choreographers' demands and John's judgment—she knew everything and told nothing. She became the centrifugal force holding this threadbare, quarrelsome and highly effective organization together.

It wasn't sainthood, but it would do. And whatever was behind the improbable, illogical impulse to make dances, Lauren took it as a clear sign that some intangible intelligence existed somewhere. Sister Leonarda would like this, she thought. Sister Leonarda would approve.

During this season in her life she suffered the little puncture wound that brought her into the emergency room where she met her future husband. Robin was the resident on duty in the ER when she arrived asking for a tetanus booster. Patient flow was very slow that morning.

Robin moved deliberately, sat down beside her before he touched her or looked at the foot and engaged her in a conversation about puncture wounds and feet as though there were no more fascinating things in the universe. Within a matter of minutes she was telling about the dancers and giving him synopses of their best performances. Then she found herself telling him what it was like to drive through an upstate New York whiteout. His attention felt intelligent, clean, focused—so when he dropped her entire foot to soak in a bedpan of soapy water and told her to keep it there while he saw a toddler in the next examining area, she sat still.

From where she perched she could hear the alternating musical calm of Robin's voice and the jagged hysteria of the child's mother. Her baby, it seemed, had spiked a fever so high that it threw the infant into a seizure. The baby's yowling made Robin's words indecipherable but the mother's voice rose on a nearly hysterical edge that carried her every word to the adjacent examining areas. Then suddenly, silence. Lauren leaned forward to peer through the dividing curtains and saw Robin taking the infant's temperature with an instrument inserted into an ear. He held her in a nursing position, snugly against his chest, and he sang, *Stewball was a racehorse, and I wish he was mine. He never drank water. He only drank wine.*

The baby's eyes locked on Robin's, who began to waltz, and then her face broke into a smile whose shimmering quality didn't seem to originate at the baby herself. She had seen that smile before, Lauren thought, but she honestly couldn't remember where, so distracted was she by the way Robin's hips moved.

The mother's mood tracked along behind the baby's and she grew calmer. Robin kept singing, but now his words were directed at the mother. He sang, *I bet on the sorrel and I bet on the bay. If I'd bet on old Stewball, I'd be a free man today. This baby's temp's high now, around a hundred and four. And in somebody this tiny that's cause for concern but not panic. Is she drinking anything? How much Tylenol's she had?* He kept smiling at the baby and holding her close. Her fingernail-sized eyelids began to droop and her doughy little feet hung like sandbags. Lauren listened while Robin's voice rocked on in the same rhythm as his body. The baby began to snore. The mother began to cry, softly.

He returned to Lauren soon after this and lifted her foot out of the bedpan.

"Is that baby okay?" she asked tentatively.

"Oh," he said. "I've seen six almost identical sets of symptoms this week. I cultured the first three and kept the first two in here to observe. They run the same fever pattern at exactly the same trajectory: it's a four-day cycle and I'm pretty sure that tomorrow is going to be worse for that baby and mom than today. But then the fever's going to break and they can certainly weather it at home with Tylenol and sodium-laced fluids."

"You seem so confident."

"The real giveaway to the pattern is the parent—if they cry like that, it's this particular infection. This week, anyway. It changes with weather and the particular microbe du jour."

"Is crying typical? I mean, in the parent?"

"Oh, God, yes. That's how most of them know to come in. It's not when the baby cries because babies cry all the time. It's when the parent cries. That means everybody's crossed some kind of line and they need help. You know, it wouldn't hurt to keep soaking that foot. When did you say you last had a tetanus booster? I might want to put a stitch in before we check you out. You know?"

The shot took about thirty seconds to administer and then he hopped up beside her on the sheeted table and they fell into conversation again. She stayed there, waiting while he came and went to see a deep cut that needed stitching, a broken leg and an aspirin overdose. His happy calm never left him.

"What about the stitch?" she asked after two hours of this.

"Oh, a stitch isn't really a good idea. In a puncture there's less chance of infection if it's left open." He grinned, not exactly apologetic about this reversal of medical advice. He asked her for her telephone number and she gave it to him; he wrote his own on a prescription pad and pressed it into her hand.

The next day she set it on her desk and let it sift down among the piles of folders. She'd been drawn to him. A lot. But she wasn't going to go digging down to find the number and she was going to ignore the elevated levels of interest she felt when the telephone rang. If the paper with his telephone number surfaced on its own, she told herself, if it floated up when she pulled a file, that would be a sign. She would maybe call him if that happened. She found herself humming "Stewball," thinking over and over about Robin's elastic and competent ER manner, reconstructing the way he had leaped easily onto the table by her side. These memories had the effect of making her shyer about calling him rather than more eager.

It took him three days to call, and when he did he asked her to go on a picnic. She hated picnics—soggy, sand-sprinkled food and crawling things. She said yes.

On the appointed day he drove a mere twenty minutes out of their urban world, parked by an unlikely patch of woods and led her to a meadow bordered by a rocky little creek. He had brought pickled garlic and ham wrapped in cold pancakes.

"I'd say I saw this menu in *Gourmet* or something, but the fact is I was afraid to plan—thought you might back out on me. The ham and pancakes were already in the refrigerator," he admitted sheepishly. An interesting man, Lauren thought: he knew what *Gourmet* was, he owned a hamper, he had odd leftovers and he blushed.

The afternoon melted into an evening with a gibbous moon. Robin pointed out two possums waiting at the edge of the clearing for the humans to leave so they could rummage for leftovers. She would not have been able to see them but he knew where to look. Such beautiful forearms, she thought, and looked away. He pointed out an old skunk path, a squirrel nest, a foxhole—used and abandoned—that were invisible to her before he showed them to her .

He had grown up hunting all these animals with his father, he explained, in Virginia's Blue Ridge Mountains. His father had died during his first year at college. His mother had vanished many years before that, swept away by some other man whose name had never been spoken in his father's house. Brothers and sisters? There were none.

He asked about Winston and Henry, about her parents. What did their home look like now? What was in her father's basement workroom? Her mother's kitchen? Winston's childhood bedroom?

He wanted to know about the dancers, the studio. She began with what had struck her first about the dancers' world—the way it smelled: old eggplant parmigiana sandwich ground into indoor-outdoor rug under spilled coffee on the stairs. Sweaty clothes. Varnish.

She described the expansive feel of the studio's dusty shafts of light at the end of the afternoon and the narrow feel of the dancers' proscribed lives. "They don't even know who the president of the United States is," she laughed. "He doesn't matter because he doesn't choreograph or dance."

"Why is that appealing?" he asked, sincerely confused. She said she didn't know, and was immediately seized with the impulse to kiss him. She did this. They kissed again as he dropped her before her apartment. He tasted like toasted nuts and dirt.

But then she started to think of where this kind of feeling led. She knew she herself was no longer the fool who'd happily strapped on the stiletto heels and zipped up the tight orange dress. Why wouldn't shaking things up in her life be a good thing? She test-drove several imagined scenes in her mind, some involving only herself and Robin, others involving members of her family and Robin. The scenes interfered with her peace of mind.

He called: she let the answering machine pick up every message. Whenever the telephone rang in her apartment she felt a little rush of happiness swarm through her chest and down to the hand that would reach for it. But something stopped her every time, and the hand floated above the receiver until the answering machine picked up again. He called every day the week after the kiss, then once a week, then not at all. She had let him go.

It was Henry who brought her back to him.

Fifteen

Though she knew that Henry kept in touch with *Bon-matsuri,* insect song, and Asagao's thoughts, until the night the military plane flew over their parents' home, Lauren had been lulled into complaisance. Henry was gainfully employed, independent, apparently able to navigate the real world without shocking lapses. She still saw him every week. They still built the snow house on January 14 and sailed the lantern boats on July 21, but by now she thought of these things as parts of normal life. She had not seen the piles of newspaper articles clipped and stacked in Henry's study, this one about nuclear proliferation in Third World countries, that one about twelve-year-old child guerrilla fighters in Central America, the majority about fighter plane costs and technology: stealth devices that evaded radar, cruising speeds that evaded heat-seeking missiles. She didn't find them until it was too late to matter.

The Cooper siblings met at their parents' home for family dinners every five or six weeks and more often when Winston was home from college. On the night that Henry went to sleep again, Warren was out of sorts and finding fault with everything in his reach. The salad was rusty, the meat overdone, the potatoes gluey. These things were the norm in his household, but it wasn't his habit to notice. Tonight he complained bitterly.

The conversation might have stuttered around the potatoes, but a whining screech overhead brought their father to his feet and into the yard. He searched the sky until he found the blunt military silhouette howling above them. He came back to the table and said the name of the airplane, grunting as he sat down again.

The plane was low enough, the engines heavy enough, to vibrate the glassware on their table. The whining quality to the plane's noises had changed to a deep rumbling, like a rolling series of explosions. "Is something burning?" Lauren asked anxiously. Everyone at the table shook their heads no.

"That plane," Warren muttered.

"What about it?" Lauren asked.

"I know the sound of that engine like I know the sound of this house's oil burner. I helped design it. It contains some of the most sophisticated technology on the planet. But its time may be over. Our time may be over."

"Who's 'us'?" Annie asked. "I don't understand."

" 'Us' is me. And people like me, the old-fashioned engineers with their second degrees in chemical engineering instead of finance. Nobody wants to pay for research anymore—too expensive and time-consuming. The money people run companies like mine now, and they've got their noses firmly ground into the next quarter's earnings. You can't build world-class technology if all you worry about is next quarter's earnings."

He had fallen earlier that week, a jarring whacking fall to his knees when he'd missed the tread on a stair riser. He had been following after his wife like a cranky pet, padding after her into a neighbor's garage through its ill-lit back entrance, calling out to her impatiently because she'd gone so far ahead of him. He had not seen the stair. Now his neck hurt him terribly though he refused all help but aspirin. Lauren's mother had described the scene to her: the dimness, the cracking thud, the ensuing silence, the shoes scrabbling as he rose again, slowly. Lauren watched him lift a fork to his lips now and turn white with pain. He would not acknowledge it, though.

"Can I get you some more aspirin, Dad? Has it been four hours yet?"

He shook his head dismissively, and she could see that even this simple physical movement was difficult for him. Why did her father's almost animal-like stoicism make him look so vulnerable to her?

"The money people can't see that cash won't protect you as well as a good set of missiles. Evil exists," her father said with sincere regret—an emotion she knew her father didn't often indulge because it was, to his mind, a waste. "And only guns tend to fight it effectively."

No one had anything to say to this. Lauren speared a browned lettuce leaf and watched her father's face finally gain some of its color back as the spasm in his neck relaxed. A jagged little stab of grief for her father went through her. He looked terribly gray.

They sat in the growing darkness, eating mashed potatoes and imagining evil—but right behind the general agreement that evil existed, all consensus among the little group vanished. Each Cooper at the dining room table saw a different face, a different form, as he or she imagined evil. Another whine overhead drew all of them but their father back out into the yard.

"What is it?" Lauren asked her father, yelling the question back into the kitchen where Warren stacked dishes in the dishwasher.

"That's just a weather plane." He flapped one hand, dismissing it.

"How can you tell?"

"Different engines."

"How do you know?"

"Well, their sound, of course. They don't sound at all alike."

Then the force of their private considerations drove the Coopers apart from one another physically. Each drifted into a different part of the house on one pretext or another until Annie sent Lauren to gather everyone for coffee.

Months earlier, Lauren had found a book in a used bookstore on the shelf labeled ORIENTAL. The book was a collection of photographs of ice houses decorated for the January festival. She had scooped it up feeling something she could accurately call glee, and though she'd meant to keep the book until January's *matsuri,* last night's fighter plane discussions had left her uneasy. If she wrapped the book today and took it as a surprise for Henry the first thing tomorrow morning, they would both feel better. She drove along humming, imagining his excitement when he saw the 1940s snow house on page fifty-six, which looked exactly like their own snow house from 1965. That year she had been fourteen years old. She and Winston had gotten into a fight because he wanted to put a snow fireplace in the living room, arguing that Eskimos built fires in the centers of igloos so why shouldn't they build one in their snow house? He hadn't won the argument in 1965, but in the 1966 snow house they had included a fireplace complete with mantel, and it had been quite lovely lined with burning tapers.

Henry didn't answer her knock. She let herself in with the key he kept, against all advice, in the mailbox. His coat hung by the door; his wallet lay on the kitchen table.

"Henry!" she called. "You couldn't still be asleep! Come on! I have a surprise for you! If you aren't decent tell me now because I'm coming in your bedroom!"

The bed was empty. Her heart rate picked up. Could he be in the bathroom, even though she couldn't hear the shower or any running water? She flew through the rooms until she came to his body on the kitchen floor, breathing shallowly. She shook him. She put a cold washcloth on his face, and then when he didn't respond she felt frantically for a pulse. She couldn't find it immediately, but that, she tried to tell herself, was because her hands were shaking so hard. There! A warm but thready flow along one of the veins. "Henry, you have to stand up," she insisted. "Jesus," she breathed. "Jesus, Mary and Joseph." She called her parents' home, where Winston answered. Their parents had left for work and he was alone. He came immediately, and together they wrestled Henry down the stairs and to the hospital emergency room, where she found Robin on duty.

That was how she was returned to Robin's orbit. When she saw him she felt such relief—such gratitude! "Robin!" she yelled down the corridor. "Robin!" He had been examining a form at the check-in desk and he twisted around at the sound of her voice. His face lit spontaneously, happily when he saw her, then returned to professional impassivity when his eyes moved past her to Henry. He hurried to their side.

She and Winston were dismissed from the triage area while Robin examined their brother. No one came out for an hour and a half except a nurse who asked if Henry had any history of heart disease.

Winston was near hysteria. "Christ, what could he be doing in there? Why do they want to know about heart disease? Do you think Henry's having a stroke or a heart attack or something?" His heels clicked as he paced. "All I can get when I try to reach Mom and Dad are answering machines."

"We don't need to tell Mom and Dad anything yet," Lauren began. She felt an unreasoning faith in Robin.

Just then Robin approached them, looking altogether too calm for announcing mortally serious news. He said, "Can I speak with you for a moment?" and crooked a finger toward a small office.

"Is he all right?" Winston demanded.

Robin motioned them to chairs. "Hello, Lauren." He smiled.

"You know each other?"

"I came in once for a tetanus booster."

"How is Henry?" Winston asked.

"His vital signs were reading very much like a coma patient when he first came in," Robin said, and Lauren could see he was alert in the way a cat can be alert—all stillness but the tail going like mad in the rear. "But other things were not at all like a coma. There are some allergic reactions that look like this, and that would have been my diagnosis because when we gave your brother a shot of epinephrine he became responsive to us—talkative even."

"So it was an allergic reaction?" Winston pressed.

"How long has your brother been listening to this Japanese person? This Asagao?" Robin answered.

"Asagao?" Winston replied. Both he and Lauren sat back. A full thirty seconds passed.

"When your brother was able to talk we asked him how he was, and if he could tell us what precipitated the coma-like state he was in. He told us that someone named Suriyu Asagao had had a shock."

"Have you been talking with him about Asagao for the last half hour?" Lauren asked.

"The last hour I'd say," Robin replied. "So. Your brother says that he can hear Asagao but Asagao doesn't know that he exists. Does this sound familiar?"

Robin's manner was so unlike that of the medical people surrounding Henry in his teenaged years, and he'd posed the question as if Asagao were an acquaintance rather than a pathology. Lauren took a deep breath and said, "Yes."

"How long has your brother had this person in his mind?"

"Since, maybe . . ." She turned to Winston but he sat stonily. "Maybe since he was thirteen."

"That's clinically a bit early."

"For what?" Winston demanded.

"For symptoms associated with schizophrenia, such as hearing voices. They typically surface closer to sixteen or seventeen."

"Asagao isn't a voice in his head," Lauren said. "He's more like . . . a memory. An inclination. It's not like Henry has conversations with an imaginary friend. Or anything."

"So I gathered from speaking with him."

"What are you going to do? What can we do?"

Robin leaned forward and put his chin in his hands. The posture made him look much older. "Your brother says that Asagao was upset by a conversation about missiles. Planes. Does that make any sense to you?"

Winston shook his head side to side no; Lauren shook her head up and down yes. "Winston," she said, twisting to face her brother, "you saw how upset Henry was at dinner after that plane went over." Lauren turned to Robin. "My father has always worked for companies developing military technologies, and last night at dinner he was talking about his work a little. It's a normal reaction to be uneasy with that. I would describe Henry as a deeply committed pacifist. You see, Henry was upset himself—this Asagao thing is beside the point."

Robin considered this for a moment and switched tack. "How long has your brother had skin sensitivities?" he asked.

"Skin sensitivities?" they asked together.

"About a third of your brother's back was covered with a kind of purple mottling. At first I thought they were burns. But they're just some kind of dermatitis—possibly related to an allergic reaction. That's one of the reasons we used the epinephrine."

They were silent. Robin swiveled to face her directly, not looking toward Winston at all. "Tell me. In your opinion is Henry capable of harming himself or other people?"

"Absolutely not."

"Is there a possibility of your brother having drug dependencies?"

"Oh, God, no."

"Did he in the past?"

"Nope."

"He's had no history of venereal disease or endocrinology problems?"

"Nope."

"I have a choice here. I could release your brother and tell him he has to return for an appointment with a neurologist, or I could admit him to the psychiatric unit now for more tests." Robin rearranged a pile of folders on his desk and they all sat in silence.

Terrible pictures swept through Lauren's mind—Henry alone in a bed on a white ward with white nurses. "Release him," she said.

Robin said, "Though I can discharge him saying he has had a possible allergic reaction, I also have to make a psychiatric diagnosis because of his friend Asagao."

Lauren nodded. Winston said nothing. Robin looked at Winston. "Winston!" Lauren barked. "Winston!"

"Lauren . . . What's wrong with his skin? What caused him to fall asleep like this?"

Robin pushed his chair away from them and stood. "Are you both at least twenty-one?"

"I am," Lauren answered.

"I'm having blood tests run and I'll have to check early results before I can release him."

Lauren watched Robin's face carefully, saw him running through different plans in his mind. Should he release this man onto the streets or keep him? Certainly worse cases than this had walked out the door, and done it without a sibling on either side of them, too.

"All right," he said at last. "If you want to speak to your brother, he's in exam area three, up that aisle on your right. I suggest he see an endocrinologist and I want your assurance that he'll follow up with a neurologist." Lauren nodded emphatically as he continued. "I understand that you feel confident that there isn't any complication here from drug use, but you understand that I'll be ordering the tests that can establish that for Henry's medical records." Robin left them.

She turned to her brother. "Snap out of it, Winston, and start helping me here. Henry is not going to be admitted!"

"Lauren, it sounds like Henry's getting confused, like he's feeling things that he thinks Asagao is feeling. I'm afraid for him."

"I'm more afraid for him if he gets checked into the psychiatric ward. What will his medical records look like? Who will give him health insurance? And what good are those people anyway? They'll treat him like . . ."

"'These people' are professionals who are trying to take care of him. You're just taking care of yourself. Not Henry," said Winston.

She sucked in a breath and got him in her sights. She said, "If I were you, Winston Cooper, I would be afraid to walk on the streets after saying something like that to me, because if a truck hit you before you got to confession, you'd go straight to hell."

"Shut up, Lauren. Just shut up. Let's go talk to Henry." They made their way down the linoleum corridor in a spiky silence.

Henry greeted them cheerfully. His rumpled pajamas looked

terribly worn in this clinical atmosphere, and it hurt Lauren's heart a little to see frayed threads on the sleeves and the beginning of a tear on one knee. Henry was humming and swinging his paper-slippered feet over the side of the examining table. His hair stood up directly from his head, giving him a shocked expression. She caught Winston's terrified look out of the corner of her eye and sighed. How had it come to be that Henry was still the most constant sympathetic intersecting space between her and Winston? And here we are once again, she thought, marching to Henry to ask him to solve the problem even when Henry himself is the problem.

"Henry, the doctor who saw you said that he could admit you or you could go home. What do you want to do?" Winston asked.

"What?"

"You have to decide a few things," Winston said briskly. "Come on. Clear your mind. We're in a spot here, Henry."

"You are so stiff, Winston. Bending would be better," Henry told him gently.

"No more of that wood and water stuff, Henry. You are going to get yourself locked up in a psychiatric ward if you don't watch what you say," Lauren said.

"I do watch. You know I do." Henry lowered his voice and leaned conspiratorially toward them. "Asagao didn't mean to hurt me or cause any difficulties. He was just frightened by the planes. But you know, he still has no idea I'm even aware of him even though my thoughts seem to be leaking into him somehow. Isn't it interesting? He's calmer now—it's fine."

"Did that epi shot drive him off?" Winston asked.

"What's going on with your skin, Henry? Robin said you had stuff that looked like burn scars. Have you developed any new allergies?" This from Lauren.

Henry only shrugged.

Winston said, "The doctor says he has to give you a psychiatric diagnosis, which means that you can't leave unless you are signed out into someone's care. He says you need to see a few more doctors."

"I know. That's what he told me," Henry responded. "He seems like a very good doctor. Don't you think? I like him."

"So what should we do?" Winston was asking, but Lauren broke in impatiently.

"We check Henry out and leave," she insisted.

"Henry?" Winston asked again. "What should we do?"

"I'm perfectly fine. I can leave."

"I'll go home with you," they both said at once. Lauren turned to Winston. "You have to go home to Mom and Dad and act like you just went out with some friends or something. You can't stay with Henry or they'll get suspicious. I will."

"Mom and Dad should know," Winston protested. "I want to stay with Henry."

"Just shut up and do what I say for once, will you, Winston?"

"Always the same—pushing your own agenda with no consideration for how it makes other people feel!"

"What are you talking about? Did you sleep through your childhood?" she snorted.

"Enough," Henry said gently. "Childhood's over."

"Childhood's never over," Lauren replied.

"The child is father to the man," Winston added.

"You aren't children," Henry urged. "Lauren, you're an adult with a responsible job. Winston, you're graduating from college in a matter of weeks."

"So what?" Winston and Lauren said together, at once, and Henry laughed. Lauren and Winston didn't.

Winston turned to his older brother. "Henry, what should I do? Should I tell Mom and Dad?"

"Do as Lauren says. Mom and Dad would worry."

Robin took Lauren aside as they were signing the papers. He said, "It's possible that I'm making a mistake because I trust you too much." It was a question.

"No, of course you aren't. You're being a good doctor." She hesitated. "A good friend."

"The tests I ordered take a long time to culture but they'll be back in seven days. Hospital protocol says the patient has to hear them directly from the doctor so I can't mail them or leave a telephone message. I think you should come too."

"There's nothing wrong with me." She tried for a light tone.

"I'd feel better if I knew that somebody in Henry's world was getting the same information that Henry was getting—that's all."

"Okay. I understand. I'll come with him."

She did not tell Winston about this follow-up appointment. When the three of them reached Henry's apartment, Winston was clearly anxious. She walked him out to the car as he was leaving. "Don't worry," she told her younger brother.

"'Don't worry, don't worry,' you say, but it feels like you just want to kick dirt over this!"

"Lay off, Winston. Just back off."

They stood glaring, confused at the way time had suffered a little tear through which once again, against their own wills, they had dropped back into first and third grade, respectively.

"He makes you feel helpless," Lauren observed, struggling to be exact and fair and clear. It was the only way she knew back to a workable peace with Winston. At its most successful the approach even led to something like friendliness. "He makes me feel that way, too."

Winston said, "You're just afraid of Henry going completely around the bend and leaving you here, alone with me. And Mom and Dad." That made him grin, his eyes still bright with tears.

Lauren laughed out loud. "What a thought!" She laughed louder. "What an idea! Alone with you!"

"Nightmare." Winston grinned. "Absolute nightmare."

Winston climbed into his car and pulled away from the curb. She watched until he got too far away for her to see his rear lights. They winked one last time; he turned and was gone.

All that week Lauren woke in the hours between midnight and dawn to the whine and then the vibrating rumble of military aircraft. It pulled her to the window, but all she could see as she tried to peer upward was her own reflection in the black glass, her own face tipped toward the distant sound.

Sixteen

She and Henry went together to get the laboratory results, which showed no traces of drugs or infections. Henry's thyroid was beginning a slow climb toward hyperactivity, and Robin repeated the advice about the endocrinologist.

"Does that explain the . . . what happened?" Lauren asked.

"No. It doesn't. It only rules out some hormonal possibilities. Henry, you need to see your internist and get a thorough physical. Because you responded to the epinephrine I'd advise you to get an allergist's opinion. And you need to be entirely open with the internist about events like this one. Have you called for an appointment with the psychiatrist?"

"Not yet." Henry was smiling cheerily. "But I will. I promise."

"Stay in touch," Robin said to them as they were leaving. "Really."

Henry twisted around to give him a big smile and say, "We'd love to. Why don't you come to my place for dinner on Wednesday? Winston will still be in town. I'll make my famous coleslaw. I'll boil lobsters. You'll come, won't you?"

Robin hesitated just an instant, just long enough to see Lauren's alarm. "I'd love to," he said. Henry turned on his heel and started talking menu. Before they left, Robin had agreed to be in charge of gingerbread for Wednesday night. "Do you like it with whipped cream or applesauce?" he asked Henry. Lauren had already turned to leave.

As he snapped his seat belt into place Henry said, "He's nice, isn't he? You know, I just pick up these vibes. He likes you a lot, Lauren."

"You don't have any famous coleslaw."

"You don't know everything about me." Henry saw that this unnerved her, and he added, "Come on. How mysterious is it that I know something about coleslaw? Henry Cooper's deep dark secret. I didn't offer to make smashee sushi. Doesn't that make you happy?"

"You're making fun of me. And you don't intend to see a psychiatrist, do you, Henry?

"You know, I have this feeling he wanted to invite you out for dinner but he knew you'd say no." Henry grinned. "He inspires faith—as a doctor, I mean. Don't you think?"

The dinner went well. More than well; it was fun. Robin seemed to genuinely like her brothers and she had never seen Winston take to anyone so well, so quickly. Robin called Henry two weeks later and invited the three siblings to his house. Henry accepted warmly on his and Lauren's behalf, declining for Winston, who would be back at school.

Henry loved almost everything about Robin: Robin's cooking, Robin's refusal to stick to the standard diagnostic texts and perspectives, Robin's house (which looked like a chicken coop from the outside and a museum of natural history on the inside), Robin's collection of pottery.

At that first evening at Robin's their host wasn't home when they arrived. "I'm so sorry," Robin had said, juggling bags and keys as he hurried up his walk to them. "I was helping a friend find something."

"What?" Henry asked as Robin led them to a kitchen. Copper pots swung from the ceiling; more pots were strewn over the walls.

"A raccoon penis."

"Pardon?" Lauren said.

"I have a friend at the natural history annex of a museum at Harvard. He's cataloguing burial remains and he lost a raccoon penis bone that was somewhere in about a square acre of Mimbres Indian burial remains. He thought my background in anatomy would help. Also, he knows I'm a sucker for that kind of problem."

"How did they know the bone was there?"

"The rest of the raccoon was there."

"But penises don't have bones," Henry said.

"Quite right, unless you're a raccoon or a coyote. I started hanging out at the museum because of the pottery in the collection. Beautiful, beautiful things. Those pots up there are copies of some in the MOMA collection. And one is real—a gift from my friend at the annex, who was given it by one of the tribal representatives." Robin didn't stop moving as he rambled on, raising his voice to be heard over the running water and copper pot collisions.

"Where's the raccoon you were looking for from?"

"New Mexico or Arizona." Robin's hand plunged into his pocket. "Oh, my God," he sighed.

"What?"

"I took it with me. I have the bone with me! I *told* Nicky that the security system over there is worthless!" He held a little stick-shaped fragment between his thumb and forefinger for them to inspect. "I guess I'd better wash up. Put this thing somewhere more sterile than my pocket."

"Why would they bury a raccoon with a person? Why did they do that?"

"Nicky says the tribal representatives won't tell him. It's secret."

"So. You found the raccoon penis."

"Oh, yes. It was there all along right under his nose. He thought it was a finger joint."

"And then you walked out of the museum with the artifact."

"I did." Robin set it down gingerly on the counter and washed his hands. "I'll get it back to him first thing tomorrow."

After dinner Robin herded them into the living room and brought out coffee. "You collect insects?" Henry asked, indicating two large glass cases hanging on the wall.

"Mostly butterflies, as you see. But I like insects, yes."

"Me, too."

"Don't get started, Henry."

"No, no. I won't. I'll go do dishes." He exited, and soon the splashing and pot-clanging shielded their conversation from being heard from the kitchen.

"Did you invite us because you were worried about Henry?" she asked.

"No." Robin smiled. "When I discharged him, technically Henry stopped being my patient. And he inspires this faith."

"Henry said exactly the same thing about you."

"I invited you because I wanted to see you again, and if I asked you out by yourself you'd have said no. Wouldn't you have?"

"I'm sorry I didn't call you back," she said.

"I accept your apology. Why didn't you call me back?"

"I was very busy."

"Why do people think that lying to someone hurts him less than telling him something he doesn't want to hear?" He shifted around in his seat to look at her more directly. "Henry says you haven't dated anyone for years."

"Henry said that?"

"He dropped by at the end of a shift last week. We had a beer."

"What's your interest in Henry?"

"He dropped by of his own accord. One of the things I like about him is how he feels about Asagao. I like Asagao," he added.

"Asagao doesn't exist. And he is none of your business."

"Maybe. Henry says Asagao is confused. Lost. He blames it on the leukemia he says killed Asagao one year after the blast. Confusion, disorientation—these are actually diagnostic symptoms of the end stages of leukemia. Other stuff, too. Everything he says about radiation effects, white blood cell counts, dermotological burns, psychological effects . . . it's all accurate, Lauren. He says there's nothing he can do for Asagao because Asagao is stuck between lives, unaware even of the fact that he somehow got attached to Henry's life. He says Asagao doesn't know where he is."

"How can you say all these things, as a neurology resident, and be so calm about my brother?"

"I have no idea. But I am. I guess I see Asagao as a part of Henry. Just that. People isolate parts of their personalities in much stranger ways than Henry is doing with this *hibakusha* guy, Lauren. His way seems gentle, generous and, I have to add, mysteriously well informed. Did he study Japanese or anything related in college? Did your family talk about the war a lot?"

"He's an engineer, Robin. He studied engineering. And my family does not talk about the war."

"See me next week," Robin replied. "Pick a night."

She barely hesitated. "Monday," she said, and a smell filled her head.

His entire person snapped to attention. "What did you just smell?" he asked her.

"Nothing. How do you know I'm smelling anything?"

"It's eye movement. Eyes travel up and down in reaction to a scent memory; back and forth in reaction to a visual memory. You just went up and down. Smell."

"It wasn't a memory. I actually smelled it. Don't you smell it?" He shook his head no. "Are there . . . ?"

"Olfactory hallucinations?"

"I guess that's what I'm asking."

"There are. Yes."

"What do they mean?" she asked.

"Different things. They might mean you have polyps in your nose. What did you smell?"

"Ash. Camphor. Pine."

"Really? From when? What are you remembering?"

"Nowhere. I don't have that memory." For no reason in particular Lauren smiled at him. The smell seemed to fill her chest, cool camphor followed by the bite of ash. She coughed.

Robin says you two went out for a beer," she said to Henry later that week. It was a question.

"Raccoon penises!" Henry laughed. "Isn't he something?"

"Beer. Did you go out for a beer with him?"

"I did," Henry said happily. "I didn't even tell him I was coming. Walked into his office and there he was practically being assaulted by that pediatrician with the long legs."

"What pediatrician with the long legs?"

"Oh, you didn't meet her probably. She was running up and down between X ray and the emergency room the night I was there, doing everything she could think of to get his attention. He didn't even look up. But he looks at you."

"Come on, Henry. You're making this up to see if you can get a reaction out of me. Robin told you that we went out on a date before you met him in ER, right? And you've decided that I need to get out more, so you're trying to pique my interest."

"He didn't tell me you already knew him," Henry said, and this sounded to her like the truth.

"Really?"

"He didn't. Maybe I made up the leggy pediatrician but not the part about how he looks at you. You look back, too."

"Looking doesn't mean anything."

"Date him, for God's sake. You want to. I can see that. I just can't see why you won't."

"Well, if you must know, I already have another date with him planned for the beginning of next week. So there. You win."

Robin came by the studio with flowers, exciting a wave of ribald jokes from the dancers, none of whom had ever seen a man show up asking for Lauren. But he made himself irresistibly likable as time went on and he became a familiar part of the company landscape, offering medical advice to aching dancers, remembering someone's attachment to Black Jack gum, guiding another to an osteopath who actually solved her problems. Within a matter of weeks the dancers greeted him loudly and happily whenever he appeared.

Lauren was not so socially adept, and it took much longer for people at the hospital to have any idea that she was not just a regular emergency room problem. She asked him about pediatricians with long legs and romantic designs. He looked puzzled. "Never mind.

Just something Henry made up. I knew he made it up. I guess he's more capable of deception than I'd thought. Hah."

"What?" he asked. She had gotten his full attention just at a moment she didn't want it. "You're blushing. What thing that Henry made up?"

"A joke."

"Henry made a joke? He doesn't make jokes."

This was an accurate reading of Henry, she thought, and it made her smile at Robin. Her smile appeased and distracted him and she was able to change the subject.

The next afternoon when the dancers had gone, Lauren made her way up to the large studio and stood directly before the wall of mirrors to examine herself. Her hands were inky. The toe she twisted on the ground was scuffed. William had let her have a bite of his egg-parm sandwich that afternoon and a tomato stain on her chest marked the occasion. She tipped her head and caught her own face in a mirror on the wall—bent hawky nose and high forehead anchored by almost black eyes under brows that could, without exaggeration, be called furry.

"I could look at you happily for years," she heard someone say. She twisted around to see Robin, standing in the doorway just out of the mirror's range, watching her. "I'm early," he added.

"So really," Diana pressed, sitting in the office picking at a salad. "Really, how serious is it?" Diana was the company's flashiest dancer, and its best source of gossip.

"What did you think of Norman's new costumes? Didn't you just come from a fitting?"

"Oh, we'll be beautiful—they're lovely." She sighed. "All right. If you don't want to talk about the doctor, I'll just have to go up there and tell the other dancers whatever comes to mind since I have no actual information to share." She pitched the lettuce into the trash. "How I hate eating this shit. When I stop dancing it's going to be endless meatballs."

The telephone rang, Lauren picked it up, and Diana lingered to eavesdrop because the caller was clearly Robin.

"Well," she said when Lauren had hung up. "I know where this is headed."

"What?" Lauren blushed.

"You watch out," Diana said. "Marriage often involves babies. Permanently broadened rear ends. Anemia."

"I'll watch out." She stood. "I have to give these forms to William. Excuse me."

Diana followed her up to the studio, where Lauren couldn't stop herself from craning her neck to look at herself from another angle. The company members, astute to this kind of assessment, gave her a wolf whistle. "Not a bad rear," Diana said. "Though you've got that bustline, too. Some men like those. So, this is your last chance to have any input into what I say about you and your doctor friend. Speak now or forever yadayayada."

"Tell them I'm in love."

"They want something more interesting. Something more concrete."

"Diana." She smiled. "Tell them what you will. I place my reputation in your hands." She tripped lightly back down to her office, where she stacked boxes of tacks for another hour before drifting out to the parking lot to look for her car.

That night she asked Robin to marry her and he said yes. He said it as simply as if she had asked if he wanted a cup of coffee.

She had never been so happy in her life.

• • •

One thing Ishiru and I shared was our deep knowledge of work's sweetness. How pleasant, how full of light and generosity, were the hours we spent in our trades. We made the world more beautiful, and this is a great thing.

Here in the Void, in the Kingdom of the Dead, I have no work. I wander and look, and I think I search for Ishiru, because that is what any sane man who had lost her would do. But I am confused. From here I can solve nothing; open nothing. I am at a distance, yet the sense of planes and dropping bombs remains lodged in me. I cannot remember the moment of my own death but I remember Ishiru's. I cannot remember what the altars in my adopted family's home held, but I can remember the silhouette of the B-san and the rivers of fire that were once Hiroshima's canals. And children. I sense children near me, though I cannot seem to see them or converse with them. They must be the children who died there in those alleys and roads and fields. Or perhaps they are children from far, far before that—or even the children who have yet to die. Influences flow up and down and back and forth in the river of time, and from the perspective of the Dead it is easier to see how the future and past are not so one-in-front-of-the-other as one thinks in life.

That does not seem obvious to someone still in the flow of life, so I offer the raccoon woman as explanation: There was once a raccoon who lived in the country where the B-sans came from, lived in a desert place in a corner of this country. The raccoon died, and his spirit wandered with me for a time here in the Kingdom of the Dead, which is how I know that this raccoon's only unhappiness was that upon his burial his penis was somehow separated from his body. This happens. Birds of prey, coyotes, humans—all these things disturb the Dead. But the loss of his penis left the raccoon inconsolable, unable to settle into a new life anywhere. And so we met, two gakis *wandering in the same in-between world.*

But the raccoon gathered his courage and decided that to wait for the penis's return would be a waste of life. His nature was essentially sanguine, making it possible for him to set aside this hope of reunification with the penis and choose a new life. His reincarnated form was a woman who worked as an animal control officer in a place called Pittsburgh, Pennsylvania. This woman enhanced her material well-being by passing bad checks, shoplifting and setting up separate accounts in her own name with money that the city of Pittsburgh put in her hands to deposit for her department. That was her raccoon karma, the stealing. She could not help it.

Then, a miracle! In the deserts of the Southwest the parts of his body had been dug up by a group of archaeologists! The parts, it seemed, had been separated only by a matter of ten yards—the distance a stupid coyote had carried the raccoon's bony parts when he'd found them one dry June afternoon. The archaeologists reassembled the body, joining the penis with its old self! This happened, of course, many years after the poor raccoon had passed on to become the lady in Pittsburgh, Pennsylvania. But the penis's return to her former self had a happy effect. This woman, who liked her husband well enough but had no carnal joys herself to speak of, became a great lover. I do not think she ever gave up her raccoon ways, but she was a happier woman if not a better one. So you see, time does not really run simply back to front, past to future. Things that happen to the remains of our past selves change our present selves.

But this story is not all happiness, for attachment is never a story of simple happiness. That raccoon woman, poor woman, fell more deeply in love with her husband because of this new desire and she missed him so terribly when he died that she wandered again as a gaki *for long after her own death, once again held between lives by a yearning she could not control. I met this raccoon woman again after her thief-lover-woman life. You see, I have been here for a long time.*

I loved my own Ishiru like this, and so I know her fate in my very skin. I have wandered, confused, looking for what I have lost, though what remains of my waking mind knows I will not find it until I stop looking and accept that it is gone. I will find nothing until this acceptance—only longing. Lately I have been terribly distracted by a longing feeling that is new. It longs for children—not any children, but children whom I seem to know. Sometimes I think that I have simply found one of Ishiru's old feelings and made it my own, because she was practically eaten alive by her desire for children. And she never got a child in the lifetime I shared with her. Now you see my sad state. I not only long for what I, Suriyu Asagao, long for; I also long for what my beloved longed for. So many attachments blocking The Way! So much memory shackling me to this confused and wandering state. I cling and cling to it.

After the bomb, when the streets were fire and rubble and gangsters, I never took the hippon *that they sold in the alleys. There were other ways to lose your waking mind besides the* hippon *but none of them interested me. I had to remember. They sold* duburoku *knowing that the methylated spirits leave those who drink it blind. I would not risk my sight—neither my inside-mind sight nor the sight that showed me the remains of Hiroshima. I clung to sight because for a long time it was the last possession that linked me to Ishiru. What if I took the* hippon *or drank the* duburoku *and lost my inside-mind sight? What if I could not remember her long neck and her crooked teeth? I do not have enough stomach to imagine this. What if other parts of my mind left me, and I could not remember her passion for me, the smell of her skin during love or in sleep? What worth would consciousness have without this?*

And the parts of her that made others not care for her, I loved them best. She was as others said she was—stubborn and narrow and difficult.

But these things I understood to be the undersides of other, lovelier, things. My Ishiru, to me, was a faithful warm spirit who had the bad fortune to watch and listen too closely when dark things passed by.

And so her ways were not soft or modest, but I knew these ways to be attached to her strong feelings for me so I was content with them. I loved them. Strangers said she looked at them with white eyes, bold eyes, but I knew she meant no offense. It was her always-looking spirit. My Ishiru had to see—she could not keep her eyes down as a modest woman should. She made much noise, and protested things she did not like loudly, which is not the Japanese way for a woman. I know that other men turned away from her bold ways and pitied me. An undesirable woman, they thought. But I so loved her.

The next night Winston, Henry and Robin went to a movie together. After dropping Henry off, Robin offered to drive Winston back to his parents' house, where he was staying on a weekend visit.

"So really, isn't Henry looking . . . good?" Winston had waited until the moment they pulled up to his parents' door.

"Are you asking for my professional assessment?" Robin asked. "I don't have a professional assessment."

"Well. How about a personal assessment, then."

"Personally, I like Henry a lot."

"You wouldn't be so cavalier if you were in my position."

"What position is that?" Robin asked.

"If you were his brother. You know. If you were . . . responsible for him."

"I'm going to be his brother. His brother-in-law. Yours, too."

Winston shut the car door he had opened. He turned an utterly uncomprehending face to Robin. "How?" he finally managed.

"In the usual way. I'm marrying one of your siblings," Robin replied. He grinned.

"My God. I mean, it's just such a shock. I don't think Lauren has ever had a date in her life."

"Well, her romantic history, whatever it was, is over. And her future is me." Robin was still smiling. "Come on, Winston. You're supposed to congratulate me and tell me that I'm a lucky man. Then I say, 'I know,' and then maybe we'll even do something with a little drama, shall we? Hug, perhaps?" Robin leaned forward and hugged Winston. "And you're supposed to hug me back," Robin added as his future brother-in-law sat woodenly in his embrace.

"Well, good luck," Winston finally managed, lifting his arms and applying them to Robin. "Do Mom and Dad know yet?"

"Nope. We'll tell them next. We knew you'd be thrilled—I wanted you to know as soon as possible." Robin winked in a way that was hard for Winston to decipher. It seemed friendly, though. It was high-spirited, certainly.

"I am, Robin. Really. I'm so pleased. And lucky to have you in our family."

"Much better." Robin beamed. "That's good. Thank you, Winston. I'm pleased to have you as well."

Winston took this amazing news to Henry, who was not amazed.

"I can't believe she hooked him!" Winston sputtered. "I mean, he's charming. Makes a good living. And she's so crabby and short-tempered. I just don't see the match."

"Lauren is an interesting woman, and she has deep kindness," Henry said. "She isn't bad-looking, Winston. You just don't pay attention. She's striking, actually."

"'Striking' is just a code word for not normal-looking. She's got a jaw that wouldn't attract any attention if it were on a mule. I'll say nothing about the matching temperament. Eyebrows that could double as a rug. And really, how wide is her range of interests? She hasn't stepped foot outside that dance company office for years."

"The things she is that irritate you will make Robin happy," Henry said. "They're the reasons he wants her."

Robin and Lauren were married in the dance studio. A motley collection of dancers, male and female, stood up as her maids of honor; Robin was backed by his friend Nicholas, Henry and Winston, and two scrub nurses and Triage Three from the emergency room third shift.

Seventeen

Three happy years passed. The dancers thumped above Lauren's head. The choreographers they attracted got better, the payroll got stable, and she earned a reputation in the larger dance community of the United States as a Keeper. Other dance company managers in other cities were driven off by the long hours, low pay and crumbling infrastructure of meager funding. Not Lauren. She shouldn't have been surprised when she picked up the telephone one morning and heard an acquaintance who managed a large Los Angeles company offer her his job.

"My board asked me who they should hire to replace me and I said you," he said. "Look, just come out and talk to them. They've got money, Lauren. You wouldn't have to scrounge so much like you have to in Boston."

"Where're you going?"

"Financial management."

"No."

"Yes. If I never see a nonprofit office again in my life I will be a happy man. I've had it." He named a salary figure that stunned her into a long silence. "Don't say no without thinking very seriously first," he finished.

She set the telephone back in its rocker and was still sitting there with a hand on it when Diana poked her head into the office, then her whole self. "What's the matter?" she asked.

"Would you move to Los Angeles if someone offered you more money to go there?" Lauren asked her.

"More money and what else?"

"I don't know."

"Then neither do I." Diana sat down. "So you got another offer. Shit. I knew this was going to happen."

"Don't mention it to anyone. It's not actually an offer. Just a conversation. I'm not taking it seriously."

But that night she looked serious when she told Robin about it. He was horrified. "Everything in my field is going on in Boston! I have one of the best possible positions in the country for someone like me!"

"Well, I didn't say yes, Robin. I just said I'd think about it."

"I thought you loved your job."

"I do."

"Why change a job you love?"

"Because jobs don't stay lovable forever. You have to keep moving. Meeting more people and doing new things."

"Well . . . I don't know what to say. I didn't expect this. What about Henry?"

Indeed. What about Henry. And so, when the Los Angeles manager called her again she said she was flattered, but he might want to call Harry Wu in Chicago—she'd heard that Harry was looking for something new.

Though Diana swore she'd told no one that other job offers were coming her way, Lauren could feel the dancers' attitudes toward her become more solicitous. They flattered her daily by comparing her to other managers they had known and finding her infinitely wittier, more flexible, more human, more imaginative in finding ways to keep them on stages and paid regularly.

"You told them," she accused Diana at last.

"Only William," she admitted. "Look, you are the best manager the company's had in fifteen years. I inherited all the gossip when I got here five years ago and I think I know what I'm talking about. And you side with us against John. We like you."

"John thinks I side with him against the dancers," Lauren replied.

"See? What did I tell you? Don't leave us."

She told Los Angeles she wasn't coming out to interview. They hired Harry Wu. Lauren buckled down to the upcoming season and told herself she was better off sticking close to Henry and not disrupting Robin's life.

Robin himself had disrupted no Cooper sibling patterns. He had been absorbed into them. Every July he joined the siblings when they sent boats downstream for the *Bon-matsuri* Festival of the Dead. Sometimes the boats were plastic; sometimes plywood. One year they made simple platforms just large enough for rice-paper shades and a candle. Once Robin wove boats from rush, modeling them from pictures in children's books with titles like *Holidays from Around the World.* They bore little toys and plates of dainty food.

Every January fourteenth they brought plastic sheets and sleeping bags, sesame candy and thermoses of hot drinks, and drove to Henry's. There they found his ice house lit with dozens of flickering candles, snow chairs and snow bunks waiting for them all.

The fact was that Asagao had become an accepted and undiscussed part of the sibling group: a shadow brother. Their parents continued to live outside the confines of the world where Asagao was normal; the siblings and Robin lived inside it. This made Henry normal, and them normal by extension. In short, it served their purposes.

Winston had come East to do graduate work on medical equipment design but switched when his father introduced him to some engineers in his firm who were working on fighter plane wings. All they had to do was show Winston their laboratory. His first morning with his father's colleagues left him as breathless and glassy-eyed as a man who had just come from an illicit assignation.

"It's fabulous," he told Lauren. "They're so far ahead of what's being taught in universities. They're the people who are making the world what it is—the ones who shape things."

"Exactly," Lauren replied.

Winston snorted at her. "I'll do you a favor, Lauren. When the research and development I'm associated with saves your life on a passenger plane someday, I won't call you a narrow-minded sanctimonious crunchy-granola prig."

Lauren and Winston didn't speak to each other for two weeks after this exchange; then Henry intervened and convinced them both that they had committed the sin of pride, and they should get over it. They started speaking again.

Winston took the job working on fighter plane design. Never an urbanite, he immediately bought a house in a suburb north of the city. He met Melanie in a hospital elevator and married her three months later. On the day he first saw her she was crying, coming from seeing a friend who had delivered her first child; he had come to congratulate a colleague in the same situation. Melanie was a beautiful woman, and the sight of her crying all over her tailored black silk suit completely undid Winston. He managed to persuade her to have a cup of coffee with him in the cafeteria, and then to allow him to pursue her with all the determination he had ever brought to disassembling a collection of machine parts.

Their parents were pleased with the conquest—the preoccupied, spiky Winston capturing this friendly and ebullient young beauty. Warren read it as the natural result of determination and strategy. "Of course she would say yes to Winston," he said to anyone who would listen. "He's a serious man. An engineer. A practical man and a responsible provider."

Melanie seemed to have no complications—no darknesses. The tears in the elevator had been shed because she'd come from the nursery, whose rows of tomato-faced sleepers had seemed beautiful to her. She sold high-end lingerie for a couture house that specialized in it, and all the male Coopers found this work exotically glamorous—it hadn't occurred to any of them that people made their living that way. In the course of his first long conversation with Melanie, Warren had discovered that her job offered substantive investment and retirement benefits as well as an impressive salary. Goodness, he thought: smart as well as exotic.

Unlike most bridegrooms, Winston took an immediate interest in the details of the wedding ceremony and reception.

"I want some kind of Jell-O salad at the reception," he announced one evening.

"Winston, no one has seen Jell-O salad at a wedding reception since 1960," Lauren said.

"Exactly. That's its charm. Bridal attendants in full-length pale blue. White gloves. Groomsmen in tuxedos. Sit-down dinner and a band."

"That's nice," Robin said.

"That's a waste of money," Lauren said.

"It's romantic," Henry said, "and it's wonderful to see someone who knows exactly what he wants. What about Melanie? Does she have the same idea of the wedding?"

"Melanie says she is busy, on the road half the days in the month preceding the whole thing. She leaves it in my hands, happily leaves it in my hands."

"Did you mention Jell-O to her?" Lauren asked.

"I did."

"And her reaction?"

"She wanted green." Winston grinned.

"She's perfect," Henry said to his brother. "I'm so happy for you, Winston."

Winston beamed back at Henry and Robin before Lauren's eye-rolling overcame his goodwill. He said, "No offense, Lauren, but not everyone wants to get married the way you did, with paper plates and rented bubble machines and the dancer friends dressed for the red-light district. It made Mom and Dad very uncomfortable, if you want to know. That, and of course the fact that there was no priest involved."

"Oh, I loved the lights!" Henry protested. "And the bubbles in the lights, floating!"

"A marriage is a traditional event," Winston went on. "A religious event."

"It is." Henry nodded. "Very. And yours will be beautiful. As Lauren and Robin's was, in its own way."

"Thank you, Henry," Robin said. "I loved it myself."

"You're a good man, Robin," Winston said, setting his arm around Robin's shoulders. "I am going to consider naming our second child after you." Winston had had two beers. He didn't normally drink, but happiness had eroded some of his exacting habits.

"Who gets the first child named after her?" Lauren teased.

"I don't know. We've agreed that Melanie gets to name the first child. It's only fair. She is the one, after all, who has to deliver it."

The first child was named Iphigenia. They called her Iffy. When she was almost two Melanie became pregnant again. "I want six at least," Winston said when they announced the pregnancy at a family dinner.

"This is the last," Melanie responded, "unless Winston is willing to carry the next four himself."

"It would be the greatest honor," Winston said. "I would so love it."

Robin and Lauren had no child to name. In their public lives, even within the Cooper family, they didn't speak of their efforts or their failures. The longer they did not speak of it the more invisible it seemed to become, a private loss covered by extremely busy work lives.

Robin—orphan and only child—had wanted a child immediately. Lauren convinced him to wait, to let it be just the two of them for the first year of marriage. In fact, his first words to her when they were alone after the marriage ceremony were "We'll have three. No, four." She knew he meant children, and a brief sharp panicky stab froze her where she stood. Then she thought, Oh, for Christ's sake, Lauren—so much wood in your nature! which made her laugh at herself. "Sure." She grinned at her new husband. "We could do that."

She began suggesting revisions to the dance company's employee policies that would make a pregnancy leave possible. No one, in all the years the company had existed, had tried to have a child while employed here. She would be the first.

But the second year passed without a pregnancy, and then the third. They started using temperature charts and reading advice books. Then, doctors. Robin did the reasonable first thing and checked sperm count and mobility. There were no visible problems, and so they were condemned to the long search for hidden ones. "Have you ever been pregnant?" the fertility specialists asked her. She lied.

What did it matter, she thought. I'll be pregnant again soon. The past was not relevant.

More tests; no revelations. Their marriage began to feel like a hostage of her body temperatures, her ovulation cycles. They rushed to their bed or to the doctor's office when the thermometer sent them. Three attempts at artificial insemination failed. A good deal of the happiness seeped slowly, unstoppably, out of their physical life together. It will happen, Lauren thought. I have been pregnant before and I will be again. She found herself praying in the car when she was at stoplights; she began to dream babies.

Then, gradually, the weight of disappointment began to change her thinking. We will give up, she began to think, and we will learn to live in this newly discovered state—washed up into a permanently childless universe. Lots of people lived here, she told herself. You don't need a child to be a happy person, she murmured to herself. But she didn't believe that; she was coming to feel that a childless life was a kind of terrible sentence. And in yet another corner of her mind, the part Asagao would have called her sleeping mind, she feared babies as very dangerous creatures. Just because they came, this part of her mind said to her, did not mean they would stay.

She continued to go through the motions, thinking all the time that Robin, too, regarded them as motions and had given up. But he hadn't.

"We could get more aggressive with drug therapy," he said to her one night.

"You mean I could take the kind of drugs you have to monitor every minute to make sure they don't destroy your kidneys," she replied.

"Yes. I understand that, Lauren. I appreciate the risks of what I'm suggesting."

Tell him now, she thought to herself. Tell him that it has to be him and not you because you've already been pregnant, and that it would be fruitless to take the dangerous drugs. But she didn't.

She told him nothing. She could see Robin's bitterness and his sense of being unfairly resisted, his certainty that she had placed herself firmly between him and his desires. She could feel her own resentments tangle and stop her tongue. How enraged might he be if she told him now, after all this time? Robin would insist on an accounting; she would have to produce reasons and apologies. And so the impulse to withhold was stronger than the one to step forward, and she remained silent.

She went, as she had always gone, to Henry.

"Perhaps there isn't any other way out of this than talking to Robin," he suggested. "Tell him more."

"Tell him that I've been pregnant?"

"Yeah. And I'd tell him about Sally."

"And what exactly would that accomplish?"

"I just have this feeling that what happened to Sally has got a hold on you. That it's reached forward from way back then and it's changing what can happen now."

"And this hold on me is keeping me from getting pregnant?"

"Maybe."

"You want me to believe that my fallopian tubes are attached to thoughts in my head."

"Well. I'd say that your future was attached to your past. That's how I'd say it."

"Well, in that case, what good would talking to Robin do? That doesn't change the past. I'll tell you what I imagine the conversation looking like: it starts with Sally, who was a baby, and it rolls into the all-consuming topic of babies, which to us means the topic is fertility and then, because we're getting everything out in the open, it all ends with my mentioning that I've been lying to the specialists we've been seeing and that I have indeed been pregnant. So Robin looks at me and thinks I hid things and I lied and I betrayed him. Meanwhile I have a hard time thinking that I held back anything that mattered, really."

"You're getting afraid of each other, you and Robin."

Henry didn't have to explain. She knew he meant that she was afraid that Robin would not accept a childless life, or that she couldn't accept a childless life, and that their marriage would end.

"Lauren, it'll be fine. You'll have a baby and live happily ever after, paying its college tuition bills until the day you die," Henry said, patting her shoulder and moving to sit beside her.

"Oh, Henry. You walk around thinking the best of everyone. Everything will be fine and nobody will hold anything against anybody in the end and we can deal. You're such a ninny sometimes. I wonder you don't get into more trouble than you already do."

"It's true. I'm a lucky person," he said, still patting her. "I am."

Lauren and Robin made love less frequently. They argued more and more bitterly over smaller things. He grew distant and more judgmental, utterly foreign to her experience of Robin. He clearly blamed her, confirming all her worst fears. She withdrew even further.

Some of Lauren's Roman Catholic habits resurfaced. She said rosaries, reciting Hail Marys as she sat on hold on the telephone, reciting them stopped in traffic or standing at the stove. She mentioned this to Robin, who told her that repeating virtually any phrase changed brain wavelengths in ways that calmed. "It's more effective, however," he added absently, "if the person repeating the phrases believes that they have some spiritual significance." She switched to poetry, found that it didn't have the same calming effect, and went back to Hail Marys and Acts of Contrition.

She and Robin were more and more alone when they were in one another's company. If he asked me to now, right now, she thought, I would try again. If a new doctor asked me if I'd ever been pregnant, this time I would say yes, yes, I have been. This time I wouldn't refuse more aggressive infertility treatments. I would say yes to everything.

But Robin did not ask her. Instead he began a residency in a neurological specialty that swung him back into erratic and often double-stacked shifts. Sometimes an entire week would pass without their speaking for more than a few minutes. He had chosen this route, she was sure, as a way of avoiding the increasing unhappiness between them.

She worked longer hours; the company became even more of a refuge. They were getting famous. John had his pick of choreographers and he chose, for the coming year, a contrasting pair: Joe Morel, just on the edge of what everyone predicted was going to be international acclaim; and Isobelle Isacio, a woman whose name was already in the history books as a foundation stone of modern dance.

That was how Lauren came to be standing in the airport at gate number twenty-seven, waiting to meet Isobelle Isacio. She scanned the crowd, searching for the choreographer in the stream of passengers. Dozens, no, hundreds, of children seemed to trail along after burdened adults. Fully half of the women in the airport looked, to Lauren, to be pregnant. She heard herself reciting the Hail Mary and stopped, concentrating on her search for a match to the press photograph she'd received of Isobelle. The press package had said that Isacio was a first-generation immigrant from Portugal, that she had started her own company in 1966, when she was only twenty-one years old, and that her career had essentially been a parade of triumphs. Now she scattered her dances among companies from Paris to Los Angeles.

Lauren had rushed here, looking up from her desk in shock to see how close she had come to missing the choreographer's plane entirely. The calm of her office, the cathedral-like heights and shimmering quality of the studio light had lulled her. Now she stood, awkwardly scanning the crowd. Finally she saw a thick woman with a waist-length mane of rough white hair watching her, walking slowly toward her. The woman held no purse or luggage and seemed entirely unencumbered. Lauren looked her up and down before dismissing her as a possibility.

The woman walked to Lauren and stopped deliberately before her, extending a hand to be shaken. "Belle Isacio. Pleasure. You would be Lauren Cooper?"

"I am." Lauren's eyes widened.

"You didn't expect a dumpy gray-haired lady, I'm sure." Isobelle smiled faintly. "Nevertheless, I am she. We'll get my luggage now." They walked to the luggage carousel. An enormous trunk-like object rolled around on the belt. "You'll carry that?" she said, and Lauren obediently picked up the gigantic thing and staggered with it toward her car. The distractions of Isacio's luggage and her manner did not blind Lauren to the way the woman moved, like thoughts through an uncluttered mind. She had been fooled by the square build and lumpy hair.

Once established in the motel room closest to the studio, Isobelle motioned Lauren to a seat. Lauren took it reluctantly. "You'll come by the motel before class to pick me up? Ten?" Isobelle's eyebrows fanned into little arches.

"Earlier if you'd like."

"Later is better."

"Class is usually at ten."

"Tomorrow we can start later."

Lauren hesitated. Schedules meant everything to John and a late class meant a ruined day to him. "Of course," she said.

"And this motel. I'd like it changed."

"To what?"

"Something less like an institution whose rates vary from fifteen minutes to four hours."

"Other people who've come to work with us have liked it because it's so close to the studios."

"There are always cabs. Perhaps you could arrange for me to intrude on some generous patron's hospitality."

"I couldn't say. Right at this moment, I mean." Lauren considered. Isacio had arrived so exhausted that her full physical powers had been obscured. Now that she had a point to make she summoned them. She seemed suddenly light, pliant, full of deeply realized color. The silence that followed was awkward for Lauren; useful for Isobelle.

"If you like, I can put you up in my own apartment," Lauren finally offered. "You'll have less privacy but it won't be a motel room. I realize they can be sterile." Lauren assumed that Isobelle had an idea of what dance company managers could afford to live in, and fully expected the choreographer to refuse graciously before angling for a board member's spare wing. But to her amazement, Isobelle agreed.

"Tonight I will stay where I am," she said. "I prefer not to move again tonight. I'll look for you around ten tomorrow morning. Thank you so much."

On the drive home, Lauren stopped to let a pregnant woman with a toddler in tow cross at an intersection. She leaned over the wheel, staring at them. Once home she drank a large scotch, pulled off her clothes and climbed into bed. Robin wasn't due for another three hours. She would put Isobelle in the spare bed on the first floor. He might not even notice her.

I'll come to dinner. I'll make dinner for all of you," Henry said when Lauren told him that Isobelle Isacio was sleeping in her spare bed. "How can you complain about having such an interesting person right there at your disposal?"

"It's more like I'm at her disposal."

"Whatever. Lauren, I have got to meet this woman."

"Why?"

"I just do. You know, she's supposed to be quite a personality. I read a profile of her in the *Times* last week."

"Yeah. I have such a glamorous job. Now if only we could get hot water in the bathrooms around here I'd know I was in heaven."

"How about tonight?"

"I don't know, Henry. She does what she wants. She may have other dinner plans."

"She's checked out of the motel already? Give me the number of the telephone up in the studio."

"She doesn't interrupt rehearsals for telephone calls, Henry. What are you going to do?"

"Invite myself and get her to promise to let me cook dinner for you."

"She'll never answer. She doesn't even allow me up there to deliver messages when she's working."

But she did answer, and she talked to Henry for a quarter of an hour while the dancers moved back and forth across her field of vision, watching her.

She hung up and asked for the last movement again. They performed it. "No," Isobelle sighed, not speaking to the dancers but to herself. "You were beautiful, my dears, but it's something else." The dancers stood on. "We will break. We will, in fact, end."

The dancers moved toward the studio door in a clump. Isobelle sat in the center of the studio and began the tape again. She remained there all the rest of the afternoon, the music seeping down through the floorboards of an otherwise empty building—only Isobelle in the studio listening and dancing, and Lauren below her.

Lauren listened to the music and watched the autumn light reach the huge maples outside her window and flick them to life. The telephone's ring startled her almost out of her seat. Robin's voice. "I can't be home until late. Sorry."

"Oh." She hadn't been aware of how much she wanted him to be home that night until she heard his voice saying he would not be there. "Fine."

"Are you all right? You sound odd. Like you're underwater."

"I'm okay. I was just concentrating on something when you called."

"Hmm." Robin waited for more. "Winston beeped me four times today."

"What's wrong? How's Melanie?" Melanie was in the first trimester of her second pregnancy.

"Oh fine. But he can't be convinced. She has heartburn; he thinks she's dying. There's this stubborn part of him that doesn't trust the idea that she's fine—she's just pregnant."

"He called you because she has heartburn?"

"No, no. He called me because he wanted to know how you were but he didn't want to be bothered getting into a conversation with you."

"Why not?"

"Because he's all cranked up and he knows he'd just stumble into a fight with you about one thing or another. He didn't have time for a fight."

"He said all this to you?"

"Of course he didn't," Robin sighed.

"Then how do you know?"

"Look, I can't be home for dinner but I'll try by ten."

She forgot to tell him that Isobelle was staying at their apartment. She worked on until the silence distracted her—the footsteps above had ceased. Within a minute Isobelle appeared at the office door, her bag in one hand.

"I've checked out of the motel and would be happy to leave whenever you like." Her tone indicated that that moment had already arrived. "Your brother Henry is preparing something for us with smoked cheeses, and I am looking forward to it."

Lauren and Robin's apartment was in the city's Italian section on a street directly abutting the harbor. It had been a cheese factory in its youth and they owed their unusually low rent to its idiosyncrasies. The better part of the apartment was below sea level, where the ricottas had been stored, and this affected the way it smelled in certain weathers. Large windows spanned both of its levels and looked out onto a busy street at the apartment's front; its back was as windowless as it had been for a hundred and fifty years, but the entrance was wide and airy. The front door opened directly onto a landing at the top of a spiral staircase. This dropped just behind the front windows and down into the apartment's main floor. During the warmer months tourists pressed their faces directly against the glass to see the building's interior and make out its purpose, which was not immediately clear from the street.

Henry was already at work in the galley kitchen alcove. He and

Isobelle greeted each other with eerie familiarity, picking up a conversation that they must have begun in the studio only that morning, their very first conversation, yet they moved around each other verbally and physically with the familiarly of a long-standing intimacy. He handed her a grater and a chunk of Gouda and she simply took it, set to work by his side and suggested they should bake a few heads of garlic as well as whatever else they had already agreed to do. They left Lauren standing idly by.

"Here," Henry said to her, turning abruptly and setting a glass of wine in her hand. "When's Robin due home?"

"He's not able to get home until late."

"Ah."

"Robin?" Isobelle asked.

"Lauren's husband."

"I see. I didn't know you were married, my dear." The choreographer scanned the room, grater still in her hands. "I don't see any pictures of you with a husband. I do like this photo." She strolled back to a table at the apartment's entranceway. "This one of you and I assume this is Henry as children. The other boy?"

"That's our brother Winston," Henry told her.

"And the crutches and cast?"

"Lauren broke her leg that winter."

"Is that the injury that's your limp today?"

"Yes."

"How did you break the leg?"

"A fall."

Henry broke in. "She dove off a barn roof thinking she had to save Winston's life. He was wedged at the gutter line though, completely safe. Lauren flew right over the edge."

"Ah."

"Do you have siblings, Isobelle?" Lauren asked.

"Not one."

Dinner was a lengthy affair involving three courses, two bottles of wine and an entire pot of coffee.

"And now, my dears, I must acknowledge that my dinner companions are much younger than I, and I must go to bed," Isobelle said at last. "Let me help with these dishes before I retire."

Her companions ordered her to leave the dishes right where they were. Lauren thought she saw a slight limp as the older woman crossed the room to leave them.

All the next day traffic ran up and down the stairwell between her office and the studio where Isobelle worked with the company. First was Elena, John's wife. John had made Elena's admission in the company a condition of his accepting the role of artistic director. She hadn't auditioned against heavy competition, like the other dancers, and so they marginalized and abused her. To make matters worse, in a company known for its dancers' beauty, her cow-hocked walking gait, buck teeth and fuzzy hair became stock punch lines to any number of company jokes. This treatment unraveled what skills she might have had before arriving.

"Isobelle said my bones stuck out and my movement was gluey!" Elena wept. Lauren patted her back and made grunty kind noises. Then came Peter, the company's most handsome dancer, also told his services would not be needed for this particular dance. He gathered up his things and left silently. At this point Lauren abandoned her mounds of numbers and photos and stepped into the studio's entrance, remaining as invisible as possible.

William stood in an arabesque in the studio's center, what was left of the company around him. Isobelle spoke quietly. She said, "Bigger," and his body, which looked to Lauren to already be stretched to its limits, did indeed get bigger. "Thank you," Isobelle said, and William returned to the ground, recognizably himself again.

"Do you all do ballroom of some kind?" No one answered. "A two-step, please," Isobelle ordered the waiting pianist. He began a halting Missouri Waltz. "No, no, no. Something more like . . ." Isobelle demonstrated with her body how the music should sound. The pianist switched to Chopin. "Much better. Now." Isobelle turned to the dancers. "Show me something partnered."

Diana was the company's gift to the spotlight. She had an actor's sensitivity to where the audience's eye would rest, and how to make her way into that precise place. Now she selected William from among her colleagues and stepped into his arms. She lifted her upper body to his own in a handsome arc, pinned her breastbone to his and drew him along in a skimming circle. Diana tilted her head to drape her white-blond hair conspicuously down William's glistening black upper arm, accomplishing exactly the effect she hoped for. Lauren reminded herself to tell Diana that later. She would be pleased to hear she succeeded. The two dancers floated in a circle around the studio, stapling perfect little square steps each to the next.

Lauren crept back down the stairs and waited to hear about the rest of the day from whatever gossip stopped in her office on its way out. The last dancer to pass through Lauren's office was William. "Well. How was your day?" she asked him politely. He looked feverish. Though he'd been off the studio floor for thirty minutes his skin still had a slick of sweat, and his eyes had the shiny, inward-turning look of someone in the midst of a streptococcus infection. "William," she repeated. "William, I said, 'How was your day?'"

He sat down in the office's only other chair. "She's wonderful," he answered. "She danced a little for us. You'd never think it to see her standing around with a cup of coffee or something but when she moves she's . . . unhinged-looking sometimes. She kind of vanishes."

"What do you mean?"

"I don't know." He laughed nervously.

"How's Diana doing with her?"

"Oh, Diana's hustling away. I mean, the roles aren't cast yet, are they?"

Isobelle herself appeared at her door when the dancers had gone.

"I know John hoped to have dinner with you," Lauren told her, taken a bit by surprise. "I thought you'd be out with him now, in fact."

"I told him to go home." Isobelle sank into a chair, heavily. "Nothing I have to say to him would change anything yet. I'm still making decisions."

"So you told him you wouldn't have anything to argue about until Friday?"

"I don't argue with company directors who ask me to set dances, dear. I simply set dances. And this is an unusual group. It will be difficult, but a pleasure. John was in no state to discuss artistic issues today. Apparently there's some upset about a critic alluding to his weight in a review."

"Why did you ask them to do ballroom?" Lauren asked.

"I wanted to see if anyone could create that kind of insular, us-alone-in the-world romance that ballroom is about. True love. Perfect love. The Invisible Engine of the Universe. I've always adored dancers who could summon up that old Astaire/Rogers illusion that if you can just dance well enough that the person you love the most will materialize in your arms and love you forever. You know. It's what the classic pas de deux is about, really. Astaire did it as beautifully as Baryshnikov."

"Well, did you see what you were looking for?" Lauren persisted.

"You were there, my dear." Isobelle leaned forward.

"You mean William and Diana?"

"William has an open airiness that Diana lacks. An ethereal quality where Diana is more concrete—more flesh and blood. She's like a kind of mass that whips him around her." Isobelle smiled and then added, as though this second idea were directly connected to the first one: "John tells me he has engaged Joe Morel to set a new work on the company right after I leave."

"You don't like him?"

"You misinterpret my tone."

"Well, correct me then."

"He danced in my company for a year. An interesting dancer. Now a fascinating choreographer."

"His résumé didn't mention your company."

"Well. We all have the right to tailor our histories. So many merely factual histories are inaccurate, really."

"Tell me why he's fascinating."

"Mr. Morel has that wonderful capacity to make his dances look like things he has uncovered—not made. He's always on the lookout, Mr. Morel. A true hunter's spirit."

"What does he hunt?"

"My dear, I certainly can't name it. It has a happy shifting quality. It's the thing we hope for. Whatever it is." She rose heavily. "And now I am ready to go home."

"I'd love to drive you but this proposal keeps me at my desk. Let me call a cab. You have a key?"

"No matter. Henry and I are dining together. He had some restaurant in mind he thought I'd adore."

When Lauren reached her own home four hours later she found Isobelle asleep, crumb-strewn plates and two coffee cups on the table. Robin lay snoring in their own bed. Asleep, he looked terribly young, like a teenager, though in fact he was in his early thirties. So, she thought. Isobelle has met Robin.

Eighteen

They were woken in the middle of the night by a telephone call from Winston. "She's bleeding!"

"Calm down, Winston." Robin's feet swung over the bed and hit the floor before the word "bleeding" was entirely out of Winston's mouth. "Is this bleeding or spotting?"

"For heaven's sake, it's blood! Blood! She's got a temperature! She's so hot!"

"Have you called Mel's OB-GYN?"

"Yes!"

"What did she suggest?"

"She said to go to the hospital for an ultrasound right now."

"That sounds like very reasonable advice. And it doesn't necessarily mean that the OB-GYN thinks anything is really wrong. It's precautionary."

"Nobody tells someone to get out of bed in the middle of the night and go to a hospital if they think that nothing is really wrong!"

"The OB-GYN's medical training tells him to respond exactly as he did when told what you told him. It's just standard procedure—a precaution to screen out the small percentage of cases that actually need hospital backup. Winston, the truth is that OB-GYNs are always sending women to the hospital for anything at all because they have such calm medical lives they need the excitement to make themselves feel important."

"Robin, could you come with us? Could you meet us there? We've called the next-door neighbors to come over and be here in the house in case Iffy wakes up. I know I've been a pain in the ass during this pregnancy—I was so frantic that I actually called Henry tonight before I called you. He promised me you wouldn't mind. Robin, I don't trust hospitals, or what happens in the middle of the night in emergency rooms. I don't know enough to know how to help Melanie."

"I don't mind, Winston. I'll meet you there. Henry was right to tell you to go ahead and call. Which hospital?"

Lauren struggled out of bed and started searching for a sweatshirt. But as they dressed the telephone rang again. Lauren picked it up and spoke without waiting to hear the caller identify himself.

"We're coming, Winston. Just calm down." She hung up before the caller could get in a word. It was only much later that it occurred to her that it had been Henry and not Winston on the line.

A squinting Isobelle met them in the hallway, roused by all the telephoning. They sent her back to bed and proceeded to the hospital, where they found Melanie and Winston being led to an emergency room examining area. Melanie was calm; Winston actually seemed to have foam at the corners of his lips. He was yelling at the admitting nurse, who was clearly about to eject him from the examination area just as Lauren and Robin entered. "Amelia," Robin called cheerily. "This is my brother-in-law Winston." This didn't mollify Amelia, who had her finger on the call switch to summon a security guard. Robin dipped his head to meet hers, talking softly until Amelia nodded and turned on her heel. Then he led them back to Melanie, who sat in an examining area under a tangle of wires that stretched over her abdomen and into various bleeping instruments. They settled in, staring at the digital readouts tracking fetal heart rate and waiting for someone from radiology to wheel Melanie away for an ultrasound. "Isn't that high?" Winston kept saying about the number.

"All fetal heart rates are high compared to adults," Robin reassured him.

Melanie smiled at Robin; they liked each other with an uncomplicated ease that was foreign to the Cooper siblings.

Within an hour the placenta had been declared intact, the baby certified as healthy, and all four of them were heading for the exit door.

"You have a calming influence on Winston. On Henry, too, for that matter," Lauren told her husband as they drove home.

"On you, too," he added.

"Yes. Me, too."

"Give Henry a call tomorrow and ask him what Winston said when he telephoned him in that panic." Robin yawned as they climbed back into bed. "I'd have loved to be a fly on the wall. I don't understand why Winston didn't have morning sickness and abdominal cramping in the first trimester—he's a cartoon perfect textbook case of hysterically induced pregnancy symptoms in the father."

They were at ease with each other, opened by the relief that follows events that could have been terrible but in the end were not. Lauren allowed herself to imagine telling Robin about Sally, about the bloody hallway where she and Henry had found their mother, about the weeks and weeks when they thought this baby their mother carried was going to kill her. And her own pregnancy—its brevity; its convulsive bloody end. But once home, Robin fell back so quickly into sleep that she said nothing.

The next day Henry neither picked up his telephone at home when Lauren called nor responded to messages. His cell phone seemed to be switched off. At five o'clock Lauren decided to drive to his apartment, and though his car sat in the driveway, no one answered her knock. She took a deep breath and rifled through his mailbox to find the key that he kept there despite her complaints about lax security.

Even before she got the door open she had imagined and rejected several terrible possibilities, but still his prone form on the living room floor felt like a bright cold blow inside her chest. His left eyelid was half open. A little spittle cut a channel down one cheek and when she shook his shoulder and shouted, it changed course. As his head flopped over, the rivulet ran upward toward the half-open eye.

She told herself not to make Robin responsible for every decision, to make her shaking fingers punch out 911, but the fingers flew to his number despite her.

"It's just like the other time," she whispered.

"What? I can't hear you, Lauren! Speak up!"

She took some quick breaths to unlock her throat. She said, "It's like the time Winston and I took him to the emergency room. He won't wake up, Robin!"

"Call an ambulance. I'll be here when you arrive. Tell the medics everything you know—tell them that after an apparently similar episode, he responded to epinephrine. Do whatever they tell you to do. Give them full, accurate information. Do you hear me? If you lie, it could hurt Henry. Tell them everything you can think of that could be relevant."

"Yes."

"I'll call your parents."

"No!"

"Okay. But, Lauren, I will greet the ambulance at the door, and if Henry is in trouble I will tell your parents because they're his parents. I'm also calling Winston right now. This isn't in your control anymore."

When admitted, Henry was breathing but unresponsive, and just as before, the examining doctor asked about Henry's skin. "There's an inflammation I'm not familiar with," the doctor said. "Before I got a close look I thought it was a burn, but it's not a burn. It's like . . . I don't know."

"That's exactly what I saw the day you brought him to the emergency room," Robin whispered to her.

"But the inflammation went down the very next day," she said.

Lauren stood frozen in fear as they wheeled Henry off for tests. Within an hour Winston and their parents joined them, reserved and pale, turning more and more to Robin to interpret what the doctors said and to speak for Henry on their behalf.

The first softening grays of the morning found them sitting in an exhausted circle around Henry's bed in a private room Robin had secured. When a nurse switched on a hallway light directly outside the door, its light refracted through the hanging fluid containers of his IV and skittered across the ceiling. Henry's eyes flew open, trained quite clearly on the flickering streaks; then he turned his head and smiled broadly at them.

"Henry, what happened?" Robin was the first to speak.

Henry seemed to remember something and his smile vanished. "Is the baby all right?"

Lauren knew what he meant at once. "Yes. The baby is fine. So is Melanie."

Henry's smile returned. "I was sure she would be," he sighed. "I told Winston she would be."

"I'm here, Henry." Winston stood up and moved to the foot of Henry's bed.

"Henry, tell us what happened," Robin insisted.

"There was so much blood," Henry replied. He leaned forward. "And fire." Henry looked up abruptly, distracted by the lights splintered across his ceiling. "You know I saw those lights and I thought they were fireflies." He looked up then, saw Robin, and smiled delightedly. "We'll have a firefly party when the baby comes." He lay back. "It will be firefly season."

"I didn't know Henry was interested in fireflies," their father said to no one in particular. He sounded confused, frightened. No one replied. Instead they stood more quietly in a little circle around Henry's bed.

The admitting doctor's shift had ended long ago and his replacement wandered in now, alerted by the nurses that Henry's condition had changed. He insisted that they all leave the room.

"I need to get your father home and let him sleep. You call us if anything at all changes," Lauren's mother said to her. "Do you promise?"

"You go on with them," Robin urged Lauren. "I'll get in touch with the radiologist who read the films they took last night and I'll tell you as soon as they know anything."

Lauren would not leave. "What are you going to tell the doctors?" she asked Robin when they stood alone just outside Henry's room.

"Anything I think will help them," he answered. "Everything I know."

"What if it only makes things worse for him?"

Robin had done a double shift already that week and he was facing another one now. He turned impatiently. "You can't be afraid of information."

"I am not afraid of information. I'm afraid of doctors."

"Lauren, the first time I saw this happen I was overly influenced by you, and by how appealing and talkative Henry is—how normal he seems. But now it's clear that what I saw the night I met Henry is a pattern rather than an isolated incident. It can't be treated with mere observation this time. I was probably wrong to let him go so quickly. I made the wrong decision. I was wrong." He turned on his heel and walked away from her.

A kindness, Lauren thought, any kindness at all between us now, however small, would turn all this around. She took a step toward Robin's retreating figure but stopped. She should have touched him when he was standing in front of her, she thought.

These closed instincts, she thought, they will be the death of you, Lauren Cooper. Too much wood in your nature. Not enough water.

She sat down in an orange plastic chair in the hallway. It was several minutes—maybe a half hour—before she could rise and return to Henry's room.

The hospital hallways were coming into their daylight lives, with bustling staff and the smell of coffee from the nurses' station pushing back the bleachy sheet smells. She pressed on to Henry's room. "Henry." she asked quietly, "Where's Asagao?"

"We kept Winston's baby here with us." Henry smiled. "She had one foot out the door though, when we got her." He was whispering.

"Do you mean Asagao is talking to you now? That you talk to him?"

"Oh, no. No." He leaned toward his sister conspiratorially. "It's the same: he still really doesn't know that I exist, but I think he feels me here. He just doesn't know what I am—I'm just like an impulse to him or a taste. But, Lauren." Henry leaned forward and whispered, "I can see things from Asagao's mind—not just hear his thoughts but get behind his eyes."

"See what?"

But Henry's eyes had returned to the wall, where they tracked the moving lights.

A nurse entered the room. "Well, we're doing much better now, aren't we?" she crooned at Henry. "Your sister needs to go home now and give you some rest." The nurse shooed Lauren out, but as soon as she was out of sight, Lauren returned to Henry's room. She fell asleep in the chair by his side, and woke to find her mother had returned.

"Lauren?" she said, touching a shoulder with one hand and offering a paper cup of coffee with the other. "I dropped your father off and came back. He hates hospitals so."

Lauren took the paper cup. "Thanks."

"This isn't the first time this has happened to Henry, is it?"

"Come on, Mom. Have you ever sat in a hospital room with Henry before?"

"The night he was born I did. And the night after, too." Her mother sighed. "And the night that he first stayed in the sanatorium. They say people make up imaginary friends to protect them if they're frightened or if they feel alone. I keep wondering if I left Henry frightened or alone somehow."

Lauren patted her mother's arm. "You didn't. I swear you didn't."

"All those years I watched you three carrying the little boats. All the years I looked out the window and watched you sneak out to your snow forts with candles. You know, I always dug out the thermoses from the basement and bought extra milk. Cookies. I knew it was coming. I hated it but I went down into that basement and got out the two thermos bottles and cleaned them and waited, and they always were used. I always hoped they wouldn't be used."

"I didn't know that. About how you got things ready."

"Henry had to have known. I guess he was protecting you from getting any pictures in your head of a crazy mother helping him do those crazy things."

"Why did you do it if you hated it, Mom?"

"I don't know. Probably for the same reason that you went out with him and stayed in the snow forts all night. The same reason you kept flipping through that *Disaster, Disaster, Disaster* library book like there was a clue in it that you needed to find."

They sat on together through the day, keeping watch on Henry.

Lauren went home. Isobelle had decamped for New York and left a note with her cell telephone number taped to the refrigerator. Lauren dropped her clothes as she walked to her bed and fell into a deep sleep. She dreamed she saw Sister Leonarda waving frantically, yelling, "Run!" though she felt the nun was looking past her, into dark patches of woods and high grains. All night she listened to the screaming nun and ran and ran, craning her neck. In the morning she woke exhausted.

Over the next twelve hours Henry sat up, held conversations with various nurses and doctors and ate fourteen cups of cherry Jell-O. The crisis, if there had indeed been one, was declared over, though there was the remaining mystery of what had happened to Henry. He remembered that there was a family dinner scheduled for Saturday and insisted that they gather even though he wouldn't be released in time to come.

They promised to gather for dinner as planned. Lauren and Robin came separately because he didn't get off a shift at the hospital until seven. When Lauren arrived she found Winston and her father in the living room, circling the large computer screen that dominated the room and making admiring exclamations and gestures. "New program!" her father called to her as she walked in.

"Great!" she called, walking past them to the kitchen, where a very pregnant Melanie was stirring something on the stove while her mother watched.

Melanie's face was blotchy, puffy; her ankles swollen. "I'm ready to have this baby," she sighed, "and get my mind back. Do you realize I just put the petunia pot in the refrigerator?"

Lauren dipped her face out of view and swept a pile of green beans together to snap. She said, "Robin couldn't catch the radiologist this morning to talk with him about Henry's films but he promises to have spoken to him by the time he gets here tonight."

Everyone nodded.

"Great," Melanie offered. "I'm sure there's an explanation."

Another silence gathered, the silence around the possibility that there would be no explanation, or worse, an explanation that made everything bleaker. "Robin!" they heard the men call out from the living room. They listened to the door and footsteps, and looked up hopefully to greet Robin as he strolled into the kitchen. Robin smiled at them all, then smiled again, separately, at Lauren. She smiled back. She realized again that just seeing him made her feel happy. But right behind the happiness was a new reserve. She struggled to keep the first thoughtless happiness at the sight of him, at the pleasure in his looks, at his reception at the hands of her family, who uniformly liked him. "Robin," Winston had once said to her, "is the child that Mom and Dad always wanted. Thank goodness you married him."

Robin bent down to offer Iphigenia something that he had held behind his back—a bouquet of blown-up surgical gloves. She received them joyously, then ran into the garden to destroy them at leisure. As soon as they were seated around the table for dinner, Robin cleared his throat and touched on the subject that everyone else wanted to but wouldn't.

"Henry's doctors think it's fine for him to leave tomorrow," he began. "He flies through a basic neurology exam. I know because I gave him one myself, though I'm not his doctor. The radiologist says his films aren't remarkable. They do show an unusually active diencephalon—mid-brain."

"Is that good or bad?"

"Neither, necessarily. Henry's just on the outside edge of what is called 'normal.'"

"So he's fine?"

"He looks relatively normal when you're looking at a film of his brain."

Annie Cooper broke the ensuing silence by insisting that they all look at her new garden lights now that evening had come. The little copper lanterns glowed from behind rhododendrons and vibernums, their effect purposefully diffuse. "Back away and try to look at the total effect," she said. Light sparkled from the small moving stream circulating into and out of her pond. A luminous ray hung suspended in a Japanese maple. All the plants in the small orbit of the lights had been strategically placed to highlight contrasting color; the space farther away fell off into darkness, no colors at all. Only shapes and varying degrees of darkness.

"It's lovely, Annie," Robin breathed. Then he added, to no one in particular, "It looks like the UBOs on a magnetic resonance image."

"What?" Melanie asked, rocking Iffy in her arms and standing just beside Lauren.

"Unidentified Bright Objects. It's what radiologists call bright spots in the brain that magnetic resonance images show."

"What are they?" Melanie asked.

"They think it might be caused by retained fluid. Nobody knows, really. It's something electrical, though."

"You mean neurologists don't know what they are?" Lauren asked in amazement.

"That's exactly right."

"Does Henry have them?" Annie asked.

"Oh, Henry has lots of Unidentified Bright Objects. His PET scans are like impressionist canvasses. They're in color, you know. Depressed brains are actually darker than normal scans. They show up in these deep blues, dark purples, greens like that." Robin gestured toward the rhododendron leaves—almost glowing now in the garden lights. "And manic brains look like little Christmas trees, with patches of bright reds and yellows. Oranges. That's closer to Henry—but not quite Henry. His neurologist called it the 'vibrant, active engagement of mania.'"

"Henry is not manic," she said dryly. "Henry is not depressed."

"We know, Mom," Winston said.

"Unidentified Bright Objects in the brain," Melanie repeated, as if she hadn't heard Winston's exchange with his mother. "What a lovely idea."

"Medical technology is moving so rapidly," Warren offered. "I'm sure it will have answers to all this soon. Or the answers might come from some affiliated effort. Look at how war intelligence work led to the computer—how all our work sending satellites and men into outer space has led to discoveries that were unexpected and wonderful."

"Maybe," Robin said.

"Enough," Annie said. "Whatever it is, it's God's will."

Melanie yanked at the front of her blouse, whose buttons had wadded to the left of one breast as Iffy tugged. "If our brains were easy enough to understand, after all, then we'd be too stupid to ask anything about how they worked. Maybe if we look at outer space long enough it will help us figure out Henry's Unidentified Bright spots."

"That's an idea," Lauren said. "The brain as a mirror image of the universe."

Her mother sniffed. "It's cold out here. Come in. Come in, everybody. There's chocolate cake."

That night Lauren asked Robin for more details from his conversations with hospital staff. "Did Henry tell the doctors about Asagao?"

"No. But I did. And he did talk with most of the nursing staff about different kinds of insect eating and mating habits, and drew pictures of cages that were best for different festivals."

"What's going to happen to him? Medically, I mean."

"Well, Henry and I talked a bit about that. His doctors have prescribed some of the predictable starter psychopharmaceutical solutions. Henry agreed to everything, then when I asked him if he'd really take them, he admitted that he wouldn't. He says there's no reason. And he says that these seizures only happen when Asagao is frightened and that Asagao's getting much calmer."

"Does that mean he's had seizures that we don't know about?"

Robin nodded. "I think so."

"Do you think he should take the pills?" Lauren asked.

"Yes."

"Do you think he's ill?"

"No."

"Then why do you think he should take the pills?"

"Because I'm a little frightened," Robin said, "and I don't know what else to do."

"Then we have to make Asagao brave," Lauren said.

Nineteen

"'Waste No Happiness,'" Isobelle said. She was back for a third visit, working with the company and staying, once again, in Lauren's apartment. Her contract limited her to four visits with the company, but it was clear that Isobelle did not intend to pay any attention to the agreed-upon schedule.

"But that's not the name of the dance we described in the grant proposal," Lauren protested.

"The funder does not care what we call it. They just want it to exist. And that is the dance's name."

"It sounds like the moral of a story."

"I understand your objection. But unless William Harrison becomes a different kind of dancer entirely, the name will have to stand."

"But he's just one of the dancers in a larger company."

"He's setting a tone. Diana's picked it up and pushed it along. I know all that frumpery about the company's collegiality and the absence of stars. But William and Diana simply do not fit unobtrusively into a corps. So I'm going to set them in plain view and let them go."

"I thought choreographers liked control," Lauren sighed.

"We do. But control, in cases like this, could be described as responding with alert exactitude to what's in front of you," Isobelle said. "The way William moves summons up whatever is at the root of joy. But there's desperation in everything he does as well. The combination is exactly right. Fragile. Bright. Otherworldly. And Diana has a gift for spotlighting his best moments."

"Is the piece done, then?" Lauren asked hopefully.

"No. It's begun. We did what we have for John this morning. He's had to stay away because his wife is so vocal about being removed from the piece that it could have influenced his impressions. I wanted it to settle into its own shape before he was admitted to the studio." Isobelle stretched and took a deep breath, then coughed. "My God. The smell of old armpits and dancers' underwear in here! How I hate the nonprofit world."

"But you chose it."

"I did not choose it, my dear, any more than I chose my ear for music, my fuzzy hair or my boxy body. There are whole worlds of things that you simply deal with because you find, with and without careful examination, that they are you. Isn't it time for lunch? What's the most expensive restaurant within a fifteen-minute drive?"

Lauren named one.

"Get your car keys," Isobelle said. "Take us there."

"Are we celebrating something?" Lauren asked.

"I'll leave that up to you."

Isobelle had taken on a tone of high hilarity, and Lauren didn't trust it. The choreographer ordered wine and then consumed half a roast chicken stuffed with portobello mushrooms, a root vegetable gratin, an arugula salad, espresso and a slice of flan. Lauren had ordered a sandwich and tapped her fingers on the table, waiting for Isobelle to be done.

"You are wasting a clear and present happiness," Isobelle said to her. "This flan is the reply to all desire."

"Really?"

"Well. Not the reply to *all* desire, perhaps. But it is immensely satisfying in its own way." She sighed happily and pushed the plate away. "It does leave me a little earthbound; chicken and flan are spiritual experiences of the lower order. But there's nothing like them when they're well done. Your brother Henry would understand what I mean."

"Back to the studio?" Lauren asked hopefully. She had left all her preparations for the next board meeting sitting undone on her desk and they pulled at her even at this distance.

"No. Take me to the airport. I'll catch the next shuttle."

"But didn't you schedule rehearsal through the afternoon?"

"Go back to the studio and send them all home. I am satisfied with them at the moment. I'm satisfied with everything at the moment, and I don't want to disturb my state of mind. I'll come back in two weeks, after Morel's spent some time with them. No point in my going much further until he's come and gone."

"Why?"

"He changes things. You'll see." Isobelle stood. "Enough talk of Mr. Morel. I don't want to create a reputation for him to fail to live up to."

"Or succeed in living up to," Lauren added distractedly. Her mind tacked back and forth between two different ways of presenting financials to her board. She hadn't decided which one to use.

Isobelle opened a wallet and removed an American Express card. She waved it at a waiter. "To the airport, please," she said to Lauren when the bill was settled. "I'm going home."

"Isobelle," Lauren ventured, as they sat stuck together in the Callahan tunnel. "Are you afraid of things?"

"Of course I am," Isobelle replied breezily.

"What are you afraid of?"

"The decay of the body, naturally, and what follows: losing the stage. And dying, of course, but less so that. I don't think about that. Thought is, to my mind, an overrated activity. It admits prevarication, doubt, fear. The body is clearer."

"That doesn't sound right," Lauren said.

"That, no doubt, is because you haven't danced."

"Maybe."

"I'm working with a San Francisco–based company next week. Please tell Henry that I have not forgotten, and I will get the lanterns in Japan town."

"Henry wanted lanterns?"

"For this year's *o-bon.* We were talking about what is available here on the East Coast for those kinds of occasions. The West Coast is better—Henry and I agree entirely on that." Their car popped up out of the tunnel and into a shockingly bright afternoon. "USAir," she said. "Thank you very much."

Henry's driver's license had been taken away for six months when the word "seizure" appeared on his medical records. Lauren saw him much more frequently as a result. She and Winston kept him in groceries and made it difficult for him to avoid appointments with the people he'd promised to see: endocrinologists, neurologists. When asked if he was taking the medications prescribed, though, he would cheerfully admit that he threw them all away.

"Why do you do that?" Lauren demanded one day as she picked him up for a grocery run.

"They muddy my thoughts."

"You know I've had three dreams since you went into the hospital this time with Sister Leonarda in them," Lauren told him.

"Me, too. I've had two."

"Really? What does she do in your dreams?"

"She's waving at me so hard her wimple is half off and she's yelling, 'Run! Run!' It makes me think of how she used to say that trucks tend to hit people who don't get to confession." He laughed. "What's she doing in the dreams you have?"

"I don't remember."

"Lauren," Henry said.

"Yeah?"

"Don't be frightened for me."

"Of course not." She grinned.

"Because whatever happens to me, it's fine with me and I want it to be fine with you."

"What would happen to you, Henry?"

"I feel like I'm getting drawn by something. I know it might make me seem distant sometimes."

"You mean being distracted, or thinking Asagao's thoughts, or what?"

"All that. And maybe there are other ways I seem to go away from you, or exclude you. I think I'm going to seem like I'm getting worse, but I want you to know that I'm not. I'm just looking."

"Looking at what?"

"Just looking. And I want you to know that it's fine with me. I want it."

"You want what?"

"I want to go . . . look," Henry ended. And he would say no more about it.

Ishiru was fourteen years old when she married me, a gangly boy of sixteen. Her family loved the older customs, the ones even before the Shinto ceremony. And so Ishiru walked in a parade from her father's house to my uncle's house and she wore white—the color of death. Her brothers and uncles surrounded her with torches and lanterns whose light drove spirits and demons away. She was vulnerable to spirit people, you see, because between the two houses she had no name, no family, and they might possess her body.

I watched their arrival from the road before our home. They moved toward me, my Ishiru's robes flowing around her in streams the color of the inside of a shell except where the torchlight hit them, and then they were as white as light itself. For three days after she arrived at my family's house she continued to wear white. And on the third day she could cast it aside and be my wife. On that day I said to her, "We are both born on this day. Not only you." And this was true. She was like a spirit, like something coming to me truly from another lifetime.

My adoptive family had made paper butterflies, which symbolize happy marriage, and tied them to every surface in the house. When Ishiru turned quickly in the center of the little house the breezes from her robes moved their wings.

She was thirty-four years old when she died. We lived together for twenty years whose happiness was blemished only by the lack of children to honor us.

Ishiru would say mono no aware, *meaning simply that this is the way of it, it is the suchness of things which must be accepted. But I knew it was a grief in the center of her life, a heavy scouring thing that once it had made a smooth place in her it lay down there to stay forever. I accepted it with a calmer heart than she. We never lived to the old age that would make our childlessness most terrible; that was how I saw it. For her it was different. It did not matter how long or short her life was to make this childlessness a most terrible thing.*

People would call my Ishiru's life short. She died seventy minutes after the pica-don. *I was almost nineteen hundred meters from the blast center, but she was only eight hundred. I ran and ran, directly back toward her into the flames, but nothing I did or wanted mattered by then.*

The only building that withstood the center of the blast was the Jesuit church. The Black Robes made it of stone because they were terrified of earthquake. They wasted all that stone on the fear of earthquakes. It did not protect them in the end, but it stood when everything around it fell and burned, and there it was at the corner of my eye as I ran back toward Ishiru, so strange to see a wall of stone still erect and blank and there. It stood behind her as she turned to me with her hands lifted up.

Pictures of that moment made their way into books for children, which is unfortunate because things enter the mind through the eyes, travel like the light that brings them to their destination and then drop down roots so they are impossible to dislodge. If the flower returns to the root, as they say, then so does the terrible dream. So does the terrible memory.

Even the smells of that time have great power over me. On that day Hell came to the surface of the earth and became the alleys we walked down, littered with ragged children frying fish and soybean sludge in motor oil. Emaciated twelve-year-old girls blew through the streets like tiny kites, all become panpans *in tight bright clothes calling out to the conquerors, the enormous Americans in Eisenhower jackets and porcupine haircuts: Hey, Big Boy. Wanna date, Big Boy? Hey! Hey!*

The streets were inhabited as well by the orphan furoji *who returned to the ashes that had been their homes and their families. Parents gone, many found that relatives had stolen their homes and inheritances and so they fled the corrupt adult world, preferring to make their way on the street than go to the orphanages.*

No more kimono-making for the seamstresses of Hiroshima. Now they make Eisenhower jackets for the Murakami-gumi *and* Oka-gumi *gangsters of Hiroshima, who think they must look like the conqueror General to do what they do. No more silk, because during the war the iron clamps that held the silk weavers' looms together were stripped and melted into munitions. So the Eisenhower jackets are not of silk, and this at least is a small justice.*

My Ishiru was always the protector of littler ones when she was alive, and after the pica-don *when the streets became full of gangsters,* furoji, panpans, *bullies who demanded two yen before they let you sit by their diesel-can fires, I thought often of how she would react to these scenes. I thought that if I had more of the true Japanese spirit I would have stopped much of what I saw. Ishiru would have. Yet for being this brave person people said she lacked true womanly Japanese virtue.*

In that lifetime's last year I told myself to stop looking around every corner for her and accept her death. I offered chinkon *to her spirit but she would have been freed from the earth even without it because her spirit was pure. I lit incense and looked for her in the smoke of every fire, knowing as I did that all incense—even the smell of the fish frying in diesel oil on every alley's entranceway, maybe—summoned the viewless spirits. They come to devour the smoke. But my Ishiru never appeared to me. Perhaps she avoided the smoke because she did not like to be near* Jiki-ko-ki, *the incense-eating goblins who belong to the lowly fourteenth of the thirty-six classes of* gaki. *These ones wander as* gakis *because they sold bad incense in their lifetimes. When this thought occurred to me, I stopped burning incense and lingering by the street fires.*

I have come to think that her spirit never for an instant wandered as a gaki, *like I do now. She had no unfinished business with me; we knew each other's hearts, and though that was not enough for me it was enough for her. She was not greedy; she was free.*

Accept that she has left this lifetime, I said to myself. Do not shame her with unworthy longing and wishing; remember her courage. Remember all the times she pushed into a crowd to defend a dog or a small person during the terrible early years in the war. She came home one day with a red fist mark on her cheek that a bully gave her when she stepped between him and a young girl he was touching, a modest and good young girl who cried while the bully laughed. My wife spit on him and stepped between him and the girl and he punched her in the face, a small woman! But that was how it was in those years. Dark years.

That bully stood first in the draft lines; he was in a hurry to die and he did. He died, his proud mother told us later, in Burma. She looked forward to the Bon-matsuri, *the Festival of the Lanterns, when she could set his boat upon the water laden with his favorite dumplings and a flickering candle, and watch it make its way back to the sea. But such a spirit, I was sure, would never achieve peace after death—he would come back in some terrible form, something that bit or stung or leaped upon people in dark passageways.*

When I first realized that I was a spirit bound to the earth and wandering lost I felt great fear that I would meet this bully, but I have not met him.

This little man was more fearful of his manhood being insulted than he was afraid of death. This is a strange and powerful cowardice, this fear of not being man enough, and in the end it often leads to many people being exploded. He is the kind of soldier who stood taller when his superiors told him that if his ship were to be hit by American torpedoes he must abandon it with the utmost decorum or the world would laugh at him—the Americans would take movies of him and show them in New York. That is what they told the soldiers. Worse than death, to be laughed at in New York movie theaters.

That is what this fool believed.

PART 3

Many of Us Who Survived Changed in Our Minds

Twenty

That week Joe Morel came into town to begin setting an original piece on the company. Lauren had ironed out a list of demands through his manager in New York so she got her first glimpse of him when a silver Miata came to a tread-ripping stop in front of the studio. A thick, disheveled figure swung its door open and kissed the driver good-bye. The driver wore a lot of white linen and a very expensive haircut. The ends of her flip were near surgically straight, with the faintest purple line running in a circle around the hair at shoulder level. She tipped her head back to kiss him, and the hair blew back away from her face like feathers. He pulled a dance bag out of the back and picked his way over the duct tape holding down the indoor-outdoor rug at the building's entrance. Lauren sat waiting stonily in her office at the top of the stairs, not replying when he began calling from the third step. He was an hour late.

The door to Lauren's office stood open at the top of the first flight of stairs and he strolled through, setting the bag down and knocking lightly on her doorjamb to announce himself. "I'm Morel," he said.

"Wonderful to meet you. The dancers have been warm for an hour," she said coolly.

"Well." He shrugged, the smile unaffected by her displeasure. "I'll go introduce myself to the dancers. No, no. Don't get up. I'm sure I can find my own way."

"An *artiste,*" Lauren muttered to herself. "Another narcissist."

Late that afternoon the friend in the pretty new automobile reappeared to sweep him away, and Lauren made a point of catching William as he skipped past her door. "So?" she said.

"So what?"

"So how was today? What do you think of him?"

"His head looks like somebody made it out of cement," William said. "How old is he, anyhow? He smokes! He smokes cigarettes in the studio, during rehearsals! Disgusting. And he actually brought a six-pack of beer into the studio in the middle of the afternoon. Banged an empty can on the piano to keep time."

"What was he like to work with?"

"Didn't I just answer that question?" William blew an exasperated gust of air from his nose. "He concentrates so much on the women. At least he did today. John and Peter and I were told to sit still and keep quiet."

"Diana!" she called, seeing her passing by the door. "Diana, come here."

"What's the matter?"

"How was today?"

Diana laughed a nervous, tinkly, utterly uncharacteristic laugh.

"He has a very direct way of setting movements," William said, one eyebrow shooting sarcastically upward on the word "direct."

"What? What?" Lauren asked.

"He just wants to know what we can do," Diana replied coolly. "And he's quick."

"She means he puts his hands all over them," William sniffed. "And he's impatient as hell. He yells at them. He's the masterful man for them."

"I don't think it'll be a bit different when he works with you and John and Peter tomorrow," Diana said.

"We'll see," William called over his shoulder.

"Boys," Diana said, pursing her lips dismissively. It was clear she was not including Morel in her sweeping assessment.

"I don't think Morel is William's type," Lauren said.

"William's just cranky because he was ignored by a great choreographer."

"Is he a great choreographer?"

"If he isn't now he will be soon. And William thinks so, too, which is why he is so cranky about the day's neglect. Isobelle spoiled William, putting him in the spotlight."

"Isobelle put you there too, Diana."

"But I had to work my ass off to get there, and William just strolled centerstage."

Diana at that moment had the look of a creature who had to chase and pin down other living things in order to live. That other living thing, it seemed, was the center of a stage. "I'm not going to have to convince the choreographer of what I can do and who I am this time," she said. Then, feeling generous, she added, "William's got nothing to worry about. Choreographers take one look at his wingspan and reset their works on his arms. He isn't grateful enough for what God just dropped in his lap." Diana stopped, got a controlling grip on the feelings that colored her tone. She smiled carefully. "But I don't want to sound like a shrew and a harpy. Do I?" She smiled a full-out stage smile.

Lauren grinned at her. "You don't have to flirt with me, Diana. I'm just the manager. And I kind of like the shrew and harpy sound—it distinguishes you."

"Good thing." Diana flung herself into a chair. Unlike anyone else in the company, Lauren could get away with teasing Diana. They were allies: she respected Diana's work; Diana respected hers.

"How's Peter doing?" Lauren asked. Peter had been in the company two years. He suffered from a degenerative eye disease that hadn't stopped his career yet but kept him in a chronic state of anxiety because some choreographers didn't want to work with him.

"You mean is he afraid his eyesight will get him kicked out of the piece? He was. So he told Morel about the bad peripheral vision thing immediately. Morel asked him to do some floor work and then he put him in some patterns with us. He said he was satisfied and I was amazed he cut Peter that slack. Peter's such a slob."

"He is?"

"Well, compared to the rest of us. He smokes too much grass. He eats too many hamburgers. He's got this tendency to stiffen up, move like a lobster. He doesn't have the patience to warm himself up right."

Lauren brought the subject back to the choreographer. "Do you think this Joe Morel guy is . . . I don't know . . . salacious?"

"You mean the touching stuff that irritated William? It's sexual but it's not gratuitous. It isn't in fun, either. Maybe sexual's not the word I mean. All I mean is that it feels necessary. And it's very . . . gratifying." Diana laughed nervously again. Diana hardly ever laughed, and was not anybody Lauren thought of as nervous. "William's just jealous."

"Don't all choreographers touch you?" Lauren asked.

"No, no, no. Isobelle Isacio, for example, would never touch a dancer. She intones from ten feet away. She models. She lectures. She sings. She inspires. She doesn't touch. But if Morel has something to say to you, he puts his hands on you." Diana sighed. "Come on. Work's over—come have a drink with me."

"Now you sound like Isobelle," Lauren said.

"Do I? I'm not sure if I'm pleased, but I might be." An hour later, sitting with a scotch in her hand, Diana said, "So. How much are you paying Isobelle?"

Lauren named a paltry figure, and Diana sat up directly. "That's all? I'm amazed."

"Why?"

"She's got a reputation as having a very expensive life. She's got this mansion in Connecticut and a great apartment in New York. Does lots of entertaining."

"How do you know all this stuff?"

"How can you not? Really, for an intelligent person who talks to people all day, you don't get much information, Lauren."

"I guess not."

"You've got to get more involved in the daily stuff, my dear. Come up tomorrow and look at Morel work. It's very interesting."

"Okay," Lauren said. "I will."

The next day Lauren made her way upstairs to the studios about an hour into rehearsal. No one noticed her entrance because the group was focused entirely on Patrick, heavily muscled and the largest of the group, throwing Mary in a slow sweep upward and away from his body toward the waiting John. The others held their places anxiously. It was an unusually far toss, no body contact of any kind in its middle section. Lauren saw a thick manila rope stretched behind them. It rose from a barre at one side of the room to a hook in the ceiling at the other, waiting.

Morel instructed. "Just land her in the palms of your hands full in the chest and Diana will move in to brace her lower body. Now. One two one two one two GO two one two . . ."

Mary was swung gently, eerily upward. Her arched body reached the crest of the swing and began the descent. Patrick released her. Mary's arms remained folded wing-like against her rib cage just as she'd been directed. Peter reached upward to receive the shock of her weight, but when her chest reached him he pulled his hands away as if they'd been stung. She tumbled full into his center of gravity, the momentum of her fall carrying them both to the studio floor in a tangle topped off with Diana, holding on doggedly to Mary's feet.

Morel was in the middle of it first, unwrapping and rearranging until the two dancers sat dazed, side by side. From her distant vantage point Lauren hadn't been able to see anything at first, when the press of company members hid the fallen dancers from her entirely. Then Mary's and Peter's heads rose shakily above the concerned onlookers.

"They're squishy!" Peter said, the moment it was clear that no one needed immediate medical attention. "I was just . . . shocked. The surprise jerked my shoulder off to one side and I lost my center of balance. I didn't expect them to be so . . ."

"What?" William asked.

"Her breasts," Diana said. "He's never touched a breast."

Peter actually wrung his hands. "Mary, I'm so sorry! It won't happen again. I promise you. I promise. I was just . . . so surprised. You know I would never do anything to jeopardize you. I just . . ."

Mary stood at her full height but she still trembled. "I'm fine," she insisted though her voice shook as well as her legs, and when Morel tried to rerun the sequence she was so clearly unfocused that he pulled her out of the passage and put Diana in her place. Mary stood by and watched the part vanish from her life.

"Don't jump," Morel interrupted Diana in the middle of a phrase.

"Like this." He demonstrated what he wanted: a gentle curve. At least one toe touching the floor for every inch of the phrase. Diana nodded. "Now," Morel said, still talking to Diana, "Elena's going to swing you on her back. Come here," he beckoned to Elena. "Your hips aren't over your ankles," he corrected, setting her body in place with a few deft pushes. "There." He led Diana to Elena, who crouched and waited. He twisted them back to back and hooked Diana's arm through Elena's elbow. "Swing up on her back—face the ceiling and just roll up onto her." Diana hesitated. "She's ready," Morel assured her. Diana hesitated again.

Morel sighed. "Come here," he said, turning on his heel and facing Mary, who had thought herself unnoticed until this instant. Mary stood and walked to him. He turned her so her back was to him. He ran his hand down her legs, bending them and positioning the feet in an exact duplicate of Elena's posture. Then he pushed her back flat, holding her collarbone in one hand and her tailbone in the other. He said, "This is what I want." He hooked his arm in Mary's elbow as if they were going to square dance and then swung himself in a slow roll onto her back. He faced up; she faced down. Mary turned her head toward the mirror to see what he was doing. She saw his head tip back, his hair fall down around her shoulders and blend with hers while his backbone slowly arched away from her own flattened spine. Then he twisted his upper torso to one side, the chest revolving toward the mirror. He bent both legs at the knee, opened his thighs and left one foot to point decisively down, the other to extend outward as if a string attached to the ankle was being swung away from Mary. "Hold still," he ordered her. The studio was utterly silent except for the sounds of Mary's and Morel's breathing and the scuff of their feet on the sprung wood. All the noise and attention and air in the room seemed to have been sucked into what they were making. Stationary, Morel was a scruffy, stubby presence. Moving, he was not.

Lauren was suddenly aware that her face felt hot. She tried to look away. She retreated to the mats on the sidelines but she couldn't leave.

He held the position for perhaps five seconds. "I'm rolling off on three. Brace the right leg for the roll," he said to Mary; he counted and dismounted. "Thanks," he said to her. He turned to Elena and Diana. "That's what I want."

Lauren stood, no longer looking at the dancers. She was turning on her heel to leave when a sickening crack stopped her. Diana lay folded in an unnatural tangle. Her face was white and then whiter, and then as they all watched she vomited on the studio floor. Two strides and Morel had the leg and foot in his hands. He applied gentle pressure in three places. Diana screamed in response each time. "We'll need an ambulance," he said in a conversational tone.

Lauren practically fell the length of the stairs, into her office and to the telephone. The ambulance arrived within seven minutes. Morel was the only member of the group with more native authority than the brusque medical team, and he disregarded all their firm insistence that no one go with them but the patient. He stepped in, gently and irresistibly setting a burly medical assistant to one side to accomplish this. Lauren got the name of the hospital and walked heavily up the long flight of steps back into her office. The dancers filed silently past her on their way to their dance bags and home. Rehearsal was over.

William marched into her office. "He did it on purpose," he said.

"Who?"

"Morel."

"Morel didn't do anything," she said.

"He turned away from Diana knowing that she would push herself to get his attention back again. Take some chances and be more reckless."

"Getting distracted for a moment is hardly a hostile act designed to break a dancer's bones."

She saw an internal argument pass over his darkened face. "It's not just that." He stopped, his hands dangling in an unusually graceless attitude. "There's something wrong about him," was all he could manage.

"I'm going to the hospital to see her," Lauren replied. "Coming?"

"No. I just can't look at her in a hospital bed. But I'll see her as soon as I can."

Was this what Isobelle had been warning her about when her eyebrows did that funny thing at the mention of Morel's name? What else had Morel disrupted or broken, Lauren wondered, in his brief career?

That night Annie called her to tell her that Sister Leonarda had died in her sleep. "I thought you'd want to know. Poor old lady," she said. "People we still know in the parish said she got impossibly cranky toward the end. Still. God rest her soul."

Twenty-one

The flesh takes so long to let go of us, Sister Leonarda had thought every day all through this long year. Meanwhile her hips ached. Her hands swelled. Wherever she walked, a noise like sand grinding beneath the caps came from her knees. She knew it was chips and cracks rather than sand because the Father Superior had sent her to an osteopath when he saw her struggling stiff-legged up a short flight of stairs. The osteopath had recommended gym membership for the sake of the weight-lifting equipment, the shortest route, he said, to building musculature around the degrading joint and offering it the support it needed. "What did he recommend?" the Father asked her the day after the appointment. "Complete rest for at least two weeks," she replied. She went to bed.

Her face and neck were dotted with scars where basal cell carcinomas had been sliced out of her skin. Her aging uterus had developed fibroids, which felt like an inflamed band of muscles stretching around her hips to her lower back. Her eyes faded. Her stomach failed her regularly.

Enough, she insisted every night as she prayed. Why must it be so slow and so pocked along the way with all these little diminishing humiliations? Hadn't she served Him as well as she could? Hadn't she lived a life of true religious sensibility? Yes, there had been lapses in her perfect faith, moments of frustration and darkness, but hadn't she been told that crises of faith were unavoidable parts of the contemplative life? Really, she sighed and panted, struggling up stairs on particularly stiff days. Really. Such a tenacious hold the flesh had—stubbornness to rival any spiritual force.

So she waited. She was not afraid of judgment—she had argued and sung and muttered alongside and with Jesus Christ since she was thirteen years old and had accepted him totally. The Sister's Jesus wasn't a beatific fellow with Episcopalian features and one philosophically raised palm, the fingerpads like points on an infinite plane. Hers was not the image hanging in every Catholic hallway in America until the Second Vatican Council. Her Jesus followed the trajectory of her own mortal life, young with her in youth, stooped with her now as she approached death. And when she complained about the back or the knees He'd complain right back in her mind. He had, He would remind her, lived the life of the flesh. If she got out of hand and her manners with Him fell off the track, He'd whack her with the bottom line: He had paid a debt He didn't owe because she and all those other humans had one they couldn't pay. That was how the first priest she'd ever really listened to had explained the exchange, and these words knitted together all her native confusion into the baggy shape that had carried her faith all these years.

Her Jesus had grown into a crabby and generous presence that restrained her when she was about to say something too ridiculous to her First Communion candidates; He guided her when she woke at three o'clock in the morning, believing that when she died there would be no heaven or hell or greeting face of God—only worms. No, no, He'd say. Haven't I been here with you, proving Myself? Don't be a fool. A person is what she believes. Don't believe in the worms. Choose Me.

But she would be petulant. Then her Jesus would stomp around and maybe even leave for a little while, but He always came back. He loved her and He wanted her to choose Him.

Her Jesus wore a baggy leisure suit during the week, a Brooks Brothersish boxy suit on Sundays and generally shorts and an L.L. Beanish thing on top for Saturdays. He was always clean but not always pressed. He forgot things. He favored crew cuts. She talked out loud to Him all the time but she knew others had different Jesuses or didn't think it possible that her Jesus was not only present but communicative, so she never spoke up to Him when others were in the room. Her Jesus knew this and said the most provocative and sometimes hurtful things to her when there were people around so she couldn't talk back. Her Jesus had a temper, and He might always forgive in the end but He'd remind her for weeks or years of mean things she'd said to students; of lapses in her kindness; of too strong attachments to the physical world of eighteen-ounce milk chocolate Fribbles, which in her native Maine had been called Awful Awfuls.

Well, what was she to do, having been given the body that God designed and the mind and character He provided?

These other people had sometimes noticed how the Sister's face would darken or screw up in the middle of a conversation about some subject that contradicted her expression. They did not know that her face was responding directly to Jesus rather than to what they had just said, and wanting to be free and unhampered by the prejudice that people felt toward individuals who spoke directly to Jesus, she did not tell them. She felt a special sympathy for others who she felt were also speaking directly to their Jesus in ways that the general population would not approve.

On her bad days her Jesus wore thorns. He did this whether or not it was a grimy wimple day or a crisp haircut and new wimple day. Thorns go with everything, He'd said. She was not in a position to correct Him. On her good days He wore warm light—not the blinding stuff—so He could be seen through it.

When the Sister complained that He wore the thorns too much He told her she should have more good days. He only wore what she wanted, He said. She didn't believe this, and because she didn't believe Him He wouldn't talk to her for weeks. She'd go back and forth and so did He—talking, not talking. They always talked again after a while because there was too much ingrained habit and too much to say to keep up the silence. And in fact, the Sister did have a religious nature.

She would not, absolutely would not, go to the Father Superior for comfort or support. That moron, she thought, then crossed herself and apologized directly to her Lord for the disrespect she felt for the superior He had placed in her life and whom she must accept with grace. Of course, the Father Superior was supposed to be taking her confessions, and more and more of her complaints and offenses could not be offered up through him. *Bless me, Father, for I have sinned. It has been seven days since my last confession. I have cursed the Lord for letting these goddamn fibroids bleed me half to death. I have mocked the Father Superior behind his back and compromised his authority in my dealings with young students, who have heard me say that he has bananas for brains.*

Her solitude was another burden. She borrowed the rectory car and drove right into the next county to make her confessions to strangers. On the way back she stopped at a Friendly's and ordered Fribbles and hamburgers. She noticed that as she got older her appetites were becoming more, not less, demanding. This was an unpleasant surprise. If the demands her body made only got shriller as the years went on, where might it finally lead her? There it was again, the towering authority of the flesh: the obstacle that was, in the end, necessary to the spirit's creation. The Sister imagined a future full of fleshly demands. Was it the body that wouldn't let go, or the orbiting planets that pulled at it along with the tides and the menses? She was ravenous and short-tempered; moderate and patient by turns.

She must accept it. She would not accept it. She tormented her students. She was ashamed, and struggled her way back to kindness with her students.

So lonely. Her loneliness seemed to her like another sin. Shouldn't her life have brought her closer to her Lord and Savior, the only husband she would ever know? If she were closer to Him why was she so alone? Why didn't He do something about these fibroids? Most of the contemplative life, the holy life, she knew, depended upon vast plains, effluvial landscapes, full of patience. You hope and pray. You try not to drift too far or give in to anything in the meantime.

Some days her body left her at peace and had nothing to say to her at all. Ah, happiness. God will forgive you, she told her students on these days. He loves us as He loves himself. Her Jesus wore light and enjoyed Fribbles.

And then on the bad days full of pain she would think, What if He hates Himself and that explains why I feel this pain? These days were followed immediately by car trips to adjoining counties, confessions, Fribbles and hamburgers. She bought whole quarts of raspberries and ate them herself, sometimes with the ice cream, sometimes not.

Her back troubled her and kept her sleepless, and when she did sleep her dreams were confusing and anxious. She dreamed of raspberry patches, and farmers who guarded their fields with shotguns. She dreamed of Awful Awfuls, and then her dreams, like her waking eyesight, would get fuzzy. The worst moments, though, the moments she had the most trouble banishing, were those when she thought that perhaps Jesus's death had only been that: a death, and not a gift to those who were freed by it. Then she would shake her head vigorously to set loose the sense that something foreign was in it.

One afternoon in the middle of a class for seventh-graders, the Sister suffered a terrible dizzy spell and fell flat on her face at the front of the room. She scared them all out of their wits. After that she was told she could no longer be allowed students. The head father presented this loss as a gain: the students were clearly too much of a strain for her; they had become a threat to her health, he said. But they had never been a threat to her health. In fact, as she tried to live outside the classroom her pains and aches worsened. The students had been keeping her well. Why couldn't the idiot head father see that as her decay accelerated, they were the clearest reason for taking a shower and walking as briskly as she could, head up and shoulders back—walking right over that crackling knee and yammering pelvis.

"I need the students," she said to the Father Superior after twelve weeks of this torment. "I'm still able and willing. Please don't waste me."

But he did waste her. He nodded sympathetically and assured her of his total understanding of her position, his deep regard for her. Then he reminded her of her vow of obedience and of her hierarchical relationship to him, who represented God's will in her life. But he understood nothing, and certainly had no regard for her! He was a secret cringing anxious bully who had always disliked her, probably feared her, and was pleased to set the steps in motion that would lead to her incarceration in a nursing home for old nuns.

Indeed. She would burn the whole place down first, she thought. She began trying to recall all her old students and this is when the Cooper children came back to her. At first she remembered their names wrong: Harry and Laura. No, no, she thought. Hilton? No.

Then it straightened out in her head: Henry. And the little sister, Lauren, and that odd other one . . . Salem? No, no. Some cigarette thing, though—Winston! She remembered that the Henry boy's Jesus came to him in the shape of the Japanese person and his sister was upset all the time. The sister was the one in trouble, she thought—the boys really were perfectly all right.

She tired of thinking of her students, who seemed even from the distance of time to be unsolvable problems. She found herself reading women's magazines or watching soap operas in the afternoons. The articles on how to have the perfect sexual climax might as well have been written in Hindustani. The mannequin-like flickering images on the afternoon dramas had problems that struck her as easily soluble—dump the guy, marry the guy, have babies, don't have babies. The only drama here, she thought, was the burning question of how long the audience could tolerate the characters' stupidity. No doubt advertisers all over America were at the edge of their seats.

The world had changed. She would not. So she sat through the long afternoons dreaming of flowers, fields, shotguns, explosions, waiting for her body to leave, wondering whether there would be ice cream for dessert that night. French vanilla she hoped, with a few scoops of lime sherbet for bite. That was her favorite.

On the afternoon that Diana broke her foot, the Sister sat in a patch of sunshine with a bowl of ice cream, finished it, set it down beside her, fell asleep, and was finally, finally, released.

Twenty-two

A small bone in Diana's foot was broken—such a tiny thing to undo an entire woman. An unlucky freak accident, Lauren said. When the painkillers wore off Diana found herself shorn from her body. She couldn't dance; she couldn't even walk. She settled into a serious rage.

Lauren volunteered Robin as a case manager and motivator. He stopped in her hospital room, talked to the osteopath and radiologist who were assigned to her, and calmed her with optimistic interpretations of what they had to say. In fact, the doctors had said she should not dance again. But Robin had known the dancers too long to bother to tell Diana anything about what she should or shouldn't do—he knew she'd dance on it no matter what. "I don't have to save it for the end of my career," she hissed at Lauren. "It's here. I'm there."

Morel worked on without Diana, layering thicker and thicker patterns into his dance. Lauren was drawn to watch every day at some point. She found herself trying to explain the fascination to Henry one evening.

"I don't like the way you're talking about this man," Henry sniffed. "And I don't like the fact that wherever he goes, things break."

"Who says that?"

"Isobelle has a few stories. He's like a conduit for bad spirits. Or maybe he's a bad spirit himself."

"It's amazing to me that you take what Isobelle says about him at face value, Henry. Do the words "professional jealousy" have any meaning for you?"

"Nobody said I took Isobelle at face value," he sniffed.

Lauren kept drifting upstairs to the studio. She watched Morel set a happier second movement, quick and living after the terrible first movement when the dancers seemed on the edge of damaging themselves. John went around clutching his head, whispering things about the bills and injuries, the loss of Diana. "We don't have a replacement! Diana had the largest part!" Lauren ignored him and continued to visit the studio regularly to sit in Morel's orbit.

Meanwhile Elena, moved to a highly visible position with the full support of an authoritative choreographer, was transformed. She still wasn't pretty; she was something more. It struck Lauren that something in Elena had been invisible before. Watching her skim through a line of fellow dancers, she could see someone who'd been tethered and was now set loose.

Every day Lauren visited Diana at home, where she recuperated. Diana had temporarily dismissed her lover and alienated most of the people who could be called her friends. Lauren, however, was immune to her abuse and patient with the complaints against the doctors, against her own body, against John.

"The only one you've let off the hook is Morel."

"Don't be ridiculous. He had nothing to do with it," Diana

sniffed. "You just tell that bug-eyed Elena that I'll be back and the role isn't hers for good. She's got it on loan."

"All right," Lauren answered, though they both knew the role would never be Diana's.

"God help me, Lauren. I'm turning into a bitter, warped character. You know, I worked for fifteen years to have a chance to dance the thing that Morel set on me. It took me that long to be good enough to catch his eye and then good enough to do the kind of dancing he wants. And there I was, finally there, so old that my ankle and leg weren't elastic enough anymore to do it."

"You do it, Diana. You did it. Morel said you were just going too far."

Diana snorted, disgusted at Lauren's meager understanding of her world. "You have to go too far to get there. That's where 'there' is."

Lauren could not argue with this and so said nothing.

"You want to leave now," Diana said. "I can see it in the way you're bouncing a little." She hobbled to a chair and flung herself down. "See ya."

"I wasn't leaving. Where's your coffee? Don't you have any coffee?"

Diana relaxed, clearly relieved that Lauren was not going to accept this permission to leave. "Freezer."

"Fine. I'll make coffee."

"Thank you," Diana said. "Thanks, Lauren."

Twenty-three

For the first time since he had met the Coopers, Robin missed *Kamakura matsuri.* Though he pleaded work as an excuse, he had always worked and always been a doctor and always been there for the *Kamakura matsuri,* so the explanation had a hollow ring. Other disruptions threatened: Winston was lobbying, since the holiday was indeed a children's holiday, to include Iffy. No one overtly protested, but it was clear to Henry that there was something about this shift that Lauren resisted, some violation of the sibling pact that she could not bear to see happen quite yet.

"One more year with just us," Henry said to his brother. "You know we love Iffy. But one more year of waiting will only make it sweeter for her next year. Yes?"

Winston had never been able to resist Henry's diplomacy. He relented and started looking around for rice ball recipes and the best greens—he was usually in charge of these decorations.

In fact, Lauren adored Iffy and wanted her to come; or rather, she both wanted her there and didn't want her there. It was becoming difficult to simply enjoy Winston's family as her own childless state pressed down on her. She hoped that this selfish reaction was a phase and would pass, but in the meantime the idea of an affectionate, unoffending, purple-snowsuited Iffy playing in the ice house with them could reduce her to tears. Robin's defection did not help. So she made it hard for Winston and said nothing to him at all about children and this particular *matsuri.*

Also, the weather was not cooperating. Unseasonably warm temperatures were blowing in off the lakes from Chicago and had made their way across the mid-Atlantic states and into New England. Reports reaching the Cooper siblings early January 13 suggested that the expected snowfall could be sleet or rain by the time it reached their ice house.

Mid-morning of *Kamakura matsuri* found Henry and Lauren arranging the pine boughs Winston had brought over the night before, shopping for candles and finishing snow-house furniture. Winston had called to say that last-minute work on the rice balls and sesame cookies would delay him a bit. The ice house itself had been roughed out the day before.

"He said he'd be over here helping with the final touches on the house! Why didn't Winston plan better?" she complained. "It's not like we don't all have jobs."

"He has a family as well as a job. Iffy has a sore throat, and Mel's at the end of a pregnancy. Why are you acting like you don't know these things? Also, Mel doesn't understand *Kamakura matsuri* and doesn't know why he has to spend the night. Remember last year?"

Last year Melanie had asked Winston to be home by ten. He'd stretched it to eleven, but he had left them then and gone home to his wife and child. They had made jokes about it at the time, but it was strangely disturbing to be in the house without Winston—even more like the end of something than the milestones of their marriages, their graduations, their jobs, the birth of Iffy.

"He can bring Iffy. He can bring Melanie, too," she protested. "I don't care. I really don't."

Henry looked at her just long enough before answering to make it clear to her that he knew she was lying and he appreciated the effort though he wished she didn't have to do it. "Melanie would never come. She hates the cold and views the whole thing kind of like some kind of weird bachelor party for the Coopers. She's not exactly a nature girl, Lauren. And she says Iffy is too young, which is probably true."

"Winston wouldn't even sneeze if Melanie told him it was a bad idea."

"Winston has a different kind of marriage than you do," Henry replied.

Lauren's mouth fell into a fish-like circle while she wondered how visible the inside of her marriage was to her brother. "What do you mean?" she asked.

"I mean Winston and Melanie seem to crash along more in the same direction than you and Robin do. I mean you don't look happy lately," Henry said, continuing to pat at an alcove detail. "I mean Robin isn't here tonight and your only complaint is 'Where's Winston?'"

"I'm happy."

"All right," Henry replied. "You're happy."

Just then they heard tires in the front drive and a slamming door. Winston skipped around to the back garden bearing cups and thermoses and little metal tins, yelling something they couldn't hear. As he drew closer they made out, "Hey, look! I found these great little steamers that can fit over candles and I got us some dumplings this year!" He stepped into the ice house. "Next year will be so much fun with Iffy here. Mel still doesn't want anything to do with it." He studied their work. "Lauren, what's up with that couch you're building? It's collapsing in the middle."

All three turned to consider the couch. It sagged in the middle, just as Winston had said.

"It's fine," Henry said.

Winston chattered on, setting up his little candleholder and steamer as he talked. "We need a kid, after all, this being *Kamakura matsuri* and us not being kids anymore. So. We need some kids. And I, at least, have one to contribute, unlike you two slackers. Are there special kid *kamakura* outfits? I'd love to dress her up in something. I had no idea dress-up was such a blast. Maybe I should have had dolls or something when I was a kid. That duck head I tried to get on her last Halloween! God, she was cute, but she just screamed until I let her wear the Viking helmet. So in the end she was a Viking duck." He whistled cheerfully.

Lauren stepped away from her brothers, her eyes shut tight because suddenly she was sure that if she let it start she would cry and cry and cry.

"She looks awful," Winston said to his brother when he noticed Lauren's condition. "What's the matter?"

"Nothing."

"Oh, right. That's why her face looks like a tomato."

"It's partly my fault," Henry sighed. "I said something about Robin not being here."

Lauren's tears started in earnest.

"What does that have to do with anything?" Winston demanded.

"I don't know. I think it might have to do with kids." Henry sat down on the unfinished ice sofa.

"But they don't have any kids," Winston protested. Then, "Oh." The two brothers stood awkwardly by their sister, their arms bouncing vaguely at their sides. Finally Winston said, "Is your door open, Henry? I'll go get some Kleenex. Okay? I'll just be gone a second."

When Winston was gone Lauren said, "At first it was because Robin wanted a baby. But way back then I never even imagined I might not be able to get pregnant. We've been failing at this for years, and all the while behind my own back I was getting to want it more and more and more. I know just how Robin feels—he feels robbed. Abandoned."

"But you've been pregnant," Henry said reassuringly. "You can get pregnant."

"That's another problem."

"Why?"

"I know you said you thought I should talk to Robin and tell him more about what's happened. But I didn't. And now it feels like I can't go back and undo what I didn't do then."

"What difference does it make? Why is it ever too late?"

"Sometimes it is too late. I'm not sure if this is one of the times but it might be, Henry. From Robin's point of view, see, maybe the worst thing I did was lying to the fertility specialists when they asked if I'd ever been pregnant. I was so sure I'd get pregnant soon and it was none of their business. But Robin's not going to look at it that way. He's a doctor. He's going to think that there might have been something they could have advised us to do, or there might have been a difference in treatment, if I'd been honest. I've misled Robin, who trusted me so completely, who thinks of me as utterly honest."

"Robin's not somebody who gets all knotted up in what happened before he even knew somebody. And he's not a blaming person, Lauren."

"No, he wasn't. But things change. Henry, this means so much to him. It's impossible now for him to look at me and not see this person who's keeping him from having children. And if I tell him everything now it will be so clear that I haven't been open. How would that change his feelings?"

"Not all marriages are built on openness, Lauren. Why does he have to see you as open to him?"

"Maybe he doesn't. But that would be a different marriage than the one he thought he had. Wouldn't it?"

"I don't know."

Winston reappeared, carrying a cardboard box of tissues and a glass of water. "Here," he said, spilling half the water over Lauren as he tried to get the glass in her hand. "Oh, God, I'm sorry! Let me get a towel." He turned to start away again.

"Forget it, Winston. I promise to stop crying. You don't have to go hide in the kitchen anymore." She blew her nose. "I can't see a thing. Light those other candles, will you? And give me one of those dumplings."

"They're not warmed through."

"Who cares? Henry, can you drink bourbon at *Kamakura matsuri?*"

"It's not traditional. Hot chocolate is traditional."

"I know that," she sighed.

It started to rain into the ice house. This year's design did not have any ceilings—they'd been rejected as too cave-like. A cluster of drops bounced off some ice and directly onto the candle Winston had lit beneath the dumplings. It sputtered out.

"Jesus," Winston muttered. "Now what?"

"Don't worry—I have a tab tent," Henry said. "And see? I've set hooks here for it. I knew the weather might get bad." He shook out a canvas square.

"Here, Winston. Hold that up. No, no. On the other side. There. Come on, Winston. You can see the hook, right? Just stretch it."

Struggling with the torn canvas and cold metal rings served as a kind of bridge back to more normal conversation. Finally the tent was up and dangling over their heads. The three siblings settled once again on the snow sofa. Winston relit his burner, and they huddled under the green canvas listening to the *pwonkpwonkpwonk* of enormous raindrops. Within five minutes the *pwonks* had hardened into *pwhacks,* and hail the size of cherries bounced off the tent, ricocheting at them from the ice house walls.

"I'm going in. Or I'm going home," Winston declared.

"Winston, don't give up! Who knows what the weather will do next? It could be great. It could be magical," Henry pleaded. He wasn't joking. Right after he said "magical" the center of the tab tent gave way in a tearing rip, dumping slush directly onto their heads.

"Come on, Henry," Lauren said, shaking ice from her hair, *"Mono no aware,* you know? Sometimes things are just not meant to happen. This year, it was *Kamakura matsuri."*

"We've never missed one," Henry said sadly.

"We've just been lucky. That's all," Lauren replied. "It's amazing, when you think of it, that we got this far."

"Right," Winston said. "Mel would kill me if she knew I was staying out in this. Iffy's sick already. Look, you two, I'm bagging it. Okay?"

"Sure, Winston. We understand," Henry said. "Lauren's right. This just isn't a *Kamakura matsuri* year and we can be fine with that."

"Lauren." Winston turned to her. "I didn't mean to say anything callous when I went on and on about kids. Happiness can make a person a little less alert to other people's troubles."

"It's good that you're happy, Winston. I don't begrudge you your babies."

"If you want a baby, Lauren, I'm just sure you'll get pregnant."

"You bet."

"I was only trying to be encouraging."

Henry broke in. "Let's carry this stuff inside. Come on, Lauren. Help Winston make a graceful exit here."

Henry was right. Winston was, in his own way, trying, and she was indulging herself in bitterness and self-pity: such terrible temptations. She wiped her nose, gathered up the dumplings and followed her two brothers into Henry's apartment.

Her higher moral plane collapsed as soon as Winston was gone and she had changed into some of Henry's dry clothes. There wasn't any bourbon but she'd found some sake, which she now sipped from a ceramic cup. "So there goes Winston back to his fluffy, funny little daughter and his sunny Melanie and his simple, straightforward marriage."

"You didn't want a sunny Melanie and a simple marriage. You wanted someone who would come to *Kamakura matsuri* and accept Asagao as a member of our family. That's Robin. Not Melanie."

"Right."

"And now you want a baby."

"It's like a chronic low-level fever, Henry. I dream babies. They pull me along after them if I see them in the street. It must be a chemical my uterus is directing at my brain. It hurts."

"I know."

"Do you want a baby?"

"No. But I know what it feels like to have that fever feeling."

"What do you want, Henry?"

"Sometimes . . ." Her brother hesitated before plunging on. "Sometimes I get so lonely. I know you and Winston would throw yourselves in front of trains for me, and I love you both. And Mom and Dad and Iffy and Robin and Mel. I know I'm not alone. But I'm missing something that I need to breathe easily. The only thing that makes me feel calm, entirely right with myself, is being in Asagao's mind. It's strange, isn't it? Asagao isn't just an idea in my head. He's out there—like your baby."

"But you say you can be in his mind now. Why are you still so lonely if that's all you want?"

"He's still in one world, unaware of me in another. I want him to see me," Henry said.

"Well, he can't. He's dead."

"Yes. He's dead. But that doesn't mean that I can never be in his mind in a way that he's aware of."

"What? You mean you can meet him when you die and go to the Great Void?" She laughed.

Henry picked up something from a table and fiddled with it. He said, "You'll have a baby, Lauren. She won't always just be an idea in your mind."

"Well, that's very reassuring."

"No, I mean it. Nothing can take up so much room in your head without a reason. What's all this longing for, anyhow, if it doesn't mean something? There has to be something enormous out there, making us want it."

"I don't know, Henry."

"It's hard to live with something missing," he said, shaking his head.

Lauren understood this to mean that desire was just something you had to live with, but it wasn't what he meant.

Twenty-four

Two weeks later Henry disappeared. It took her about a week to notice that he hadn't returned her calls, but as soon as this occurred to her, she got in her car and went to his apartment.

No one answered her knock. She took her key and entered. She went to his bedroom. All his clothes hung, as they always hung, in order of their age: newest to the right, oldest to the left. His drawers were similarly neat.

She walked into the kitchen and plucked the telephone from the receiver. She hesitated, but finally she called Winston.

"Winston, have you heard from Henry in the last day or so?" she asked hopefully.

"What's wrong?"

She had alarmed him already. "Nothing. Probably nothing."

"Just tell me," Winston insisted.

"It's only that I can't get hold of him. I usually don't have trouble tracking him down is all."

"Where are you?" Winston was instantly his managerial self, in charge. This irritated her so much that it banished some of her anxiety.

"I didn't call to summon you to the rescue, Winston. It might be nothing at all. I just don't know where he is."

When Henry didn't answer calls that day or the next and another visit found his apartment still empty, Winston called the police.

The police were a deeply discouraging experience. "Did he have money trouble?" they asked. "Women trouble? Man trouble? Was he a gambler? What about drug and alcohol use?" No, no, no, no, they replied. "Well," the police said, "we'll get a man on it if he doesn't show up in forty-eight hours. In the meantime call all the hospitals. File a report."

"That's all?" Winston asked in disbelief.

"Look, sir, this man you've described is an adult. You say he holds a responsible job. I mean, I know you say your brother's been in psychiatric care, and we'll treat the case accordingly, but every year hundreds of people just choose to vanish. How well do you know your brother, sir?"

Winston lost his temper. The officer with whom he lost his temper told him to control himself, wait awhile and get back in touch if Henry did not appear. "Give it two days," he said kindly. "He'll probably have a good explanation when he shows up."

"Well. It's not a murder. It's not bank robbery," Lauren said quietly when Winston raged against this total indifference.

"Whose side are you on!? Nobody walks off the face of the planet if they have people who care about them, and will worry about them."

"I think the policeman was telling us that they do," she said.

Henry's telephone rang. Neither of them moved to pick it up. The answering machine clicked on and they heard Isobelle Isacio saying,

"Look, Henry, if you're still interested in going to that exhibit with me next Wednesday, give me a call . . ."

Winston scrambled to the telephone and snatched it up.

"Isobelle? It's Henry's brother, Winston. Have you heard from him recently?" Isobelle had. Henry had called her from a pay phone somewhere three days before. She didn't know where. It hadn't occurred to her to ask.

Lauren took the telephone from Winston. She said, "Did he sound odd when you talked with him? Did he say anything odd?"

"No. Mostly we talked about food. Have you noticed his appetite getting more aggressive? He was in New York for some client meeting and I had him to dinner two weeks ago. He ate half of a Lady Baltimore cake, and that was after seven lamb chops."

"But did anything sound . . . odd?"

"I know what you're getting at, Lauren," Isobelle sniffed. "You don't have to evade."

"What?"

"Trust me. Asagao is a decent individual. As is Henry. No harm has come to him. You underestimate your brother, my dear. He is probably sitting at some table even as we speak, deciding whether to begin with the crevettes or simply go straight to the clafouti."

For three more days they telephoned hospital emergency rooms and police stations. Then they told their parents, who repeated every call that Winston and Lauren had made. They all went to work every day but if they accomplished anything they were not aware of it. Everyone called everyone else every few hours.

When Henry appeared again he came first to Lauren. He was perhaps ten pounds lighter than he had been before he left: the effect was ethereal rather than haggard. He wore linen, stylish cuts of linen, and his silhouette was entirely unfamiliar in the high-contrast late-afternoon light in the office doorway until he stepped forward and she could see him move. "Henry!" she cried. She lifted up her head from where it had sunk on a pile of folders. "Henry, where have you been?"

His face screwed into its most concentrated expression. "I don't know," he answered at last. "Isn't that strange?" He looked as though it had just occurred to him that he could not account for the last two weeks of his life.

Lauren rose briskly and approached him. "Empty your pockets. Do you have your wallet?"

He patted his sides and rear and produced a wallet. He emptied everything onto her desk: a paper parasol from a Chinese restaurant mixed drink, twenty credit card receipts from expensive restaurants all over New England, three receipts from restaurants in Albuquerque, a boarding pass, a licorice button. He held it up. "They were wonderful!" he said. "I remember the licorice!"

"Henry, you went to Albuquerque?"

"Apparently."

"Look at the money you've spent in restaurants! Who was with you?"

"Asagao." Henry actually hung his head. "Or rather, Asagao's thoughts. He's obsessed with food," he offered.

"You look so thin," Lauren said. "Why are you so thin?"

"I don't know. I shouldn't be. I've been eating, it seems, nonstop."

"Henry. Look. We have to contact people. Winston. Mom and Dad. The police."

"Why the police?" He was amazed.

"Well, we filed a missing person report on you. You don't understand, Henry! We were so frightened!"

"I didn't mean to worry you. Oh, Lauren, I'm sorry." Henry hugged her, and this kindness cut through her.

"Henry, you don't know where you were! I don't know what to do anymore."

Henry hung onto her hand. "It's changing," he whispered.

"What's changing?"

"Asagao's getting less confused, and I'm getting more confused. It's like we're switching. Maybe that's a good thing. I don't know."

Henry began twisting a bit of cloth that had fallen from his pocket. He looked at her imploringly, and her own conviction that she couldn't help him filled her chest like so much sand.

It was decided that Henry needed observation in a clinical setting. Lauren protested weakly. For the second time Henry was committed during her watch. But then, she thought, her watch was scheduled to last the rest of her life. She was bound to fail.

She felt an illogical certainty that when Henry suffered it was because she had done something wrong. She had left him exposed, somehow, and endangered. The doctors called what he had done a seizure and gave him a combination of anticonvulsant drugs.

"A seizure? Did he have any spasms? Are they saying he's epileptic?" she asked Robin.

"They're referring to spasms in his brain. Not large muscle spasms that are visible to the naked eye. They're bursts of electrical energy that interrupt or redirect neural paths in the brain, and one of their presenting symptoms is an inability to account for time—like not knowing where you've been. It can be localized or global. That's clearly what's happened to Henry."

"Why? Why does the brain do that?"

Robin shrugged.

The doctors might call this electrical energy but she called it Asagao. That was what there was too much of in Henry's brain. She got so angry thinking of Suriyu Asagao that she had trouble breathing. She realized that she had a concrete picture in her own head of this imaginary person. It was based on the photograph in *Disaster, Disaster, Disaster,* but it wasn't always, in her mind, that burned and ragged figure. In her mind, Suriyu Asagao often appeared sitting outside with a group of other neatly dressed, happy Japanese people, watching Charlie Chaplin dance across the side of a building on a summer night, an outdoor impromptu neighborhood drive-in, everyone eating slices of baked sweet potato and dried seaweed. His happiness as he watched Charlie Chaplin and licked his plum ice made her even more angry.

It was the old scabby problem: if Henry was the trouble, she could not turn to Henry. Winston might work. Then again, they might stumble into some incendiary exchange that left them both more charred than when they began. But it was in considering Robin as a source of perspective and support that she became most unhappy. A year ago Robin would have been a refuge and partner, but the new coldnesses and hesitations that had sprung up all around them had changed that.

Now she was alone.

Twenty-five

Had she suspected that something as commonplace as a failure of imagination could so damage a marriage, she would have considered her options and come up with something more original. But her judgment was not at its peak and she plotted a traditional course back toward Robin—the Romantic Dinner. This, she realized later, was the strategy of the already exhausted person.

The Romantic Dinner strategy was like painting by number: making the right reservation at the right restaurant, keeping it a secret from the beloved, shopping for a suitably Romantic Dress, wondering if she should do something different with her hair, trying to figure out eyeshadow and gloss. This activity kept her from considering the reasons they needed a Romantic Dinner at all. It kept her from considering whether it was the right plan for a man like Robin and a moment in a marriage like this one. Again, failure of imagination.

She actually called Diana in to consult on the hair, clothing and makeup. Diana set her straight about a number of misconceptions, took her to a new hairdresser, and sat her down afterward to offer some hands-on direction about eyebrow plucking.

"It's like getting up in drag," Lauren said to Diana, staring at her plucked and altered face in the mirror.

"All women, when they are dressed, are in drag," Diana sniffed. "We are all female impersonators of sorts, trying to look like what we think our audience is looking for."

"What if your audience is your husband, though?"

"You're not serious," Diana sighed. "Historically, they're the *primary* audience. I've never had a husband but I've had a few close approximations, and the way I see it, they're the toughest to surprise. And surprise is the name of the game."

Lauren looked in the mirror again. "He'll be surprised," she said.

"Good. Use it," Diana replied. "For whatever purpose you have in mind."

All Lauren had told Robin was that she'd pick him up after work and that he shouldn't be on call. For most men that would have been explanation enough, but Robin, too, suffered a failure of imagination. So when she appeared in a skin-tight silver bodice above sweeping layers of net and tulle, he stopped dead in his tracks. "What is this?" he said lightly, "A new kind of *matsuri*?"

She had practiced the smile against the chance that the moment proved to be awkward. Sadly, it was. Robin rallied, however and told her she was beautiful. "I place myself in your hands," he said. "Happily in your hands," he had added. But just then his beeper went off, he picked it up, motioned to her with his finger. "Sit here," he said, gesturing to a chair in the lobby. "I'll be right back."

He reappeared fifty minutes later, making it impossible to reach the restaurant in time for their reservation. There was valet parking—

she had checked. The maître d' pursed his lips and noted how late they were. Lauren agreed, apologized profusely, slipped a twenty-dollar bill into his hand and assured him that anything he could do would be heroic. The maître d' sighed, said they should wait at the bar just a moment. He found them a bustling corner near the kitchen where her skirt kept being billowed out by rapidly passing waiters and then stepped on.

Mono no aware, she thought grimly to herself. It's just the suchness of things.

The talk floated along on a thin surface right up to the moment before the check came. They covered the food, the wine, her dress, his schedule that day, her schedule the next week. Then Robin asked, "Lauren, why are we here? What's that dress all about?"

"We're here for fun. The dress symbolizes Romance."

"You don't look like you're having fun."

"Are you having fun?" she countered.

"No."

"For Christ's sake, Robin. I mean, I'm trying here."

"Trying what?"

"Trying to make you happy. Trying to repair some of the damage we've done to ourselves over the baby thing," she admitted miserably.

"Since when did a new dress and a haircut change anything important? The bottom line to this situation is that you don't want a baby. I do. We won't change unless that changes."

"That's not the way it is at all, Robin. I want a child as much as you do. I think I want one more."

"You don't act it."

"What am I supposed to do?" She set the pen down with a sharp little crack.

"How can you ask that?" He was openly angry now. "There were more tests, more therapies we could have tried. You refused."

"I would have done anything that I thought would have changed things. But I don't think the problem is with me."

"But all my first tests came back normal," he protested.

"Robin, I don't think that the problem is my inability to get pregnant. The reason I think this is that I've *been* pregnant. That's why I think it's you. That's why I didn't think it would help to keep doing stuff to me."

He stared. He pushed himself a little farther away from the table and from her. "Why did you tell the doctors that you had never been pregnant?" His voice was flat.

"Do you think it would have changed anything?"

"Fertility isn't my area of expertise, but I assume they wouldn't have asked the question if the answer didn't impact treatment."

"Well, that's a very logical line of thought," she said.

"You have no right to use that tone. I've been open and responsible all the way through. You haven't. You have no right to bitterness."

"You didn't used to be somebody who talked about feelings as something you had a right to or didn't have a right to," she said. "You didn't used to be somebody looking for a chance to judge. It's a very unattractive position, the moral high road."

"Well, I guess we both look a little different to each other than we used to look."

"I was seventeen, Robin. I miscarried. Only Henry ever knew. I didn't want to bring it back to life. I was sure I'd get pregnant and it wouldn't be relevant."

"But it might be very relevant." He paused. "What caused the miscarriage? That information could be important."

"Who knows why some pregnancies end like that? If I'd told you that I'd miscarried when all this began, I still wouldn't be able to answer questions like that. What good would it have done?"

"Okay. What else?"

"What do you mean, what else?"

"Is there anything else?"

"No."

"I think Henry would disagree."

"All right. I'll play. What does that mean?"

"The last time we were at Henry's for dinner he asked me to get him something from his room. There was a picture on the bureau that I'd never seen before. It was you when you were very little, and the boys, and Annie and Warren, and you were holding a baby. Why did Henry put that picture there and send me in for something he didn't need? Who's the baby?"

"Why didn't you ask Henry when you found the picture?"

"I was a little skittish of it, maybe. Actually, I thought I should ask you. So I'm asking."

She crunched her napkin into a ball and set it on the table.

"Come on, Lauren."

"We had a sister. She died when she was only a few weeks old."

"Why wouldn't you have told me that?" He was stunned.

"I don't know."

"You just wiped it out of your memory?"

Her voice was steely when she answered. "I never wiped anybody out of my memory. It would be easier if I could."

"Why did Henry want me to see this picture, do you think?"

"I think Henry believes that it's Sally, the way I felt about her dying, that is keeping me from getting pregnant."

"That doesn't make any sense," Robin replied.

"Not medically, no."

"Are you saying that you think he's right?" Robin asked.

"The thing about Henry is, he usually is," she answered.

"You mean he thinks you're afraid to have a baby?" She didn't answer him. He went on. "Tell me what happened to the baby."

"They called it sudden infant death syndrome. She was just lying there in her crib one morning. She wasn't moving. When I touched her she was like wood, really solid and cool. I had woken up and gone to warm the bottle that Mom kept in the refrigerator. We usually were the first in the family to wake up. That morning I tiptoed out of the room thinking that by the time I ran it under hot water in the kitchen and brought it back to the room, she'd be awake. She always was. I can remember the bottle felt warmer than her skin."

"You were the one who found her?"

Lauren nodded. "Mom had a terrible pregnancy and delivery. Then she had problems recovering, and in the middle of the night she'd started bleeding again. If Dad hadn't gotten her to the hospital that night she probably would have died. Henry knew they'd left—Dad had woken him and told him. But I didn't know. We were alone."

Robin was silent for a few minutes. Then he said, "How many conversations have I had with your mother, your father, your brothers, where her existence would have naturally come up in the course of things and it just . . . didn't." He was clearly amazed. "It makes so many of those conversations look different."

"They aren't different," she said.

"Did Asagao arrive right after this baby died?"

"I don't know exactly when he arrived. But it was after Sally. Yes."

"You didn't say this to anyone who was treating Henry for psychosis? It didn't occur to you that it was relevant to his diagnosis? You all—all of you in the family—kept this secret?"

"It wasn't a secret."

Robin shook his head briskly. "Years. We spent years trying to get pregnant. And you've been pregnant, but you said nothing."

"Robin, I went to doctors for tests. I tried. Sometimes sharing every detail of your past doesn't make anything in your present better."

"What did she look like?" Robin said at last.

"I don't remember."

"I don't believe you," he said.

"She was blond. Not like us. Round. Thighs like little tires piled up on top of one another. I was the first person she smiled at." She re-arranged her silverware. "Henry baptized her that morning."

"How often do you think of her?"

"I don't know. Maybe every day."

"Every day?!"

"Not like I stop and think, Oh, that reminds me of the time . . . and I've got a specific picture in my head: you know, a baby with blue corduroys and a spit-up stain and it's late afternoon. Nothing that concrete. It's more like the way you feel if you've had a dream that you don't remember but it changes the way you feel the next morning. And then maybe sometime in the afternoon something will cross your path that suddenly makes you remember a feeling from the dream. Then it fades again. I remember Sally like that aftertaste feeling."

"I don't remember things that way."

"Yes you do. You just don't remember remembering them."

"Now you sound like Henry."

"Robin, tell me something. Did you apply for the neurology residency to avoid being with me? I mean, it was just like beginning medical school all over again. And at that point you had choices and you could have started something with half the number of hours. You didn't have to apply for that residency. You wanted a family."

"But I didn't think you did."

"So you were trying to stay away from me? From home?"

"No. I wanted to learn more in that area. Lauren, you didn't say a word about my doing it."

"You never asked me."

"No. No, I guess I didn't." He stood. "Isn't it funny?" he said. "One day your marriage is one thing and the next day it's something different. Maybe a lot different or maybe only a tiny bit different, but for a while it's impossible to know which." He started for the door. "I'll get your coat and the car. I'll be out front."

But when she had made her way to the lobby and out the door and the valet pulled up in their car, she could not get in. The idea of being in the car and staring directly ahead in silence while Robin did the same in the seat beside her, stopped her hand as it reached for the door handle. Now, when it was too late for it to be her friend, her imagination kicked in. She could see herself back in the apartment, undressing, lying down in the darkness beside him. She withdrew her hand from the car handle and stepped back.

"What is it?" he asked impatiently. "Lauren, I need to get some sleep. I have an early start tomorrow. Get in."

She shook her head from side to side.

"Okay." He shrugged. "Do you have enough for a cab?"

She nodded.

"You're sure you don't want to get in?" he asked again. Again she shook her head from side to side. "All right," he said. Then he was gone, and she stood alone on the curb.

When she did call a cab she directed it to drop her at the studio. Still trailing her tulle and net, she trudged up the stairs to the large studio and lay down directly in the middle of the sprung wood ballroom floor. Headlights from occasional cars in the rotary below bounced off the mirrors. She hadn't turned on any lights.

William was the first dancer in the next morning. He found her asleep on the floor. She asked him to take her home and he did, not asking any questions.

When she opened the door to her apartment she found a note from Robin. "I waited," it said. "You didn't come."

Lauren made herself coffee and sat, still in her Romantic Dinner attire, in a chair facing the street. She had taken the little ravaged part of her that was the reaction to Robin's residency application and put it away right until the moment she spoke of it to him. She'd told herself it didn't matter about the residency. She'd told herself that the pregnancy would come or not; it would be all right either way. She'd dismissed the idea that Sally had anything to do with her life now. She'd watched Robin cool and sadden and look at her across more and more distance and said to herself, It's nothing.

She thought, Now what? Now what? Now what? but no answer came to her.

Twenty-six

When Lauren finally stood up and took off the silver and gold costume, the only plan that made its way through her rumpled state of mind was to work. So she did that. In the weeks that followed she and Robin shared the house like polite acquaintances, which caused her equal parts rage and grief. She wore herself out with it, staggering under the contradictory pushing and pulling of these feelings.

Henry was released from the hospital and returned to the workaday world of jobs and travel arrangements and deciding what to eat for dinner. The first week he was home she and Winston alternated evenings at his apartment. They learned his boss's name and got his telephone number to use in case of an emergency. They made copies of any part of his schedule at work that they could check in on to make sure Henry remembered it. They squabbled behind his back.

"He can't travel three weeks in a row," Winston hissed when she penciled in a job in Portland, Oregon.

"Says you," she replied casually. "Work is good for people."

"He's not people," Winston argued. "And he's not you. You solve everything with work."

"Don't be an asshole, Winston. He can handle it."

Henry entered the room at this point, carrying a teapot and three cups. He looked at them unhappily. "What's the matter now?"

"She just told me I was an asshole."

"Well. Perhaps you were behaving a bit like an asshole," Henry said mildly.

"PMS," Winston snorted.

At this, to both men's amazement, their sister burst into tears, which threw Winston into a panic. His hands flapped uselessly, anxiously, in front of him as he pleaded, "I'm sorry! Lauren, please, stop crying! Oh my God, is this going to be something that happens a lot? Lauren, what the hell's the matter? It couldn't be me—I'm like this all the time and you don't cry. It's the baby thing, isn't it? It's stuff with Robin."

Henry sat with his brow furrowed and his hands folded neatly on his lap, regarding his siblings in silence.

"Henry!" Winston demanded. "Say something!"

"Something has to change," Henry said at last.

"What?" Winston asked. "What can you do? Lauren, look, this will just resolve itself. I'll get you a drink of water," he said, rising and rushing to the kitchen.

As soon as her younger brother was out of earshot she turned to her older one. "Henry, I told Robin about Sally and about the miscarriage. He says I'm secretive and I lied to the fertility specialists and that our entire marriage looks different. Not different in a good way."

Henry moved to sit beside her. He patted her knee.

"I've made so many mistakes, Henry. I can see him mulling it all over, feeling like I've backed him into a place he can't stay in. I feel like I've been backed into a tight place myself. It's hard to do much thinking here."

She took the glass of water that Winston held out to her upon his return. "I'll be fine. I'm sorry I upset you." This last to Winston.

"You didn't upset me," Winston said, clearly lying. "It will be fine. I tell you, as soon as you two stop worrying about getting pregnant and stop trying, you'll get pregnant. I've heard dozens of stories. It works." He nodded hopefully.

Lauren smiled politely, already gone in her mind. She hugged both brothers good-bye.

"I'm going to talk to Robin," Winston said to Henry when she had left. "It just sounds to me like he's blaming Lauren for something she can't change and it's not doing either of them any good."

"Leave him alone, Winston. Don't say anything. We can't understand all these things. Interfering could do damage."

"Why do you say that?"

"It's the way these things work."

About to remind Henry that he was the only unmarried sibling, perhaps the least qualified to describe how "these things work," Winston stopped himself. After all, this was his older brother Henry speaking. He said, "I hate to see her like that. She doesn't get weepy. She gets pissed off or bossy or judgmental or at least purposeful, but she doesn't cry."

"Not habitually," Henry agreed.

And when Winston, too, had left him, Henry took the medicine bottle that he had promised his family he would open every day and he opened it. He poured out the two pills he had told them he would take and flushed them down the toilet. He sat down on the bathtub rim and closed his eyes and there, again, were his fireflies before his eyes, and the fields where they had been pursued so long ago on the long dragon's spine of volcanic islands rising from the sea.

"Something has to change," Henry repeated to himself. "If I could remember, I would know what it was." Then he thought, Remember what? But he didn't know. This failure made Henry so tired he had to lie down.

Lauren had returned to her office and worked through the night, stopping for a nap on the cot at the back of her office. Twice she walked up the stairs to the largest studio to flip on all the lights and sit in the center of the mirrored room. If Robin came home that night, he didn't call the office looking for her. Perhaps he didn't even leave the hospital, she thought. Probably he just slept in the resident bunks. Easier to think this than think that he had come home, found her gone, and done nothing.

She put on a pot of coffee at first light and sat waiting for the reassuring sounds of dancers' feet. John would be in first, before everyone else, playing tapes and working out his class details. She waited uneasily until she was rewarded at eight-thirty by the sound of his familiar steps. The day was beginning just like yesterday and the day before and the month before that. She was here at work just like she had been here a hundred mornings before.

She rallied, went through another pot of coffee, dispatched five administrative problems one by one. She strolled up the stairs into the studio feeling better, looking forward to telling the dancers she had covered their parking tickets—they would be grateful.

Joe Morel swung his head around when she came in. The spinning line of bodies he'd set off just before her entrance kept right on going to the masking-tape line he'd set to end the phrase. William is right, she thought, looking again at Morel's head. Cement. He met her eyes and smiled. To her surprise, the smile set off a kind of electrical current in her chest that ran directly down between her legs. He seemed to see this, and his smile changed to a much more serious expression.

She backed out of the studio, his eyes still locked on her, and hurried down the stairs to the safety of her office. What was happening to her?

She dialed Robin's pager and punched in the company number. He did not return the call. She dialed the emergency room desk but he was not on duty there. She had him paged, and finally heard his voice on the other end of the line. "Come home tonight," she pleaded.

"I agreed to do a shift for Jeffrey Wong."

"Take back the offer."

"I can't. I promised." He sighed. He added, "This is awkward. Isn't it?"

"What are you saying?"

"That things look different. That's all."

"I love you," she said.

"I know that," he answered. He didn't say he loved her. What he's thinking and not saying, Lauren thought, is that I don't love him enough.

She hung up, defeated. She would not go back up to the studio. Suddenly even the prospect of the neat stacks of work here on her desk could not free her from this restless anxious shifting yearning. She had left the important things to drift, she thought to herself.

Twenty-seven

Winston tended to do what he said he would. In this case he went to the hospital and had Robin paged. He had never done this before, so Robin was race-walking as he approached, stethoscope dangling and the sides of his white coat lifting like wings beneath his arms. "What's happened?"

"Nothing. Nothing at all," Winston assured him, sitting down in one of the orange plastic chairs in the hallway. "I just wanted to say something about Lauren, you know, without her being around to hear it."

Robin sank down in the chair next to him. "What?"

"Have you ever seen Lauren cry?" Winston asked.

"Well, sure." Then he considered. "Maybe. I don't remember."

"You'd remember. Before recently, I'd only seen her cry when she got three bees stuck up her jacket sleeve and they all stung her at once.

She didn't even cry the afternoon she fell off the barn roof and broke her leg."

"What made her cry recently?"

"She told us about wanting a baby."

"She said she wanted a baby?" Robin asked.

Winston nodded. "And we got the clear impression, though she didn't offer details, that you do too, and that things aren't going well. Between you, I mean. As well as the baby thing. Or because of the baby thing. It wasn't clear." Robin didn't respond so Winston stumbled on. "I don't want to intrude, but I have money to spare and I know that residents don't make anything, and Lauren, God help her, has never known how to make money, and I know that things like infertility treatment aren't always covered by the insurance plan and that also adoption can cost a bundle and you should know that I'm in a position to ease up any tension there might be around the financial side of things. I mean if some things are possible but you need money to make them happen, I can make them happen. I'm just looking for a way to help," he finished lamely.

Robin sat dumbly, his face clinically impassive—he had been taken entirely by surprise. Winston stumbled on. "Her face when she cried—like she had broken plates in her head or something. It would help me if you let me help somehow. I just don't know what to do."

"Tell her that."

"Oh, God no. She'd bite my head off. But I knew I could talk to you about it."

"She's not all that unreasonable, Winston," Robin said.

"Look, I know her to the bone, and I have no intention of being lectured on how I condescend to her."

"All right. Here's a question for somebody who claims to know her totally. If she were unhappy in her marriage, what would she do?"

"You mean, would she be unfaithful?"

"I don't know if I mean that. Maybe I do."

Winston blew out a puffing sound of dismissal. "Don't be ridiculous. Once she's attached to something, she couldn't be unattached with any kind of crowbar. I don't think she's physically capable of infidelity. So. Is that your way of saying that you think she's unhappy?"

"We don't seem to be happy at the moment."

"Forget about it. It's just part of marriage. I make Melanie miserable all the time but we're as happy as can be. Lauren's on edge, I see that. But believe me, what's making her like that is most likely not you. Unless you count the possibility of her being miserable because she thinks that you're unhappy. You know?" Winston twisted in his seat so he could better slap his brother-in-law on the back. "She adores you. As she should. You're the best thing that every happened to her."

"Why, thank you, Winston."

"Frankly, I was surprised she nabbed you."

"It's more the reverse."

"Hunccccckkh." Winston expelled the snort in a way that showed he appreciated Robin's gallantry but did not believe the lie.

"Winston, the fact is that I occupy a much smaller place in her mind than she does in mine. Her mind had this permanent, unmovable furniture in it when we married. Henry takes up all this space. You do. Work does. Even Asagao does. I can't help but think that things would be better between us if I had more room in her head."

"Well, if you two had a child, that would do it. Babies reshuffle everything—there would be less room for Henry and the damn dance company. More room for you. So . . . I mean it about the money."

"I don't think money's the solution, Winston, though I am touched that you offered it." He put his arm around his brother-in-law's shoulder.

Then an awkward silence, Winston clearly dissatisfied and not ready to end the conversation.

"What is that lumpy thing sticking into me?" Winston asked. Robin stood and yanked it out—a black-and-red plastic figure holding a crystal ball. "Modern medical technology," he said, holding it up for inspection. "The wizard is good on fevers for males between three and seven. I've found that extreme fevers treated with Tylenol alone react more slowly than fevers treated with Tylenol and the wizard. The average reduction is greater with the wizard too—about point-nine degrees greater. Also he's good for basic neurologic eye-focus checks. Reflexes. He's a clear visual cue."

"Really. And the lump in your other pocket?"

Robin shoved his free hand into this pocket and pulled out a graying puffy ball that had once been white. "Stuffed kitten," he sighed. "I have a couple of them because they work well on girls between one and ten, but they're problematic. The nurses hate them because they absorb dirt and fluids. They actually make some boys hostile—if you happen to get one who's busy establishing his masculinity, the kitty can be interpreted as a challenge. Also, kitties don't yield consistent results like the wizard does. That wizard's results are quantifiable. But not the kitties'. I keep meaning to turn them in and get some princesses or queens made in a plastic that can stand up to bleach baths . . . see how they do clinically. But the fact is, I find the kitties comforting. I usually have one when I'm here in ER but it's for me, not patients."

"Can I see that kitty?" Robin handed over the little animal, and Winston set it on his knee. He stroked its head as he sat. "Henry will get entirely on his feet and he'll take up less space in her head," Winston said, patting away. The words were meant merely to comfort; the speaker himself didn't seem convinced. "We could get a wizard for Henry," he suggested. "And a kitty. Maybe they'd accomplish something that neurology can't."

"I think of Asagao as this part of Henry that can only come out as

Asagao," said Robin. "It's occurred to me that Asagao is something that we shouldn't fiddle with."

"How can you say that? You're a doctor. You're supposed to offer some mechanical explanation for what happens in Henry's brain."

"Well, there's the brain and then there's the mind. We can only look at his brain. I told you that I'd reviewed Henry's films with the radiologist. And the diencephalon is abnormal. Not abnormal in a way that every radiologist in the world who saw it would write 'damaged' in the report—there are significant variables within the boundaries of 'normal,' and Henry could be read as just being on the far end of that curve. Lots of people live there and manage just fine."

"You told us at that family dinner that there were lights in his head but that all brains had lights in them. You didn't say anything about damaged diencephalons."

"Unidentified Bright Objects, is what I said. Pockets of electrical activity. A lot of brains present like that—even brains in normal-functioning people."

The two men sat on shoulder to shoulder, one holding the grayish stuffed kitty and the other the plastic wizard, until Robin's pager went off again and he rose to respond. He forgot to retrieve the kitty, and Winston still held it between his thumb and index finger, still stroking its head, as he walked back to his own car and made the short drive home to his wife and children.

Henry meanwhile had risen up and gone off to catch fireflies. His own neighborhood was mowed and trimmed in ways that discouraged insect life. He had to drive twenty miles before he found the kind of landscape that might contain them. Then he settled comfortably on a tuft of moss and waited.

Finally, an hour after twilight, tiny flashes. He considered the fireflies' positions. He knew they lit themselves to attract mates. He also knew that once firefly lovers had found a match that they would flash back and forth until the female was inseminated, and that she would then darken herself and vanish in the night. A lonely flasher kept up his vigil, blinking hopefully under an uncoiled fern. Other flashes. Clusters and the occasional Milky Wayish stream of flickers.

Then Henry's small corner of the universe was plunged again into darkness—the fireflies dimmed and scattered. The tiny photinus specimens had seen what they feared was the signal of the much larger photuris—a predatory female who flashed not for love but to deceive and attract smaller males, whom she then dismembered and ate. But in fact it wasn't such a predator. It was one of their own, revving up his electrical charge in order to impersonate the huge cannibal female and frighten away all the nearby males, leaving him unchallenged in the field of love.

The simple strategy worked. A cloud of glittering lovers came to him, and Henry stepped out of hiding with a little fine-mesh cage and scooped them all up, just as knowledgeable insect hunters had been doing for centuries. He released them, thinking he would give himself the pleasure of catching them again. The flickering absorbed him utterly and he stayed on, watching the stars that rose after the firefly hours ended, and still on while the moon finished its time and the sun washed the darkness into progressively lighter grays. Morning found him happy, stiff, alone, thinking of nothing in particular.

Then it occurred to him again that he had forgotten something. But what? His perfect happiness was shattered by this sudden awareness that he did not know what he had forgotten—and then he remembered.

He must go home. There was a way to do everything he should do, and he saw it clearly at last. Those were the things that he had forgotten but now remembered.

Twenty-eight

The next day Lauren found John at the barre in the large studio at seven-thirty when she arrived. John was never up this early: no dancer was ever conscious at this hour.

"John?"

John gasped, swung a fully extended toe slowly upward and said, "If he's sleeping with her I'll kill both of them."

"Who?"

"Morel. My wife."

"Well. That would solve my publicity problem for the at-home season. We'd finally get coverage on the eleven-o'clock news. Of course, you'd be in jail and Elena would be dead." John didn't smile. "He isn't sleeping with her, John. Even Diana says he's not sleeping with her, and Diana knows everything. It's just the dancing."

"There's no such thing as just dancing. You know he offered her a position in his company in New York?"

"Really?"

"I don't know what drew my attention to that man in the first place. I don't know why I hired him."

"She didn't say yes, did she?"

"She hasn't 'decided' she says. Can you believe that? She hasn't 'decided'! Of course that means she's going to say yes. I would say yes. Any idiot would say yes!"

"Well, what would be so terrible about going to New York?"

"Lauren. Look at me." John's leg swung down from the barre, his foot slapped the sprung oak floor. He sagged there, swaying above his splayed toes for a few moments before discouragement overcame him and he just sat down. Lauren walked over and settled beside him. He said, "I'm not an up-and-coming red-hot sensation. I'm at the edge, the wrong edge, of my dancing life, and I'm not a choreographer. You know what that means. It means that my future is all behind me. It means that New York is not my oyster. She'll be moving into the crest of her career, but what will I be doing?" They listened to the thickening traffic noises outside the studio windows. "Dance has been like my religion. What will happen to me when I can't get on a stage?"

"You'll do something else. There's lots of places here besides the stage. The dance world isn't going to disappear just because your place in it changes, John."

"Call Isobelle," John said suddenly. "Fabricate some reason for her to show up here this week. Maybe she knows of some openings in New York I may be interested in. Isobelle's faced things like this."

"Just call her, John."

"No. I'm not good at telephone conversations. I want her in my space, my studio when I expose these kinds of . . . difficulties to her. You don't know how she can be if she thinks you're vulnerable, Lauren. It's terrible. Still, over the years I've thrown a few things Isobelle Isacio's way and she knows it. She'll help me."

"But what about us? You're going to just quit?"

"Really, Lauren, any honest person can see that this company was here before Elena and I arrived, and it will be here after we leave. You don't need one of the five flashiest choreographers in the country to head a repertory company—you just need somebody who can pick and train dancers good enough to attract the flashy choreographers. Besides, don't you read the reviews? They say I'm gaining weight." He rose, groaning. "Goddamn knees. Goddamn groin tear." He hobbled to the door.

Later that day Lauren found herself resisting the urge to go up to the studio because if she was going to be honest with herself, she had to admit that she would only be going to test her physiologic reaction to Joe Morel. She remained at her desk and paged Robin. He didn't return the calls. She called Henry, who sounded sleepy but cheerful. She hung up satisfied with his well-being. Finally she gave in and walked up the steps to the studio.

Morel circled the company with the churning, perfect flow of a running collie, all explosive blur beneath a quietly balanced head. He spoke to them as he circled them, explaining what he wanted. All their heads turned with him as he circled.

Under his influence the dancers moved in ways she had never seen them move before: Elena, for example. Now, in Diana's role, she offered up a performance that was immaculately precise, sparkling with happy authority. Lauren watched for a full minute before she was even sure it was Elena and not some member of his New York company here to help him. Meanwhile John, too, had climbed the stairs and stood by Lauren on the mats at the side of the studio door.

"I hate that man," he hissed to Lauren. "But there he is, giving them the moments you dance for to begin with. What an asshole."

Morel didn't turn or acknowledge her entrance in any way she could see, but she felt sure that a stream of his attention had attached to her the moment she entered. When she rose to leave, his head swiveled around like an owl's, the body just a half second behind it, and he fixed her with a brilliant smile. Again, the same current running inside her body to the same destination. It's an illusion, a small warning voice inside her said. You are confused.

As he left that day Morel stopped purposefully at her office doorway. "What did you think?" he said to her. She was acutely aware of his hips, their swiveling ball jointish symmetry. "I don't know," she said. He smiled.

William had been following only a few feet behind the choreographer. He stuck his head in when Morel moved on, both eyebrows jolted up in suggestive little arches.

"Go away, William," she said. He did. She picked up the telephone and dialed Isobelle's New York number; the choreographer picked it up on the third ring. They talked about costumes and the rest of the season's schedule before she got to her point. "Isobelle, I'm supposed to ask you to come to town on business so that John can take you by surprise with questions about possible job opportunities in New York."

"For whom?"

"For John, of course."

"And why is John interested in New York?"

"Because Joe Morel has offered Elena a spot in his company and she tells John she is thinking about saying yes."

"My, my. My, my."

"What does that mean?"

"Not a thing."

"Isobelle."

"Everywhere he goes. Bing, bop, bang."

Lauren could see Isobelle's arm floating in the air, the hand bouncing on the last three words. "Another way to think of it, Isobelle, is that he has given Elena a chance at real attention as a soloist, and that maybe John is ready for a switch."

"Your optimism is one of the things that makes you such an inventive and durable administrator, my dear. You are a treasure, and you are quite right. Tell John I'll be in town the sixteenth and I will pretend that his job queries are entirely unexpected. By the way, are you coming this weekend?"

"Coming?"

"I've asked Henry to join some guests spending the weekend at my Connecticut country house. I told him to feel free to extend the invitation to you and your Robin if he chose." She paused. "Ah. I imagine he didn't choose."

"Henry said yes?"

"He said no when I first asked. Then he called me at the crack of dawn this morning and said yes."

"So . . . ?"

"So, we'll have a lovely time. Ring whenever. Ciao."

Lauren stared at the walls in her office for another hour. Robin would be on rounds now, she thought, checking the clock. Or would his rotation have changed? Was he on emergency room staff this week? These days she hated being home. She tried not to call the hospital. She would not fall back on Henry. She let the answering machine pick up more calls than she normally did. Winston, uncharacteristically, had called six times this week, but since he hadn't sounded like there was any emergency in the offing, she had not called him back.

She found that if she planted her left hand on the telephone that this satisfied her impulse to dial Robin or Henry just enough to leave her mind clear and able to work. She sat like that, one hand at the keyboard and the other on the telephone, until she became so tired that she could go home and face her own apartment.

Twenty-nine

About seven people had been invited, an assortment who appealed to Isobelle or her husband. He liked musicians. Her preferences were more catholic.

Her "country house" was a fifteen-acre estate in a county that could be called economically diverse. Wealthy Manhattanites had discovered these hilly pasturelands about fifteen years earlier, and built among the farmers whose families had struggled here for as many as twelve generations, not always successfully. The local grocery store was stocked with Italian olive oil–based crackers, smoked oysters, organic brown rice, pigs' feet, Wonder bread and a full assortment of Frito-Lay products. The aisles' contents were arranged socioeconomically.

"My next-door neighbor," Isobelle announced at dinner that Friday night, "has taken a mysterious dislike to me and mine, and has strung barbed wire all along our eastern property line to make it clear that he will brook no trespass upon his cowpies. So—consider yourselves warned. He's a very crabby man. His wife has a garden touch like Demeter's—beautiful things. I shall make peace with him through her, and depend upon them as a source of cilantro as the summer moves on toward tomatoes."

"It's not just crabby, Isobelle," her husband added. "He's strange."

"Don't be ridiculous," Isobelle sniffed.

"What's his name?" Henry asked.

"His name? Edward Simon."

At this very moment Edward Simon was cursing a piece of machinery whose third spark plug would not fire. He yanked it. Corroded into uselessness. He would have to stop work, just stop everything when the weather looked like it was going to turn wet soon, and go into town for a new one. His truck refused to start. He got out in a high rage and picked up the largest rock he could find. He threw it at his truck. A spiderweb of cracks opened in a circular pattern around the impact point on the windshield's passenger side. Now he would have to replace the windshield, because nowadays even the least little itty-bitty fucking goddamn line in the thing made them flunk your vehicle at inspection, and his inspection sticker, he saw, had expired last week. He cursed the sky and fields and the idle machine that stood before him like a stubborn animal. More time lost, and this year of all years he had grown strawberries! Goddamn strawberries! If they get wet even ten minutes before you pick them, rot, rot, rot! Months of labor, all that acreage given over to it, all the seedlings, worthless! And the price of the seedlings! Edward Simon started kicking tires and bumpers. He wore heavy boots that left dents behind in the bumpers.

The truck started the second time he tried. The first driveway he passed was Isobelle's, the second another New York weekender, the third a New York weekender. All their land was more level than his—

all their land was less rock-infested. His own land heaved up rocks from beneath the surface every night as he slept. Their land, from the looks of it, was unadulterated nitrogen-rich earth, dark as hardwood ash. He had to look at it every day now, sitting unused and serving its owners as mere scenery. Weekend scenery at that. Some of them had even plopped down these iron and copper messes they called sculpture right in the middle of prime acreage. Next thing you know, they'll be hiring pricey consultants to help them house-train pet livestock. He'd heard they kept pigs on leashes.

His wife, the Demeter of the vegetable garden, had been unfaithful to him with the owner of the fourth driveway. This had happened several years ago, and some days he could shoot past this driveway without pain. Not today. Today it seemed to him that not a crop had gone right since the betrayal. It was rain, rain, rain, or drought. It was bugs or fungus. In his memory it had been bounty and ease before the infidelity—endless difficulty after it. She said she was sorry. She said it was long over, but the pictures he had formed in his own mind of what she had done with the other man had settled like so much grapeshot in places where it couldn't be dug out.

By the time he got to town he was so overwrought he could not immediately remember why he had come. Then he remembered, bought the spark plug, drove back past the reminder of grief, past the fertile waste, back to his own land. He got the machinery started.

He would just stay away from the house today, he decided. He would be better off staying away from his wife until this terrible feeling wore off some. He loaded his shotgun and set it by him in the tractor cab. The last time he'd been in that field he'd seen deer in the rows, eating his profit. Edward thought of deer as large rodents. They had multiplied since the scenery lovers had moved into the county. They retreated during hunting season to the New York weekenders' properties, swarming out after hunting season like vermin to gnaw at every living thing in the county—no natural enemies around to keep their numbers down. Most of the farmers around agreed with Edward—it was a public service to kill them. He'd averaged one a week this season, not even bothering to skin and butcher the last one. He just dragged it off his field and left it to the scavengers. So he set off to the fields this day, a suffering man.

Most of Isobelle's guests that weekend were her husband's musician choices, but her butcher had also been invited, as had a young contender for the next Olympic fencing team. Isobelle had met him at the club where she had recently begun fencing lessons. In preparation for this weekend she had borrowed enough foils for each of her guests, and they spent the next morning squatting and hopping toward each other with little mesh grates over their faces and padded chests that looked vaguely bumblebeeish. "Don't hop! No, no! Never hop!" the young fencing hopeful cried in alarm. "Roll! Heel to toe! Roll smoothly forward, smoothly back. Like this. Toe up." He demonstrated with one toe arched ceilingward. "Approach. Retreat. Approach. Retreat. Double approach. Double retreat. You see?"

But the fencing expert couldn't control the musicians; they did not acknowledge the centuries-old discipline that he revered. In fact, by the looks of their middle sections, they didn't acknowledge the disciplines of any sport at all, and the confusion deepened when he tried to teach little quick epées and lunges. Only Isobelle faced the young fencer with respectful concentration.

"Level the point of your foil at my eyes," he told her, and she complied instantly. "Drop the pummel to about one and a half fist lengths from your waist. There. Close. Relaxed. Now—lunge." Isobelle had a stunning, feline lunge. The heaviness of her body vanished. It flashed toward her opponent, her foible ending directly at his heart.

"Very good," the young man said, sincerely pleased. "Wonderful. Like the owl to its mouse!"

Henry was content to watch them through the early afternoon while the musicians scooted away to find a piano or two.

They had a late lunch that went on for hours. Then Henry went to his room to get a sweater. When he came down again Isobelle was fencing on with her young guest. Beethoven rolled down the stairs from the second floor. Henry strolled out onto a perfect early evening: soft aromatic air, pink light that seemed to radiate upward from the earth rather than down from the setting sun. Off he went, hands in pockets, taking the first path that veered away from the foot of the drive. It led into the woods. It took him to a pretty little bridge over a creek. He crossed.

The barbs on the fence glinted separately. He saw their little reflective flashes before he found the long reels of wire that held them. He stepped off the path and toward the barbs, trampling fern and tangled grass to reach them. He heard some kind of farm equipment buzzing in the distance, past the fence, as he slipped between the barbs and followed the sound. It led him to Edward Simon, who stopped his tractor the moment he saw plumes of corn waving six inches above Henry's head in the adjoining field. Edward saw a moving patch of brown among the stalks. The plumes moved in a little wave that crested above the trespasser's movements.

Edward picked up his shotgun, determined to kill any deer who approached his corn. He saw another piece of brown something among the stalks and raised the gun to his shoulder, training it just about ten feet ahead of where he'd seen the bit of movement. He would feel better, he knew, after he killed it. The light was behind his target, and angling so steeply that colors and features were impossible to distinguish. Henry stepped out of the row and into sight. He waved, but the finger coiled around the trigger had already begun to squeeze. Edward thought, It's a man, but his thoughts didn't travel down to the finger in time. He fired.

Thirty

Lauren woke that Saturday morning exhausted by some relentless pattern of dream she could not remember now that she was awake. She could feel its anxious aftertaste, though, driving her up out of bed and to coffee, to the spiritual refuge of her desk and the studio.

Saturdays in the office were her favorite. Dancers seldom showed up on weekends and the building was empty but for her. Everywhere she walked in the empty spaces her movements echoed and the familiar smells parted before her: sweat and old dance shoes, leotard elastic, bits of dropped eggparm sandwiches. Coffee.

When the telephone rang late that afternoon she assumed it was Winston or Henry, who knew she often spent Saturdays here. She sighed, prayed that it was not one of her parents, and lifted the receiver.

"Lauren, I found this note in my box at the hospital addressed to both of us. Henry wrote it. He signed it, anyway." Robin's voice was strained. "Where is Henry?"

The simple happiness Lauren felt at hearing Robin's voice lasted only the moment it took to understand his tone. Something was wrong with Henry. "This weekend? I don't know. Home. No. Isobelle invited him to her house in Connecticut—she told me just Thursday. He isn't even in town. Did he leave this note before he went?"

"He must have put it there on Friday because it was here when I checked at about seven this morning."

"That's odd." She waited for Robin to go on. "Well. What does the note say?"

"I'll show it to you. I'll come to the office."

"You can't just tell me?"

"Stay there. I'll come."

Robin's expression when he arrived was grim. She had been hoping for tenderness, and his face deflated the happiness she had been preparing secretly, behind her own back, at the prospect of seeing him. He handled the letter he set on her desk as if it were a small animal that tended to bite, attentive and brisk with it. "Open it," he said.

Dear Robin and Lauren,

I have sent this same note to Winston to explain, and to remind him that I love him, as I love you.

I've thought about this for a long time, how to stop longing for what's just out of reach. I can only find out what will happen if I go, so that is what I'm doing.

For a long time I have also thought that I would be able, if I went, to change your own paths in ways that smooth them. I know

I can't do that from here. What I can do from there remains unknown.

Think of me as happy and well. If you can find it, I would love plum ice on my lantern boat.

Henry

Thirty-one

After the bomb many of us who survived changed in our minds. Doctors sent by the Americans said that our minds' fears made us imagine symptoms in our bodies. They did not understand that when the contamination you suffer is invisible, the invisible everywhere becomes very powerful.

Some doctors noticed that people who had been called schizophrenic before the bomb became now what the doctors called "sane" and that others who had been "sane" were now acting in ways the doctors called "schizophrenic." They also called these people paranoid because they were so afraid all the time about so many things. But then, these people had seen the bomb; what they saw was inside their minds and could never be taken out. I think about the days after the bomb, when the inside of my heart was disordered and broken, and it seemed to me that the explosion happened inside me.

I must say that these are not happy ideas and I try to deny them the attention they demand. It is hard to banish thoughts, however. If I could control them I would not have in my mind the picture of myself touching Ishiru's arm and seeing the skin come off her body in my hands. Nor would I welcome back any memory of myself as I ran back, maddened, toward the blast and toward her. She'd been outside with no wall to shield her from the tsunami of heat and light, the five-kilometer-high mass of clouds that climbed like a kind of dark light into the sky before its summit broke open and apart into a mushroom, boiling clouds erupting from its underside.

I thought, This must have some meaning. Then the thought went away and I did not have it again for many months. This idea comes back sometimes but I have not ever found meaning in the pica-don. *Later, much later, my idea changed shape like the funny twisted pottery and metal bowls that survived the blast. The idea had taken on a* hibakusha *shape. It was a question now: How could I possibly have survived when you were not with me? Perhaps I didn't. Perhaps afterwards I was not alive, but something else.*

When I found Ishiru I did not recognize her but she recognized me and called out my name. And still, until she began to weep, I was not sure it was her. A man I did not know stood a hundred yards from her with a camera in his hands. He pointed it, and when his bulb flashed I fell down and stayed very still even as my mind assured me that it was only a flashbulb and a camera. Get up, my Ishiru said to me then, and see what I am before I leave you. Get up and listen to me say again that I love you, because I am leaving you soon. Then I touched her and felt her blackened skin fall into my hand. But she wept no more because she was done with weeping then. All around us dying people cried out for water. Cries came from the wreckage of buildings. I remember one little girl standing alone, stunned, all her clothes burned from her body and her face barely a face anymore, a perfectly preserved doll clutched to her chest, the doll's skin still pink and intact, her little doll dress quite spotless.

Here is something that many hibakusha *felt. Ishiru felt it. She said to me, If one of us must die I am glad that it is I who leaves this life. I am satisfied, she said. She believed that her death protected me, whom she loved. You must understand that all* hibakusha *who lived a part of their lives in this end-of-the-world place have believed that one person's death protects another from death.*

I would like to think of memories as things that flow from mind to mind in the shifting weather of history and mood. Some memories stand like a plant in the fields, breezes blowing at the details of the images or rain washing over them. Others are like castles or kingdoms full of kites and shrimp-stuffed tofu and all the deep attachments. The cicadas sing and beautiful paper flowers fill the torch-lit festival nights. I have these memories to give, and in my mind I toss them into the currents that carry the raccoon-lady spirit and the genbukusha *who died that day and the dancers and poets who comfort us when the warriors burn our cities.*

PART 4

Chinkon

Chinkon: . . . the ceremony for enabling the soul of a person hovering between life and death to achieve repose—either through urging it not to leave the body, or to return to the body if it had already left. . . . In subsequent usage the word also came to signify the pacification or even restraint of souls which had become restless, wayward, and dangerous to the living—whether because of being neglected or because their owners had died unnatural or violent deaths. Chinkon suggests a gentle atmosphere of respect and love, and above all a combination of continued connection with the dead and peaceful separation from them. It means "Requiem" or "Consolation of Souls."

—ROBERT LAY LIFTON,
Life After Death

Thirty-two

Henry was buried in a Catholic service. Lauren's parents insisted that the coffin be closed, and though this was a relief to her, she struggled with the desire to pry open the shellacked black lid and lay her hand on his chest. She wanted to feel the rise and fall that would reassure her, as it had when she stood at his bedroom door as a little girl who had dreamed of Henry's death, that he was well and she lived on under his protection.

She had gotten the call from Isobelle; she had been the one to tell everyone. Her parents received the news in a silence that felt silvery to Lauren—papery and worn, just the fragile skin of something. "Mom?" she called into the silence. "Dad? Mom, did you get Dad on the other telephone?" Then she heard a click, and she called out their names again.

"Your mother had to hang up, Lauren," her father's voice said.

"We'll call you as soon as we can." She had never heard his voice fail him. It shook wildly now. "Don't worry. Don't come rushing over here. Winston's at a radar convention in Germany, isn't he? Who's going to call Winston?" This last question was offered up in a horrified whisper and Lauren realized that her father was afraid. The idea of telling Winston of Henry's death terrified her father.

"Oh, Dad. I'll call. Don't worry. I'll do it."

Her father did not resist; if he had she would have argued. Little as she wanted her voice associated with this news, it was unimaginable to her that anyone else would carry it to Winston, who at this moment was sitting listening to a lecture on long-range software modifications for different temperature zones. She called Melanie and told her; got the telephone number of Winston's hotel. "Look, Lauren," her sister-in-law said. "He'll call me as soon as he gets off the telephone with you. Given that it was Henry . . . I think you should pick him up at the airport. Bring Robin—Robin calms him. Okay? Then bring him home to me."

It was the middle of the night in Germany. She called anyway.

"Who is this?" a half-asleep Winston demanded.

"It's me, Winston. I have to tell you something about Henry." She told him. They sat on opposite sides of the Atlantic holding their telephones and saying no more for a full five minutes. Then Winston said, "I don't believe you."

"I know."

They sat in silence for another few minutes. Then he said, "We're alone, Lauren."

She knew what he meant. He meant that in their own minds, Henry's and Lauren's and Winston's, the sense of a triumvirate with clear individual roles had persisted into adulthood—and now it was destroyed. Winston was no longer one of three. "I was at his apartment last week," Winston said. "You know, a year ago I brought these half-finished plans to him for the cottage I wanted to build on my property. He knew I meant for him to live in it, but we didn't talk about it in detail. I wanted the design to be his own, but he wouldn't finish those plans. I've been carrying those unfinished plans to him about once a month. If I had finished it, maybe just gone ahead and not waited for him to make decisions, maybe he would have been living there and closer to me every day and maybe he wouldn't have gone and this wouldn't have happened."

"There's a letter, Winston. He left one at the hospital for me and Robin, and it said that he was sending you a letter that said the same thing. He seems to be saying good-bye in it." She read it.

"What does this mean, about changing paths in ways that smooth them?"

"I don't know. But this whole note thing, Winston, I think it means Henry knew he was going to die."

"But you said it was a crazy farmer. You just said this person thought Henry was a deer and that the police called it a terrible accident. You don't plan encounters like that."

"That's true," she said to Winston now. But she didn't believe that what had happened could accurately be called an accident. She had already examined that idea and discarded it. She believed that when Henry had accepted Isobelle's invitation he could already see the farmer's facial expression, the exact look of the blowing corn, the exact place in the fence that would lead quickly to the man who had been ruined by rage. She thought this because she herself had seen these things in the dream she'd been having since childhood. No, no, she countered in her anxious conversations with herself. The place was merely an idea, just a part of her sleeping mind that had risen up enough to be seen—only a part of herself. Ideas were not things. This dream was only an idea from the sleeping world.

Why was she still here, and Henry gone? The question left the most terrible residue in her mouth, and a tightening band at the base of her throat.

These were *hibakusha* thoughts, she told herself, the kind that Henry had warned she would have—guilty thoughts.

"Did you tell Mom and Dad yet?"

"Yes."

"Did you tell them about this note?"

"It's only been a few hours, Winston."

"You didn't tell them about the note," he said. She nodded. She knew he couldn't see a nod but she couldn't speak. He said, "I'll go to the airport right now and I'll get on the first thing I can."

When she saw her surviving brother at the airport she barely recognized him. He was disheveled and his face was mottled and puffy. He looked like he'd been drinking, but Winston did not drink. Robin stood firmly by her side at the gate, holding her hand and keeping his eyes fixed on Winston, who was talking about something that had to do with baggage terminals. He smelled of new sweat, airplane air and airplane soap. She pictured him sitting in his seat on the flight, becoming aware that he was unraveling, making his way down the aisle, standing in the tiny airplane bathroom, trying to scrub his armpits and get his face back to normal with cold water. Failing.

"Do you want to go alone?" Robin had asked her only an hour before. "Or should I come?"

She turned dumbly to him, unhearing, unresponsive. Since Henry's death she had felt no hunger, though she ate. No cold: though she felt full of a vast cool space, it did not make her cold. She had burned herself on a teakettle because she had left an insensate finger too long on its heated surface. She looked down and saw the red puffy burn site now, in fact, but thought, I don't feel that. She could observe herself looking at a mark on her body and thinking, *That should hurt.*

She knew when Robin asked her if he should come that he had wanted her to say, "I need and want you to come with me," and that she hadn't been able to summon this. "Melanie said you should come," she had said instead. "I think Winston would be grateful if you came."

Now she listened to Winston as if he were at a great distance, speaking to Robin and saying, "You know, all the way back I had these terrible chest pains and I thought, well, Robin is a doctor and he'll be right outside the gate when I land and as long as he's there I don't have to worry. Where's Mel? Home? Oh, my God, of course. It's the middle of the night, isn't it? I mean, the kids are asleep! She's waiting for me?" The outlines of her brother's rumpled physical self had temporarily dissolved. The spiky, confrontative Winston had given way to a man who sagged as he struggled down the corridor, looking so sad he could hardly breathe much less make his way to the baggage carousels.

Robin opened his arms, saying, "This won't last forever." Winston stepped into them.

"What will we do? What will we do?" Winston cried then. And Lauren watched them and thought how strange it was that the two people in the world with whom she had the most complicated and heated connections both looked to her right now like projections on a screen. She walked with them to retrieve Winston's suitcase. She guided the car out of the parking garage, paid a person an amount of money, drove through the Callahan tunnel, up over the North End and then down to Chinatown and the turnpike. She got off at the right exit and made all the appropriate turns, arriving at Winston's home without remembering much of the trip. She sat with Winston and

Melanie and Robin in the kitchen for an amount of time, went with Robin back to her own home.

The only sensation to make its way to the surface during the weeks that followed was the achingly deep desire to have placed her hand on Henry's chest before he was buried. She was aware of Robin watching her anxiously and saying nothing. She was aware of eating food and going to bed and rising in the morning, but she didn't taste food or experience rest.

She went back to work and did things, but she could not have said what. Robin's attentions, his care, his questions, drove her deeper into unresponsiveness. Robin wrote her a prescription for an antidepressant. She accepted the bottle and tossed one pill into the toilet each day, just as Henry had done. Her senseless state wore on.

Robin watched her. He knew she threw the pills away and he said nothing because he didn't believe he should have given her the pills in the first place. The tangle of his own *hibakusha* feelings muddied his judgment. Robin was suffering his own thoughts, which ran something like: If I had intervened more aggressively with Henry, he would be alive. He couldn't talk about this with Lauren.

For her part, Lauren had stopped speaking unless it was necessary. She would not make love. She went more and more often to the studio to stare out windows rather than stare out of them at home, because she knew in some distant thinking part of herself that it upset Robin to find her sitting transfixed. Winston invited them to his home almost every day, was clearly in need of her and Robin, but after the first two weeks she stopped responding to him as well.

Winston had no Robin-like compunctions about respecting her period of grief; he was not too nice to demand things that he wanted from her. He got fed up. He showed up at her door one evening after she'd let weeks pass without returning his telephone calls. When she didn't respond to the knocks he yelled, "I saw your car on the block so I know you're home! Answer the door, Lauren!" She had retreated out of view of the front windows when he first knocked and he had seen a bit of movement as she drew away. This made him angrier. He marched to his car, popped open the trunk and removed a few tools. Within minutes Lauren could hear him dismantling the hinges to her front door. She thought about calling the police and reporting a break-in, but she didn't have the energy to deal with what would happen when they arrived, so she was still sitting on her bed when Winston finished hoisting the door out of the frame and tipping it to one side.

"You shouldn't have done that, Winston. You have to put the door back before you leave," she said dully.

"What is the matter with you?"

"What is the matter," she countered, "with you?"

"Cut it out, Lauren. I'm not asking you to feel fine. We don't feel fine and we're not going to feel fine for a while. But I tell you it helps to fake it if that's all you can manage at the moment—to pretend you're married, and employed, and that you sleep at night and work during the day. I've talked to Robin. I know what you've been like. And if you think I pay any attention to that psychobabble about 'giving people space' or 'letting grieving take its time' you can forget about it. You are not the only person in the world who lost Henry."

"Thank you for your thoughts and feelings, Winston. Don't forget to fix the door as you leave."

"Lauren, think of Robin. Think of your job. You're going to want them to be there for you on the other side of this. You have to protect them."

"Stop telling me what I have to do," she said. Winston only glared. She tried not to look at him, but she couldn't not look at him. "You're asking for too much."

"What you're calling 'too much' is the bare minimum for getting through."

"You know, Diana said something like that to me once. Something about how you had to go too far to get there because that's where 'there' is. I don't think I'm interested in going anymore, though."

She saw three bright tracks make their way down Winston's face, cutting through the dust left after his struggles with the front door. She felt an actual pang—an edged and sharpened unhappiness on her younger brother's behalf. She struggled back away from the feeling, trying to tamp it down, to extinguish it before it burst into flame. "Oh, Winston! Don't cry," she pleaded.

"You have to come back," he said. "It's just us, now."

"I didn't go away." She stretched out a hand and set it on his head. He stopped crying. "Don't worry. Come on. I'll help you rehang the door. Give me a screwdriver."

When he was gone she found she could not simply sit and stare as she had been doing before he came. She was left restless and shaken loose. What to do, what to do?

My Ishiru told me once that men blew up living things because they could not make any breathing thing out of their own flesh, like a woman makes a child, and this affected their minds in strange ways. If they had grown a human being in their own bodies and cared for it in its infancy, she would say, they would not so often argue that it was necessary to drop bombs on human beings. As to blowing things up, the attraction some men have to planes and guns and bombs, she spoke of this as a kind of sexual confusion. Many kinds of grief, she used to believe, made their ways into lives as kinds of sexual confusion. I imagine she was right. After the pica-don *I saw many things of a sexual nature happen that could not have happened, I am sure, unless the world had been exploded.*

My wife never said these things beyond the edges of our tatami mats, and we were married many years before she said them to me. She said them because the war was closing in on us and we were not sure of our lives. She said them because she loved me and she wanted me to know her mind. She did not count me among the men who blew things up in order to feel alive. I think, though, that other men could feel these ideas in her and it did not please them. Other men wondered at my deep happiness with her.

Then she died and I was in Hell alone, where I wandered among the living ghosts of Hiroshima's alleys and cardboard houses. For a time I did what was possible without knowing for sure what exactly it was that I did. I stopped speaking. I remember watching a man, a silent man, breaking apart the funeral tablets of his ancestors with an ax. Even the sheepdogs that roamed about did not bark. The trees, the plants, all that lived seemed numb, without movement or color. Hiroshima was a splintered bit of the end of the world. We hibakusha, we survivors, we were failed suicides.

I do not remember my own death, which did not come for me for more than a year. Almost all we hibakusha died in the confusion that comes at the end of the blood cancer that the pica-don made, a cancer called leukemia. They called many of us schizophrenic. They said our minds had been damaged.

I had hoped, as I died, that my first sight when next I held consciousness would be Ishiru, with whom I hoped to share eternity. And I did see her, but it was not her. The crooked teeth and long neck she wore in life were nowhere to be found. She moved in a way I would call fluttering, and white masses flowed away from her to either side of what I think was her self. "Ishiru!" I cried, "I know it is you because I smell your skin. I smell it not as a memory but as it scented the air I breathed in life."

Ishiru spoke to me but not in words. Still, I understood her. She said, "I have waited for you, my Asagao. I waited to remind you of how I loved you before I returned to life."

"Do you return as a butterfly, my beloved?" I cried, for my father had always said that butterflies were the spirits of good people. "How will we *speak together all through the long nights if you are a butterfly when I find you in my next life?"*

"You need not worry. We will find a way to speak, however you find me."

"Will I find you?"

"Of course you will find me, beloved. But you will not know me when we see one another again. And I will not know you. All the love I feel in my next life will have clinging to it the darkness that came when I lost you—everything I come to care for will cast your shadow. What you have been to me will follow and guide me at once. I will find you again."

"And I will truly find you?"

"I am sure of it."

"But we shall not know one another when we meet again?"

"Asagao, we never have remembered one another, but see how we have managed to become lovers again and again. So you must release me from waiting now, and trust."

I did not have the stomach to release her of my own will. I am ashamed to say that I tried to capture her but could not. I grabbed at the white wings, the spray of little lights in her wake. She eluded me. And then, just above my head, she changed again. She became not a butterfly but a stream of shining particles that whipped from side to side like the neck of an animal seeking something, and then they found what they sought. They vanished.

I am kept from my next life, I fear, by my refusal to accept that when I see her, our spirit memories will be asleep to one another. I will accept it soon, though, I know, and then I will move from this plane to another.

The Buddhist priests say that love is the greatest obstacle to the Way. This is what makes me sure I am a bad Buddhist. The Black Robe Bodhisatva they called Jesus says that love itself is the Way, and that idea better matches my experience among the living.

But then, his followers eat him. So what can we make of that?

• • •

At one A.M. Lauren gave up on hopes that Robin would return home to sleep between shifts. He wasn't coming. He hadn't come home now for longer than it took to change clothes or eat in more than a week. She scrawled a note: "Went to the office."

Then she rose and made her way through a drizzle down black reflective city streets to her car. She drove silently past the lights of Quincy Market, down into the bowels of the expressway tunnel, up again and onto the long ribbon of turnpike and then to the parking lot, the little alley dividing the old federal brownstone from a drugstore.

She had settled in long enough to review a pile of new promotional photographs before she noticed a line of light flicking down the stairs from the largest dance studio. A steady soft thumping began just over her head. She sat bolt upright, aware that she was frightened. How interesting, she thought, in the part of her that was hardening and distancing and seeing things differently. I feel something. She listened more carefully. Handel. What vandal or thief would break into a dance studio to listen to Handel? And though she was less frightened now, she still armed herself with a heavy metal flashlight before marching up the stairs to confront the intruder.

It was Morel. His hand flew to his heart when he saw her. "You look like a ghost! When I walked past your door I just thought someone had left a light on in the office," he said. "It didn't occur to me that anyone would actually be in there at this hour."

"I've been working odd hours."

"Your brother," he replied, nodding. "I know. I'm sorry about your brother. I've meant to drop by your office to say that but, as you say, you haven't been keeping predictable hours."

"What are you doing here?"

"I come here often in the middle of the night when I'm in town. In New York I live in my studio, so I'm used to having the space to work in whenever I want. It's a challenge on the road. Motels. But I've always loved working like this, imagining all those sleeping people on every street in the city, everyone around me unconscious." He smiled but not at her.

"How did you get in?"

"I have John's key. He knows my nighttime habits and took pity on me."

He dug into a pocket and produced it—held the little piece of glittering metal toward her.

"No, no. Keep the key," she said, "until your work here is done."

"Thank you." A car entered the rotary beneath the studio's windows, and its lights bounced from the mirrors into Morel's face. The car beams tracked across the room, flicking from Morel's face to his hand and the key.

"Why don't you have the overheads on?" she asked.

"I like the light from the street."

"But you can't see what you're doing," she protested. She stepped toward the wall and the light switch. Morel intercepted her, reached out and stopped her hand with his own.

Something like an electric current passed through her hand to the arm, the chest, then downward. Her face twisted upward, startled, and she found his face directly before it, looking at her with perfect concentration. Moreover, it felt familiar, as if it were an expression she had known always. She did not step away.

He kissed her. Then she was not aware of any actual thoughts, any words in her mind that would have named what she was doing as sex or adultery. It was simply a cascade of effects leading to an end that felt like a splintering implosion. In the aftermath she lay very still, her eyes closed and her senses snapped loose, and behind her closed eyes she felt the presence of something like gently swirling particles, blowing and tingling, moving in deep quiet to the limit of her skin. The sensation didn't make her afraid, though in some part of her mind she knew that it should have. She was aware of feeling fully alive for the first time since the telephone call from Isobelle's country house.

And after he had left, she thought, I'm going to live.

In the week that followed she avoided Morel on the one day he was in town. She found herself shaken loose from her old insensibility in ways that were terrible. She became newly aware of and vulnerable to Robin's grief. She became, again, palpably aware of the fact that she loved her husband and that this feeling was, in some mysterious way, unbearably painful. Robin was kind to her as he had been kind a hundred times—an attempt at a joke or a quiet touch, only today it cut her to the heart where a matter of days ago she had not even felt it. How could he be so kind to her? She could not drive more than a couple of miles without pulling over to the side of the road, blind with tears. Tears salted everything she cooked, stained all her clothes and flowed through every conversation. Sometimes at work she simply hung up the telephone mid-conversation to weep.

When she finally faced Morel again the encounter was startling for its lack of feeling. She saw him first, coming toward her in the stairwell leading from the office to the studio. She felt the cloth of his shirt brush her shoulder. But this figure walking up to the studio held no meaning for her whatsoever, and she could tell by Morel's first searching and then confused expression that his own experience was the same.

At the end of the day he appeared suddenly in her office, his body awkwardly propped against a doorjamb and his expression still searching, still surprised. She had never seen him physically awkward, and the sight amused her. "It's all right," she began. She thought but did not say, I don't want anything from you. I don't want you to expect anything from me.

"This is my last contracted day with the company," he began. "I got on a plane this morning eager to see you—sweating, in fact, I was so eager. I was going to ask you to come to New York. To keep seeing me."

"But now you don't think that's a good idea," she finished for him. He said nothing in response so she continued. "It's not. I wouldn't have said yes if you'd come here still wanting to say it. You feel like it went from so much to nothing at all. Right?"

Morel hesitated a moment. "Yes," he admitted. "But not like anything else I've experienced. Not casual."

"I know. I know exactly what you mean."

"I'm sorry it feels like this now. I don't understand what happened. It was extraordinary."

"Yes." She only wanted him to leave. She knew what he meant, but the fact that their encounter had indeed been extraordinary was irrelevant to her now. She was remarkably free of all kinds of reactions that only a short while ago would have dominated her entirely.

"It could come back," he said hopefully. "It might come back."

She shook her head decisively. It was not going to come back. It was done with them. "You'll miss the last hourly shuttle if you don't get going," she said. "Good-bye."

He dropped the key to the studio on her desk before he turned to go, and then it was entirely, completely, over. She didn't understand, but she wasn't afraid.

Thirty-three

Three weeks later she looked in the mirror and wondered why her breasts were so swollen when it was the week after rather than before her period. Then it occurred to her that her period hadn't happened. In the following week the smell of coffee began to bother her. She stopped at a drugstore on the way to work and bought a pregnancy kit. At the end of the afternoon she locked herself in the office bathroom, pulled the kit out of its paper bag and followed the instructions. The test stick turned blue—the pregnant color. A thick wave of tiredness moved up her body. When it reached her shoulders she put her head down and fell into a deep sleep.

She woke an hour later. Dusk. A light rain.

She would simply tell him immediately, she decided. The moment she got in the apartment she found Robin in the kitchen slicing vegetables. She dug in her briefcase and pulled out the little blue stick. She held it up.

Then she watched his initial joy fade as he counted the weeks and calculated the last time they'd made love in relation to that narrow window of opportunity. "It's not me," he said at last.

"No. It isn't."

"I can't believe it. I can't believe it."

"Robin," she began, but he cut her off with a violent shake of his head.

"I don't need to listen to you. I don't want to hear what you have to say."

"But I'm pregnant. You have to listen."

"You're mistaken. I do not."

She stepped toward him and he turned on her. "If you come any closer I will hurt you. I may hurt you badly, in fact. Just step out of my way."

She did this. Ten minutes later he came out of their bedroom with a duffel bag stuffed with his possessions. "I'm staying in the residents' dorm for a while."

"What's 'a while'?"

"I have no idea."

Then he was gone.

Thirty-four

Robin stayed away, occasionally returning to the apartment to retrieve a book or article of clothing, and choosing his times to be fairly sure that Lauren wouldn't be in. He'll talk to me in a week when he cools down, she thought. He'll talk to me in a few weeks.

But an entire trimester went by in this paralyzing fashion, broken by notes or brief answering machine messages on practical matters. *Remember the oil bill. Please renew my* JAMA *subscription when the notice comes. Leave my mail on the kitchen table in a pile.* This was what he said to her. Never, *Are you in love with this other person?* Never, *Do you still love me?* Never, *Apologize for what you did. Say you're wrong!* Only, *There's a book of Winston's that I left under the bed that I'd like you to return to him, please.*

Only a few months ago such a breach would have terrified her. Now she accepted it with grief and calm.

As the pregnancy deepened she grew both physically and mentally slower. Her nausea regularly worked up to a disgusting pitch until the fifteenth week, when it vanished utterly. Still, the baby managed to keep her awake half the night every night, thinking and squirming and jabbing fists or feet into her ribs. Moreover, Lauren was certain that the child had begun to eat parts of her mind.

First, the baby ate specific words. Language like "door" or "tuna fish" flew out of her head, leaving her pointing to what she meant and saying things like, "wooden rectangle that swings open and shut" or "dolphins get killed accidentally when it's caught." Then sequencing became harder to maintain. Lauren could get a letter that needed John's signature written, and she could go up to the studio to get him to sign it, but once there she generally could not remember why she had climbed the steps even when the letter was clutched in one hand. She would retreat again to the office, holding the letter and struggling to remember why she had woken as if from a dream to find herself on the stairs, going she knew not where.

Some of the sorrow that had darkened her mind was eaten, too. Thoughts of Henry softened. She dreamed of Robin, and her dreams were happy. She only remembered the breach in their marriage when she woke. In sleep, she was still newly in love with him. Everything between them was clear and light. In her dreams he had never applied to new residency programs, they had never stood by and watched the joy drain away from their physical lives, she had never sexually betrayed him.

One night she woke suddenly, ravenous and wide-eyed. Two A.M. She lay still and pretended to sleep. She got up and ate a sandwich. She lay down again. Finally she rose, got a broom and started cleaning floors. She poked the broom under the bed and when it emerged, one of Robin's little plastic wizards was hooked in the bristles. She brushed the berobed figure off and brought him into the bathroom, where she stuck him under a stream of running water. She set the wizard by her bed with his gaze fixed directly on her and she lay down again. "Make the baby go to sleep," she said to the wizard. "Help me get some rest."

She did not wake until the sun was so high there were no shadows on the city streets. She dressed, dropped the wizard in a pocket and drove with him to the hospital. There a few inquiries directed her to the cafeteria, where she found Robin sitting alone in a wide band of sunlight by the windows, eating a bowl of cereal and flipping through a pile of folders. She sat down directly opposite him and set the wizard on the table at the edge of his folders. His eyes tracked from the wizard to her face. Robin looked worn and grubby. Three smears of clotted blood showed where he had nicked himself shaving. A line of gray dirt was visible around his cuffs. He saw her looking at them; he turned the cuffs up. "I wondered where this one was," Robin said, accepting the wizard. "How are you feeling?"

"Robin, you don't understand what happened."

"Yes, I do."

"No, you don't. I didn't have an affair. It was more like walking into some kind of explosion. It was like getting caught in a spasm."

"Is that what you call it when you describe it to yourself?"

"Henry was dead. I couldn't feel anything. You and I were so distant from one another."

"I was never distant."

"You were maybe hanging in there by a thread. A little breeze would have carried you off, much less the windstorm I was in when Henry died."

He sat silently, tense; deeply unhappy. "You didn't tell me about the miscarriage. Or about Sally," he said.

"Robin, in my family, Sally isn't real. She's like a ghost. No one had spoken her name out loud in our house since I was maybe nine years old. And as to my miscarriage, I was a coward and a fool to keep things from you that I know you would have wanted to know. I wanted a baby more, I think, than I wanted you. More than I wanted peace of mind or anything else I could think of."

"Do you think what you're saying now is supposed to undo what has happened?" Robin's feelings twisted up into his face. "I don't even know you."

"That can be rectified."

"You were supposed to say that I *do* know you," he said. She had surprised him.

"Robin, something's shifted in me and I want something to shift in you, too. I'm stepping forward here. You should pay attention to what I'm doing because it's what you've always wanted from me. Things that I was afraid of all my life have happened, and I'm still here and they're not in my way anymore. They're behind me. I'm in love with you. I always was, but now it's . . ."

"It's what?"

"Not the same. Do you realize that a part of me was always waiting for you to disappear and I didn't even know it?"

"I was never going to disappear."

"The joke on me is that now you really have disappeared. I wake up every day looking for you. Take a chance on me, Robin." Her hand brushed his and he jerked it away.

"I already did."

"I am so sorry that I hurt you, Robin, but I can't get a new past and neither can you. I have the future to offer you, and that's what I'm doing. It's a different future than the one I had to offer you only a matter of weeks ago. And there's a baby in this future." She rose and pushed herself away from the table. "I love you. You can have this child with me. Or not. Right now I'm giving you the power to decide which, but that power won't be in your hands forever."

Once she was out of sight his own anxious, exhausted momentum carried him out of the cafeteria and back to his office, where he automatically flicked on the X-ray panel lights and clipped a series of brains up to examine. The film could not hold his attention. He couldn't keep the data on the presenting symptoms straight, or the prescribed drug trail, or the family history.

He found himself striding along in the corridors, vaguely retracing his rounds route. There in a chair outside room 23A sat a compact little man wearing wing-tipped shoes: Mr. D. H. Miriam, husband of room 23A's occupant, his patient Mrs. D. H. Miriam. Mrs. Miriam had been admitted because she could not sleep. At first her legs had jiggled and then she started pacing and finally, unable to stop moving, she had surrendered to whatever was happening to her and pushed the furniture in the living room to the walls so she could dance all night. A simple check of the *Physicians' Desk Reference* had noted this unusual side effect to a psychotropic medication in amounts that Mrs. Miriam had exceeded long before the dancing began. Robin had admitted her to observe while they tapered off the medication and found an alternative.

"Doc! Good to see you," he greeted Robin. "Sit down." Mr. Miriam patted the other chair, and Robin obeyed, coming to rest by the old man's side.

"How are you, Mr. Miriam?" he asked.

"I'm glad to see you. Is there a cafeteria around here? I could use an ice-cream cone in the worst way." Robin began to give Mr. Miriam directions to the cafeteria. "What I meant, really, Doc, is that I could use a conversation with you along with the ice cream. Come on. I'm buying."

They strolled companionably to the cafeteria, Mr. Miriam choosing a Nutty Buddy and Robin a frozen fruit bar. "What I wanted to say," Mr. Miriam began, peeling the Nutty Buddy wrapper off in a long spiral and taking a nip at the chocolate topping, "is that I want you to be my wife's doctor and I want you to tell her not to take pills. Which she knows already, but coming from a doctor it has more ka-boom."

"I read her records, Mr. Miriam. She's been diagnosed as depressed. Pills can help those conditions."

"They aren't looking at her. They don't know her. They just want to slap a word on her that fits a pill. The woman is not depressed."

"What would you call it?"

"The woman has suffered from occasional active, aggressive states of despair. There is no pill for it. I know. I've been there."

"I don't understand."

"You're a young man, but it's possible I may be able to explain so I'll go on. We lost a son, the most beautiful young man I'd ever seen in my life. He was kind, too, and in the young it is very rare indeed to find kindness. But he had it. Vietnam came, and when he came home without his legs, we noticed that a good deal of his heart was also missing. He was lost. He was defenseless, so six months later when he got sick, the infection just took him away.

"We went through losing him twice, and the first time I thought, *She's so strong. She's my rock.* But the second time she wasn't a rock. She isn't sick; she's just human."

"What do you want me to say to her, Mr. Miriam?"

"Tell her we should take in a foster kid. Tell her it's not over, and we can fall in love with someone new. Tell her that."

"Okay, Mr. Miriam. I can talk to her."

The Nutty Buddy and the frozen fruit bar had met their respective ends. Mr. Miriam stood. "Thank you for helping my wife," the man said. "You're a good boy." Then Mr. Miriam leaned over and hugged Robin, giving him a dry, cool kiss on the cheek as he stood again. He stopped a few feet away to say, "You know, even if I had to lose him all over again, I'd do whatever I could to get him back. I'd do it even knowing what it was going to feel like to lose him. Isn't that an amazing thing?"

Robin nodded. Amazing.

His hand dropped into his pants pocket and found the wizard, which he withdrew. He spit on the little plastic head and polished it idly against his chest. "Well," he said to it at last. "What should I do?"

The dance studio's line rang three times before Lauren picked it up. "It's Robin," he said. "Lauren, if I got home around six would you be there?"

"Yes."

When Robin's key turned in the door she was stepping out of the shower. When she walked into the bedroom he was sitting on the bed. They faced each other quietly.

The middle trimester had left her rounded and firm, iconically feminine. "Robin, feel this." She opened his hand and laid it palm down on her abdomen. "Wait." She was rewarded by the bright shock in his face when the baby kicked. He snapped his hand away. Then he put it back.

Robin had not seen her body during the last months as its center had rounded and tightened into an egg-shaped drum. "You aren't even recognizable," he said when he saw her now.

She was not entirely recognizable to herself. This complicated her responses to Robin, made her feel as if this were the first time they had ever been lovers. She couldn't predict herself or him, and their physical reactions to one another startled both of them.

"That was frightening," she said to him much later as they both lay covered in sweat.

"Jesus," he responded. "What's happening to us?"

"I don't know," she said. "But something happened."

She said these words in perfect happiness, but directly behind them she could feel other things. Lauren swung her legs over the side of the bed and set them gingerly onto the floor. "I don't feel right," she observed, not alarmed—only commenting.

"Not right how?" Robin asked, still prone.

"Do it. Try to stand up," she suggested.

Robin swung his own legs over the bed. "I can't feel my feet," he observed. He stood. "I think my legs are shaking but I'm not sure. I can't really feel them, either."

"They're shaking," Lauren assured him. She stood up too, disoriented and giddy.

So they began the mysterious trip back to each other.

Thirty-five

She felt a blow—some hand or foot trying to knock a rib out of its way. The jab snapped her upright. Such a strange sensation, to be struck from the inside of one's own body.

Passing a mirror that afternoon she saw that the baby had moved into what had once been her waistline. She had to formally tell her family members what they probably already knew.

"I knew it!" Winston said when she told him and Melanie that she was pregnant. "I knew it wasn't just that you'd gained twenty pounds! But Melanie said it would be rude to ask and what if I was wrong."

"Twenty pounds?"

"Oh, yes. You've gotten rounder all over," Melanie assured her. "I'd say puffy but I don't want to hurt your romantic illusions about pregnancy being a period of glowing beauty. Here." She pulled

Lauren over to a mirror. "Look at your face. Pink and white and kind of purplish, all in spots. Pregnancy glow my ass. Do your legs and feet hurt yet?"

"The baby just started kicking me," Lauren told them.

"Oh, isn't it the weirdest thing you've ever felt?" Melanie cried. "And it tingles! Like having a little battery in the middle of your body. What did Robin say?"

"He's ecstatic, of course."

She called her parents and told them she was pregnant. "Oh, Lauren," her mother cried, "I was right! I was sure that you and Robin were trying all along when years went by and there weren't any announcements! I prayed to the Immaculate Virgin Mary for you! I believe that this is the first time in my life that my prayers were actually answered! I prayed to Mary that whatever you needed for your happiness would come to you."

"Thank you, Mom."

"And your father said you were just gaining weight! Men!"

The dance company's home season sold out, and a touring season just big enough to hold them in the black had been scraped together. It took them as far west as Chicago and as far south as Tulane University. Diana returned to the company with every part of her body except the foot stronger than it had been before the accident. John went to New York, found three young hopefuls and returned with them in tow. Elena moved to Brooklyn and began the following season with Morel's company. She and John adjusted to the commuting. He was steady and cheerful—he did not cast himself in a single piece after she left. The board approved Lauren's hiring an assistant to carry the company through a brief pregnancy leave and make it possible for her to come back to work without having sole responsibility for the entire operation.

As the pregnancy reached its last weeks Lauren's pelvic bones popped apart and she had difficulty walking. She and Winston were consciously trying to infuse their relationship with Henry's old peaceful influence. They were keenly aware of their dependence on each other.

The day Lauren's daughter was born she had driven to Winston's house. She found him in the cottage he had gone ahead and built, even though Henry could never need it now. He was sitting in it, looking over landscaping plans at a makeshift desk of sawhorses and an unhung door.

"He did the lighting design before he died," he told her as soon as she crossed the threshold. "It's just been installed. See the floods on the landscaping? And the way the light sources inside are hard to even locate? Cool, huh?"

"It's beautiful, Winston. Henry would have loved it."

"Iffy's already fallen in love with it. I'll give it to her as a playhouse. Melanie says it's perfect for girl sleepover parties."

"Ah."

"And Mom and Dad are planning to stay here when their kitchen is being remodeled. I guess I could see a time in the future when they would live here—when it got to be too much for them to run their own house."

"I didn't know their kitchen was going to be remodeled."

"Their kitchen is being remodeled." Winston pushed the plans to one side.

Her water broke.

"Oh, God," she said.

"What? What?"

"Do you have the telephone line run out here yet? I think I want to call my doctor. I don't know what to do."

"Didn't they teach you that at the classes Robin made you take?" Winston's voice cracked.

"If they did I don't remember. Do you have a telephone?"

She didn't call her OB-GYN. She called Robin, who told her that some doctors would suggest that she check in to a hospital right now and get induced, and others would suggest that she hang around and wait for contractions. "Well, what do you think?" she asked him.

"How do you feel?"

"Besides the fact that there's a steady drip going down one leg and all over the floor, I feel normal."

"Maybe you should wait then."

"You're not much help here, Robin. What do you mean, 'maybe'?"

"I meant maybe yes. Maybe no."

"I'm calling my OB-GYN, and Winston is going to take me to the hospital."

"I'll meet you in maternity."

"This could take forever; just pretend I didn't call. I promise I'll beep you if I'm induced or if the contractions get serious. I promise." She hung up on him before he could say anything else. "Come on, Winston," she told her brother. "You're taking me to the hospital."

"My car seats! I have to get a towel!" Winston was looking at the puddle around her feet in horror.

"So get the towel. My God, Winston, did Melanie give birth without your seeing anything at all? It's just fluid, for Christ's sake."

"What's that?" Winston asked in horror. A red, almost magenta, trickle joined the clear liquid pool at Lauren's feet.

"I'd say that was blood," Lauren replied.

"Oh, my God!"

"Winston, everything will be fine. Completely fine." Her tone was relaxed enough to calm Winston, and she sent him off to tell Melanie that he was taking her to the hospital. He returned with four towels, which he layered on the passenger seat. A contraction buckled Lauren over in half just as she was about to get in. She turned away from the car door and vomited into the lawn.

"The contractions are supposed to be weak at first!" Winston protested.

Lauren managed to get herself into the car but she couldn't get the seat belt on. Winston pressed himself between her belly and the dash, found the clip and buckled her in. His hands were shaking.

"Winston, nobody dies giving birth nowadays. Almost nobody, anyhow. Calm yourself. You'd think you were the one whose water just broke."

She had three more contractions by the time they reached the hospital, one requiring that they pull over to the side of the road so she could open the door and vomit onto the pavement. Winston was clearly relieved to turn her over to the nurses in maternity, who greeted her cheerfully.

"Dial Robin's beeper," she gasped. "You don't have to worry about a thing. Go on home, Winston."

"No. No, I'm not leaving."

"All right. If you're not going to leave you're going to have to pretend to be less nervous."

"I'll try." Winston looked so anxiously helpless at that moment, so much like the five-year-old boy who had sawed apart bedboards and dismembered electrical outlets, that Lauren felt a pang. She smiled at him until the next contraction cut her off.

Robin trotted down the hall toward them. "How many centimeters?" he called as he ran along.

"I have no idea. Not many, I'd guess."

"Come into the exam room for a second and I'll be able to tell."

Robin did a quick dilation measurement: four centimeters. He went back to his office and returned with two brown paper bags. "I've been getting ready for this," he explained. "They told us at the class to find some kind of distracting way to spend the time while you waited for the delivery." Inside the bags were dance magazines, news magazines, a game of Scrabble and a game of Stop and Shop. "You did say you used to like Stop and Shop," he protested when she swept them to one side. "Cards, then. Come on, Winston." Robin grinned at his brother-in-law. "How about a round of Old Maid?"

"Don't you have to be on duty?" Lauren hissed. "I am busy here, Robin! I don't have time for a card game! Maybe you could find some reason that Winston has to go home, too."

"I do not have to be on duty," Robin said. "I wouldn't miss this for the world, and everybody in this hospital who knows me knows that. I have coverage for the next two weeks, every minute, if I want it. I'm not going anywhere."

"Maybe I could do some errand?" Winston suggested. They sent him home.

Three hours later the contractions were not regular, and Lauren's cervix was not one millimeter more dilated. "The membrane has been broken for hours, Lauren," Robin said soberly. "We should do the Pitocin."

"Who's this 'we'?"

"It's up to you. Certainly. And the OB-GYN on duty."

"You're not going to cave in to that hierarchical doctor crap on me now, Robin. You're going to back me up, no matter what the OB-GYN on duty wants."

"Yes. Of course."

Four hours later, still no more dilated, Lauren agreed to the Pitocin. Fetal heart monitors were attached and her abdomen became a lacework of wires. Two minutes after the Pitocin drip started, crashing full-scale contractions began washing over her every two minutes. She barely had time to recover from the last before the next approached. The pain was so obliteratingly total that she lost awareness of anything but it. The only way to meet the waves of pain, she found, was to duck—to sink down as deeply into them as she could get as they gathered energy and approached and try her best to get them to break over rather than into her. It was the difference between being on the surface as they collapsed into curls and foam, and being in the quiet, slower body of water beneath the movement—inside it.

"Why isn't this going anywhere?" she gasped, clutching the sides of the gurney. Her eyes sought out Robin, sought out the furniture and the monitor and the chair—all the things on the surface that had vanished in the last contraction.

"It's probably the state called hypertonic uterine inertia," Robin said. "That just means that the uterus contractions aren't efficient—they're originating all over the muscle at the same time, like a heart that's gone into atrial fibrillation."

"You mean it's like a heart attack in my uterus?" Robin nodded. It was. "What do I need to do?" she gasped again.

"Do? I don't think there's anything you can do. You just have to wait until the uterus gets its electrical impulses organized and starts contracting at the top and moving in a wave to the bottom."

"All right. I think I can do that."

"You mean you can wait?"

"No. I mean I can get the uterus to do that."

"It's an involuntary muscle, Lauren. It's like the heart. You can't make your uterus do a thing."

"I'm going to make it do that thing, that wave thing from top to bottom."

The anesthesiologist on duty approached to introduce himself.

"You have a long way to go, dear. I'll check back before the end of my shift," he said, clapping Robin on the back as he hurried out.

"Here comes another one." Her face closed. She sank down and waited for it.

"That contraction was different," Robin said, watching her anxiously. "What happened?"

"I can feel it move from the top to the bottom," Lauren hissed. "I'm too far along for an epidural, aren't I?"

Robin examined her quickly. "Yep," he answered. "Too far. Too late."

Her face closed again. "Shit," she said.

He waited for her to come back from the pain. She returned.

"Remember, no unnecessary episiotomy," she gasped. "You're in charge of that—no unnecessary episiotomy. Okay?"

"I love you." He smiled. She vanished again, going down. Then one of the monitors plunged and Robin's calm disintegrated. "Her blood pressure's gone!" he yelled. "Assist in here! Assist!" Lauren lost awareness of anything, even the pain. She could feel people rushing into the room. Her arm was jabbed. She could see Robin again. The room had emptied as quickly as it had filled—everyone had moved to the emergency delivery of triplets in the next room over. Screams from the mother and bustle from the staff could be heard through the walls.

"Nobody dies giving birth, anymore, Robin," she said when his face came into view again. She could see that something had happened to her that made him afraid, though she did not know what it was. "You know that. I am fine."

"You're crowning!" he answered. A nurse moving from room to room heard him and called a nurse practitioner in. The OB-GYN was too occupied with the screaming mother of triplets to come to this relatively normal delivery. The nurses stood at the foot of Lauren's bed. They called out, "Push! Push!"

Lauren raised herself on her elbows. "Shut up, shut up, shut UP!" she demanded. "Everybody leave me alone!"

"We're fine," Robin said placatingly to the nurses. "I'll call if anything happens."

The nurses obeyed him, reflexively honoring his white coat and doctor ID tag where they would have brushed a civilian father into the hallway. The baby appeared seven minutes later, and was laid on Lauren's chest.

"What a bloody mess," she breathed. "Is there supposed to be this much blood?"

"I think so," Robin answered, in tears, "but I don't remember enough of my OB-GYN rotation to know."

It was a few moments short of midnight. Lauren swore she and the baby were leaving by nine A.M., but that she would agree to stay put until then. Robin convinced her to let the staff check the baby's vital signs. She insisted on taking the baby back to bed with her rather than putting her in the nursery. They lay spooned together and slept for two hours before waking to find Robin by their side, snoring in the visitor's chair.

"She's so quiet," she said, waking him.

"That's just the first few hours," he mumbled. "She's in shock. But she'll recover tomorrow or the next day and cry for three months. That's what happens. Go back to sleep now while you can."

The baby woke her two hours later, crying. Lauren held her up to look her in the face, and the newborn looked right back, her little eyes widening in what looked like amazement at what she saw. "I do look pretty shocking, don't I?" Lauren whispered. Robin was not in his chair by her side. The hallway lights had been dimmed, and the nursing station lights were too far away to make her clearly visible as she slipped out of her room, the baby in her arms, and limped out of the maternity ward, waddling slightly to accommodate the pads between her legs.

Robin had a narrow cubicle stuck at the back of the radiology department. She found him there with a glowing series of images set in a row on the light box. There was a cot in the cubicle, and a desk heaped with MRI files and CAT scan reports. The images now hanging to the side of his desk were, as they usually were, of a head, its brain lit up into lobes and swirling patterns.

He reached out for the baby and she passed the little bundle to him. He looked down. "We have to name her to check her out of the hospital."

Lauren leaned forward to read the name written on the bottom of the film image that sat on the light board. She could make out the outlines of the skull and the lobes of the brain. Two darker patches marked the eye sockets. "This is Henry," she whispered.

"I know."

"Why is Henry out here?"

"I look at him at least once a week," Robin confessed.

"What do you look for, Robin?"

"I don't know anymore. I just keep doing it, though. I used to find it disturbing, but now it's comforting."

The lights in Henry's mind floated like things caught in the whorls of the brain's lobes. Most were like dots of light; some glowed like colored lanterns. The brain stem looked like a channel leading out to an enormous darkness beneath the brain. Lauren imagined the little lights bobbing along and away, out of their endlessly circling whorls and on to some other place. Some unknown place.

"Unidentified Bright Objects," she said.

"Yes," he answered. "I know." Meaning, she realized, not that he knew what the term meant to a radiologist, which he did, but that he too was mystified about these lanterns and their destinations, which all seemed to lie beyond the dark channels of the mind.

Thirty-six

After the paper flower lanterns have been carried to the graves to greet the visiting dead, after the Market of the Dead has opened and begun selling its paper lotuses and honorable boiled food and honorable cooked food, the little stick bundles of hashi *are lit to welcome the ghosts. Then the temple gongs call people to the festival of Yakushi-Nyora, who is the Physician of Souls. The people cast their offerings into alms chests and send up prayers for their own particular dead. The insect sellers cry out behind the rows of tiny cages and dancing gotcha-gotchas. Paper flowers lit from within by tiny clay lamps float above the stalls, and their flickering makes them seem utterly alive, more like their insect than their rooted vegetable brethren. I loved the Festival of the Dead above all other festivals.*

The courting-age young girls and boys love this festival best, too. They love it for its bon odori, *the dance that is the one time in the year when they are allowed to touch one another in a public place, in a pri-*

vate way. The Dead are not so alive to them as their own hopes for love. The young dancers anticipate it as a moment of romance—the moment perhaps when they will meet the one who will love them forever. They are so young that this idea makes them only full of happy anticipation.

So at the appropriate time, the elders fall back to give the dance to these eager seeking youth. They may be in costume or disguise. They may not be. Every time I danced it I could feel the spirits' happiness inside my own body. Usually I felt it in my scalp, but occasionally it inhabited the chest. The night I first touched Ishiru's hand as I took a place beside her in the dancing line, I felt a happiness so large I knew it could not be mine alone. It was theirs, too, the Dead who came to be amused and greeted and bid farewell. Perhaps it was happiness spilled over into my life from previous lives of my own, as well as the lives of our honorable spirit visitors.

In the evening shadows of the festival's last day the priests feed the gaki, *the Hungry Spirits, who come to the terrible Circle of Penance. We come to the Gakido to make offerings of* segaki *and thus encourage the citizens of the unseen world to leave us. They do not belong with us, though they are tempted—we, too, are sometimes tempted. But they must leave.*

Then one day I found myself at the Gakido. This was the first Festival of the Dead I had attended as a spirit, though I had died so many years ago. I found myself moving along the river of paper lotus-blossom lanterns between the Market of the Dead and the graveyards of Hiroshima. I smelled the senko's burning perfume and saw the little boats being prepared. I passed doors with the stick pushed through the holly leaf and the fish head nailed to the planks to keep away the evil Dead.

I will tell you how the segaki *and the* Bon odori *dance came to be. There is a story that Dai-Mokenren, the great disciple of Buddha, was permitted to see the soul of his mother in Gakido, which, sadly, is a place of eternal hunger. Mokenren filled a bowl with his mother's most beloved foods and offered it to her, but when she lifted it to her lips, it licked up into her face as flames. Mokenren begged the Buddha to spare his mother from the hunger torment, and the Buddha granted his wish. Mokenren's mother danced with joy to be finally, for that moment, unhungry.*

That is why on the fifteenth day of the seventh month the Dead are offered foods and dances. On this night they can be satisfied. When I found myself for the first time at the Bon-matsuri *as a spirit, I passed those of the seen and the unseen world at once, and I looked among them for Ishiru. But I will tell you a shocking thing. I saw among the Dead not my wife but a Black-Robed Sister sensei floating here among the lanterns. The Black-Robed Sister saw me, and what is more amazing, she looked directly at me and called out! I cannot say I liked or trusted the Black Robes I knew in life. I had never seen a female Black Robe and I found it a very unnerving thing. She hooted and waved when I turned aside my gaze and tried to become small. It was a terrible* Hwaaanck! Hwaanck! *sound, like a duck being hit with a paddle.*

"HwaankHwaank! *Idiot!" she yelled at last. "Come here! Don't you see me? I'm telling you to get over here right now!"*

Such glowing eyes! How I retreated before she began another howling. She screamed, "Blockhead! I'm calling you!"

"Yes, Honorable Sister," I mumbled. And I approached her because she seemed elder to me and because she wore the authority of the sensei in her tone and carriage. I had no defense against her that was as strong as she herself was.

"Henry forgot his statue of St. Joseph! He didn't take the St. Joseph! This, of course, probably explains how he got lost." The Sister waved a little doll in her hand, one of the Catholic dolls that represents their spirit helpers, the saints.

"Honorable Sister, may I respectfully ask why you are here and not in the Christian heaven?"

The Sister looked confused. "I don't know," she said. "I did know.

But now I've forgotten. I thought I would see Henry. He told me to look for you and I had some errand to do. The errand had something to do with a woman with a name like Isis or Ishtar. Isotope? That's too electrical or chemical. The name had a slushy sound."

My hands flew to my heart. "Is it Ishiru? Did this Henry person give you an errand that concerns a woman named Ishiru? Do you know something of her destiny?"

The Black Robe flapped a hand at me. "Don't bother me right now. I've got to collect my thoughts!"

"Sister, who is the person who sent you?

"Well, Henry Cooper, of course," she snorted. "Who else would wander around a pagan backwater like this but Henry Cooper! Ah! I remember! I'm to tell you where this black-haired woman is now."

"Is it Ishiru?"

"Is it a woman who spent her last life finding beautiful stones?"

"That is Ishiru!"

"That's the woman, whoever she is." The Sister's face took on that look that I had felt so many times from the other side of my own face—the look of a confused Spirit. "I am confused," she said at last. "I only know that I needed to do what I have just done." The Sister did not look anxious. She must have been an old spirit. She said, "It was only a moment ago, it seems, that I lay in a cool room with a painted blue dresser."

"Oh, Honorable Sister," I comforted her. "Tell me where Ishiru went. Tell me what she said."

"I can't do it with words," the Black Robe told me. "But I can show you."

"Show me, Honorable Sister."

"Very well. I'll show you. Don't be afraid."

I felt myself changing, becoming a stream of tiny particles, each buzzing and rushing. I felt surges and sparkling electrical bumping.

I was leaving. I would forget everything that I knew at this moment—

forget my Ishiru and the insect trade and plum ice and the pica-don *and the Black-Robed Sister, and if I saw any of these things again, I would not recognize them as parts of my own past. Oh, Ishiru! Good-bye now to my waking memories of you. What will be the new shape, I wonder, of the part of my mind that is devoted to you, to the glowing stream of boats at* o-bon, *to the tastes of sliced baked sweet potato, of plum ices and fried tofu stuffed with shrimp! How sweet are our lives!*

I cling backward toward every pleasure my waking mind recalls, but the direction of my own spirit resists. I go on.

I vanish.

ACKNOWLEDGMENTS

Several survivors and observers of the atomic blast helped shape Asagao's vision of that experience. Most important among them were Robert Jay Lifton, who wrote *Death in Life: Survivors of Hiroshima,* and Robert Jungk, who wrote *Children of the Ashes.* Thanks also to Kyoko and Mark Selden for their *The Atomic Bomb: Voices from Hiroshima and Nagasaki.* For background on professions like the insect trade I am indebted to Lafcadio Hearn, whose reports on life among the Japanese at the turn of the century were one of the Western world's most interesting windows into that time and place. I am especially grateful for his *In Ghostly Japan, Out of the East, Exotics and Retrospectives* and *Glimpses of Unfamiliar Japan.* Bless him for turning to Japan for a home when the United States didn't suit him.

I wish to thank Liv Blumer, my agent, who treated this book like a first-born child, and Jennifer Hershey, my editor and most indefatigable and generous reader, for getting it into the world. Among the friends and guides who read versions or supported me as I worked, I count Fred Ramey, Arthur Golden, Ellen Ruppel Shell, Sally Arteseros, Susan Schotz, Connie Brown, Susan Soranno, Terry Grobe, Bobby Ganong and Mallory Digges. Leslie Epstein and Barbara Goldfinger were teachers who influenced me in ways that can be seen in this book's final form. And, of course, my colleagues and students at the Maimonides School have been a kind of North Star to me as I worked.

I'm deeply grateful to them all.

Sharon Pywell